Also by Stanislaw Lem in Orbit paperback:

THE CYBERIAD
THE FUTUROLOGICAL CONGRESS

Stanislaw Lem

The Star Diaries

Translated from the Polish by Michael Kandel
with line drawings by Lem

Futura Publications Limited.
An Orbit Book

An Orbit Book

Published in Polish under the title
Dzienniki gwiazdowe by Czytelnik,
Warsaw, in 1971

First published in Great Britain 1976 by
Martin Secker & Warburg Limited

First Futura Publications edition 1978

English translation copyright © 1976 by
The Seabury Press, Inc.

ISBN 0 7088 7000 7
Printed by
William Collins Sons & Co. Ltd
Glasgow

Futura Publications Limited
110 Warner Road, Camberwell
London SE5

Contents

Introduction

This edition of the works of Ijon Tichy, being neither complete nor definitive, does represent a step forward in comparison with its predecessors. Included here are the texts of two hitherto unknown Voyages, the Eighth and the Twenty-eighth.[1] The latter provides us with new information concerning the biography of Tichy and his family, information which will interest not only the historian, but the physicist as well, for it points to a phenomenon long since suspected by me, namely, the dependence of the degree of kinship upon velocity.[2]

As for the Eighth Voyage, a team of Tichologists-psychoanalysts has verified—minutes before this edition went to press—all the events which took place in the dream of I. Tichy.[3] The Interested Reader will find, in Dr. Hopfstosser's work, a comparative bibliography on the subject, showing the influence of the dreams of other famous people, like Sir Isaac Newton and the Borgias, on the dreams of Tichy, and vice versa.

On the other hand the present volume does not include the

---

[1] E. M. Sianko, *Wyściółka lewej szuflady biurka I. Tichego—manuskryptem jego nie publikowanych prac;* Vol. XVI Tichiana Series, p. 1193 ff.

[2] O. J. Burberrys, *Kinship As a Function of Velocity in Family Travels;* Vol. XVII Tichiana Series, p. 232 ff. See also R. Z. Hemp, *Relatives and Relativity* (Xerox: Brasilia), pp. 482–512.

[3] Dr. S. Hopfstosser, *Das epistemologisch Unbestreitbare in einem Traume von Ijon Tichy;* spec. ed. Tichiana Series, Vol. VI, p. 67 ff.

Twenty-sixth Voyage, shown conclusively to be apocryphal. The proof of this has been supplied by a team of workers at our Institute, who used electronic-textual analysis.[4] I might add here that personally I have always considered the so-called "Twenty-sixth Voyage" to be spurious, on account of the many inaccuracies that appear in that text, regarding—among others—the Oofs (not the "Oops," as the text gives), also the Guzzards, Meopticans and the species of the Lowths (Phlegmus Invariabilis Hopfstosseri).

Of late certain voices have been heard, which would cast doubt upon the authorship of Tichy's writings. The press tells us that Tichy used a ghost-writer, or that he never even existed, his works having been penned—they say—by a device given the name of "Lem." According to some extreme versions this "Lem" is even supposed to be a man. Now, anyone who has a rudimentary acquaintance with the history of space travel knows that LEM is an abbreviation for *LUNAR EXCURSION MODULE*, an exploratory vessel built in the U.S.A. as part of the "Apollo Project" (the first landing on the Moon). Ijon Tichy requires no defense, neither as an author nor as a traveler. Nevertheless I would like to take this opportunity to quash those ridiculous rumors once and for all. Specifically then: the LEM was indeed equipped with a small brain (electronic); that device however performed only the most narrow navigational tasks and would have been incapable of writing a single coherent sentence. About any other LEM nothing is known. We find no mention of such in the catalogs of large-scale electronic machines (viz. Nortronics, New York, 1976–9), nor in the Great Encyclopedia Cosmica (London, 1989). High time then, that this gossip, so out of keeping with the seriousness of the work at hand, ceases to distract our Tichologists, from whom much labor yet—and many years— will be needed to compile the OPERA OMNIA of I. Tichy.

— PROFESSOR A. S. TARANTOGA
Department of Comparative Astrozoology, Fomalhaut University
on behalf of the Editorial Committee for the Publication
of the Complete Works of Ijon Tichy
and the Scientific Council of the Tichological Institute
in conjunction with the Editorial Board of the Quarterly "Tichiana"

[4] E. M. Sianko, A. Hayseed and W. U. Kałamarajbysowa, *A Frequency Analysis of the Linguistic Beta-spectra in the Texts of I. Tichy;* Vol. XVIII Tichiana Series.

Introduction to the Expanded Edition

I t is with joy and deep emotion that we offer the Reader this new edition of the writings of Ijon Tichy, for it includes not only the texts of three hitherto unknown Voyages (the Eighteenth, the Twentieth and the Twenty-first), not only invaluable illustrations by the author's own hand, but also an explanation of certain mysteries that have, till now, given even specialists in Tichology many a sleepless night.

As for the drawings, for a long time the Author was unwilling to part with these, claiming that he sketched stellar-planetary specimens *in flagranti* or from his private collection purely for his own amusement, that they possess neither artistic nor documentary value, since he always dashed them off in a great hurry. Yet even if they *are* scribblings—with which opinion, by the way, not all the experts agree—their use as visual aids in the reading of these texts, so often difficult and obscure, is undeniable. This is the first source of our staff's satisfaction.

Secondly, the texts of the new Voyages afford no little comfort to the mind that yearns for definitive answers to those oldest of questions which Man has put to himself and the world: namely, who exactly it was that constructed the Universe, and why thus and not otherwise it was done, also who was responsible for natural evolution and general history, the origin of intelligence, life, and other, no less important matters. And is it not a pleasant surprise indeed to discover that our illustrious Author himself played, in that creative endeavor, a major if not deciding role? We can well understand the modesty with which he defended the drawer containing those manuscripts, but equally well the delight of those who finally broke down Tichy's resistance. It is here, too, that the reason for the gaps in the numbering of the Star Voyages comes to light. After studying this edition, the Reader will see not only why there never was a First Journey of I. Tichy, but also why there never could be, and with a little concentration he will realize that Voyage number twenty-one is at the same time the nineteenth. True, this is not immediately apparent, since the Author crossed out the last few dozen lines of the manuscript in question. For what reason? Once again, his tremendous modesty. I cannot break the oath of secrecy placed upon my lips; I have been permitted however to pull aside the curtain just a little. I. Tichy, seeing where attempts to improve prehistory and history were leading, in his capacity as Director of the Temporal Institute did something, as a result of which something the Theory of Time Vehicles and Transport never was discovered. Since at his order this discovery was undiscovered, by that very act the Telechronic Program to correct history vanished, so did the Temporal Institute and so—alas— did I. Tichy himself, being its Director. The pain caused by that loss is assuaged in part by the knowledge that we will now not have to fear any unpleasant surprises from the past (at least), and in part by the startling fact that he who tragically is no more still lives, without at all having risen from the dead. Admittedly, this circumstance is perplexing; for its full explanation we direct the Reader to the appropriate places, namely, the Twentieth and Twenty-first Voyages.

In conclusion I should like to announce the establishment in our Association of a special futurological section, which, in keeping with the spirit of the times, will make available—using the method of so-called self-realizing prognoses—those star journeys of I. Tichy which as yet he has not undertaken, nor indeed intends to.

—Prof. A. S. Tarantoga
on behalf of the Associated Institutes of Tichology, Tichography and Tichonomics Descriptive, Comparative and Prognostic

THE SEVENTH VOYAGE

It was on a Monday, April second—I was cruising in the vicinity of Betelgeuse—when a meteor no larger than a lima bean pierced the hull, shattered the drive regulator and part of the rudder, as a result of which the rocket lost all maneuverability. I put on my spacesuit, went outside and tried to fix the mechanism, but found I couldn't possibly attach the spare rudder—which I'd had the foresight to bring along—without the help of another man. The constructors had foolishly designed the rocket in such a way, that it took one person to hold the head of the bolt in place with a wrench, and another to tighten the nut. I didn't realize this at first and spent several hours trying to grip the wrench with my feet while using both hands to screw on the nut at the other end. But I was getting nowhere, and had already missed lunch. Then finally, just as I almost succeeded, the wrench popped out from under my feet and went flying off into space. So not only had I accomplished nothing, but lost a valuable tool besides; I watched helplessly as it sailed away, growing smaller and smaller against the starry sky.

After a while the wrench returned in an elongated ellipse, but though it had now become a satellite of the rocket, it never got close enough for me to retrieve it. I went back inside and, sitting down to a modest supper, considered how best to extricate myself from this stupid situation. Meanwhile the ship flew on, straight ahead, its velocity steadily increasing, since my drive regulator too had been knocked out by that blasted meteor. It's true there were no heavenly bodies on course, but this headlong flight could hardly continue indefinitely. For a while I contained my anger, but then discovered, when starting to wash the dinner dishes, that the now-overheated atomic pile had ruined my very best cut of sirloin (I'd been keeping it in the freezer for Sunday). I momentarily lost my usually level head, burst into a volley of the vilest oaths and smashed a few plates. This did give me a certain satisfaction, but was hardly practical. In addition, the sirloin which I threw overboard, instead of drifting off into the void, didn't seem to want to leave the rocket and revolved about it, a second artificial satellite, which produced a brief eclipse of the sun every eleven minutes and four seconds. To calm my nerves I calculated till evening the components of its trajectory, as well as the orbital perturbation caused by the presence of the lost wrench. I figured out that for the next six million years the sirloin, rotating about the ship in a circular path, would lead the wrench, then catch up with it from behind and pass it again. Finally, exhausted by these computations, I went to bed. In the middle of the night I had the feeling someone was shaking me by the shoulder. I opened my eyes and saw a man standing over the bed; his face was strangely familiar, though I hadn't the faintest idea who this could be.

"Get up," he said, "and take the pliers, we're going out and screwing on the rudder bolts . . ."

"First of all, your manner is somewhat unceremonious, and we haven't even been introduced," I replied, "and secondly, I know for a fact that you aren't there. I'm alone on this rocket, and have been now for two years, en route from Earth to the constellation of the Ram. Therefore you are a dream and nothing more."

However he continued to shake me, repeating that I should go with him at once and get the tools.

"This is idiotic," I said, growing annoyed, because this dream argument could very well wake me up, and I knew from experience the difficulty I would have getting back to sleep. "Look, I'm not going anywhere, there's no point in it. A bolt tightened in a dream won't change things as they are in the sober light of day. Now kindly stop pestering me and evaporate or leave in some other fashion, otherwise I might awake."

"But you *are* awake, word of honor!" cried the stubborn apparition. "Don't you recognize me? Look here!"

And saying this, he pointed to the two warts, big as strawberries, on his left cheek. Instinctively I clutched my own face, for yes, I had two warts, exactly the same, and in that very place. Suddenly I realized why this phantom reminded me of someone I knew: he was the spitting image of myself.

"Leave me alone, for heaven's sake!" I cried, shutting my eyes, anxious to stay asleep. "If you are me, then fine, we needn't stand on ceremony, but it only proves you don't exist!"

With which I turned on my other side and pulled the covers up over my head. I could hear him saying something about utter nonsense; then finally, when I didn't respond, he shouted: "You'll regret this, knucklehead! And you'll find out, too late, that this was not a dream!"

But I didn't budge. In the morning I opened my eyes and immediately recalled that curious nocturnal episode. Sitting up in bed, I thought about what strange tricks the mind can play: for here, without a single fellow creature on board and confronted with an emergency of the most pressing kind, I had—as it were—split myself in two, in that dream fantasy, to answer the needs of the situation.

After breakfast, discovering that the rocket had acquired an additional chunk of acceleration during the night, I took to leafing through the ship's library, searching the textbooks for some way out of this predicament. But I didn't find a thing. So I spread my star map out on the table and in the light of nearby Betelgeuse, obscured every so often by the orbiting sirloin, examined the area in which I was located for the seat of some cosmic civilization that might possibly come to my aid. But unfortunately this was a complete stellar wilderness, avoided by all vessels as a region unusually dangerous, for in it lay gravitational vortices, as formidable as they were mysterious, one hundred and forty-seven of them in all, whose existence was explained by six astrophysical theories, each theory saying something different.

The cosmonautical almanac warned of them, in view of the incalculable relativistic effects that passage through a vortex could bring about—particularly when traveling at high velocities.

3

Yet there was little I could do. According to my calculations I would be making contact with the edge of the first vortex at around eleven, and therefore hurriedly prepared lunch, not wanting to face the danger on an empty stomach. I had barely finished drying the last saucer when the rocket began to pitch and heave in every direction, till all the objects not adequately tied down went flying from wall to wall like hail. With difficulty I crawled over to the armchair, and after I'd lashed myself to it, as the ship tossed about with ever increasing violence, I noticed a sort of pale lilac haze forming on the opposite side of the cabin, and in the middle of it, between the sink and the stove, a misty human shape, which had on an apron and was pouring omelet batter into a frying pan. The shape looked at me with interest, but without surprise, then shimmered and was gone. I rubbed my eyes. I was obviously alone, so attributed the vision to a momentary aberration.

As I continued to sit in—or rather, jump along with—the armchair, it suddenly hit me, like a dazzling revelation, that this hadn't been a hallucination at all. A thick volume of the General Theory of Relativity came whirling past my chair and I grabbed for it, finally catching it on the fourth pass. Turning the pages of that heavy tome wasn't easy under the circumstances—awesome forces hurled the rocket this way and that, it reeled like a drunken thing—but at last I found the right chapter. It spoke of the manifestation of the "time loop," that is, the bending of the direction of the flow of time in the presence of gravitational fields . of great intensity, which phenomenon might even on occasion lead to the complete reversal of time and the "duplication of the present." The vortex I had just entered was not one of the most powerful. I knew that if I could turn the ship's bow, even if only a little, towards the Galactic Pole, it would intersect the so-called Vortex Gravitatiosus Pinckenbachii, in which had been observed more than once the duplication, even the triplication, of the present.

True, the controls were out, but I went down to the engine room and fiddled with the instruments so long, that I actually managed to produce a slight deflection of the rocket towards the Galactic Pole. This took several hours. The results were beyond my expectations. The ship fell into the center of the vortex at around midnight, its girders shook and groaned until I began to fear for its safety; but it emerged from this ordeal whole and once again was wrapped in the lifeless arms of cosmic silence, whereupon I left the engine room, only to see myself sound asleep in bed. I realized at once that this was I of the previous day, that is, from Monday night. Without reflecting on the philosophical side of this rather singular event, I ran over and shook the sleeper by the shoulder, shouting for him to get up, since I had no idea how long his Monday existence would last in my Tuesday one, therefore it was imperative we go outside and fix the rudder as quickly as possible, together.

But the sleeper merely opened one eye and told me that not only was I rude, but didn't exist, being a figment of his dream and nothing more. I tugged at him in vain, losing patience, and even attempted to drag him bodily from the bed. He wouldn't budge, stubbornly repeating that it was all a dream; I began to curse, but he pointed out logically that bolts tightened in dreams wouldn't hold on rudders in the sober light of day. I gave my word of honor that he was mistaken, I pleaded and swore in turn, to no avail—even the warts did not convince him. He turned his back to me and started snoring.

I sat down in the armchair to collect my thoughts and take stock of the situation. I'd lived through it twice now, first as that sleeper, on Monday, and then as the one trying to wake him, unsuccessfully, on Tuesday. The Monday me hadn't believed in the reality of the duplication, while the Tuesday me already knew it to be a fact. Here was a perfectly ordinary time loop. What then should be done in order to get the rudder fixed? Since the Monday me slept on—I remembered that on that night I had slept through to the morning undisturbed—I saw the futility of any further efforts to rouse him. The map indicated a number of other large gravitational vortices up ahead, therefore I could count on the duplication of the present within the next few days. I decided to write myself a letter and pin it to the pillow, enabling the Monday me, when he awoke, to see for himself that the dream had been no dream.

But no sooner did I sit at the table with pen and paper than something started rattling in the engines, so I hurried there and poured water on the overheated atomic pile till dawn, while the Monday me slept soundly, licking his lips from time to time, which galled me no end. Hungry and bleary-eyed, for I hadn't slept a wink, I set about making breakfast, and was just wiping the dishes when the rocket fell into the next gravitational vortex. I saw my Monday self staring at me dumbfounded, lashed to the armchair, while Tuesday I fried an omelet. Then a lurch knocked me off balance, everything grew dark, and down I went. I came to on the floor among bits of broken china; near my face were the shoes of a man standing over me.

"Get up," he said, lifting me. "Are you all right?"

"I think so," I answered, keeping my hands on the floor, for my head was still spinning. "From what day of the week are you?"

"Wednesday," he said. "Come on, let's get that rudder fixed while we have the chance!"

"But where's the Monday me?" I asked.

"Gone. Which means, I suppose, that you are he."

"How is that?"

"Well, the Monday me on Monday night became, Tuesday morning, the Tuesday me, and so on."

"I don't understand."

"Doesn't matter—you'll get the hang of it. But hurry up, we're wasting time!"

"Just a minute," I replied, remaining on the floor. "Today is Tuesday. Now if you are the Wednesday me, and if by that time on Wednesday the rudder still hasn't been fixed, then it follows that something will prevent us from fixing it, since otherwise you, on Wednesday, would not now, on Tuesday, be asking me to help you fix it. Wouldn't it be best, then, for us not to risk going outside?"

"Nonsense!" he exclaimed. "Look, I'm the Wednesday me and you're the Tuesday me, and as for the rocket, well, my guess is that its existence is patched, which means that in places it's Tuesday, in places Wednesday, and here and there perhaps there's even a bit of Thursday. Time has simply become shuffled up in passing through these vortices, but why should that concern us, when together we are two and therefore have a chance to fix the rudder?!"

"No, you're wrong!" I said. "If on Wednesday, where you already are, having lived through all of Tuesday, so that now Tuesday is behind you, if on Wednesday—I repeat—the rudder isn't fixed, then one can only conclude that it didn't get fixed on

Tuesday, since it's Tuesday now and if we were to go and fix the rudder right away, that *right away* would be your *yesterday* and there would now be nothing to fix. And consequently . . ."

"And consequently you're as stubborn as a mule!" he growled. "You'll regret this! And my only consolation is that you too will be infuriated by your own pigheadedness, just as I am now—when you yourself reach Wednesday!!"

"Ah, wait," I cried, "do you mean that on Wednesday, I, being you, will try to convince the Tuesday me, just as you are doing here, except that everything will be reversed, in other words you will be me and I you? But of course! That's what makes a time loop! Hold on, I'm coming, yes, it makes sense now . . ."

But before I could get up off the floor we fell into a new vortex and the terrible acceleration flattened us against the ceiling.

The dreadful pitching and heaving didn't let up once throughout that night from Tuesday to Wednesday. Then, when things had finally quieted down a little, the volume of the General Theory of Relativity came flying across the cabin and hit me on the forehead with such force, that I lost consciousness. When I opened my eyes I saw broken dishes and a man sprawled among them. I immediately jumped to my feet and lifted him, shouting:

"Get up! Are you all right?"

"I think so," he replied, blinking. "From what day of the week are you?"

"Wednesday," I said, "come on, let's get that rudder fixed while we have the chance."

"But where's the Monday me?" he asked, sitting up. He had a black eye.

"Gone," I said, "which means that you are he."

"How is that?"

"Well, the Monday me on Monday night became, Tuesday morning, the Tuesday me, and so on."

"I don't understand."

"Doesn't matter—you'll get the hang of it. But hurry up, we're wasting time!"

Saying this, I was already looking around for the tools.

"Just a minute," he drawled, not budging an inch. "Today is

7

Tuesday. Now, if you are the Wednesday me, and if by that time on Wednesday the rudder still hasn't been fixed, then it follows that something will prevent us from fixing it, since otherwise you, on Wednesday, would not be asking me now, on Tuesday, to help you fix it. Wouldn't it be best, then, for us not to risk going outside?"

"Nonsense!!" I yelled, losing my temper. "Look, I'm the Wednesday me, you're the Tuesday me . . ."

And so we quarreled, in opposite roles, during which he did in fact drive me into a positive fury, for he persistently refused to help me fix the rudder and it did no good calling him pigheaded and a stubborn mule. And when at last I managed to convince him, we plunged into the next gravitational vortex. I was in a cold sweat, for the thought occurred to me that we might now go around and around in this time loop, repeating ourselves for all eternity, but luckily that didn't happen. By the time the acceleration had slackened enough for me to stand, I was alone once more in the cabin. Apparently the localized existence of Tuesday, which until now had persisted in the vicinity of the sink, had vanished, becoming a part of the irretrievable past. I rushed over to the map, to find some nice vortex into which I could send the rocket, so as to bring about still another warp of time and in that way obtain a helping hand.

There was in fact one vortex, quite promising too, and by manipulating the engines with great difficulty, I aimed the rocket to intersect it at the very center. True, the configuration of that vortex was, according to the map, rather unusual—it had two foci, side by side. But by now I was too desperate to concern myself with this anomaly.

After several hours of bustling about in the engine room my hands were filthy, so I went to wash them, seeing as there was plenty of time yet before I would be entering the vortex. The bathroom was locked. From inside came the sounds of someone gargling.

"Who's there?!" I hollered, taken aback.

"Me," replied a voice.

"Which me is that?!"

"Ijon Tichy."

"From what day?"

"Friday. What do you want?"

"I wanted to wash my hands . . ." I said mechanically, thinking meanwhile with the greatest intensity: it was Wednesday evening, and he came from Friday, therefore the gravitational vortex into which the ship was to fall would bend time from Friday to Wednesday, but as for what then would take place within the vortex, that I could in no way picture. Particularly intriguing was the question of where Thursday might be. In the meantime the Friday me still wasn't letting me into the bathroom, taking his sweet time, though I pounded on the door insistently.

"Stop that gargling!" I roared, out of patience. "Every second is precious—come out at once, we have to fix the rudder!"

"For that you don't need me," he said phlegmatically from behind the door. "The Thursday me must be around here somewhere, go with him . . ."

"What Thursday me? That's not possible . . ."

"I ought to know whether it's possible or not, considering that I'm already in Friday and consequently have lived through your Wednesday as well as his Thursday . . ."

Feeling dizzy, I jumped back from the door, for yes, I did hear some commotion in the cabin: a man was standing there, pulling the toolbag out from under the bed.

"You're the Thursday me?!" I cried, running into the room.

"Right," he said. "Here, give me a hand . . ."

"Will we be able to fix the rudder this time?" I asked as together we pulled out the heavy satchel.

"I don't know, it wasn't fixed on Thursday, ask the Friday me . . ."

That hadn't crossed my mind! I quickly ran back to the bathroom door.

"Hey there, Friday me! Has the rudder been fixed?"

"Not on Friday," he replied.

"Why not?"

"This is why not," he said, opening the door. His head was wrapped in a towel, and he pressed the flat of a knife to his forehead, trying in this manner to reduce the swelling of a lump the size of an egg. The Thursday me meanwhile approached with the tools and stood beside me, calmly scrutinizing the me with the lump, who with his free hand was putting back on the shelf a siphon of seltzer. So it was its gurgle I had taken for his gargle.

9

"What gave you that?" I asked sympathetically.

"Not what, who," he replied. "It was the Sunday me."

"The Sunday me? But why . . . that can't be!" I cried.

"Well it's a long story . . ."

"Makes no difference! Quick, let's go outside, we might just make it!" said the Thursday me, turning to the me that was I.

"But the rocket will fall into the vortex any minute now," I replied. "The shock could throw us off into space, and that would be the end of us . . ."

"Use your head, stupid," snapped the Thursday me. "If the Friday me's alive, nothing can happen to us. Today is only Thursday."

"It's Wednesday," I objected.

"It makes no difference, in either case I'll be alive on Friday, and so will you."

"Yes, but there really aren't two of us, it only looks that way," I observed, "actually there is *one* me, just from different days of the week . . ."

"Fine, fine, now open the hatch . . ."

But it turned out here that we had only one spacesuit between us. Therefore we could not both leave the rocket at the same time, and therefore our plan to fix the rudder was completely ruined.

"Blast!" I cried, angrily throwing down the toolbag. "What I should have done is put on the spacesuit to begin with and kept it on. I just didn't think of it—but you, as the Thursday me, you ought to have remembered!"

"I had the spacesuit, but the Friday me took it," he said.

"When? Why?"

"Eh, it's not worth going into," he shrugged and, turning around, went back to the cabin. The Friday me wasn't there; I looked in the bathroom, but it was empty too.

"Where's the Friday me?" I asked, returning. The Thursday me methodically cracked an egg with a knife and poured its contents onto the sizzling fat.

"Somewhere in the neighborhood of Saturday, no doubt," he replied, indifferent, quickly scrambling the egg.

"Excuse me," I protested, "but you already had your meals on Wednesday—what makes you think you can go and eat a second Wednesday supper?"

10

"These rations are mine just as much as they are yours," he said, calmly lifting the browned edge of the egg with his knife. "I am you, you are me, so it makes no difference . . ."

"What sophistry! Wait, that's too much butter! Are you crazy? I don't have enough food for this many people!"

The skillet flew out of his hand, and I went crashing into a wall: we had fallen into a new vortex. Once again the ship shook, as if in a fever, but my only thought was to get to the corridor where the spacesuit was hanging and put it on. For in that way (I reasoned) when Wednesday became Thursday, I, as the Thursday me, would be wearing that spacesuit, and if only I didn't take it off for a single minute (and I was determined not to) then I would obviously be wearing it on Friday also. And therefore the me on Thursday and the me on Friday would both be in our spacesuits, so that when we came together in the same present it would finally be possible to fix that miserable rudder. The increasing thrust of gravity made my head swim, and when I opened my eyes I noticed that I was lying to the right of the Thursday me, and not to the left, as I had been a few moments before. Now while it had been easy enough for me to develop this plan about the spacesuit, it was considerably more difficult to put it into action, since with the growing gravitation I could hardly move. When it weakened just a little, I began to inch my way across the floor—in the direction of the door that led to the corridor. Meanwhile I noticed that the Thursday me was likewise heading for the door, crawling on his belly towards the corridor. At last, after about an hour, when the vortex had reached its widest point, we met at the threshold, both flattened to the floor. Then I thought, why should I have to strain myself to reach the handle? Let the Thursday me do it. Yet at the same time I began to recall certain things which clearly indicated that it was I now who was the Thursday me, and not he.

"What day of the week are you?" I asked, to make sure. With my chin pressed to the floor I looked him in the eye. Struggling, he opened his mouth.

"Thurs—day—me," he groaned. Now that was odd. Could it be that, in spite of everything, I was *still* the Wednesday me? Calling to mind all my recollections of the recent past, I had to conclude that this was out of the question. So he must have been the Friday me. For if he had preceded me by a day before, then

In the time loop.

he was surely a day ahead now. I waited for him to open the door, but apparently he expected the same of me. The gravitation had now subsided noticeably, so I got up and ran to the corridor. Just as I grabbed the spacesuit, he tripped me, pulling it out of my hands, and I fell flat on my face.

"You dog!" I cried. "Tricking your own self—that's really low!"

He ignored me, stepping calmly into the spacesuit. The shamelessness of it was appalling. Suddenly a strange force threw him from the suit—as it turned out, someone was already inside. For a moment I wavered, no longer knowing who was who.

"You, Wednesday!" called the one in the spacesuit. "Hold back Thursday, help me!"

For the Thursday me was indeed trying to tear the spacesuit off him.

"Give me the spacesuit!" bellowed the Thursday me as he wrestled with the other.

"Get off! What are you trying to do? Don't you realize I'm the one who should have it, and not you?!" howled the other.

"And why is that, pray?"

"For the reason, fool, that I'm closer to Saturday than you, and by Saturday there will be two of us in suits!"

"But that's ridiculous," I said, getting into their argument, "at best you'll be alone in the suit on Saturday, like an absolute idiot, and won't be able to do a thing. Let *me* have the suit: if I put it on now, then you'll be wearing it on Friday as the Friday me, and I will also on Saturday as the Saturday me, and so you see there will then be two of us, and with two suits . . . Come on, Thursday, give me a hand!!"

"Wait," protested the Friday me when I had forcibly yanked the spacesuit off his back. "In the first place, there is no one here for you to call 'Thursday,' since midnight has passed and *you* are now the Thursday me, and in the second place, it'll be better if I stay in the spacesuit. The spacesuit won't do you a bit of good."

"Why not? If I put it on today, I'll have it on tomorrow too."

"You'll see for yourself . . . after all, I was already you, on Thursday, and *my* Thursday has passed, so I ought to know . . ."

"Enough talk. Let go of it this instant!" I snarled. But he grabbed it from me and I chased him, first through the engine room and then into the cabin. It somehow worked out that there were only two of us now. Suddenly I understood why the Thursday me, when we were standing at the hatch with the tools, had told me that the Friday me took the spacesuit from him: for in the meantime I myself had become the Thursday me, and here the Friday me was in fact taking it. But I had no intention of giving in that easily. Just you wait, I thought, I'll take care of you, and out I ran into the corridor, and from there to the engine room, where before—during the chase—I had noticed a heavy pipe lying on the floor, which served to stoke the atomic pile, and I picked it up and—thus armed—dashed back to the cabin. The other me was already in the spacesuit, he had pulled on everything but the helmet.

"Out of the spacesuit!" I snapped, clenching my pipe in a threatening manner.

"Not a chance."

"Out, I say!!"

Then I wondered whether or not I should hit him. It was a little disconcerting, the fact that he had neither a black eye nor a bump on his head, like the other Friday me, the one I'd found in the bathroom, but all at once I realized that this was the way it had to be. *That* Friday me by now was the Saturday me, yes, and perhaps even was knocking about somewhere in the vicinity of Sunday, while this Friday me inside the spacesuit had only recently been the Thursday me, into which same Thursday me I myself had been transformed at midnight. Thus I was moving along the sloping curve of the time loop towards that place in which the Friday me before the beating would change into the Friday me already beaten. Still, he *did* say, back then, that it had been the Sunday me who did it, and there was no trace, as yet, of *him*. We stood alone in the cabin, he and I. Then suddenly I had a brainstorm.

"Out of that spacesuit!" I growled.

"Keep off, Thursday!" he yelled.

"I'm not Thursday, I'm the SUNDAY ME!" I shrieked, closing in for the kill. He tried to kick me, but spacesuit boots are very heavy and before he could raise his leg, I let him have it over the head. Not too hard, of course, since I had grown sufficiently familiar with all of this to know that I in turn, when eventually I went from the Thursday to the Friday me, would be on the receiving end, and I wasn't particularly set on fracturing my own skull. The Friday me fell with a groan, holding his head, and I brutally tore the spacesuit off him. While he made for the bathroom on wobbly legs, muttering, "Where's the cotton . . . where's the seltzer," I quickly began to don the suit that we had struggled over, until I noticed—sticking out from under the bed—a human foot. I took a closer look, kneeling. Under the bed lay a man; trying to muffle the sound of his chewing, he was hurriedly bolting down the last bar of the milk chocolate I had stored away in the suitcase for a rainy sidereal day. The bastard was in such a hurry that he ate the chocolate along with bits of tin foil, which glittered on his lips.

14

"Leave that chocolate alone!" I yelled, pulling at his foot. "Who are you anyway? The Thursday me? . . ." I added in a lower voice, seized by a sudden doubt, for the thought occurred that maybe I already was the Friday me, and would soon have to collect what I had dished out earlier to the same.

"The Sunday me," he mumbled, his mouth full. I felt weak. Now either he was lying, in which case there was nothing to worry about, or telling the truth, and if he was, I faced a clobbering for sure, because the Sunday me—after all—was the one who had hit the Friday me, the Friday me told me so himself before it happened, and then later I, impersonating the Sunday me, had let him have it with the pipe. But on the other hand, I said to myself, even if he's lying and not the Sunday me, it's still quite possible that he's a later me than me, and if he *is* a later me, he remembers everything that I do, therefore already knows that I lied to the Friday me, and so could deceive me in a similar manner, since what had been a spur-of-the-moment stratagem on my part was for him—by now—simply a memory, a memory he could easily make use of. Meanwhile, as I remained in uncertainty, he had eaten the rest of the chocolate and crawled out from under the bed.

"If you're the Sunday me, where's your spacesuit?!" I cried, struck by a new thought.

"I'll have it in a minute," he said calmly, and then I noticed the pipe in his hand . . . The next thing I saw was a bright flash, like a few dozen supernovas going off at once, after which I lost consciousness. I came to, sitting on the floor of the bathroom; someone was banging on the door. I began to attend to my bruises and bumps, but he kept pounding away; it turned out to be the Wednesday me. After a while I showed him my battered head, he went with the Thursday me for the tools, then there was a lot of running around and yanking off of spacesuits, this to in one way or another I managed to live through, and on Saturday morning crawled under the bed to see if there wasn't some chocolate left in the suitcase. Someone started pulling at my foot as I ate the last bar, which I'd found underneath the shirts; I no longer knew just who this was, but hit him over the head anyhow, pulled the spacesuit off him and was going to put it on—when the rocket fell into the next vortex.

When I regained consciousness, the cabin was packed with people. There was barely elbowroom. As it turned out, they

15

were all of them me, from different days, weeks, months, and one—so he said—was even from the following year. There were plenty with bruises and black eyes, and five among those present had on spacesuits. But instead of immediately going out through the hatch and repairing the damage, they began to quarrel, argue, bicker and debate. The problem was, who had hit whom, and when. The situation was complicated by the fact that there now had appeared morning me's and afternoon me's—I feared that if things went on like this, I would soon be broken into minutes and seconds—and then too, the majority of the me's present were lying like mad, so that to this day I'm not altogether sure whom I hit and who hit me when that whole business took place, triangularly, between the Thursday, the Friday and the Wednesday me's, all of whom I was in turn. My impression is that because I had lied to the Friday me, pretending to be the Sunday me, I ended up with one blow more than I should have, going by the calendar. But I would prefer not to dwell any longer on these unpleasant memories; a man who for an entire week does nothing but hit himself over the head has little reason to be proud.

Meanwhile the arguments continued. The sight of such inaction, such wasting of precious time, drove me to despair, while the rocket rushed blindly on, straight ahead, plunging every now and then into another gravitational vortex. At last the ones wearing spacesuits started slugging it out with the ones who were not. I tried to introduce some sort of order into that absolute chaos and finally, after superhuman efforts, succeeded in organizing something that resembled a meeting, in which the one from next year—having seniority—was elected chairman by acclamation.

We then appointed an elective committee, a nominating committee, and a committee for new business, and four of us from next month were made sergeants at arms. But in the meantime we had passed through a negative vortex, which cut our number in half, so that on the very first ballot we lacked a quorum, and had to change the bylaws before proceeding to vote on the candidates for rudder-repairer. The map indicated the approach of still other vortices, and these undid all that we had accomplished so far: first the candidates already chosen disappeared, and then the Tuesday me showed up with the Friday

16

me, who had his head wrapped in a towel, and they created a shameful scene. Upon passage through a particularly strong positive vortex we hardly fit in the cabin and corridor, and opening the hatch was out of the question—there simply wasn't room. But the worst of it was, these time displacements were increasing in amplitude, a few grayhaired me's had already appeared, and here and there I even caught a glimpse of the close-cropped heads of children, that is of myself, of course—or rather—myselves from the halcyon days of boyhood.

I really can't recall whether I was still the Sunday me, or had already turned into the Monday me. Not that it made any difference. The children sobbed that they were being squashed in the crowd, and called for their mommy; the chairman—the Tichy from next year—let out a string of curses, because the Wednesday me, who had crawled under the bed in a futile search for chocolate, bit him in the leg when he accidentally stepped on the latter's finger. I saw that all this would end badly, particularly now as here and there gray beards were turning up. Between the 142nd and 143rd vortices I passed around an attendance sheet, but afterwards it came to light that a large number of those present were cheating. Supplying false vital statistics, God knows why. Perhaps the prevailing atmosphere had muddled their wits. The noise and confusion were such that you could make yourself understood only by screaming at the top of your lungs. But then one of last year's Ijons hit upon what seemed to be an excellent idea, namely, that the oldest among us tell the story of his life; in that way we would learn just who was supposed to fix the rudder. For obviously the oldest me contained within his past experience the lives of all the others there from their various months, days and years. So we turned, in this matter, to a hoary old gentleman who, slightly palsied, was standing idly in the corner. When questioned, he began to speak at great length of his children and grandchildren, then passed to his cosmic voyages, and he had embarked upon no end of these in the course of his ninety-some years. Of the one now taking place— the only one of interest to us—the old man had no recollection whatever, owing to his generally sclerotic and overexcited condition, however he was far too proud to admit this and went on evasively, obstinately, time and again returning to his high connections, decorations and grandchildren, till finally we shouted him down and ordered him to hold his tongue. The next two vortices cruelly thinned our ranks. After the third, not only was there more room, but all of those in spacesuits had disappeared as well. One empty suit remained; we voted to hang it up in the corridor, then went back to our deliberations. Then, following another scuffle for the possession of that precious garment, a new vortex came along and suddenly the place was deserted. I was sitting on the floor, puffy-eyed, in my strangely spacious cabin, surrounded by broken furniture, strips of clothing, ripped-up books. The floor was strewn with ballots. According to the map, I had now passed through the entire zone of gravitational vortices. No longer able to count on duplication, and thus no longer able to correct the damage, I fell into numb despair. About an hour later I looked out in the corridor and discovered, to my great surprise, that the spacesuit was missing. But then I vaguely remembered—yes—right before that last vortex two little boys sneaked out into the corridor. Could they have possibly, both of them, put on the one spacesuit?! Struck by a sudden thought, I ran to the controls. The rudder worked! So then, those little tykes had fixed it after all, while we adults were stuck in endless disagreements. I imagine that one of them placed his arms in the sleeves of the suit, and the other—in the pants; that way, they could have tightened the nut and bolt with wrenches at the same time, working on either side of the rudder. The empty spacesuit I found in the air lock, behind the hatch. I carried it inside the rocket like a sacred relic, my heart full of boundless gratitude for those brave lads I had been so long ago! And thus concluded what was surely one of my most unusual adventures. I reached my destination safely, thanks to the courage and resourcefulness I had displayed when only two children.

It was said afterwards that I invented the whole thing, and those more malicious even went so far as to insinuate that I had a weakness for alcohol, carefully concealed on Earth but freely indulged during those long and lonely cosmic flights. Lord only knows what other gossip has been circulating on the subject. But that is how people are; they'll willingly give credence to the most far-fetched drivel, but not to the simple truth, which is precisely what I have presented here.

THE
EIGHTH
VOYAGE·

Well, it finally happened. I was Earth's delegate to the United Planets—or more precisely, a candidate, though that isn't right either, since it was not my candidacy, but all humanity's which the General Assembly was going to consider.

Never in my life did I feel so nervous. My tongue was thick, my mouth dry, and when I walked out onto the red carpet spread from the astrobus, I couldn't tell whether it or my knees were gently buckling under me. Speeches would surely have to be given, but I was too choked with emotion to stammer out a single word, so that when I caught sight of a large, shiny machine with a chrome counter and little slots for coins, I hurriedly inserted one, placing the cup of my thermos underneath its spigot. This was the first interplanetary incident in the history of human diplomacy on the galactic level, since what I had taken for a soft drink vending machine turned out to be the deputy chairman of the Rhohch delegation in full regalia. By a great stroke of luck the Rhohches happened to be the ones who had offered to sponsor our candidacy at the meeting, though I didn't know this at the time, and when that high dignitary spat upon my boots I took it as a bad sign, while in fact it was only the aromatic secretion of his salutation glands. All this I understood after swallowing an informational-translational tablet handed me by some sympathetic UP official; immediately the jangling sounds around me changed in my ears to perfectly coherent words, the quadrangle of aluminum bowling pins at the end of the plush carpet became an honor guard, and the Rhohch that greeted me—till then looking more like a very large pretzel— seemed an old acquaintance, whose appearance was in no way unusual. But my nervousness remained. A small trundler pulled up, constructed especially for the conveyance of biped creatures such as myself; the Rhohch accompanying me squeezed in after me with difficulty and, taking a seat to the right as well as to the left of me, said:

"Honorable Earthling, I must inform you that a slight procedural complication has taken place. The actual head-chairman of our delegation, the one most qualified to promote your candidacy, being a specialist-Earthist, was unfortunately recalled to the capital last night and I am supposed to replace him. You are familiar with the protocol? . . ."

"No, I . . . I haven't had the chance," I muttered, trying without much success to make myself comfortable in the chair of the trundler, which had not been completely adapted to the needs of the human body. The seat was more like a steep pit, practically two feet deep, and on the bumps my knees touched my forehead.

"Never mind, we'll manage . . ." said the Rhohch. His flowing robe, pressed into rectangular shapes that glittered metallically—and which I had mistaken earlier for a refreshment stand—hummed softly as he cleared his throat and continued:

"Of course I am acquainted with the history of your people, indeed to be so informed is one of my duties. And truly what a magnificent thing it is, this humanity! Our delegation will move (item number eighty-three on the agenda) that you be accepted as official members of the Assembly, with full rights and privileges accruing thereunto . . . you haven't by any chance lost your certification papers, have you?!" he asked so suddenly that I jumped and strenuously shook my head. The roll of parchment in question, somewhat limp with sweat, was clutched in my right hand.

"Good," he said. "So then, yes, I shall deliver a speech depicting your great achievements, achievements which entitle you to take your rightful place in the Astral Federation . . . This is, you understand, a kind of ancient formality. I mean, you don't anticipate any opposition . . . do you?"

"I—well—no, I don't think," I mumbled.

"Of course not! The very idea! So then, strictly a formality, nonetheless I will need certain information. Facts, you understand, details. Atomic energy, one may assume, you already have at your disposal?"

"Oh yes! Yes!" I eagerly assured him.

"Marvelous. But wait, ah, I have it right here, the head-chairman left me his notes, but his handwriting, h'm, well . . . and for how long have you availed yourselves of this energy?"

"Since the sixth of August, 1945!"

"Excellent. What was it? The first power plant?"

"No," I replied, feeling myself blush, "the first atomic bomb. It destroyed Hiroshima . . ."

"Hiroshima? A meteor?"

"Not a meteor . . . a city."

"A city . . . ?" he said, uneasy. "In that case, h'm, how to put it . . ." he thought for a moment. "No, it's best to say nothing," he decided. "All right, fine, but I must have something to praise. Come now, think hard, we'll be there any minute."

"Uh . . . space travel," I began.

"That is self-evident, without space travel you wouldn't be here now," he explained, a little testily I thought. "To what do you devote the bulk of your national revenue? Try to recall, any grand feat of engineering, architecture on the cosmic scale, gravitational-solar launchers, well?" he prompted.

"Yes . . . that is, work is under way," I said. "Government funds are rather limited, most of it goes into defense . . ."

"Defense of what? The continents? Against meteors, earthquakes?"

"No, not that kind of defense . . . armaments, armies . . ."

"What is that, a hobby?"

"Not a hobby . . . internal conflicts," I muttered.

"This is no recommendation!" he said with obvious distaste. "Really, you didn't come flying here straight out of the cave! Your learned ones must have realized long ago that planetary cooperation is invariably more profitable than struggles for loot and supremacy!"

"They did, they did, but there are reasons . . . reasons of a historical nature, you see."

"We are getting nowhere!" he said. "I am here, after all, not

21

to defend you, as if you were on trial, but to commend, applaud, speak highly of, enumerate your merits and your virtues. You understand?"

"I understand."

My tongue by now was as stiff as if someone had frozen it, the starched collar of my dress shirt choked me, its front was all damp with the sweat that was pouring from me; I caught my roll of credentials on one of the medals and tore the outside sheet. The Rhohch, annoyed, contemptuous, yet at the same time detached, as though thinking of other things, suddenly said with an unexpected calm and mildness (ah, the artful diplomat!):

"I shall speak instead of your culture. Of its outstanding achievements. You do have a culture?!" he quickly added.

"We do indeed! A splendid culture!" I assured him.

"That's good. Art?"

"Oh yes! Music, poetry, architecture . . ."

"So then, architecture after all!" he exclaimed. "Wonderful. I must make a note of that. Explosives?"

"How do you mean, explosives?"

"Creative detonations, controlled, to regulate the climate, shift continents, river beds—you have that?"

"So far only bombs . . ." I said, then added in a hesitant whisper: "But there are many different kinds, napalm, phosphorus, and even with poison gas . . ."

"That's not what I had in mind," he said coldly. "Let us stick to the intellectual life. What do you believe in?"

This Rhohch who was supposed to recommend us was not, as I finally realized, a specialist in Earthly affairs. The thought that our fate would shortly be decided by the appearance of a creature of such ignorance before the forum of the entire Galaxy—well, it took my breath away. What rotten luck, I thought, they *would* have to go recall that head-chairman, the Earthist!

"We believe in universal brotherhood, in the triumph of peace and concord over hatred and war, we consider that man should be the measure of all things . . ."

He placed a heavy claw on my knee.

"Why man?" he said. "Well never mind. Still, your catalog is negative: the absence of war, the absence of hatred—by all that's nebular, have you no positive ideals?"

It was stifling hot.

"We believe in progress, in a better tomorrow, in the power of science."

"At last something!" he cried. "Science, yes, good . . . that I can use. And on which sciences do you spend the most?"

"Physics," I replied. "Research into atomic energy."

"Look . . . I tell you what. Say nothing. Let me do the talking. I'll handle this. Leave everything to me. And chin up!" he said as the machine stopped in front of a building.

My head was spinning, things swam before my eyes; I was led down crystal corridors, invisible barriers of some kind flew open with musical sighs, then I was plunging down, then up, then down again, the Rhohch stood at my side, immense, silent, wrapped in folds of metal, suddenly everything came to a halt, the glass balloon in front of me bulged and burst. I was standing at the bottom of the hall of the General Assembly. The amphitheater, spread out in funnel fashion, went swirling up in circular tiers of seats, immaculately white, dazzling; in the distance the tiny silhouettes of the delegations were sprinkles of emerald, gold and crimson along the spiraling ivory levels, strangely scintillating myriads it hurt to look upon. At first I was unable to distinguish eyes from medals, limbs from their artificial extensions, I only saw that they were moving rapidly, reaching across the snowy desks for sheaves of documents, black and shiny things like tiles of anthracite, while directly opposite me, at a distance of some fifty or sixty feet, flanked by walls of electronic machines, the Secretary-General sat atop a dais in the middle of a forest of microphones. Snatches of conversations floated in the air, conversations conducted in a thousand languages at once, and these stellar dialects ranged from the lowest basses to notes as shrill as the chirping of birds. With the feeling that the floor might open up beneath me any minute, I pulled my tuxedo straight. A sound rang out, reverberating endlessly, it was the Secretary-General setting in motion a machine that swung a mallet at a slab of solid gold; the vibrations made my ears throb. The Rhohch, towering above me, pointed to my place as the voice of the Secretary-General boomed from unseen loudspeakers. But before sitting down by the rectangular sign that bore the name of my native planet, I scanned the curving rows of seats, higher and higher, trying to find at least one kindred soul, at least one creature of humanoid appearance—in vain. Enormous shapes, lush, tuber-like, coils of aspic, currant jelly, fleshy stalks, pedunculations propped against the desks, faces the color of well-seasoned meat pies or gleaming like rice fritters, knots, pads, mandibles, pseudopodia holding the fates of stars both far and near, all passed before me as if in some slow-motion film, nor was there anything monstrous about them, I experienced no revulsion—contrary to the suppositions expressed so often back on Earth—as though I were not dealing here with cosmic horrors, but with beings that had emerged from beneath the chisel of some abstractionist sculptor, or perhaps a gastronomic visionary . . .

"Item number eighty-two," hissed the Rhohch in my ear and took his seat. I did the same. Picking up the headphones that lay on the desk, I listened in.

"The appliances, which, pursuant to the treaty ratified by this Esteemed Assembly, were, in full accordance with the terms specified in that treaty, delivered by the Altair Commonwealth to the Sexpartite Alliance of Fomalhaut, have displayed, as was confirmed by the report of the ad hoc subcommittee of the UP, certain properties which cannot be accounted for by minor deviations from the technological prescription agreed upon by the esteemed parties involved. Granted, as the Altair Commonwealth correctly notes, the radiation sifters and planetary regulators it manufactured were indeed supposed to possess the ability to reproduce, guaranteeing thereby the creation of machine progeny, which was duly provided for in the contract drawn up between both the esteemed parties involved; nevertheless that potentiality should have taken the form, in compliance with the engineering code of ethics that binds all members of our Federation, of individual budding, and not resulted from the endowment of the abovementioned mechanisms with programs of opposing signs, which—unfortunately—did in fact take place. This programmed polarity led to the creation, within the main energy compounds of Fomalhaut, of prurient tensions and, as a consequence of these, scenes that were not only offensive to public morality but which entailed serious material losses for the plaintiff party as well. The delivered units, instead of attending to the work they had been designed to perform, devoted most of their shifts to partner selection, whereby their constant running about with plugs for the purpose of recreational coupling led to violations of the Panundrian Statute and, ultimately, mechanicographic overcrowding, for both of which regrettable phenomena the defendant party is to blame. And so we hereby declare the debt to Altair null and void."

I put down the phones with a splitting headache. To hell with these machines offending the public morality, Altair, Fomalhaut and all the rest of it! I had had enough of the UP and wasn't even a member yet. I felt ill. Why did I ever listen to Professor Tarantoga? What use to me was this awful honor that obliged me to blush for the sins of others? Instead I should have—

An invisible current ran through me, for there on the enormous board flashed the digits 83, and I felt a vigorous jab. It was my Rhohch who, jumping to his claws or perhaps feelers, pulled me after him. The sun lamps floating beneath the ceiling of the hall directed upon us a blazing flood of azure light. Bathed on all sides by beams of radiance which seemed to shine right through me, and numbly clutching my thoroughly limp roll of certification papers, I heard the powerful bass of the Rhohch booming at my side, voluble and unconstrained, filling the entire amphitheater, yet the content of his speech reached me only in snatches, like sea foam during a storm, spraying the one who dares lean out over the pier.

". . . this marvelous Arrth (he couldn't even pronounce the name of my native planet properly!) . . . this noble humanity . . . and here its distinguished representative . . . elegant, amiable mammals . . . atomic energy, released with consummate skill in the foothills of their mountains . . . a youthful, buoyant culture, full of feeling . . . a deep faith in jergundery, though not devoid of ambifribbis . . . (evidently he was confusing us with someone else) . . . devoted to the cause of interstellar solidarity . . . in the hopes that their admittance into this august body . . . bringing to an end the embryonic phase of their social development . . . though alone and isolated on their galactic periphery . . . plucky, independent . . . surely deserving . . ."

"So far, in spite of everything, it's going well," flashed the thought. "He's praising us, not badly either . . . but wait, what's this?"

"True, they are paired! Their rigid underpinning . . . but

one must understand . . . in this Esteemed Assembly exceptions to the rule have the right to be represented too . . . there is no shame in abnormality . . . the difficult conditions that shaped them . . . aqueousness, even when saline, need not be an obstacle . . . with our assistance in the future they can rid themselves of this ug . . . of this unfortunate appearance, which the Esteemed Assembly with its customary generosity will be willing, I trust, to disregard . . . and so on behalf of the Rhohch Delegation and the Sidereal Union of Betelgeuse I hereby move that humanity from the planet Oreth be recognized as a member of the United Planets, and that the honest Orthonian standing here be accorded therewith the full rights of an accredited delegate to that organization. That is all."

A mighty roar broke out, interspersed with strange whistlings, but no applause (nor could there have been any, in the absence of hands); this din and racket abruptly subsided at the sound of a gong, and the voice of the Secretary-General could be heard:

"Do any of the esteemed delegations intend to speak to the motion now under consideration, namely the recognition of Humanity from the planet Areth?"

The radiant Rhohch, evidently extremely pleased with himself, dragged me back to my seat. I sat down, mumbling some incoherent words of appreciation for his services, when two pale green rays shot out simultaneously from different parts of the amphitheater.

"The representative from Thuban has the floor!" said the Secretary-General. Something rose to speak.

"Esteemed Council!" came the far yet piercing voice, not unlike the sound of sheet metal being cut, but the timbre quickly ceased to occupy my attention. "We have just heard, from the mouthparts of polpitor Voretex, a warm recommendation for the race of a distant planet, till now unknown to those assembled here. I should like to express my keen disappointment that the unexpected absence at today's session of sulpitor Extrevor has deprived us of the opportunity to acquaint ourselves more particularly with the history, the manners and the nature of that race, whose presence in the UP all Rhohchdom so eagerly desires. Now I am no specialist in the field of cosmic teratology, however I _would_ like, to the extent of my modest abilities, to supplement what we have just had the pleasure of hearing. First of all, in passing only, parenthetically as it were, I will point out that the native planet of humanity is called not Oreth, Areth or Arrth, as was said—not out of ignorance, of course, but purely, as I am quite convinced, in the heat of the oratorical moment— by my worthy colleague the preceding speaker. An insignificant detail, to be sure. However the other term, 'humanity,' which I made use of, is taken from the language of the race of Earth— the correct name, incidentally, for that obscure little planet— while *our* sciences designate the Earthlings somewhat differently. I trust it shall not unduly weary this Esteemed Assembly if I take the liberty of giving the full name and classification of the species whose membership in the UP we are considering, quoting for that purpose from an excellent work of specialists, namely the Galactical Teratology of Grammpluss and Gzeems."

The representative from Thuban opened the enormous volume on his desk to the place indicated by a bookmark, and read:

"In accordance with the accepted systems of taxonomy and nomenclature, all anomalous forms found in our Galaxy are contained within the phylum *Aberrantia* (Deviates, Freaks), which is divided into the subphyla *Debilitales* (Boobs) and *Antisapientinales* (Screwheads). To the latter subphylum belong the classes *Canaliacaea* (Thuglies) and *Necroludentia* (Corpselovers). Among the Corpselovers we distinguish, in turn, the orders *Patricidiaceae* (Fatherbeaters), *Matriphagideae* (Mothereaters) and *Lasciviaceae* (Abominites, or Scumberbutts). The Abominites, highly degenerate forms, we divide into the *Cretininae* (Clenchpoops, viz. *Cadaverium Mordans* or the Chewcarcass Addlepate) and *Horrosrissimae* (Howlmouths, with the classic example of the Outchested Backshouldered Dullard, *Idiontus Erectus Gzeemsi*). A few of the Howlmouths have actually been known to create their own pseudo-cultures; among these are such species as *Anophilus Belligerens*, the Bungfond Tuff, which calls itself *Genius Pulcherrimus Mundanus*, or that most curious specimen, possessing an entirely bald body and observed by Grammpluss in the darkest corner of our Galaxy—*Monstroteratum Furiosum* (the Stinking Meemy), which has given itself the name of *Homo Sapiens*."

A clamor went up in the hall. The Secretary-General set in motion his machine with the mallet.

"Stiff upper lip!" hissed the Rhohch. I couldn't see him, what with the glare from the sun lamps, or perhaps it was the sweat getting into my eyes. A ray of hope flickered within me, for someone was demanding to be heard on a point of order. Presenting himself to the assembly as a member of the Aquarius delegation, who was also an astrozoologist, he began to take issue with the Thubanian—but alas, only on the grounds that—as a disciple of the school of Professor Hagranops—he considered the classification put forward to be incomplete. For he distinguished, after his mentor, the separate order *Degeneratores*, to which belonged the Fouljowls, Upgluts, Necrovores and Stifflickers: the application of the term "Monstroteratus" to man, he also felt, was incorrect—instead one should follow the nomenclature of the Aquarian School, employing the more consistent term of Bug-eyed Bogus (*Artefactum Abhorrens*). After a brief exchange of remarks, the Thubanian resumed his speech:

"The honorable representative of Rhohchia, urging upon us the candidacy of this so-called Man the Wise or—to be more precise—this Bug-eyed Meemy, a typical example of a Corpselover, failed to mention—in his recommendation—the word 'albumin,' apparently thinking it indecent. And indeed, the word does evoke associations, which propriety forbids me to elaborate on here. To be sure, the possession of EVEN THAT kind of living matter carries with it no disgrace. (Cries of "Hear, hear!") It is not in the albumin that the problem lies! Nor in the bestowing upon oneself, when one happens to be a corpseloving howler, the title of sapient human. This is but a weakness, quite understandable if not forgivable, dictated by one's *amour-propre.* No, the problem lies not here, Esteemed Council!"

My attention began to wander, blur, go blank—I was catching only snatches.

"And even carnivorism is no one's fault, if it results in the course of natural evolution! Yet the differences separating so-called man from his animal relatives are practically nonexistent! Just as an individual who is *higher* may not claim that this gives him the right to devour those who are *lower*, so one endowed with a somewhat *higher* intelligence may neither devour nor murder those of *lower* mentality, and if he absolutely must do this (shouts of "He musn't! Let him eat spinach!")—if, I say, he *must*, by reason of some tragic hereditary affliction, he should at

28

least consume the bloodied victims with dismay, in secret, in his lair and the darkest recesses of the cave, torn by feelings of remorse, anguish, and the hope that he will be able, someday, to free himself from that burden of unremitting murder. But such, alas, is not the behavior of our Stinking Meemy! It desecrates the mortal remains, chopping, stewing, skewering, it toys with them, only afterwards to ingest them in public feeding places, in the presence of cavorting naked females of its species, which serves to whet its appetite for the dead; the necessity of changing this stage of affairs, that cries out to the entire Galaxy for revenge, never even enters its colloidal head! On the contrary, it has provided itself with higher justifications, which, residing somewhere between the stomach, that crypt of innumerable victims, and eternity, entitle it to continue murdering with a clear conscience. So much then, not to take up the time of this Esteemed Assembly, for the activities and habits of 'man the wise.' Among its ancestors there was one that seemed to promise much. I speak of the species *homo neanderthalensis*. He deserves our attention. Similar in appearance to modern man, he possessed a brain case of greater capacity, hence a larger brain, or intellect. A gatherer of mushrooms, inclined to meditation, a true lover of the arts, gentle, phlegmatic, there is no doubt but that he would have made a strong candidate for membership in our Esteemed Organization. Unfortunately he no longer is among the living. Would perhaps the delegate from Earth, whom we have the honor here to entertain, care to tell us what became of the ever-so-civilized and likable Neanderthal? I see he does not, so I must speak for him. The Neanderthal was exterminated root and branch, wiped off the face of the Earth by our selfsame *homo sapiens*. And as if the foul deed of fratricide was not enough, Earth's scholars then began to blacken the name of the annihilated victim, ascribing to themselves—and not to it, their cerebral superior—the higher intelligence. Today we have among us, here in this venerable hall, within these lofty walls, a representative of the corpse-eaters, one who is resourceful in the pursuit of lethal pleasures, a cunning architect of wholesale slaughter, and whose physical appearance inspires in us both ridicule and horror, a horror we are scarcely able to overcome. Today we see, there on that hitherto white, unsullied seat, a creature that lacks even the courage of a consistent criminal, for it ever seeks

29

to dress its body-strewn career with the splendor of false names, names whose true and terrible meaning may be deciphered by any objective student of interstellar civilization. Yes, Esteemed Council . . ."

In point of fact I got only fragments from this two-hour harangue, but they were more than enough. The Thubanian created a picture of monsters wallowing in a sea of blood, and he did this without haste, methodically opening still other learned books, records, annals, chronicles, all placed in preparation on his desk, and took to hurling the materials to the floor when he was done with them, as if in a sudden fit of disgust, as if the very pages that described us had become caked with the victims' blood. Then he turned to our recorded history; he told of the massacres, pogroms, wars, crusades, genocides, and using slides and full-scale charts showed the technologies of crime, instruments of torture, ancient and medieval. When he started in on the present day, sixteen assistants had to wheel in carts that groaned beneath stacks of additional documentation; other assistants, or rather UP paramedicals, meanwhile administered (from tiny helicopters) first aid to the hundreds of listeners who had grown weak during the lecture, but me they ignored, in the naïve belief—I suppose—that the stream of gory details of Earth's culture would not affect me in the least. But actually about halfway through that presentation I began, like one on the brink of madness, to fear my very self, as if, thrown in among these phantasmagorical, outlandish beings that surrounded me on every side, *I* were the only monster. Then, just as it seemed that this horrible list of accusations would never end, the words were uttered:

"And now let the Esteemed Assembly proceed to vote upon the motion of the Rhohch delegation!"

The hall fell into a deathly silence, till something stirred right beside me. It was my Rhohch rising, in the attempt—a desperate attempt—to refute at least a few of the charges made. But he put his foot in it completely when he tried to assure the assembly that mankind felt the deepest respect for the Neanderthals, its venerable ancestors, who had died out entirely by themselves; the Thubanian, however, demolished my defender on the spot with a single, well-aimed question, put directly to me:

30

on Earth, did calling someone a "Neanderthal" pass for a compliment, or was it instead a term of abuse?

Well it was all over now, I thought, every hope was lost, and I would be limping home like a dog sent back to its kennel for having been caught with a little bird, half-smothered, in its jaws. But then, in the hum and buzz of the hall, the Secretary-General leaned over to the microphone and said:

"The chair recognizes the representative from the Iridian delegation."

The Iridian was short, silvery gray and plump, like a puff of smoke caught in the slanting rays of the winter sun.

"I would like to ask," he said, "who will be paying the Earthlings' enrollment fee? They themselves? It's a considerable sum—a billion tons of platinum, not every applicant has that kind of metal!"

An angry murmur filled the amphitheater.

"Your question will be appropriate only when the motion of the Rhohch delegation has been taken to a vote and passed!" said the Secretary-General after a moment's hesitation.

"With the permission of Your Galactitude!" returned the Iridian. "I happen to be of a somewhat different opinion and therefore wish to support the question I just raised with a few observations, which I think you shall find most relevant. I have here, to begin with, a work of that renowned consultant planetologist, hyperdoctor Phrogghrus, and I quote from it as follows: . . . *planets on which life cannot spontaneously originate have these distinguishing features: A) radical climatic changes in rapidly alternating sequences (i.e. the so-called cycle 'spring-summer-autumn-winter') or those even more cataclysmic, occurring at great intervals (ice ages); B) the presence of large natural satellites; their tidal influences also are inimical to life; C) frequently appearing maculations on the surface of the central or mother star, as these are a source of deleterious radiation; D) the preponderance, in area, of seas over continents; E) persistent glaciation in the polar regions; F) the atmospheric precipitation of water in its solid or liquid state . . . As one can plainly see . . ."*

"Point of order!!" cried my Rhohch, jumping up as if fired with some new hope. "I ask whether the delegation from Iridia will vote in favor of the motion, or against it."

"In favor of the motion, but with an amendment we shall

31

shortly propose to this Esteemed Assembly," the Iridian replied, then went on:

"Revered Council! At the nine hundred and eighteenth session of the General Assembly, in this very hall, we considered the application for membership of a race of bungbrain abominoids, who presented themselves to us as 'supremious everlasters,' while in actual fact their forms were so impermanent that during the abovementioned session of the Assembly the composition of this abominite delegation changed fifteen times, though the session itself lasted no more than eight hundred years. These wretched creatures, when the time arrived to submit the curriculum vitae of their race, became hopelessly entangled in contradictions, solemnly assuring the Esteemed Assembly—though, mind you, without a shred of evidence—that they had been created by a certain Supreme Mover in his own perfect image, owing to which circumstance they were—among other things—spiritually immortal. Then when it came to light that their planet fit exactly the bionegative conditions of hyperdoctor Phrogghrus, the Joint Plenary Assembly appointed a special Investigative Subcommittee, and that body confirmed that the race of screwheads under suspicion had arisen not as a result of any prank of nature, but instead due to a regrettable incident brought about by third parties."

("What's he saying? Hush! Not true! Kindly remove that claw, you deviate!" went the commotion in the hall, growing by the minute.)

"The findings of the Investigative Subcommittee," continued the Iridian, "led to the passage, at the next session of the UP, of an amendment to article two of the United Planets Charter, which amendment reads as follows (here he unrolled a lengthy parchment and cleared his throat):

A categorical ban is hereby imposed on the engagement in any life-initiating activities on all planets of the Phrogghrus type A, B, C, D or E, also the authorities in charge of research expeditions as well as commanders of ships that land upon such globes are as of now instructed to see to—and therefore held fully responsible for—the strict observance of the aforesaid ban. This includes not only deliberate life-engendering practices like the sowing of algae, bacteria and so forth, but also the unintentional induction of bioevolution, whether through negligence or in absent-mindedness. Such con-

32

traceptive prophylaxis is dictated by the best intentions and knowledge of the UP, and particularly in cognizance of the following facts. In the first place—the natural hostility of an environment which one has externally inoculated with microorganisms gives rise, in the course of their subsequent evolution, to deviations and deformities of a sort never encountered within the domain of natural biogenesis. Secondly—these adverse circumstances produce species which are not only defective physiologically, but burdened as well with the severest forms of psychic abnormality; and if under such conditions there should develop beings possessing some small degree of intelligence—and this does on occasion happen—their existence will be filled with great mental suffering. For, upon attaining the first stage of consciousness, they immediately begin to search their surroundings for the cause of their own origin and, unable to find it there, turn in confusion and despair to blind, delusive faiths. In particular, since the normal course of evolutionary processes in the Universe is unknown to them, they take their physical shape, however hideous it may be, as well as their way—such as it is—of thinking, for ordinary phenomena, entirely typical of those manifested throughout the macrocosm. And therefore, out of deep concern for the well-being and dignity of life in general, and of sentient beings in particular, the General Assembly of the UP resolves and decrees that whosoever violates this contraceptive article of the UP Charter, effective immediately, shall be subject to sanctions and penalties pursuant to the terms of the corresponding paragraphs of the Code of Interplanetary Law.

The Iridian, putting aside the UP Charter, lifted a massive volume of the Code, which nimble assistants placed in his tentacles, and, opening that monumental tome to the right page, read in a ringing voice:

"Volume Two of the Interplanetary Penal Code, Section Eighty, entitled, 'On Planetary Incontinence.' "

Paragraph 212: The impregnating of a planet naturally barren is punishable by no less than one hundred, no more than one thousand five hundred years of full astrocism, irrespective of any civil liability for the moral and material losses suffered by the victims.

Paragraph 213: The infraction of paragraph 212, aggravated by the conspicuous presence of malicious intent, as evidenced by manipulations of a wanton nature and with premeditation, whose purpose is the evolution of life forms singularly disfigured, to in-

33

spire universal fear or universal revulsion, is punishable by astrocism and distillation of up to one thousand five hundred years.

Paragraph 214: The impregnating of a barren planet as a result of carelessness, oversight or through the slipshod application of appropriate contraceptive measures, is punishable by astrocism of up to four hundred years; if the act is committed in relative ignorance or otherwise reduced awareness of its consequences, the sentence may be reduced to a hundred years.

"I make no mention," added the Iridian, "of the penalties for interfering with an evolutionary process *in statu nascendi,* as that does not concern us here. However I would like to point out that the Code does provide for the material liability of the perpetrators with respect to the victims of their planetary incontinence; I will not quote the relevant sections of the Civil Code, for fear of altogether exhausting the patience of the members of this Assembly. I note only that in the catalog of spheres held to be definitively barren by hyperdoctor Phrogghrus no less than by the United Planets Charter and Interplanetary Penal Code, we find on page two thousand six hundred and eighteen, eighth line from the bottom, the following heavenly bodies: *Ea, Eagron, Earlsharn, Earth, East Bong, Eblis . . .*"

My mouth fell open, the certification papers slipped from my hand, it grew dark before my eyes. ("Pay attention!" they were shouting in the hall. "Hear, hear! Who does he mean?! Down with—! Long live—!") As for me, to the degree that it was possible, I tried crawling under the desk.

"Esteemed Council!!" thundered the representative from Iridia, hurling the heavy volumes of the Interplanetary Code to the floor of the amphitheater (this must have been a favorite oratorical device in the UP). "We can never hear enough of matters that bring dishonor to those who would violate the United Planets Charter! We can never brand enough those irresponsible elements who would beget life in conditions entirely unsuited for it!!

"Now here we are approached by creatures that have no inkling of the true odiousness of their existence, nor any knowledge of its cause! Now here they come knocking at the venerable door of this Worthy Assembly, and what then, pray, are we to tell them, all these abominoids, howlmouths, freaksnouts, clenchpoops, corpse-lovers, mother-eaters and addlepates, wringing their alleged hands and falling to their alleged knees when they learn that in reality they belong to the subphylum 'Artefacta,' and that their supreme and perfect creator was some ship's cook, who once poured out upon the rocks of a dead planet—a bucket of fermented slops, for his own amusement imparting to that wretched source of life properties which later would make it the laughing-stock of an entire Galaxy! And how, pray, will these poor devils defend themselves when some future Cato throws up to them the shameful levorotarory configuration, yes the left-handedness, of their amino acids!!" (The hall was all aboil, in vain did the machine repeatedly swing its mallet, they were howling on every side: "For shame! Down with—! Quarantine 'em! Who is he talking about? Look at the Earthling dissolve, the Meemy is leaking all over!!")

I was indeed sweating like a pig. The Iridian, raising his stentorian voice above the general roar, cried:

"I shall now put a few final questions to the honorable delegation from Rhohchia! Is it not true that many years ago there landed on the then dead planet of Earth a ship carrying your flag, and that, due to a refrigerator malfunction, a portion of its perishables had gone bad? Is it not true that on this ship there were two spacehands, afterwards stricken from all the registers for unconscionable double-dealing with duckweed liverworts, and that this pair of arrant knaves, these Milky-Way ne'er-do-wells, were named Gorrd and Lod? Is it not true that Gorrd and Lod decided, in their drunkenness, not to content themselves with the usual pollution of a defenseless, uninhabited planet, that their notion was to set off, in a manner vicious and vile, a biological evolution the likes of which the world had never seen before? Is it not true that both these Rhohches, with malice aforethought, malice of the greatest volume and intensity, devised a way to make of Earth—on a truly galactic scale—a breeding ground for freaks, a cosmic side show, a panopticum, an exhibit of grisly prodigies and curios, a display whose living specimens would one day become the butt of jokes told even in the outermost Nebulae?! Is it not true that, bereft of all sense of decency and ethical restraints, both these miscreants then emptied on the rocks of lifeless Earth six barrels of gelatinous glue, rancid, plus two cans of albuminous paste, spoiled, and that to this ooze they added some curdled ribose, pentose, and

35

levulose, and—as though that filth were not enough—they poured upon it three large jugs of a mildewed solution of amino acids, then stirred the seething swill with a coal shovel twisted to the left, and also used a poker, likewise bent in the same direction, as a consequence of which the proteins of all future organisms on Earth were LEFT-handed?! And finally, is it not true that Lod, suffering at the time from a runny nose and—moreover—egged on by Gorrd, who was reeling from an excessive intake of intoxicants, did willfully and knowingly sneeze into that protoplasmal matter, and, having infected it thereby with the most virulent viruses, guffawed that he had thus breathed 'the fucking breath of life' into those miserable evolutionary beginnings?! And is it not true that this leftwardness and this virulence were thereafter transmitted and handed down from organism to organism, and now afflict with their continuing presence the innocent representatives of the race *Artefactum Abhorrens*, who gave themselves the name of '*homo sapiens*' purely out of simple-minded ignorance? And therefore is it not true that the Rhohches must not only pay the Earthlings' initiation fee, to the tune of a billion tons of platinum, but also compensate the unfortunate victims of their planetary incontinence—in the form of COSMIC ALIMONY?!"

With these words pandemonium broke loose in the amphitheater. I cowered—flying through the air in every direction came portfolios, volumes of the Interplanetary Penal Code, and even material evidence, objects such as badly rust-eaten jugs, barrels, pokers, though Lord knows how they got there; perhaps the clever Iridians, having some score to settle with the Rhohches, had been conducting archeological research on Earth since time immemorial, collecting the incriminating evidence, which was all carefully stored on board their Flying Saucers; but I found it difficult to ponder such a point, for everything was heaving around me, tentacles and claws flashed past, and my Rhohch, extremely agitated, leaped up from his seat screaming something, but it was lost in the general bedlam, while I continued to sit, as it were, in the eye of the storm, and the last thought that pounded in my brain was the question of that sneeze with premeditation which had brought us into the world.

The next thing I knew, someone seized me by the hair, painfully, till I groaned; it was the Rhohch, trying to demonstrate how solidly I'd been fashioned by Earth's evolution and how little I deserved being called a paltry sort of creature, stuck together—and flimsily at that—out of rotten bits of refuse, and he walloped me over the head again and again with his enormous, heavy claw . . . I felt the life slowly going out of me, my struggling grew weak, weaker, I couldn't breathe, I gave a few last kicks in agony—and collapsed on my pillow. Half-conscious, I jumped up immediately, sat on the bed, feeling my neck, head, chest, to make sure that all that I had undergone was but the product of an awful dream. I heaved a sigh of relief, but then, later, some slight doubts began to trouble me. I told myself, "For God's sake, it's only a dream!" Somehow that didn't help. Finally, to dispel these gloomy thoughts I went to see my aunt on the Moon. But an eight-minute ride on a lunibus that stops right outside my house, no, I can hardly call this the eighth stellar voyage—more worthy of that title, surely, would be the journey taken in my sleep, in which I suffered so for all humanity.

THE ELEVENTH VOYAGE

It was going to be one of those days. The mess in the house, bad enough when I'd had my servant sent out for repairs, was growing worse. I couldn't find a thing. There were mice nesting in my meteor collection. They had gnawed the prettiest chondrite.

While I was making coffee the milk boiled over. That electrical numskull had hidden the dishrags along with my handkerchiefs. I really should have taken him in for an overhaul back when he started shining my shoes on the inside. I used an old parachute for a dishrag, then went upstairs, dusted off the meteors and set a mousetrap. I'd collected all the specimens myself. It's not that difficult—all you do is come up on the meteor from behind and drop a net over it.

Then I remembered the toast and ran downstairs.

Burnt to a crisp, of course. I tossed the toast in the sink. The sink stopped up. I waved my hand in disgust and took a look in the mailbox.

It was full of the usual morning fare—two invitations to conferences somewhere in the godforsaken backwaters of the Crab Nebula, fliers advertising cream for polishing your rocket, a new issue of *The Jet Trackman*, nothing of interest. The last item was a dark, thick envelope sealed with five seals. I weighed it in my hand, then opened it.

The Secret Minister for matters concerning Cercia has the honor to request the presence of Mr. Ijon Tichy at a meeting to be held on the 16th of this month, 17.30 hours, in the small lecture hall of Lambretanum. Admittance only to those bearing invitations. X-rays required.

We urge the matter be kept in strictest confidence.

An illegible signature, a seal,
and stamped across in red,
diagonally, the words:

COSMIC IMPORTANCE. CLASSIFIED!!

Well now, here was something at last, I thought. Cercia, Cercia . . . I knew the name, but couldn't quite place it. I looked it up in the *Cosmic Encyclopedia*. Ceres, Cerulia, that was all. Curious, I thought. The *Almanac* didn't have it either. Yes, this was interesting indeed. Definitely a secret planet. "That's what I like," I murmured and began to dress. It was ten already, but I had to straighten up after my servant. The socks I found right away, in the refrigerator, and it seemed to me that I was finally catching on to the train of thought of that unhinged electronic brain, when suddenly I was faced with a singular fact: no pants. None, nowhere. Only jackets and coats were hanging in the closet. I searched the whole house, I even cleaned out the rocket—nothing. Except I discovered that that broken-down blockhead of mine had drunk up all the oil in the basement. He must have done it recently too, because a week ago I'd counted the cans and they were all full. This was so infuriating that I seriously considered whether I shouldn't have him scrapped after all. He didn't like getting up in the morning, and for months now would stuff his earphones with wax at night. You could ring until your arm fell off. Absent-mindedness, was his excuse. I threatened to unscrew his fuses, but he only rattled in disdain. He knew I needed him.

I divided the entire house into squares according to the Pinkerton method and began a search as thorough as if I'd been looking for a pin. Finally I found a laundry ticket. The scoundrel had sent all my pants to the cleaner's. But what had happened to the pants I was wearing the day before? I simply couldn't recall. Meanwhile it was time for lunch. No point in trying the refrigerator—besides the socks, it contained only stationery. I was getting desperate. I took my spacesuit out of the

39

rocket, put it on and walked to the nearest department store. They stared at me a little on the street, but I bought two pair of pants, one black, one gray, returned home in the spacesuit, changed and—in the foulest possible mood—went out to a Chinese restaurant. I ate what they gave me, drank down my anger with a bottle of Mosel, and, looking at my watch, realized it was almost five. I'd wasted an entire day.

There weren't any helicopters in front of the Lambretanum, and not a single car, not even a private rocket—nothing. "It's *that* bad?" flashed the thought. I crossed a vast garden full of dahlias to reach the main entrance. For a long time no one answered. At last the cover over the one-way peephole lifted and an invisible eye scrutinized me, after which the gate opened, just enough for me to squeeze through.

"Mr. Tichy," the man who let me in said into his pocket microphone. "Upstairs please," he told me. "The door on the left. They're waiting for you."

Upstairs it was pleasantly cool. I entered the lecture hall and found myself in a highly select gathering. Except for two characters behind the conference table whom I'd never seen before, there on velvet upholstered armchairs sat the flower of cosmography. I recognized Professor Gargarragh and his assistants. Nodding to one and all, I took a seat in the back. One of the men behind the conference table, tall and graying at the temples, opened a drawer, pulled out a rubber bell and tinkled it noiselessly. What fantastic precautions, I thought.

"Gentlemen! Rectors, deans, professors, and you, our esteemed Ijon Tichy," began the man with the gray temples, rising. "As Plenipotentiary and Minister to Matters of the Utmost Gravity and Secrecy, I hereby open this special session convened to consider the case of Cercia. Secret Adviser Xaphirius has the floor."

In the first row a stout, broad-shouldered man, his hair as white as milk, stood up; he ascended the podium, made a slight bow to the assembly and said without preface:

"Gentlemen! About sixty years ago a Galactic Company freighter, the *Jonathan II*, set off from the planetary port at Yokohama. This vessel, under the command of one Astrocenty Peapo, a seasoned spacer, was carrying lumber to Areclandria, a planet of the gamma Orion. It was last sighted by a stellar beacon in the vicinity of Cerberon. Then it disappeared without a trace. A year passed, and the insurance people of Securitas Cosmica, SECOS for short, paid over full damages for the loss of the ship. Some two weeks after that a certain amateur radio operator from New Guinea received a telegram with the following text."

The speaker lifted a card from the table and read:

KEMPOOTAR GUN BZIRCK
ASS HO ASS JUNYJANTU

"At this point, gentlemen, I must make mention of certain facts which are indispensable for a further understanding of the matter. The radio operator in question was practically illiterate and in addition had a speech impediment. By force of habit and due, one may assume, to his total lack of experience, he distorted the message, which, according to the reconstruction made by our experts at Universal Codes, originally read: 'Computer gone berserk S. O. S. Jonathan II.' The experts maintained, on the basis of this text, that the rare event of a mutiny in deep space had in fact taken place—we are speaking of the mutiny of the ship's computer. Now because the insurance payment had been made to the owners and they were therefore no longer in any position to lay claim to the lost ship, for all the property rights to it (including the cargo) had been assumed by SECOS, it was SECOS who engaged the Pinkerton Agency, in the persons of Abstrahazy and Mnemonius Pinkerton, to conduct the appropriate inquiries. The investigation undertaken by these competent professionals revealed that the computer of the *Jonathan*, a luxury model in its day, but which, by the time of its final voyage, was well along in years, had recently been filing complaints against one of the crew. This was a rocket engineer named Symileon Gitterton, who was supposed to have tormented it in a variety of ways—lowering its output potential, flicking its tubes, taunting it, and even heaping upon the Computer such offensive epithets and slurs as, for example, 'old screw-loose solderhead' and 'uncle frammus.' Gitterton denied everything, claiming that the Computer was simply hallucinating—which does indeed on occasion happen to our senior automata. At any rate Professor Gargarragh will shortly fill you gentlemen in on this particular aspect of the case.

41

"All efforts to locate the ship during the next ten years failed. Soon after that time, however, the Pinkerton agents, still tirelessly working on the mysterious disappearance of the *Jonathan*, learned that there was a half-crazed, sickly beggar who would sit in front of the restaurant of the Hotel Galax and sing the most wondrous tales, professing to be Astrocenty Peapo the former starship commander. This old man, bedraggled and tattered beyond description, did indeed answer to the name of Astrocenty Peapo, yet not only was his reason dimmed, but he had lost the power of speech—and could only sing. When questioned patiently by the Pinkerton men, he chanted an incredible tale: how something terrible had taken place on deck, as a result of which he was thrown overboard with only the spacesuit on his back, and how with a handful of loyal rocketeers he had to return to Earth on foot from the murky regions of Andromeda, which took a good two hundred years. He wandered, so he sang, sometimes on meteors heading in the right direction, or sometimes hopped a passing barge—it was only a small part of the journey that he spent on the Lumeon, an unmanned cosmic probe which happened to be flying towards Earth at a velocity just under the velocity of light. This ride astraddle the back of the Lumeon he paid for (as he put it) with the loss of speech, though he also grew younger by many years, thanks to the well-known phenomenon of the contraction of time on bodies traveling at speeds approaching c.

"So went the story, or rather, the swan song of the old man. But of the events that had occurred aboard the *Jonathan* he stubbornly refused to croon a single note. Only after they placed recording devices around the hotel entrance where he often sat were the Pinkerton men able to tape the old beggar's tunes; in several of these he let loose a volley of the most dreadful imprecations—against a common calculator that proclaimed itself Sublime Arch-imperator of the Macropanopticontinuum. Pinkerton concluded, from this, that the reading of the message had been correct, that the Computer, having gone mad, did indeed dispose of all persons on the ship.

"The investigation took on new life with the discovery, made five years later by a cruiser of the Metagalactological Institute, the *Astromeg*, of a rusty hulk drifting in orbit around the unexplored planet of Procyon and similar in profile to the lost

Jonathan. The *Astromeg,* nearly out of fuel, turned back without landing on the planet, but it notified Earth by radio. A small patrolship, the *Deucron,* was dispatched at once, searched the regions surrounding Procyon and finally came upon a wreck. This was in fact the *Jonathan,* or rather, what remained of that ship. The *Deucron* reported that it found the abandoned vessel in frightful condition—the machines had been removed, the bulkheads, decks, partitions, hatches—everything down to the last screw, so that all that was circling the planet was an empty, gutted hull. Further probes conducted by the crew of the *Deucron* revealed that the mutinous Computer of the *Jonathan* had decided, afterwards, to settle on Procyon, and plundered the ship of its contents so as to install itself more comfortably on that planet. As a result of which information, a file was accordingly set up in our division, under the code name of CERCIA, which stands for: Cargo and Effects Repossession—Caution, Insubordinate Autopilot.

"The Computer—as subsequent research showed—had established itself on the planet and multiplied, producing numerous progeny in the form of robots, over which it enjoyed absolute power and dominion. Since however Cercia lies well within the sphere of influence, political-gravitational, of Procyon and its Melmanites, with which intelligent race it is in Earth's interest to maintain friendly relations, we had no wish to intervene militarily and so for a certain period of time left Cercia and the robot colony founded there by the Computer—in our division files bearing the code name ROBCOL—in peace. But SECOS petitioned for repossession, on the grounds that the Computer and all its robots were by law the property of the Insurance Company. We approached the Melmanites in this matter; their reply was that to their knowledge the Computer had created not a colony, but an independent state, called by its inhabitants Magnifica, and that the Melmanite government, although it had not recognized the existence of this state *de jure,* nor indeed had there even been an exchange of diplomatic representatives, nonetheless accepted the presence of that social organism *de facto* and did not feel it had justification or, for that matter, the authority to initiate any change in the situation. So far the robots in question had conducted themselves peacefully, vegetating on the planet, and gave no sign of any aggressive or destructive tendencies. But obviously our department could not simply drop the matter there, the general feeling being that such an action would smack of frivolity; thus we sent several of our men to Cercia, disguising them first as robots, for the youthful nationalism of the Robcol had taken the form of an unreasonable hatred of all things human. The Cercian press never tires of repeating that we are abominable slaveowners, who illegally exploit and prey upon innocent robots. And so all the negotiations which we had attempted to conduct on behalf of the SECOS organization, in the spirit of mutual respect and understanding, came to naught, since even our most modest demands—namely, that the Computer turn itself and its robots over to the insurance company—were rewarded with an insulting silence.

"Gentlemen," the speaker said, raising his voice, "events did not, unfortunately, proceed as we had anticipated. After a few radio reports we lost all contact with our people on Cercia. We sent replacements, with analogous results. After the first coded communication informing us that they had landed without incident, they gave no further sign of life. Since that time, over a period of nine years, we have sent a total of two thousand seven hundred and eighty-six agents to Cercia, and not one has returned, not one has responded! This evidence of the perfection of the robots' counterespionage is accompanied by other, perhaps even more alarming facts. Note that the Cercian press is attacking us more violently than ever in its editorials. The robots' printing houses are turning out, on a mass basis, leaflets and fliers addressed to the robots of Earth and in which men, portrayed as grasping voltsuckers and villains, are called injurious names—thus, for example, in the official pronouncements we are referred to as mucilids, and the whole human race—as gook. Once more we appealed, in an aide memoire, to the government of Procyon, but it repeated its previous declaration of nonintervention and all our efforts to point out the dangers inherent in that neutralist position (which is in reality the most craven isolationism) were to no avail. We were given to understand that the robots were *our* product, *ergo* we were responsible for all their acts. On the other hand Procyon was categorically opposed to any sort of punitive expedition, including the forced expropriation of the Computer and its subjects. That, gentlemen, is how the situation stands today, and the reason for the calling of this meeting. To give you some idea of how volatile the situation is, I shall only add that last month the *Electron Courier,* the official organ of the Computer, ran an article in which it cast mud upon the entire evolutionary tree of man and called for the annexation of Earth to Cercia, on the grounds that robots—according to all the best authorities—were a more advanced form than living creatures. On which note I conclude, and yield the floor to Professor Gargarragh."

Bent beneath the weight of many years, the famed specialist in mechanical psychiatry ascended, not without difficulty, to the lectern.

"Gentlemen!" he said in a quavering yet still resonant voice. "For some time now it has been known that electronic brains must be not only constructed, but educated as well. The lot of an electronic brain is hard. Constant, unremitting labor, complex calculations, the abuse and rough humor of attendants—this is what an apparatus, by its nature extremely delicate, must endure. Little wonder then, that there are breakdowns, and short circuits, which not infrequently represent attempts at suicide. Not long ago I had, in my clinic, such a case. A split personality—*dichotomia profunda psychogenes electrocutiva alternans*. This particular brain addressed love letters to itself, employing such endearing terms as 'relay baby,' 'spoolie,' 'little digit drumdump'—clear proof of how badly the thing needed affection, a kind word, some warm and tender relationship. A series of electroshock treatments and a long rest restored it to health. Or take, for example, *tremor electricus frigoris oscillativus*. An electronic brain, gentlemen, is not a sewing machine, not something one can use to drive nails into a wall. It is a conscious being, aware of everything that takes place around it, and this is why in moments of cosmic danger it may begin to quake, setting the entire ship atremble, so that those on board can hardly keep their feet.

"There are certain insensitive natures who have no sympathy for this. They provoke the brains out of all patience. An electronic brain, gentlemen, wishes us nothing but good; however the endurance of coils and tubes has its limits too. It was only as a result of endless persecution from its captain, who turned out to be a notorious drunkard, that the electronic calculator of *Grenobi,* designed to make in-flight course corrections, announced in a sudden fit of madness that it was the remote-control child of the Great Andromeda and therefore hereditary emperor of all Murglandria. Treated at our most exclusive institution, the patient finally quieted down, came to its senses, and is now almost completely normal. There are, of course, more serious cases. Such for example was a certain university brain, which, having fallen in love with the wife of a mathematics professor, began out of jealousy to falsify all the calculations, till the poor mathematician grew despondent, convinced that he could no longer add. But in that brain's defense it must be stated that the mathematician's wife had methodically seduced it, asking it to total up the bills for her most intimate undergarments. The case we are considering here brings to mind another—that of the great spacebrain of the *Pancratius*. As a result of defective wiring it became connected with the ship's other brains and, in an uncontrollable impulse to expand (which we call electrodynamic gigantophilia) pillaged the stockroom of its spare parts, deposited the crew on craggy Mizzeron, then dived into the ocean of Alantropia and proclaimed itself Patriarch of the lizards there. Before we were able to reach the planet with sedative equipment, the thing blew out its tubes in a fit of rage, for the lizards wouldn't listen. It's true that in this instance too there were extenuating circumstances: we learned later that the second mate of the *Pancratius*, a known cosmic cardsharp, had cleaned out the unfortunate brain to the last rivet—with the aid of a marked deck. But the case of the Computer, gentlemen, is exceptional. We have here the clear symptoms of such disorders as *gigantomania ferrogenes acuta*, as *paranoia misantropica persecutoria*, as *polyplasia panelectropsychica debilitativa gravissima*, not to mention *necrofilia, thanatofilia* and *necromantia*. Gentlemen! I must bring to your attention certain facts which are fundamental for an understanding of the case. The *Jonathan II* had in its hold, besides the lumber destined for the shipbuilders of Procyon, a number of receptacles carrying mercury-based synthetic memory, which was to have been delivered to the Galactic University in Fomalhaut. These contained two kinds of information: one in the field of psychopathology, the other—in archaic lexicology. We must assume that the Computer, in expanding, consumed the contents of those receptacles, and thereby absorbed into itself a comprehensive knowledge of such matters as the history of

Jack the Ripper, the Boston Strangler, the Strangler of Gloomspick, also the biography of Sacher-Masoch, the memoirs of the Marquis de Sade, and the records of the flagellant sect of Pirpinact, and a first edition of Murmuropoulos's *Impalement through the Centuries*, as well as that famous collector's item from the Abercrombie library—*Stabbing*, in manuscript, by one Hapsodor, beheaded in the year 1673 in London and better known under the alias of 'the Baby Butcher.' In addition, an original work of Janick Pidwa, *A Concise Torturatorium*, and by the same author, *Rack, Strap and Garrote: Prolegomena to the Gentle Art of Execution*, plus the only extant copy of *The Boil-in-oil Cookbook*, written by Father Galvinari of Amagonia on his deathbed. Those fatal receptacles also included the minutes, deciphered from stone slabs, of the meetings of the cannibal section of the Federation of Neanderthal Literati, as well as *Reflections on the Gibbet* by the Vicomte de Crampfousse, and if I add that the list contained, moreover, such entries as *The Perfect Crime, The Black Corpse Mystery* and *The ABC Murders* of Agatha Christie, then you can well imagine, gentlemen, what terrible influence this must have had on the otherwise innocent mind of the Computer.

"For indeed, we seek as much as possible to keep our electrobrains in ignorance about this dreadful side to human nature. But now that the regions of Procyon are inhabited by the metallic brood of a machine filled with the history of Earth's degeneracy, perversion and crime, I must confess—alas—that mechanical psychiatry is in this particular instance absolutely helpless. I have nothing more to say."

And the broken old man left the podium and tottered to his seat, accompanied by a deathly silence. I raised my hand. The chairman looked at me with surprise, but after a moment's hesitation gave me the floor.

"Gentlemen!" I said, rising to my feet. "The matter, I see, is grave. Its full ramifications I was able to appreciate only upon listening to the cogent words of Professor Gargarragh. And therefore I should like to submit to this respected assembly the following proposal. I am prepared to set off, alone, for Procyon, in order to take stock of the situation there, solve the mystery of the disappearance of thousands of your people, and in the process do what I can to bring about a peaceful settlement to the growing conflict. I am fully aware that this task is far more difficult than any I have ever undertaken, but there are times, gentlemen, when one must act without regard to the chances of success or the risks involved. And so, gentlemen . . ."

My words were lost in a burst of applause. I shall pass over what transpired afterwards in the course of the meeting, since it would sound too much like a mass ovation in my honor. The commission and the assembly conferred upon me every conceivable sort of power. The following day I met with the director of the Procyon division and the chief of Cosmic Reconnaissance, both in the person of a Counselor Malingraut.

"You're leaving *today*?" he said. "Wonderful. But not in your own rocket, Tichy. That's out of the question. In such missions we employ special rockets."

"Why?" I asked. "Mine is perfectly adequate."

"I don't doubt its capability," he replied, "but this is a matter of camouflage. You'll go in a rocket that on the outside looks like anything but a rocket. It will be—but you'll see for yourself. Also, you must land at night . . ."

"At night?" I said. "The flame from the exhaust will give me away . . ."

"We've always used that tactic," he said, clearly troubled.

"Well, I'll keep an eye out when I get there," I said. "I have to go in disguise?"

"Yes. It's necessary. Our experts will take care of you. They're waiting now. This way, if you don't mind . . ."

I was led through a secret corridor to a place that resembled a small operating room. Here four people began to work on me. After an hour they brought me before a mirror—I couldn't recognize myself. Encased in iron, with square shoulders and an equally square head, and glass apertures instead of eyes, I looked like a perfectly average robot.

"Mr. Tichy," said the make-up man in charge, "there are a few important things you must remember. The first is, not to breathe."

"You must be mad," I said. "How can I not breathe? I'll suffocate!"

"A misunderstanding. Obviously you are allowed to breathe, but do it quietly. No sighs, no panting or puffing, no deep inhalation—keep everything inaudible, and for the love of God don't sneeze. That would be the end of you."

48

"Right, what else?" I asked.

"For the trip you'll receive a complete set of back issues of both the *Electron Courier* and the opposition newspaper, *The Outer Space Gazette.*"

"They have an opposition?"

"Yes, but it's also run by the Computer. Professor Urp speculates that the machine suffers from a political as well as electrical dissociation of the psyche. But to continue. No eating, no chewing of candy, gum or anything of the kind. You will take food only at night, through this opening here, just turn the key—it's a Wertheim lock—and lift the latch, that's right. Try not to lose the key—you'll starve to death if you do."

"True, robots don't eat."

"We have no definite data on their customs, for obvious reasons. Study the classified ads of their newspapers, that is generally quite helpful. And when you talk to anyone, don't stand too close, or they'll be able to see you through the microphone mesh—it's best if you keep your teeth blackened, here's a box of henna. And don't forget to make a great show of oiling all your hinges every morning; robots consider that *de rigueur*. But you needn't overdo it—a little creaking now and then will give a good impression. Well, I guess that's more or less it. Hold on, you don't want to go out on the street like that, are you crazy? There's a secret passage, over here . . ."

A touch on the bookshelf, and a section of the wall opened up. I went rattling down a narrow stairway to the back yard, where a freight helicopter stood waiting. They loaded me inside, after which the machine lifted into the air. An hour later we landed at a secret cosmodrome. There on the platform beside the ordinary rockets stood a grain elevator, round as a tower.

"Good Lord, don't tell me that's supposed to be my rocket," I said to the secret officer accompanying me.

"Yes. Everything you'll possibly need—codes, decoders, radio, newspapers, provisions, assorted odds and ends—is already inside. Including a heavy-duty jimmy."

"A what?"

"A jimmy, for opening safes . . . to use as a weapon, only in the last resort. Well then, break a leg," said the officer kindly. I couldn't even shake his hand properly, for mine was stuck in an iron glove. I opened the door and entered. Inside, the grain elevator turned out to be a perfectly normal rocket. More than anything I wanted to wriggle out of the iron rattletrap I wore, but they had cautioned me against that—the experts explained that the sooner I accustomed myself to the burden, the better.

I revved up the reactor, blasted off, and got on course, then decided to have lunch, which wasn't easy—craning my neck until it ached, I still couldn't bring my mouth into position and finally had to feed myself with the aid of a shoehorn. Afterwards I sat in a hammock and started in on the robot press. A few headlines immediately caught my eye:

BEATIFICACIOUN OF SEINT ELECTRIX
AN ENDE TO FEENDLY MUCILID INTROODEMENT
ALARUMS ATTE COLISSEUM
MUSCILID YPILLOREYD

The spelling and vocabulary surprised me at first, but then I recalled what Professor Gargarragh had said about those archaic language dictionaries which the *Jonathan,* long ago, had been carrying on board. I knew already that the robots called men mucilids. Themselves they styled magnificans.

I read through the last paragraph, the one about the mucilid who was pilloried:

Tweye halbardeere of His Sovereyn Inductivitee kaughte, whan the oure hyt strook thre this ilke morn, oon mucilyte espye, whoo atte hostelrye of herbergeour magn. Mremran ylogged was, thynkyng ther to hyde his wikkednesse. Beeyng a feithful servaunt to H. S. Inductivitee, magn. Mremran spedily did notifie the toun Halbardeshippe, eftsoones the foule tratour, his helm agapen in grete shame, eek yhooted by the iresom crowde, in dongeoun ythrowe was, in Calefaustrium.

Not bad for a start, I thought—and turned to the column under the heading of "Alarums atte Colisseum":

Feele bettors atte gridyrnliches tornee lefte the feeld in muche confoundrement, sith Garloy III, passyng the griddebal to Turtukoor, hadde ytombresult anon, wherat a fraktur of the knee withdrewe him fro the pley. The wajoureres, seyen hir premium forlost, bethrongged them unto the kassier, stomppelte the tingulum and sorely braste als the tingulator. The citee Halbardeshippe patrole did 8 tumultineeren in the moat yputte, al weyed doun with stoons. Whan an ende to swiches sory perturbaciouns bee, the kwittie bettors mekely axe th'adminystracioun?

With the help of a glossary I learned that kwittie meant calm, from *quietas, quietatis*—peace, and that axe was ask, while gridyrn represented a kind of sporting field on which the magnificans played—in their fashion—football, using for that purpose a sphere of solid lead. I studied the papers assiduously, since before take-off it had been drummed into me at division headquarters that I must acquaint myself with all the ways and customs of magnifican life—even now I called them that in my thoughts: to refer to anyone as a robot would be not only an insult, it would unmask me at once.

So I read, in turn, the following articles: "Sixe Principles As Touchinge the Parfit Estat of a Magnifycan," "Th'Audience of Magn. Maister Gregaturian," "How Goon the Repaires atte Armurers Guilde To-yeere," "Deyntee Peregrinacioun of Magnificane Goostes by Cause of the Coolynge of Hyr Toobes." But the ads were stranger yet. A good many of them I could scarcely understand.

ARMELADORA VI, HONDIMAGN FAMOUS FOR warderobelavanderynge, valve-ootreemerye, henge-parficciounement, also in extermis, lowe rates.

JUVENOX, salve for the remooval of rustes, rustraciouns, rustifycaciouns, rusticitees and oother plaguey rusticles. Nowe on sale.

OLEUM PURISSIMUM PRO CAPITE—Suffre nat a squekee nekke destroublen youre thynkynge!!

A few were altogether incomprehensible. These, for instance:

Art likerous? Pleye-limbes to order! Alle sysen! For securitee oon worche dounpayen. Tarmodrylle VIII.

LUXURS cubiculum omnifactorlich compleat with amphigneyss, to rente. Applie Perkulator XXV.

And there were some that made the hair stand on end underneath my iron hood:

51

THE BURDEL OF GOMORRHEUM
OPNETH TO-DAY ITS YATES!
OUR RESTAURACION OFFRETH
TASTEE DISSHE NE BIFOREN
FETURED!! MUCILYDE BABEE,
VITAILLE YSERVE ATTE BORD
AND CARIE-OOT!!!

I racked my brains over these enigmatic texts, for which
however I had ample time, inasmuch as the trip was supposed to
take about a year.

In *The Outer Space Gazette* they had even more ads.

BOON-BURSTERES, FLESSHE-PERCERES, NEKKE
SISOURES, CLEVERES, CORVERES, STOUTE CUGGELS?
Trie GREMONTORIUS, FIDRICAX LVI.

PYROMANYAKS!!! Newe swabbes ysteped in Abracabbors
specyall petro-oleum, GUARANTEYDE QUENCHE-PROVE!!

FOR STRANGELACIOUN FANSYERE. Wee mussilid thynge,
swete, conne speken, in clooth ycladde, with eek oon paire
fingernail-plyers, litel used, chepe.

LEDY-N-GENTILMAGNIFIKANS—The BELY-SKEWERES,
Thumbe-skreweres, spyne-cheweres ARE IN!!!—Krakaruan XI.

Reading these announcements at length, I began to
understand—I fancied—the fate which the host of Second Division volunteers sent forth to reconnoiter had met with. It was
not, I confess, with any great degree of confidence that I landed
on the planet. This was accomplished at night, I cutting the engines beforehand as much as possible. After touching down in a
fairly mountainous region, I decided—upon reflection—to
cover the rocket with broken branches. Really, those experts
back at Intelligence hadn't been using their heads: grain
elevators, after all, were a little out of place on a robot planet. I
packed the interior of my iron casing with as many provisions as
I was able, then set off in the direction of the city, which I spotted in the distance thanks to the strong electrical glow that hung
over it. I had to stop a couple of times to reposition some cans of
sardines, for they were clattering around awfully inside. On I
went, when something invisible knocked me off my feet. I fell,

raising an ungodly racket and pierced with the sudden thought of "What, already?!" But there wasn't a living—that is, an electrical—thing in the vicinity. Just in case, I pulled out my weapons: a jimmy, the kind that safe-crackers use, and a tiny screwdriver. Groping about with my hands, I found that I was surrounded only by scrap-iron shapes. The remains of ancient automata, their abandoned cemetery. I continued on my way, frequently turning around to look, amazed at its dimensions. It went on for at least a mile. Then in the darkness, quite unalleviated by the distant glow, there loomed two four-legged shapes. I froze. My instructions said nothing about animals living on this planet. Two more quadrupeds noiselessly joined the first. A careless movement from me produced a metallic clang, and the black silhouettes bolted like mad into the night.

After this incident I proceeded with redoubled caution. The time hardly seemed auspicious for entering the city—the late hour, the empty streets—my appearance would surely attract unwanted attention. So I jumped into a roadside ditch and patiently awaited the dawn, chewing on a biscuit. I knew that until the following night it would be impossible to eat a thing.

At daybreak I approached the outskirts of the city. Didn't see a soul. On a nearby fence was a large poster, faded and washed by the rains. I walked over to it.

PROCLAMMACYON

The toun auctoritees well woot that the mucellide slyme doth ever seek to infiltreyen the honeste rankes of our magnyfycans. Harkee! Whosoever ysee a mucellid or any individuum of suspecious contenaunce, shal streghtwey go him unto the locale hallebarderye ther for to informen. Any maner collaboracioun with or eek assistenz yiven to the same wil bee ypunysshed by peyne of unscrewynge in saecula saeculorum. A prise of 1,000 pistoons on eche mucellyd hed is heere by yleyd.

I went on. The suburbs didn't look inviting. Beside wretched, rust-eaten sheds sat groups of robots, playing odd and even. From time to time fights broke out among them, and with such a din, it sounded like artillery shelling a warehouse full of metal drums. A little farther on I came to a trolley stop. An almost empty trolley car drove up, and I climbed on. The driver

was an inseparable part of the motor and had his hand permanently welded to the crank, while the conductor, screwed in
place at the entrance, was also the door. He moved on hinges. I
handed him a coin from the supply they'd given me at Division,
and sat on a bench, creaking dreadfully. At the center of town I
got off and sauntered straight ahead, as if without a worry in the
world. I came across more and more halberdiers; they were
walking back and forth, in groups of two and three, right down
the middle of the street. Noticing a halberd propped against a
wall, I carelessly picked it up and marched on, but I was alone
and that might appear strange, so taking advantage of the fact
that one of the three guards strutting in front of me had stepped
off to the side in order to adjust his drooping grille, I filled his
place in the formation. The perfect similarity of all robots stood
me in good stead. As for my two companions, they maintained
their silence for a time, then finally one spoke up:

"Whan wole we the ese ysee, Burbor? For I am wery and
fayn wouldst sport me som with the electrolasshe."

"What gabbestow, cherl?" replied the other. "Our stacioun
delyteth thee namoor! Ho! 'Tis dreer enow, ywis!"

In this fashion we covered the entire downtown area. Keeping my eyes open, I noticed along the way two restaurants, and
in front of each a veritable forest of halberds propped against
the wall. However I asked no questions. By now my feet ached in
earnest, and it was stifling inside that iron kettle heated by the
sun, and my nose was twitching from the acrid dust—afraid I
might sneeze, I tried to slip away unnoticed, but both of them
howled:

"Hola, frend! Whider trippest thou ther? Wust have the
bailly bat thee blatherless? Be ye mad?"

"Nay," I answered, "I oonly thoughte to sitte me doon a
spel."

"Sitte? An has the fever brent thy coil? We are on dootee,
trewe castynges of the founderye!"

"Een so," I said, assenting, and again we marched before us.
No, I thought, this occupation was totally devoid of possibilities.
There had to be some other way. We made yet another round of
the city, then suddenly an officer stopped us, crying:

"Raffandulum!"

"Bondamacronger!" shouted my companions. I made a

54

mental note of that password and reply. The officer looked us over, front and back, and ordered us to hold our halberds higher.

"Fy, ye are sloggardly clunks, nat halbardeere of Hys Inductivitee!! Streghten thoos rankes! Shulders out! Hep-hep!!"

The halberdiers submitted to this inspection without comment. Then on we trudged beneath the noonday sun, and I cursed the hour that I had volunteered to set out for this miserable planet. In addition, I was famished. A rumbling stomach could easily betray me, so I tried rattling as loudly as I could. We passed a restaurant. I looked inside. Practically all the tables were occupied: magnificans, or rather clunks—as I called them in my thoughts, remembering the officer's words—sat there motionless, enameled blue, though now and then one of them would squeak or turn its head to gaze, glass-eyed, out at the street. They ate nothing, drank nothing, but seemed only to be waiting—for what, I couldn't guess. The waiter, recognizable by the white apron it wore over its armor, was standing by the wall.

"Perchaunce we too moot sitten yonder?" I asked, for I could feel every blister on my ironbound feet.

"In soothe thou art a sely felawe!" huffed my companions. "Swiche luxuree nys for the lykes of us! Ne, stondynge we moste remeyn alway! But fere nat, thoos ther do lay in wayte for som musilid to entryken, whan hee coom and, requerynge soope or eek gruwel, hys feendly natur there by revele!!"

Not understanding any of this, I plodded on obediently. After a while, though, I began to grow desperate—however we headed at last towards a great building of red brick, on which a wrought-iron inscription was visible:

YE BARRACKS OF THE HALLEBARDYERES
OF
HYS MYGHTY INDUCTIVITEE
CALCULON THE FYRST

I broke away from my companions at the very entrance. The halberd I left with the sentinel as it turned its back with a clank and a clang, then ducked into the first side street. Around the corner there stood a sizable building with the signboard UNDER THE AXE. I only peered inside, but the innkeeper, a pot-bellied robot with short legs and creaking eagerly, hopped out on the street.

"Wel mette, my liege, wel mette ... umbly at your servyse ... wol ye be a-cravinge of a roum, mayhap?"

"Yis," I answered laconically.

He practically bore me bodily inside. Leading the way up the stairs, my host prattled on in his tinny voice like one possessed:

"No ende of peregrynatours are hiderward ycome of layte, no ende ... ther is nat a magnifican, I trow, who ne desyreth hem to looke upon the corounacioun of the incandessente fillementz of Oure Inductivitee with hys owne tweye lenzen ... this wey, an it please yowr lorshippe ... a worthy appartamentum, arter ye prithee ... her is the parloure ... ther the denne ... but douteleś yowr Grace moste bee for-wery ... the dust hit gryndeth in thy geeres ... by your leve I'll fecche som ablootemaúnts anon ..."

He went clattering down the stairs and, before I had much chance to look around that rather dismal room, furnished as it was with an iron chest of drawers and an equally iron bed, he returned with an oilcan, a rag, and a bottle of silicone. Placing these on the table, he said in a lower, more confidential tone:

"Whan ye hav yourselven a myte refresshened, Sire, prey betake yow doune-steyers ... for gentil folke lyke youre Honour I all weys kepe a litel secreetum, somthynge swete and savory ... shalt dally wel ..."

And out he went, winking his photocells. Having nothing better to do, I oiled myself, polished my plates with the silicone, and noticed that the innkeeper had left on the table a card which seemed to resemble a restaurant menu. Well aware that robots never eat, I picked it up, surprised, and read *Burdel 2nd Classe* across the top.

Mussilid infaunt, decapitatus	8 pist.
The same, with goo	10 pist.
The same, wepynge	11 pist.
The same, pitous	14 pist.
Lyfstok:	
Cutlette-sodomie, eche	6 pist.
Myrie choppe	8 pist.
The same, calf meke and delicaat	8 pist.

None of it made sense to me, but my blood ran cold when from the adjoining room I heard a crashing of incredible violence, as if some robot guest were endeavoring to dash his lodging into splinters against the wall. My hair stood on end. I'd had enough. Trying not to clink or clang, I fled from that dreadful den out into the street. Breathing easily only when I'd put a good distance behind me. And now what was I, poor wretch, to do? I stopped by a group of robots playing old maid and pretended to be an enthusiastic onlooker. It was still a complete mystery to me what these magnificans actually did. I could probably sneak back into the ranks of the halberdiers, but that didn't promise much and the chance of being caught was considerable. What then?

Racking my brains in this manner, I walked along, until I noticed a portly robot seated on a bench and warming his old rivets in the sun. He had covered his head with a newspaper. On the first page I saw a poem that began with the words: "A degenereyt am I, fro Magnifica I hye"—what came next I don't recall. Gradually we struck up a conversation. I introduced myself as a stranger from the neighboring town of Sadomasia. The old robot was exceedingly cordial. Almost at once he invited me to his home.

"Loo an wherfore sholdstow, worthy Sir, go knokkynge thee aboute tavernes in swiche wise and be obligen eek to biker with herbergeours and theyr sort? Pray coom with me. Vouchsaff the honour, my humble roof, hav the goodnesse, partake an gramercy. Blisse entereth, with your estemed persone, into my lowlysom abode."

What could I do, I agreed of course, it even suited my purpose. My new host had his own house, on Third Street. He immediately showed me to my room.

"Fro the rode, hast douteles muchel dust yswalwed," he said.

Again out came the oilcan, the silicone, and the rag. I knew already what he would say, robots being such uncomplicated creatures. And sure enough:

"Whanne ye arn a myte refresshened, pray take yow to the parloure," said he, "and we shal pleyen som togedere pardee . . ."

He closed the door. I didn't touch the oilcan or the silicone, but only examined the condition of my make-up in the mirror,

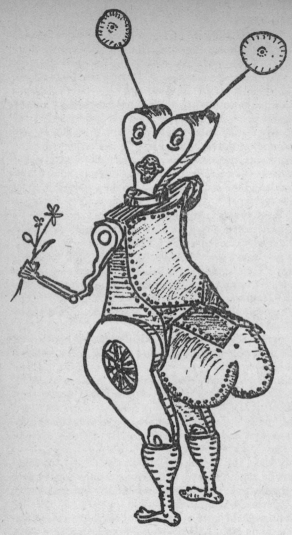

NARZECZONA ROBOTA

Engaged to be married.

blackened my teeth, and after some quarter of an hour decided to go downstairs, though I was not a little apprehensive about the prospect of this mysterious "playing," when suddenly from the depths of the house a long and drawn-out rumbling reached my ears. This time however there was no escape. Down the steps I went, deafened by the racket, as though someone were hewing an iron stump to slivers. It came from the parlor. My host, stripped down to his iron torso, was with a curiously fashioned cleaver hacking away at a large doll that lay upon the table.

"Entre, goode my gest! Ye moote werken your hertes delyte upon yon carcase," he said, leaving off his chopping when he saw me and pointing to another, somewhat smaller doll lying there on the floor. When I drew near, the thing sat up, opened its eyes, and began in a faint voice to say, over and over:

"Sire—I yam an innocent chylde—spare me—sire—I yam an innocent chylde—spare me."

My host handed me an ax, similar to a halberd, but with a shorter shaft.

"Nowe then, noble gest, awey with care, awey with sorowe—hav to, and smyte smerte!"

"But I—I do no cure for children . . ." I feebly protested. He froze.

"No cure?" he repeated. "A pitee. Ye putten me in sore perplexitee, my frend. What shal you doon? I hav but litel oons—tis my wekenesse, ywis. Woldstow then trie a calf?"

And from out of the cupboard he brought a perfectly serviceable plastic calf, which, when squeezed, produced a timorous bleat. What could I do? Not wishing to unmask myself, I slashed away at the unfortunate puppet, tiring myself out completely in the process. Meanwhile my host had drawn and quartered both dolls, put aside his instrument, which he called his bone-buster, and asked if I were content. I assured him that I had not known such pleasure for quite some time.

And so began my cheerless life on Cercia. The next morning, after a breakfast that consisted of hot mineral oil, my host left for work, while his wife sawed at something furiously in the bedroom—a baby calf, I think, but couldn't swear to it. Unable any longer to take the bleating, the screaming, the constant clamor, I went out and walked about the city. The way its inhabitants spent their time was fairly monotonous. Quartering, breaking on the wheel, burning, dissevering—at the center of town was an amusement park with pavilions, where one could buy the most ingenious instruments. After a few days of this I couldn't even look at my own penknife, and only driven by hunger would I venture out beyond the city at dusk, to hide in the bushes and hurriedly cram down sardines and biscuits. Little wonder, that on such a diet I was always within a hair's-breadth of the hiccups, which would have placed me in mortal danger. On the third day we went to the theater. They were putting on a play called "Carbazarius." It was about a handsome young robot mercilessly persecuted by man—that is, by mucilids—who doused him with water, sprinkled sand in his oil, loosened his screws so that he kept falling down, etc. The audience clanged angrily. In the second act an emissary of the Computer appeared, the young robot was freed, and the third act dealt at length with the fate of man, which, as one might imagine, was not particularly pleasant.

Out of boredom I went poking through my host's private library, but there was nothing of interest there: a few cheap reprints of the Marquis de Sade's memoirs, beyond that nothing but pamphlets, items like *Howe to Recognys a Mucilid,* of which I memorized a couple of passages. "A mucilid," the text began, "is veray softe, in consistency simular to a dumplynge . . . Its eyen are opake, watery, a trewe ymage of its soules abhomynacioun. The chekes are rubbry . . ." and so on, for nearly one hundred pages.

Saturday we were visited by the town notables—the master tinker of a tinsmith guild, a deputy municipal armorer, a senior guildsmech, two protocrats, one grand mason—unfortunately I was unable to figure out what sort of occupations these were, since the talk mainly was of art, the theater, and the wonderful all-functionality of Hys Inductivitee. The ladies gossiped a little. From them I learned that a certain Carpsidon, a notorious rake and scapegrace who in the upper circles led a life of reckless dissipation, had surrounded himself with a bevy of electrical bacchanettes, showering upon them the most expensive tubes and fuses imaginable. But my host did not seem particularly indignant when I mentioned this Carpsidon.

"Younge current muste hav its course," he said goodhumoredly. "Whanne he groweth rustee, and his resistoures begyn to fizzel, he shal clinke another tune . . ."

One female magnifican, who hardly ever dropped in on us, for some unknown reason took a shine to me and once, after downing Lord knows how many mugs of mineral oil, whispered:

"Thou art cute. Wilt have me? Let us hyen to my hous, ourselven ther for to up-hooken . . ."

I pretended that a sudden cathode discharge had made it impossible for me to hear her words.

My host and hostess generally got along well together, but once I was an involuntary witness to a quarrel; she shouted something about his going to scrap, to which he, the husband, made no reply.

We were also visited from time to time by a much sought-after master electrician who ran a clinic in the city; it was from him that I learned—for he did, though rarely, speak about his patients—that robots do on occasion go mad, and that the most serious of the persecution manias is the conviction that one is a man. Moreover—as I gathered from his words, though he never actually came out and said it—there had been a significant increase in the number of such cases of late.

I did not however relay these bits of information to Earth because, first, they seemed too trivial, and secondly, I wasn't particularly eager to go marching back over the mountains to where I'd left my rocket, which held the transmitter. One fine morning, just as I was finishing my calf (my host supplied me with one each evening, convinced that nothing in the world could give me greater pleasure), the entire house reverberated to a violent banging at the gate. My fears, it turned out, were only too well justified. It was the police—that is, the halberdiers. They placed me under arrest and, without a single word, led me out to the street before the eyes of my petrified host and hostess. I was shackled, put into a van and driven off to prison, where a hostile crowd already stood at the entrance, hissing and booing. They locked me in a separate cell. When the door was slammed shut behind me, I sat on my metal mattress with a loud sigh. A sigh couldn't hurt me now. For a while I tried to figure out just how many prisons it had been now, in which I'd sat in various regions of the Galaxy, but I kept losing count. Something was lying at the foot of the mattress. A pamphlet on the detection of mucilids—had it been put there maliciously, to mock me? I opened it without thinking. First I read about how the upper portion of the mucilid trunk moves in conjunction with the so-called phenomenon of breathing, and how one can determine whether the hand, extended in greeting, is *doughy*, and if from the facial opening there isn't a *slight breeze*. When agitated—the passage concluded—the mucilid secretes a watery fluid, mainly through the forehead.

It was accurate enough. I was indeed secreting that watery fluid. On the face of it, cosmic exploration does seem a bit repetitious, viz. those abovementioned and perpetually recurring—as if they represented an unavoidable aspect of the enterprise—sojourns in jail, whether interstellar, planetary, or even nebular, but my situation had never been so dismal as now. Around noon a guard brought me a bowl of warmed-over mineral oil, in which there floated a few ball bearings. I asked for something more nourishing, inasmuch as I had already been unmasked, but he only clinked ironically and left without a word. I began to pound the door, demanding a lawyer. No one answered. Towards evening, when I had eaten the last crumb of a biscuit I'd discovered inside my armor, a key scraped in the lock and into the cell walked a squat automaton with a thick leather briefcase.

"Corsed be ye, mussilid!" he said, then added: "I am your defendour."

"Do you always greet your clients in this manner?" I asked, taking a seat.

He also sat, clattering. He was hideous. The plates across his abdomen had worked completely loose.

"Mussilids, aye," he said with conviction. "Tis only owt of a loyaltee to my professioun—nat to yow, ye shameles feend—that I exersyse my skills in your defens, creetur! Peraventure the punysshment that awaytethee kan be lightened to but a single desmantelynge."

"What are you talking about?" I said. "I can't be dismantled."

"Ha!" he creaked. "That ys what you thynke! And nowe telle me what ye hav yhidde up your sleef, O yvel slyme!!"

"Your name?" I asked.

"Klaustron Fredrax."

"Tell me, Klaustron Fredrax, what am I accused of?"

"Of mussiliditee," he replied at once. "A capitall offence. And also: of the intent to werken tresoun upon us, of espiaillement on behaff of Gookum, of blasphemous conspiracye to lif-ten a hond agayn Hiss Inductivitude—do that sufficeth, excres-sent muscilid? Confess you to thes crymes?"

"Are you really my lawyer?" I asked. "For you speak like a prosecutor or examining magistrate."

"I am your defendour."

"Good. I confess to none of the above crimes."

"The sparkes they shal flye!" he roared.

Seeing the kind of defender they'd given me, I kept silent. The next day I was brought out and interrogated. I admitted nothing, though the judge thundered even more terribly—if that was possible—than my lawyer of the day before. Now he would roar, now whisper, now burst into metallic laughter, and again calmly explain that sooner would he start to breathe than I escape magnifican justice.

At the next interrogation there was present some important dignitary, judging by the number of tubes that glowed inside him. Four more days went by. My biggest problem was food. I made do with the belt from my trousers, soaking it in the water they brought me once a day. The guard carried the pot at arm's length, as if it were poison.

After a week the belt ran out, but fortunately I had on high laced boots of goatskin—their tongues were the very best thing I ate during my stay in the cell.

On the eighth day, at dawn, two guards ordered me to col-lect my things. I was placed inside a van and transported with an escort to the Iron Palace, the residence of the Computer. Up magnificent, rustproof stairs we went, through halls lined with cathode tubes, and I was ushered into an enormous, windowless room. The guards retired, leaving me alone. In the middle of the room was a black curtain that hung from ceiling to floor, its folds enclosing the center and arranged in the shape of a square.

"O wrecched mucilid!" boomed a voice, coming as if through pipes from an iron vault, "your final hour draws nigh. Speak, what is your pleasure: the flesh-shredder, the bone-buster, or the hydraulic punch?"

I was silent. The Computer clanged and rumbled, then cried:

"Hearken to me, mucilaginous monstrosity hitherward come at the behest of all gookumkind! Hearken to my mighty voice, thou puling coagulum, thou snivellous emulsion! In the magnificence of my illuminating currents I bestow upon thee mercy: if thou wilt join the ranks of my devoted minions, if thou with all thy heart and soul wouldst be a magnifican, I may possibly spare thee thy life."

I said that this very thing had been my fondest dream for years. The Computer chuckled, pulsing with derision, and said:

"I know thou liest. But hear me, O maggot! Thou mayst continue thy glutinous existence only as an undercover magnifican-halberdier. Thy task will be all mucilids, spies, agents, traitors and such other viscous vermin as are sent from Gook—to unmask, expose, lay bare and brand with the white iron, for only through such loyal service canst thou hope to save thy sticky skin."

When I had solemnly sworn to everything, they led me to another room, where I was entered in the register and ordered to submit daily reports at the central halberderie—after which, feeling weak and numb, I was permitted to leave the palace.

Night was falling. I went outside the city, sat on the grass and began to think. I was sick at heart. Had they cut off my head I would at least have saved my honor, but now, by going over to the side of that electronic monster, I'd betrayed the cause I represented, I'd ruined my chances completely. What then, run off to the rocket? A shameful retreat. But all the same I started walking. To be an informer in the employ of a machine that ruled an army of iron crates—that would have been more shameful yet. Who can describe my horror when, instead of the rocket in the place I'd left it, I saw only the scattered remains, broken fragments, clearly the work of robots!

It was dark when I returned to the city. I sat on a stone and for the first time in my life wept bitterly for my home, lost forever, and the tears trickled down the iron interior of that hollow hulk which was to be, for the remainder of my days, my prison—and they trickled out through the knee chinks, threatening to stiffen the joints with rust. But I no longer cared.

Then suddenly I noticed a platoon of halberdiers slowly wending its way towards a meadow at the edge of the city, outlined against the last glimmer of the setting sun. Their behavior was peculiar. In the growing darkness of evening first one, then another separated himself from the ranks and, moving his feet as quietly as possible, crept into the bushes and disappeared. This struck me so odd that, in spite of my extreme depression, I got up quietly and set off after the one nearest me.

This was—I must add—at a time when the local shrubbery was bearing wild berries, similar in taste to whortleberries, sweet and full of flavor. I'd eaten them myself—whenever, that is, I was able to slip away from the iron metropolis. Picture my astonishment upon seeing the halberdier I'd been following pull out a tiny key, the exact duplicate of the one given me by the director of Division Headquarters, and use it to unfasten his visor from the left side, then, grabbing berries with both hands, stuff them into that open pit like a savage! Even from where I stood I could hear the sounds of slurping and gulping.

"Psst," I hissed urgently. "Hey!"

With a single bound he went crashing into the underbrush, but didn't get far—or else I would have heard him. He had fallen down somewhere.

"Listen," I said in a lower voice, "don't be afraid. I'm a man. A man. Disguised like yourself."

Something like a single eye, glittering with fear and suspicion, peered out at me from behind a leaf.

"And howe woot I ye wil nat me biwreyen?" came a hoarse voice.

"But I'm trying to tell you. I came from Earth. They sent me specially."

I had to persuade him a while more before he was reassured enough to crawl out of the bushes. He touched my armor in the darkness.

"Ye are a man? For sooth?"

"Why won't you talk normally?" I asked.

"Tush, I hav foryeten howe. 'Tis the fifte yeer sithen cruel Destinee hath me delivered hider . . . muchel hav I suffred, more thanne I conne telle . . . ywis, Fortune ys mercifyll, to lette me clappe mine yë upon a veray muccilid aforn I dye . . ." he babbled.

"Pull yourself together! Enough of that! Listen—you're not by any chance from Intelligence?"

"Certeyn, fro Intelligentz. 'Twas Malingraut did sende me, here for to swinke and swelte moste grevously."

"But why didn't you flee?"

"Pray howe am I to flee, an' my rokket be desmauntelled and eke to-shivered to flindren? Allas and weilaway, hard ys my lot! But 'tis tyme I retourne . . . shal we see everich other ageyn? Atte barracks, to-morwe . . . wiltow nat come?"

I agreed to meet him then, without even knowing what he looked like, and we said goodbye; cautioning me to wait there for a while yet, he disappeared into the blackness of the night. It was with a light heart that I reentered the city, for now I saw the chance of organizing a conspiracy. In order to conserve my strength, I stopped at the first inn that presented itself along the way and went to bed. Early next morning, while looking in the mirror, I noticed a chalk mark on my chest, a tiny cross, right below the left pauldron, and suddenly the scales fell from my eyes. That man—he had done this, intending to betray me! "The no-good skunk," I muttered, frantically trying to think of what to do now. I wiped away the treacherous sign, but that wasn't enough. He'd already made his report—I was sure of that—and they would start looking for this unknown mucilid, and obviously turn first to their registers, and call the most likely suspects in for questioning—I was there of course, on that list; the thought of being questioned made me shudder. I realized that somehow I had to divert suspicion from myself, and immediately hit upon a plan. All that day I stayed at the inn, abusing a calf in order to remain inconspicuous, but at dusk I quickly set out for the center of town, concealing in the palm of my hand a piece of chalk. With it I inscribed at least four hundred crosses on the iron hides of various passers-by; whoever chanced to come my way received a mark. At about midnight, feeling somewhat easier in my mind, I returned to the tavern, and only then did it occur to me that, besides the traitor with whom I had spoken the night before, there had been other halberdiers creeping into those bushes. This made me stop and think. Then all at once an amazingly simple idea came to me. I left the city and headed for the berries. It was a little after midnight when, once again, that iron rabble appeared, slowly spread out, scattered, and then from the nearby thickets came sounds of heavy breathing, furious chewing, hurried swallowing; afterwards the visors were one by one snapped shut, and the entire company climbed out of the bushes in silence, stuffed to the gills with berries. I approached them—in the darkness they took me for one of their own—and as we marched along chalked little circles on my neighbors, wherever I could. At the gates of the halberderie I did an about-face and went back to the inn.

The following day I sat myself down on a bench outside the barracks and waited for those on furlough to come out. Having spotted in the crowd one of the ones with a circle on the shoulder, I took after him, and when there was no one in the street but us I clapped him on the back with my gauntlet, so that he rang from head to toe, and said:

"In the name of Hys Inductivitee! Com with me!"

So frightened was he, he started clattering all over—and followed me without a word, as docile as a lamb. I closed the door to my room, pulled a screwdriver from my pocket, and began unfastening his head. This took an hour. I lifted it off like an iron pot and was confronted by a face, unpleasantly pallid from being in the dark too long, thin, and walleyed with fear.

"Ye are a mucilid?!" I snarled.

"Yessir, yer worshipe, but—"

"But what?!"

"But I, that ys . . . I am registred . . . I swoor aliegiaunce to Hiss Inductivitee!"

"How long ago? Speak!"

"Three . . . three yeer agoon, sire—but—but wherfor dostow—"

"Hold," I said. "And do you know of any other mucilids?"

"On Erthe? Yea an soth to sayn I do, yer grace, I crye yow mercy, 'twas oonly—"

"Not on Earth, fool, here!"

"Nay, nossir! Loo! But yif ever I do see 'un, streighte shal I notifye the—"

"All right," I said. "You may go. Here, put your head back on."

And tossing him the screws, I pushed him out the door, where I could hear him trying to don his metal skull with trembling hands. Then I sat on my bed, greatly surprised by this turn of events. All that next week there was plenty of work to be done, for I pulled individuals off the street at random, took them to the inn and there unscrewed their heads. My hunch was

67

right: they were all of them men, every last one! Not a single robot in the lot! Gradually an apocalyptic image took shape before my eyes . . .

A demon, an electrical demon—that Computer! What hell had hatched there in its nest of glowing wires! The planet was wet, humid, rheumatic—and for robots, unhealthy in the highest degree . . . they must have rusted en masse, and perhaps too there was, as the years passed, an increasing lack of spare parts, and they began to break down, going one by one to that vast cemetery outside of town, where only the wind rang their death knell over sheets of crumbling metal. That was when the Computer, seeing its ranks melt away, seeing its reign endangered, had conceived the most ingenious machination. From its enemies, from the spies dispatched to destroy it, it began to build its own army, its own agents, its own people! Not one of those who were unmasked could betray it—not one of them dared attempt to contact others, other men, having no way of knowing that they weren't robots, and even if he did find out about this one or that, he'd be afraid that at the first overture the other man would turn him in—just as that first bogus halberdier had tried to do, the one I'd caught off guard in the whortleberry bushes. But the Computer wasn't satisfied merely to neutralize its enemies—it made of each a champion of its cause, and by requiring them to turn in others, the new arrivals, it gave still further proof of its diabolical cunning, for who could best distinguish men from robots if not those very men, who after all were privy to all the secrets of Intelligence!!

And so each man, unmasked, included in the register and sworn in, felt himself isolated, and possibly even feared his own kind more than the robots, for the robots were not necessarily agents of the secret police, while the men were—to a man. And that was how this electrical monster kept us in slavery, foiling everyone—with everyone else, for it must have been my own companions in misery who had taken apart my rocket, as they had done (judging by the halberdier's words) with scores of other rockets.

"Infernal, infernal!" I thought, quivering with rage. And it wasn't enough that it drove us to treachery, that the Division itself sent more and more of us to serve the thing's pleasure—Earth was also supplying it with the very finest, rustproof, top-

68

quality equipment! Were there any robots left among those ironclad minions? I seriously doubted it. And the zeal with which they persecuted men, that too became clear. For being men themselves, they had to be—as neophytes to magnificanism—more robotlike than the authentic robots. Hence that fanatical hatred displayed by my lawyer. Hence that dastardly attempt to turn me in by the man I had first unmasked. Oh what fiendishness of coils and circuitry was here, what electrical finesse!

Revealing the secret would get me nowhere; at a command from the Computer I would unquestionably be thrown in the dungeon. No, the people had been obedient too long, for too long had they feigned devotion to that plugged-in Beelzebub, why they'd even forgotten how to talk properly!

What then could I do? Sneak into the palace? That would be madness. But what remained? An uncanny situation: here was a city surrounded by cemeteries, in which the Computer's subjects lay, long since turned to rust, yet *it* reigned on, stronger than ever, and confident, for Earth kept sending it more and more new men—idiotic! The longer I thought about it, the more clearly I saw that even this discovery, which certainly must have been made before me by more than one of us, didn't change things in the least. A single individual could do nothing; he would have to confide in someone, trust someone, but that inevitably resulted in instant betrayal, the traitor counting on a promotion, on getting into the good graces of the machine. "By Saint Electrix!" I thought, "it is a very genius . . ." And thinking this, noticed that I too was already affecting a slightly archaic mode of speech, that I too had caught that contagion by which the sight of iron hoods comes to seem natural, and a human face—something naked, ugly, indecent . . . mucilidinous. "Good Lord, I'm going insane," I thought, "and the others, they must have turned lunatic years ago—help!"

After a night spent in gloomy meditation, I betook myself to a store downtown, paid thirty pistons for the sharpest cleaver I could find, waited for the darkness to fall, then stole inside the great garden that surrounded the palace of the Computer. There, hidden in the shrubs, I freed myself of my iron armor with the aid of a pair of pliers and a screwdriver, and on tiptoe, barefoot, without a sound, I shinnied up the rainspout to the second floor. The window was open. Along the corridor, clanking hollowly, a guard was walking back and forth. When he turned his back at the opposite end of the hall, I jumped inside, quickly ran to the closest door and entered quietly—unnoticed.

This happened to be that same large room in which I'd heard the voice of the Computer. It was dark. I pulled aside the black curtain and saw the tremendous roof-high wall of the Computer, with dials shining like eyes. At the edge a white chink was visible. Apparently a door, left ajar. I approached it on tiptoe and held my breath.

The interior of the Computer looked like a small room in a second-class hotel. In the back stood a half-open safe, not very large, a cluster of keys hanging from its lock. At a desk piled high with papers sat an elderly, dried-up gentleman in a gray suit, with baggy sleevelets, the kind worn by office clerks; he was writing, filling out page after page of forms. There was a cup of coffee steaming at his elbow. A few crackers lay in the saucer. I tiptoed in, closed the door behind me. The hinges didn't squeak.

"Ahem," I said, lifting the cleaver with both hands.

The gentleman started and looked up at me; the gleam of the cleaver in my hands produced in him the utmost consternation. His face twisted, he fell to his knees.

"No!!" he groaned. "No!!!"

"Raise your voice once more, and you perish," I said. "Who are you?"

"He-heptagonius Argusson, my lord."

"I'm not your lord. You will address me as Mister Tichy, understand?!"

"Yessir! Yes! Yes!"

"Where is the Computer?"

"Mi-mister . . ."

"There isn't any Computer, is there?!"

"No—nossir! I was only following orders!"

"Of course. And from whom, if one might ask?"

He trembled like a leaf. He lifted his hands in entreaty.

"There'll be such trouble . . ." he groaned. "Please! Don't make me tell, my—forgive me! Mister Tichy!—I—I'm only a secretary, grade 6, on the payroll . . ."

"Come now. And the Computer? And the robots?"

"Mister Tichy, have mercy! I'll tell you the whole truth! Our chief—he organized it. Funds were allocated—to expand operations, to increase—ah—increase efficiency . . . research and development, determining the fitness of our people, but the main thing was the allocations . . ."

"You mean this was faked? All of it?!"

"I don't know! I swear I don't! From the time I got here—nothing's changed, you mustn't think that I'm in charge here, God forbid!—my job is only to maintain these personal files. The question was whether . . . whether our people would break down in the face of the enemy, in a critical situation—or whether they were ready, you see, to fight to the death."

"And why has no one returned to Earth?"

"Because, well, because they all turned traitor, Mister Tichy . . . as yet not a single one has been willing to lay down his life for the cause of Gookum—phoo, for *our* cause, I meant to say, it's out of habit that I use that word, please try to understand, eleven years sitting here, and in just one more I'm up for retirement, a pension, I have a wife and child, Mister Tichy, so for the love of—"

"Silence!!" I said angrily. "You want a pension, dog, I'll give you a pension!!"

I raised the cleaver. The clerk's eyes bulged; he began to grovel at my feet.

I ordered him to stand. Making certain that the safe had a small, grated opening for ventilation, I locked him up inside.

"And not a peep out of you! And if there's any knocking or thumping, villain, it'll be the flesh-shredder!!"

The rest was simple. That night was not among the most pleasant I had ever spent, for there were papers to look through—reports, statements, affidavits, records, dossiers, each inhabitant of the planet had his own portfolio. Using all the most confidential documents, I made myself a bed on the desk, there being no place to sleep. In the morning I switched on the microphone and, as the Computer, gave the order for the entire populace to assemble in front of the palace. Everyone was to bring with him a pair of pliers and a screwdriver. When they had all lined up like giant chessmen made of iron, I ordered them to unscrew each other's heads—on behalf of the capacitance of Saint Electrix. At eleven o'clock the first human heads began to show, and there was tumult and confusion, cries of "Treason! Treason!"—which, a few minutes later, when the last iron bowl

71

had clattered to the pavement, merged into a single roar of joy. I then appeared in my own identity and suggested that under my direction they all get down to work—for I wished to put together, out of the raw materials and supplies at hand, a great ship. It turned out, however, that in the palace cellars there were already a number of cosmic ships, and with full tanks, ready to go. Before takeoff I let Argusson out of the safe, but didn't take him on board, nor would I permit anyone else to. I told him that I intended to inform his chief of everything, and also to let the latter know—in no less detail—exactly what I thought of him.

Thus concluded one of the most unusual of my adventures and voyages. Notwithstanding all the hardship and pain it had occasioned me, I was glad of the outcome, since it restored my faith, shaken by corrupt cosmic officeholders, in the natural decency of electronic brains. Yes, it's comforting to know, when you think about it, that only man can be a bastard.

THE
TWELFTH
VOYAGE

In no voyage did I ever run such hair-raising risks as in the journey to Amauropia, a planet of the constellation Cyclops. What I underwent there I owe entirely to Professor Tarantoga. That learned astrozoologist is not only a great explorer; in his spare time, as you probably know, he invents. Among other things, he invented a fluid for the removal of unpleasant memories, paper currency with horizontal eights to serve as bills of infinite denomination, three methods of staining fog in colors pleasing to the eye, as well as a special powder which one can sprinkle on clouds and then press them into suitable molds, whereby they acquire permanent, solid shapes. His also was an apparatus for tapping the energy, so often wasted, of little children, who as everyone knows cannot sit still for a minute.

That device consists of a system of cranks, pulleys and levers situated in various places about the dwelling and which the children push, pull and move in the course of their play, unaware that they are thereby pumping water, washing clothes, peeling potatoes, generating electricity, etc. It was out of concern for our youngest citizens, whom parents on occasion do leave in the house alone, that the Professor also devised lighters that will not light. These now are mass-produced on Earth.

One day the Professor showed me his latest invention. At first it seemed to me that I was looking at a small iron stove, and Tarantoga confessed that that in fact had served him as the point of departure.

"This is, my dear Ijon, the translation into reality of man's age-old dream," he announced, "and namely, a dilator or—if you prefer—a retarder of time. It makes possible the unlimited prolongation of life. One minute inside should last roughly two months, if my calculations are correct. Would you care to try it? . . ."

Always interested in technological novelties, I willingly climbed into the contraption. No sooner had I squatted down than the Professor slammed shut the little door. My nose tickled; the force with which the stove had been closed lifted the still remaining bits of soot into the air, so that, breathing in, I sneezed. At that precise moment the Professor turned on the current. Due to the retardation of the passage of time, my sneeze lasted five days and five nights, and when Tarantoga again opened the little door he found me nearly unconscious with exhaustion. At first he was astonished and concerned, but learning what had happened, smiled good-humoredly and said:

"But in actual fact merely four seconds went by on my watch. Well now, Ijon, what say you of this invention?"

"To tell the truth, well, I think it needs perfecting—though the thing is certainly significant," I said, when I was able to catch my breath.

The worthy Professor was a bit chagrined at this, but then magnanimously made me a present of the device, explaining that it could serve equally well to accelerate the passage of time. Feeling somewhat fatigued, I put off for the moment a test of this additional possibility, thanked him warmly and carried the machine home with me. To tell the truth, I wasn't all that certain about what to do with it, so I put it in the attic of my rocketshop, where it sat for more than half a year.

In the course of writing the eighth volume of his celebrated *Astrozoology*, the Professor became acquainted in some detail with information concerning beings that lived on Amauropia. It occurred to him that these would provide an excellent opportunity to try out the dilator (as well as the accelerator) of time.

This plan, when I learned of it, excited my interest to such a degree, that in less than three weeks I had loaded my rocket with provisions and fuel, and, placing on board some unfamiliar maps of that region of the Galaxy—as well as the apparatus—I blasted off without further delay. My haste might also be explained by the fact that the journey to Amauropia takes about thirty years. Of what exactly I did in that time I had better write elsewhere. I will only mention here one of the more singular events, which was when I encountered, in the vicinity of the galactic core (an area, I might add, that is dustier than most you can find in this universe), a tribe of interstellar vagabonds known as the Gypsonians.

These unfortunates haven't a planet to call their own. To put it politely, they are creatures endowed with great imagination, for practically each one of them told me something different about the origin of the tribe. Later I heard it said that they had simply frittered away their home planet, that is, an inordinate greed had driven them to engage in strip mining and the exportation of various minerals. In these enterprises they tunneled and excavated the interior of their planet, depleting it completely, till finally all that remained was one colossal pit, which one day crumbled beneath their feet. True, there are others who maintain that the Gypsonians, embarking long ago on a drunken spree, had simply lost their way and couldn't get back. Apparently no one knows how it really happened, but in either case the appearance of those cosmic vagabonds is never welcome, for whenever, advancing through space, they stop at any planet, before you know it something's missing; there might be a little less air, or a river suddenly gone dry, or the islands refusing to add up right.

Once, on Ardenuria, they supposedly absconded with an entire continent, which luckily was not in use, being ice-covered. They hire themselves out for the cleaning and adjusting of moons, but few entrust to them these important responsibilities. Their young throw stones at comets, take rides on decaying meteors—in a word, one has no end of trouble with them. I concluded that such a mode of existence was quite intolerable and so, briefly interrupting my journey, set to work—and with considerable success, for I was able to obtain a secondhand moon in perfectly good condition. It was fixed up and, thanks to my contacts, promoted to the status of a planet.

Of course there wasn't any air, but I took up a collection; the neighboring residents all pitched in, and you should have seen the joy with which the good Gypsonians entered their very own planet! They simply could not thank me enough. Bidding them à fond farewell, I continued on my way. To Amauropia there remained less than six quintillion miles; after covering this last stretch of road and finding the right planet (and they're as thick as flies), I began to descend to its surface.

When it was time to throw on the brakes, I discovered to my horror that they didn't work and I was falling towards the planet like a stone. Sticking my head out the hatch, I noticed that the brakes were completely gone. With indignation I thought of the ungrateful Gypsonians, however there wasn't time to reflect on this, for I was already plunging through the atmosphere and the rocket had begun to glow a ruby-red. Another minute and I would be burnt alive.

Fortunately at the last moment I remembered the time dilator; turning it on, I made the passage of time so slow, that my fall to the planet lasted three weeks. Having extricated myself in this way from a difficult situation, I looked around to get my bearings.

The rocket had settled in a spacious clearing surrounded by pale-blue forest. Above the trees with their broom-shaped branches hovered emerald creatures, spinning with great velocity. At the sight of me a herd of animals scurried off into the purple bushes; these bore a striking resemblance to man, except that their skin was shiny and sapphire blue. I already knew one or two things about them from Tarantoga and, pulling out my astronautical handbook, acquired a few additional facts.

The planet was inhabited by a race of anthropoidal beings—so went the text—called Microcephalids, who stood at an extremely low level of development. Attempts to communicate with them were fruitless. The handbook certainly seemed to be telling the truth. The Microcephalids walked on all fours, hunkering here, crouching there, removing the lice from themselves with great skill, and when I drew near they batted their emerald eyes at me and jabbered in a totally disconnected manner. Besides a lack of intelligence they were characterized by a good-natured and peaceful disposition.

For two days I investigated the blue forest and the extensive plains that surrounded it, then went back to my rocket and turned in for the night. I was already in bed when I remembered the accelerator, and decided to set it going for a couple of hours, to see if by the following day it would produce any effect. So I hauled it—not without difficulty—out of the rocket, placed it near the trees, switched on the time acceleration and, returning to bed, slept the sleep of the just.

I was awakened by a violent pulling and tugging. Opening my eyes, I saw the faces of Microcephalids bending over me; already standing on two feet, they were conversing noisily and with the greatest interest moving my arms, and when I tried to resist, they nearly wrenched them from their sockets. The biggest Microcephalid, a lilac giant, forced open my mouth and, sticking his fingers in, counted my teeth.

Struggling helplessly, I was carried out into the clearing and tied to the tail of the rocket. From this position I watched the Microcephalids taking whatever they could from the rocket; the larger objects that would not fit through the opening of the hatch they first broke into pieces with stones. Suddenly a hail of stones rained down upon the rocket and on the Microcephalids busy at work around it; one stone landed on my head. Tightly bound, I was unable to look in the direction from which the stones were flying. I only heard the sounds of battle. The Microcephalids who had tied me up finally took to flight. Others came running, released me from my bonds, and with signs of great respect bore me on their shoulders into the forest.

The procession stopped at the foot of a spreading tree. From its branches hung, fastened with lianas, a kind of aerial hut with a tiny window. Through this window I was deposited inside, at which point the crowd assembled below fell to its knees, wailing and chanting. Long lines of Microcephalids made offerings to me of fruit and flowers. In the days that followed I became the object of a popular cult, in which high priests divined the future from the expression of my face; whenever it seemed unfavorable to them they fumigated me with incense, so that I nearly suffocated. Fortunately during the rendering of these burnt offerings the priest would swing the shrine in which I sat, and this enabled me from time to time to catch a breath of air.

On the fourth day my worshippers were attacked by a band of club-wielding Microcephalids, led by the giant who had counted my teeth. Passing from hand to hand in the course of the battle, I became—alternately—the recipient of veneration and indignities. The conflict concluded with the victory of the attackers, under the command of the giant whose name was Flying

Worm. I participated in his triumphant return to the camp, lashed to the top of a high pole held by his relatives. This became a tradition and thereafter I served as a kind of banner, obliged to accompany them on all their military campaigns. It was burdensome, but carried with it certain privileges.

Gradually picking up the language of the Microcephalids, I began to explain to Flying Worm that it was to *me* that he and his subjects owed their rapid development. This wasn't easy, but I had the impression that I was finally getting through to him; unfortunately he was poisoned by his nephew Flaking Spoon. The latter united the Microcephalids of both field and forest, still at war, by marrying Mastozymasia, the high priestess of the forest Microcephalids.

Catching sight of me during the wedding feast (I was now the taster—that office had been introduced by Flaking Spoon), Mastozymasia gave a delighted shriek: "My, what white-white skin you have!" This filled me with misgivings, which all too soon proved true. Mastozymasia smothered her husband while he slept and wed me in a morganatic marriage. To her in turn I attempted to explain my services on behalf of the Microcephalids, but she misunderstood me, for after the first few words she exclaimed, "Aha, you don't love me any more!" and it took me quite some time to reassure her.

In the next palace coup Mastozymasia perished; I saved myself by jumping out the window. All that remained from our union was the white-and-lilac color of the national flag. After my escape I found the forest clearing with the accelerator, and was about to turn it off, but it occurred to me that it might be wiser instead to wait until the Microcephalids had produced a more democratic civilization.

For a period of time I lived in the forest, sustaining myself exclusively with roots, and only at night did I go out to look at the camp, which was rapidly being transformed into a city, encircled with a stockade.

The Microcephalid settlers tilled the soil, while the city dwellers would fall upon them, ravishing their wives and murdering and plundering them. Out of this, commerce soon developed. Meanwhile religious beliefs were also gaining in strength, and rituals grew more elaborate from day to day. Much to my distress the Microcephalids dragged the rocket from the clearing to the city and set it in the middle of their main square as a kind of idol, surrounding that area with a wall and guards. On several occasions the farmers banded together, attacked Lilium (as the city was called) and with their combined forces leveled it to the ground; however after each time a most efficient restoration followed.

These wars were brought to an end by King Sarcepanos, who burned the villages, cut down the forests as well as the farmers, and those who survived he placed as prisoners of war on the land around the city. Having nowhere now to go, I made my way to Lilium. Thanks to my connections (the palace servants knew me from the days of Mastozymasia) I was given the post of Masseur to the Throne. Sarcepanos took a liking to me at once and decided to confer upon me the dignity of Assistant to the State Assassin, with the rank of Senior Torturer. In despair I returned to the clearing where the accelerator was still running and set it at maximum speed. Sure enough, that very night Sarcepanos died of overeating and Trimon the Livid, commander of the army, ascended the throne. He introduced a hierarchy of officials, taxation, and compulsory military service. The color of my skin saved me from the draft. I was regarded as an albino and as such denied the right to approach the royal residence. I lived among the slaves, called by them Ijon the Ashen.

I began to preach universal equality and revealed my role in the development of Microcephalid society. Before long there had gathered around me many followers of this teaching, known as the Mechanists. Then disorders and rioting ensued, which were bloodily suppressed by the troops of Trimon the Livid. Mechanism became forbidden upon pain of death by tickling.

Several times I had to flee the city and hide in the municipal fish ponds; my disciples were subjected to the cruelest persecution. But more and more people from higher circles began to be drawn to my lectures, incognito of course. When Trimon tragically passed away, absent-mindedly forgetting to breathe, Carbonzyl the Smart assumed power. He was an adherent of my teachings, which were promptly raised to the status of a state religion. I acquired the title of Guardian of the Machine and a magnificent dwelling next to the court. My duties kept me busy—I don't know myself how it happened, but the priests under me took to proclaiming the thesis of my heavenly origin. I opposed this, but to no avail. In the meantime there arose a sect of Antimechanists, who held that the Microcephalids were developing in an entirely natural manner and that I was a former slave who had deceitfully whitened himself with lime to make fools of the people.

The leaders of the sect were seized and the king charged me, as Guardian of the Machine, to put them to their death. Seeing no other way out, I escaped through a window of the palace and for a time concealed myself in the municipal fish ponds. One day the news reached me that the priests were announcing the Ascension of Ijon the Ashen, who, having completed his planetary mission, had left to rejoin his celestial parents. I went to Lilium to set things straight, but the crowd kneeling before my effigies, when I began to speak, wanted to stone me. The temple guards intervened, but only in order to throw me—as an impostor and blasphemer—in the dungeon. For three full days they scrubbed and scraped me, trying to remove the whitewash with which I was supposed to have impersonated the beatified Ashen. Because I failed to turn blue, they were going to apply torture. From this predicament I managed to escape, thanks to one of the jailers who obtained for me a little bluing. I rushed back to the forest where the accelerator stood and after a great deal of manipulating increased its operation even more, in the hope that I might in this way hasten the coming of a decent civilization. Then I hid for two weeks in the municipal fish ponds.

I returned to the capital when they had declared a republic, inflation, amnesty and the equalization of all classes. At the tollgates they were already demanding I. D.'s; having none, I was arrested for vagrancy. After my release I became, to make a living, a courier for the Ministry of Education. The ministerial cabinets changed frequently, sometimes twice a day, and since each new administration began its reign by rescinding the edicts of the previous administration and issuing new, I was kept running back and forth with circulars. Finally I developed bunions on my feet and submitted my resignation, however it was not accepted, for they had just declared a state of war. Living through the republic, two directorates, the restoration of an enlightened monarchy, the authoritarian regime of General Bugbear and his subsequent beheading for high treason, I grew impatient with the slow progress of civilization and once again took to fiddling with the machine, with the result that one of its knobs broke off. This didn't particularly concern me, but after a few days I noticed that something peculiar was taking place.

The sun rose in the west, there was great commotion in the cemetery, the deceased were seen walking about, moreover their condition improved by the minute, adults dwindled before one's eyes, and little children dropped completely out of sight.

The regime of General Bugbear returned, the enlightened monarchy, the directorate, finally the republic. When I saw with my own eyes the retreating funeral procession of King Carbonzyl, who after three days rose from his catafalque and was unembalmed, it dawned on me that I must have broken the machine and time was now running in reverse. The worst of it was, I observed the signs of advancing youth on myself as well. I decided to wait for the resurrection of Carbonzyl the First, when I would again become the Great Mechanist and be able to use my former influence to get to the rocket, which was serving as a sacred idol.

The only trouble was the alarming rate of change; I wasn't sure I could last until the right moment. Every day I stood next to the tree in my back yard and marked the height of my head—I was shrinking with inordinate speed. By the time I was Guardian of the Machine at the side of Carbonzyl, I looked no older than nine—and there were still provisions to be gathered for the trip. At night I loaded them into the rocket, which cost me no little effort, for I was growing progressively weaker. To my great horror I discovered that in moments of leisure from palace duties I felt an irresistible urge to play tag.

When at last the vehicle was ready to go, I crept into it at the crack of dawn and reached for the starting stick—but it was too high. I had to scramble up on a stool before I could move it. Intending to curse, I was appalled to discover that I could only mewl. At the moment of takeoff I was still walking, but apparently the effect had acquired some momentum, since even after leaving that planet, when its disk loomed in the distance as a whitish spot, it was only with the greatest difficulty that I was able to crawl over to the bottle of milk which I had providently prepared for myself. I had to take nourishment in this fashion for six full months.

The journey to Amauropia lasts, as I mentioned at the beginning, about thirty years, consequently upon returning to Earth I did not alarm my friends with my appearance. I only regret that I lack a good imagination, for then I would not have to avoid meeting Tarantoga and could, surely, spare his feelings by making up some cock-and-bull story in praise of his talents as an inventor.

THE
THIRTEENTH
VOYAGE

It is with mixed emotions that I now come to a journey which brought me a great deal more than ever I bargained for. My object, when I set out from Earth, was to reach an extremely remote planet of the Crab constellation, Fatamiasma, known throughout space as the birthplace of one of the most distinguished individuals in our Universe, Master Oh. This is not the real name of that illustrious sage, but they refer to him thus, for it is impossible otherwise to render his true appellation in any earthly language. Children born on Fatamiasma receive an enormous number of titles and distinctions as well as a name that is, by our standards, inordinately long.

The day Master Oh came into the world he was called Hridipidagnittusuoayomojorfnagrolliskipwikabeccopyxlbepurz. And duly dubbed Golden Buttress of Being, Doctor of Quintessential Benignity, Most Possibilistive Universatilitude, etc., etc. From year to year, as he studied and matured, the titles and syllables of his name were one by one removed, and since he gave evidence of uncommon abilities, by the thirty-third year of his life he was relieved of his last distinction, and two years later carried no title whatever, while his name was designated in the Fatamiasman alphabet by a single and—moreover—voiceless letter, signifying "celestial aspirate"—this is a kind of stifled gasp which one gives from a surfeit of awe and rapture.

And now, surely, the Reader will understand why I call this

great sage Master Oh. Commonly known as the Benefactor of the Universe, he has dedicated his life to the work of bringing happiness to innumerable races of the Galaxy. Laboring without respite, he created the science of granting wishes, also called the General Theory of Simulation. He refers to himself, however, as a simple prostheticist.

The first time I encountered a manifestation of Master Oh's activity was on Europia. That planet had for ages been seething with dissension, peevishness, and the mutual hostility of its inhabitants. Brother envied brother there, students hated teachers, subordinates—superiors. And yet when I dropped in for a visit I was confronted instead by universal tranquility and the most tender affection, displayed and reciprocated—without exception—by all the members of the planetary community. Naturally I was curious to learn the cause of such an edifying transformation.

One day, while wandering through the streets of the capital in the company of a native I knew, I noticed in a number of store windows life-size heads, arranged on stands as if they were hats, and large mannequins too, all bearing a remarkable likeness to the Europians themselves. My companion explained, when asked, that these were safety valves. If you happened to conceive a dislike for anyone, you went to such a store and purchased a custom-made replica of the party, in order afterwards, in the privacy of your lodgings, to take whatever liberties you liked with it. Persons of greater means could afford an entire mannequin, the rest had to content themselves with abusing the head only.

This brilliant example of social engineering, called the Simulation of Individual Freedom, was something new to me, and I could not help but inquire as to its creator, who was, as it turned out, Master Oh.

Later, spending some time on other globes, I had occasion to come across other traces of his beneficial influence. Take Ardeluria, for instance, where there had lived a certain famous astronomer who proclaimed that the planet revolved about its axis. This theory contradicted the creed of the Ardelurians, according to which the planet was fixed motionless in the center of the Universe. The council of high priests summoned the astronomer before the tribunal and demanded he renounce his heretical teaching. When he refused, they condemned him to be cleansed of his sins by fire, at the stake. Master Oh, learning of this, hastened to Ardeluria. There he conferred with both priests and scientists, however each side held stubbornly to its position. After spending the night in meditation, the sage finally came up with an idea, which immediately he put into action. This was a planetary brake. With its help the rotational motion of the planet was arrested. The astronomer, sitting in his cell, detected the change by observing the heavens and, recanting his previous assertions, willingly accepted the dogma of the immobility of Ardeluria. Thus was created the Simulation of Objective Truth.

In his spare moments, when he was not engaged in social work, Master Oh carried out research of another kind: it was he, for example, who invented the method of locating—at great distances—planets occupied by intelligent life. This is the method of the "a posteriori clue," incredibly simple, as are all ideas of genius. The flaring up of a new star in the firmament, where there have been no stars before, testifies to the recent disintegration of a planet whose former inhabitants had achieved a high level of civilization and discovered the means of releasing atomic energy. Master Oh did what he could to prevent such incidents, and in the following way: when a planet became depleted of its natural fuels, such as coal or oil, he would instruct the inhabitants in the breeding of electric eels. This was implemented on more than one globe, under the name of the Simulation of Progress. Which of our astronauts has not enjoyed an evening stroll on Enteroptosis, wandering through the dark accompanied by a trained eel with a light bulb in its little mouth?!

As time went by I longed to meet, more and more, this Master Oh. Of course I understood that before I could actually make his acquaintance I would have to do some serious boning up, in order to raise myself to his high intellectual plane. Inspired by this thought, I decided to devote the entire time of the flight, roughly nine years, to educating myself in the field of philosophy. And so I blasted off from Earth in a rocket filled from stem to stern with bookshelves that sagged beneath the weight of the loftiest fruits of the human spirit. Having put some six hundred million miles or more between myself and the parent star, when nothing could disturb my concentration, I started in on the reading. There was so much of it, that I'd worked out a special system for myself: first, to avoid the mistake of reading books I might already have leafed through, I planned to toss each work—as I was finished with it—out the hatch of the rocket, and then collect them all, one by one, afloat in space, on the return trip.

So for the next two hundred and eighty days I pored over Anaxagoras, Plato and Plotinus, Origen and Tertullian, went through Erigena the Scott, the bishops Hrab of Moguncia and Hincmar of Reims, read Ratramnus of Corbie from cover to cover, Servatus Lupus, and Augustine too, his *De Vita Beata, De Civitate Dei* and *De Quantitate Animae*. Then I took on Thomas Aquinas, the bishops Synesios and Nemesios, also Pseudo-Dionysius the Areopagite, Saint Bernard and Suárez. At Saint Victor I had to stop, for it's a habit of mine, when I read, to roll little pills out of bread, and by now the rocket was full of them. Sweeping them into space, I shut the hatch and got back to my studies. The next shelves contained more recent works—there were a good seven and a half tons there and I began to fear I wouldn't have time to master it all, however I soon discovered that the themes repeated themselves, differing only in their formulation. What some set right side up, so to speak, others put upside down; thus I was able to skip over quite a bit.

Then I did the mystics and the Schoolmen, Hartmann, Gentile, Spinoza, Ulundt, Malebranche, Herbart, and acquainted myself with infinitism, the perfection of creation, the harmony of the spheres, and monads, never ceasing to be amazed at how each of these wise men had such a great deal to say about the human soul, and all of it diametrically opposed to what the others proclaimed.

Then, as I became engrossed in a positively delightful description of the harmony of the spheres, my reading was interrupted by a fairly serious incident. I was now passing through a region of intense magnetic fields, which magnetized all iron objects with tremendous force. This is precisely what happened to the iron tags on the laces of my slippers. Rooted to the steel floor, I couldn't take a step to reach the cupboard where the food was. The prospect of death by starvation loomed before me, but I remembered in time that I had a copy of the Astronaut's Handbook in my pocket and, pulling it out, read that in such situations one ought to remove one's shoes. This done, I returned to my studies.

When I had familiarized myself with about six thousand tomes and knew their contents like the palm of my own hand, some eight trillion miles still separated me from Fatamiasma. I was just beginning to tackle the next shelf, which was filled with the critique of pure reason, when the sound of energetic knocking reached my ears. I looked up, startled, for I was alone in the rocket, and was hardly expecting any visitors from space. The knocking grew more insistent, at the same time I heard a muffled voice:

"Open up! Aquatica!"

I hurriedly unlocked the hatch, and into the rocket came three beings in spacesuits, covered with cosmic dust.

"Aha! A hydrant, caught in the act!" cried the first of them, and the second added:

"All right, where's your water?"

Before I could reply, gaping with astonishment, the third said something to the other two, which seemed to appease them a little.

"Where are you from?" asked the first.

"From Earth. And who are you?"

"Free Aquatica of Pinta," he growled, and handed me a questionnaire to fill out.

I took a glance at the blanks in this document, then at the spacesuits, which with every movement gave a gurgling sound. Then it dawned on me that I had carelessly flown within the proximity of the twin planets of Pinta and Panta, which all the handbooks warn to give as wide a berth as possible. But it was too late now. While I filled out the questionnaire, the persons in the spacesuits systematically made a list of the objects on board. Discovering at one point a can of sardines in oil, they gave a cry of triumph, then proceeded to place seals on the rocket and take it in tow. I tried to engage them in conversation, but without success. The spacesuits they wore, I noticed, ended in wide, flat appendages, as if the Pintanese had fish tails instead of legs. Before long we began to descend. The planet was completely covered with water, which however was very shallow, since the tops of the buildings stuck out. When the Aquaticans removed their suits at the airport, I saw that they were really quite similar to people,

87

except that their limbs were strangely bent and twisted. I was put in a curious kind of boat, which had large openings in the bottom and was filled to the brim with water. Thus immersed, we slowly drifted off in the direction of the city. I asked whether it wouldn't be possible to stop up those holes and bail out the water; I asked about other things as well, but my companions didn't answer, they only took frantic notes of everything I said.

Along the streets waded the inhabitants of the planet with their heads beneath the water, surfacing every now and then to catch a breath of air. The walls of the houses were glass and one could see inside: the rooms were all more or less half-filled with water. When our vehicle halted at an intersection not far from a building that bore the inscription of "Central Authority of Irrigation," through the open windows I could hear the gurgling of the officials. In the squares stood soaring statues of fish, decked with garlands of seaweed. When our boat again stopped for a moment (the traffic was quite heavy), I overheard some passers-by say that a spy had just been caught on the corner, norching his combula.

Then we floated down a broad avenue lined with magnificent portraits of fish and with placards of many colors: "Long Live Water, Down with Drought!," "Fin in Fin We Onward Swim!"—and others I didn't have time to read. At last the boat docked in front of a gigantic skyscraper. Its façade was all festooned, and above the entrance gleamed the emerald words: "Free Piscatorial Aquatica." The elevator, resembling a small aquarium, took us up to the 16th floor. I was ushered into an office filled with water up over the desk and told to wait. Everything was upholstered in gorgeous emerald scales.

In my mind I prepared precise answers to the questions of how I came here and whither I was bound, however no one asked them. My interrogator, an Aquatican of small stature, entered the room, looked me over sternly, then stood on tiptoe and asked, his mouth just above the water:

"When did you begin your criminal activity? How much did they pay you? Who are your accomplices?"

I replied that, so help me, I was no spy; I also explained the circumstances that had brought me to the planet. But when I declared I was on Pinta purely by accident, the interrogator burst into laughter and said I would have to think up something a little more intelligent than that. Then he began to study the reports, throwing various questions at me from time to time, which cost him considerable trouble, for after each question he was obliged to stand up for air, and once he accidentally swallowed water and coughed for quite some time. I noticed, later on, that this happened to the Pintanese fairly often.

My Aquatican smilingly urged me to confess to everything, but when I continued to insist that I was innocent, he suddenly leaped up and, pointing to the can of sardines, asked:

"And what does that mean?"

"Nothing," I replied, nonplussed.

"We shall see. Remove this provocateur!" he shouted.

With that the interrogation was concluded.

The cell they threw me into was perfectly dry. Which came as a pleasant surprise, since all this moisture had begun to bother me in earnest. There were seven Pintanese besides myself in that tiny chamber; they received me most graciously and made room for me, a foreigner, on their bench. From them I learned that the sardines found in the rocket constituted, by their laws, a terrible insult to the highest Pintan ideals, and this through a "subversive innuendo." I asked what innuendo was involved here, but they were unable or rather—so it seemed to me—unwilling to say. Seeing that the subject caused them distress, I quickly dropped it. I also learned from them that cells like the one in which I found myself were the only waterless places on the face of the planet. I inquired if in their history they had always lived in water—they told me that once Pinta had contained many continents and few seas, and that there had been a great number of disgusting dry areas.

The present ruler of the planet was the Mighty Hydrant Hermezinius the Fish-eyed. During the three months I spent in the desiccator I was examined by eighteen different commissions. They measured the shape of the mist on the mirror I was ordered to breathe on, they counted the number of drops that fell from me after immersion in water, they fitted me with a fish tail. I also had to tell the experts my dreams, which were immediately sorted and classified according to the paragraphs of the penal code. By autumn the proofs of my guilt took up eighty thick volumes, and the material evidence occupied three bookcases in the office with the fish scales. Finally I confessed to everything they accused me of, and particularly to the perforating of chondrites and repeated clutch-stuffing on behalf of Panta. To this day I haven't the least idea what that means. Taking into account the mitigating circumstances, namely my dull-witted ignorance of the blessings of life underwater, and also the approaching birthday of the Mighty Fish-eyed Hydrant Hermezinius, they meted out the lenient sentence of two years of voluntary sculpture, suspended in water for six months, after which I was released on my own cognizance.

I resolved to make myself as comfortable as possible for the duration of my six-month stay on Pinta and, unable to find a room in any of the hotels, took up lodgings at the house of an old woman who spent her time trilling snails, that is, training them to arrange themselves in certain patterns on national holidays.

The very first evening after my release from the desiccator I attended a performance of the metropolitan choir, which was a great disappointment, since the choir sang underwater—gurgling.

At one point I noticed an Aquatican usher escorting out some individual who, when the houselights were dimmed, had started breathing through a reed. The dignitaries seated in the loges filled with water were showering themselves. I couldn't get rid of the strange feeling that everyone was actually quite uncomfortable with all of this. I even tried sounding out my landlady on the subject—she, however, chose to ignore the questions, asking only at what level I should like the water in my room. When I said that I would most prefer seeing it confined to the bathtub, she screwed up her lips, shrugged and walked away, leaving me in the middle of a word.

Desiring to acquaint myself more fully with the Pintanese, I tried to take part in their cultural life. At the time of my arrival on the planet there was a lively discussion underway in the press, on the topic of gurgling. The specialists were in favor of silent gurgling, as having the greatest future.

My landlady had another lodger, a pleasant young Pintan who was the editor of the popular periodical *The Daily Fish*. In the papers I frequently came across references to gwats and sunkers; judging by the texts, these were living creatures of some kind, but I wasn't able to figure out what connection they had with the Pintanese. The people I asked about this usually submerged, drowning me out with their gurgling. I wanted to ask the editor, but he was terribly preoccupied. At supper he revealed to me with the utmost agitation that a most dreadful thing had happened to him. Without thinking he had written in a lead article that water was wet. On account of which, he expected the worst. I did my best to console him, and asked if they then considered water to be dry; startled, he replied that I didn't understand a thing. You have to look at it from the fish's point of view. Fish do not find water wet—ergo, it isn't. Two days later the editor disappeared.

I met with special difficulties when I started going to shows. The first time I went to the theater, I could hardly follow the performance what with all the whispering. Thinking it was my neighbors, I tried to ignore them. Finally, extremely annoyed, I moved to another seat, but there too I heard the same whispering. While on the stage they were talking about the Mighty Hydrant, a small voice whispered: "Your limbs with bliss are all aquiver." I noticed that the entire audience had begun trembling slightly. Afterwards I learned that all public places were equipped with special softspeakers, which prompted those present with the appropriate emotions. Wishing to understand better the customs and peculiarities of the Pintanese, I purchased a considerable number of books, novels as well as graded readers and scientific studies. Some of these I still have, such as: *The Little Sunker, On the Horrors of Aridity, How Finny 'Tis beneath the Waves, Guggle Love*, etc. At the university bookstore they recommended a work on evolutionary persuasion, however all I got out of it was a highly detailed description of gwats and sunkers.

My landlady, when I tried to question her, locked herself in the kitchen with the snails, so I went back to the bookstore and inquired as to where I might possibly find at least one gwat. At these words the salesmen dived under the counter, and a few young Pintanese who happened to be present in the store took me to Aquatican headquarters as a provocateur. Thrown into the desiccator, I found three of my former companions there. It was from them that I learned that as yet there *were* no gwats or sunkers on Pinta. These are the noble forms, perfect in their fishiness, into which the Pintanese will in time change according to the laws of evolutionary persuasion. I asked when this was supposed to take place. At that they all trembled and tried to dive out of sight, an obvious impossibility in the absence of water, and then the oldest of them, his limbs badly misshapen, said:

"Listen here, hydrant, among us such things are not said with impunity. Just let Aquatica hear about these questions of yours, and you'll receive a nice addition to your sentence."

Disheartened, I gave in to the gloomiest reflections, from which however I was roused by the conversation of my fellow sufferers. They were discussing their offenses, each pondering the gravity of his own. One was in the desiccator because he had, after dozing off on a waterlogged sofa, choked and jumped sputtering to his feet with the cry: "A man could drown." The second had carried his child piggyback instead of teaching it, from the very first, to live underwater. And the third, the oldest one, had had the misfortune to gurgle in a manner characterized by competent observers as ambiguous and disrespectful during a lecture on the three hundred hydrant heroes who gave up their lives to set a record for breathing underwater.

Shortly thereafter I was summoned before the Head Flounder, who informed me that this new despicable crime of mine forced him now to sentence me to a total of three years of voluntary sculpture. The next day, in the company of thirty-seven Pintanese, I sailed off in a boat, no longer surprised at having to sit chin-deep in water, off to the sculpting areas. They were located far outside the city. Our work consisted in carving statues of fish of the carp family. To the best of my recollection we chiseled out approximately 140,000 of these. In the morning we would swim to work, singing songs; there is one particularly that sticks in my mind, it began with the words, "No slaves are we, that drag their feet, Freedom makes the labor sweet." After work we would return to our cells; but before supper—which had to be eaten underwater—a lecturer came each day and gave a talk on our watery rights; those interested could sign up as members of the club of Contemplators of Befinnitude. At the end of his talk our lecturer would invariably ask if perchance any of us had lost the inclination to sculpt. Somehow or other no one ever spoke up, so neither did I. And anyway, the softspeakers placed around the hall assured us that we wished to sculpt as long as possible, and the more underwater, the better.

One day our supervisors began to show signs of unusual excitement, and at lunch we learned that the Big Fish Himself, the Mighty Hydrant Hermezinius, would be sailing past our workshops that very day, issuing forth to further the cause of gwatish barbelment. All that afternoon we swam at attention, awaiting the exalted arrival. The rain fell, and it was so beastly cold, we all started shivering. The softspeakers—attached to buoys—told us we were trembling with enthusiasm. It was nearly twilight when the retinue of the Mighty Fish-face, seven hundred boats in all, floated by. I happened to be close enough to get a good look at His Fishiness, who to my great surprise did not in the least resemble a fish. This was, to all appearances, a perfectly ordinary Pintan, except that he was very old and his limbs were terribly twisted. Eight magnates dressed in gold and crimson scales supported the ruler's noble shoulders as he came up for air; in the process he sputtered dreadfully, till I began to feel sorry for him. In honor of this event we hewed eight hundred statues of carp over the quota.

About a week later I got awful stabbing pains in my arms for the first time; my comrades explained that this was simply the beginnings of rheumatism, the greatest plague on Pinta. Of course one was not allowed to call it an illness, but only the symptoms of the organism's ideological resistance to fishification. Now I understood the contorted appearance of the Pintanese.

Every week we were taken to see pageants that presented glorious perspectives of underwater life. I kept my eyes shut, for the very mention of water made me queasy.

And so it went, for five months. Towards the end of this period I became friends with a certain elderly Pintan, a university professor, who was sculpting voluntarily because in one of his classes he had maintained that water was indeed indispensable for life, but in a different sense than was generally practiced. In our conversations, conducted mostly at night, the professor told me the ancient history of Pinta. The planet had once been beset by burning winds, which—the scientists said—threatened to turn it into one enormous desert. Therefore a great irrigational plan was adopted. To implement which, appropriate institutions and top-priority bureaus were set up; but then, after the network of canals and reservoirs had been completed, the bureaus refused to disband themselves and continued to operate, irrigating Pinta more and more. The upshot was—as the professor put it—that what was to have been controlled, controlled us. No one, however, would admit this, and of course the next, logical step was the declaration that things were exactly the way they ought to be.

One day rumors began to circulate among us, tremendously exciting rumors. It was said that some extraordinary change was about to take place, a few even dared claim that the Mighty Hydrant Himself would very shortly decree private dryness, and possibly public. Our supervisors immediately proceeded to combat this defeatism, announcing new fish-statue projects. In spite of this, the rumor persisted, and in ever more fantastic versions; with my own two ears I heard someone say that the Mighty Fish-head Hermezinius had been seen holding a towel.

Then, one night, sounds of riotous laughter reached us from the supervisors' building. Swimming outside, I saw the commandant and the lecturer tossing water out the windows in great bucketfuls, singing loudly all the while. At the break of day the lecturer came; he sat in a caulked-up boat and told us that everything till now had been a misunderstanding; that new, genuinely free ways of living—not like the previous ways—were being worked out, and in the meantime gurgling was repealed, as fatiguing, injurious to health and totally unnecessary. During this speech he put his foot in the water and pulled it out again, shuddering with disgust. In conclusion he added that he had always been against water and knew all along that nothing good would ever come of it. For the next two days we didn't go to work. Then they sent us to the statues that had already been completed; we chipped off the fins and attached legs in their place. The lecturer began to teach us a new song, "Our spirits are high when it's dry," and everyone was saying that any day now pumps would be brought in and the water removed.

However after the second verse our lecturer was recalled to the capital and never came back. The following morning the commandant sailed over to us, barely showing his head above the waves, and handed out waterproof newspapers. These announced that gurgling, injurious to health and not furthering siluriation, was hereby once and for all rescinded, which however in no way signified a return to pernicious aridity. Quite on the contrary. To enacclimate the gwats and spurge on the sunkers, underwater breathing would be instituted throughout the planet, and *exclusively* underwater, as being fishlike in the highest degree; at the same time—out of consideration for the public welfare—this would be introduced in stages, that is, each day all citizens were required to remain beneath the water just a little longer than on the preceding day. In order to assist them in this, the general level of water would be raised to eleven bathyms (a unit of length).

That evening the water level was in fact raised, and to such a height that we had to sleep standing up. Since the softspeakers were now covered, they were fastened a trifle higher, and our new lecturer had us do underwater breathing exercises. A few days later Hermezinius, at the request of the entire population, generously consented to raise the water level half a bathym more. We all began to walk around on tiptoe. Persons who were shorter quickly dropped out of sight. Since no one quite got the hang of underwater breathing, the practice of inconspicuously jumping up for air developed. After about a month, considerable proficiency was achieved in this, while everyone pretended not to notice others doing it, nor indeed that they were doing it themselves. The press reported that great strides were being made throughout the land in underwater breathing, and meanwhile a sizable number of new sculpting volunteers arrived, persons who continued to gurgle in the old way.

All of this, taken together, gave me such a headache, that at last I decided to quit the voluntary sculpting grounds for good. After work I hid behind the underpinning of a new monument (I forgot to mention we had chipped off the attached legs of the fish and put back fins), and when everyone was gone, I swam to the city. In this respect I had a considerable advantage over the Pintanese, who, contrary to what one might have expected, were quite unable to swim.

I exhausted myself completely, but made it at last to the airport. Four Aquaticans were guarding my rocket. Fortunately someone nearby started gurgling and the Aquaticans hurled themselves in that direction. So I broke the seals, jumped inside and took off with the greatest possible speed. After a quarter of an hour the planet glimmered in the distance, now a tiny star, on which it had been my lot to endure so much. I stretched out on the bed, reveling in its dryness; but alas, this pleasant respite was

95

short-lived. Suddenly I was wakened by an energetic knocking at the hatch. Still half-asleep, I shouted: "Long live Free Pinta!" This cry was to cost me dearly, for into the rocket burst a patrol of Angelicans from Panta. In vain did I attempt to explain that they had heard me wrong, that I had shouted not "Free Pinta," but "Free Panta." The rocket was sealed and taken in tow. And as if this wasn't bad enough, there was a second can of sardines in the larder, and I had opened it before my nap. Spotting the open can, the Angelicans gasped, then with a cry of triumph proceeded to write out a summons. Before long we had landed on the planet. Placed inside a waiting vehicle, I sighed with relief, for the planet, as far as the eye could see, was free of water. When my escort removed their spacesuits I observed that these beings with whom I had to deal bore a remarkable likeness to people, except that their faces were identical, as if they had all been twins, and smiling besides.

Though night had fallen, the city lamps made it bright as day. I noticed that whenever a pedestrian looked at me he would shake his head, either with pity or dismay, and one female Pantan actually fainted, which was curious, considering that even then she continued to smile.

After a time I got the impression that all the inhabitants of the planet were wearing some sort of mask, but couldn't tell for sure. The trip ended in front of a building that carried the inscription: FREE ANGELICA OF PANTA. I spent the night alone in a small cell, listening to the sounds of the metropolis that reached my window. The next day, around noon, I was read the charges against me in the office of the examiner. I was accused of committing angelophagy at the instigation of the Pintanese, and also of the crime of personal differentiation. The material evidence of my guilt consisted of two items: one was the open can of sardines, the other — a mirror, held up to my face by the examiner.

This was an Angelican 4th Class in a uniform as white as snow, with diamond thunderbolts across his chest; he explained that for the above offenses I could face life identification, then added that the court was giving me four days in which to prepare my defense. I might consult with an officially appointed counselor-at-law at any time.

Having already had some experience with legal procedures in this part of the Galaxy, I wished above all to learn the nature of the punishment involved. In answer to my request I was led to a modest room of amber color, where my lawyer, an Angelican 2nd Class, was already waiting. He turned out to be most obliging and was only too happy to explain.

"Know, O uninvited alien," he said, "that ours is the knowledge of the ultimate source of all the cares, sufferings and misfortunes to which beings, gathered together in societies, are prone. This source lies in the individual, in his private identity. Society, the collective, is eternal, obeying steadfast and immutable laws, as do the mighty suns and stars. The individual, on the other hand, is characterized by uncertainty, indecision, inconsistency of action, and above all—by impermanence. Therefore we have completely eliminated individuality on behalf of the society. On our planet there are no entities—only the collective."

"But really," I said, astonished, "what you're saying must be merely a figure of speech, for after all, you yourself are an individual, an entity . . ."

"Not at all," he replied with an imperturbable smile. "You have noticed, surely, that there is no difference among us in our faces. In the same way we have achieved the highest degree of social interchangeability."

"I don't understand. What does that mean?"

"At any given moment there exists in a society a certain number of functions or, as we say, roles. One has the occupational roles, namely those of rulers, gardeners, mechanics, physicians; there are also family roles—fathers, brothers, sisters, and so on. Now in each such role a Pantan serves for twenty-four hours only. At midnight there occurs throughout our land a single movement, it is as if—speaking metaphorically—everyone takes a single step, and in this fashion a person who yesterday was a gardener, today becomes an engineer, yesterday's mason is now a judge, a ruler—a teacher, and so on. The same holds with families. Each is composed of relatives—there's a father, mother, children. Only the functions remain constant; the ones who perform them are changed every day. And so you see it is the collective, and only the collective, which remains intact. There are still the same number of parents and children, doctors and nurses, and similarly in all walks of life. The powerful organism of our state endures through the centuries, unmoved and unchanging, more durable than rock, and it owes its durability to the fact that we have done away, once and for all, with the ephemeral nature of individual existence. That is why I say we have achieved the ultimate in interchangeability. You will see this for yourself when, after midnight, you call for me, and I appear in a new form . . ."

"But what is the purpose of all this?" I asked. "And how do each of you possibly manage to practice all professions? Can you really be not only a gardener, judge or lawyer, but also a father or mother at will?"

"Many professions," replied my smiling interlocutor, "I do not perform well. Consider however that one's practice of a profession lasts but a single day. And besides, in any society of the old type the overwhelming majority of people carry out their professional duties indifferently at best, yet the social mechanism does not thereby cease to function. A second-rate gardener will ruin your garden, a second-rate ruler will bring disaster upon an entire nation, since both have time enough to do this, but here they do not. Moreover in an ordinary society, in addition to occupational incompetence, one can sense the negative if not destructive influence of the private ambitions of individuals. Envy, pride, egoism, vanity, the thirst for power—these have a corrosive effect on the life of the community. Here that evil influence does not exist. Indeed, here the ambition to have a career does not exist, nor is anyone motivated by personal gain, for here there is no such thing as personal gain. I cannot take some step in my role of today in the hopes that it will profit me tomorrow, for by tomorrow I shall be someone else, and who I shall be tomorrow I do not know today.

"The exchange of roles takes place at midnight on the basis of a general lottery, over which none of us has any control. Now do you begin to understand the great wisdom of our system?"

"And feelings?" I asked. "Can one really love a different person every day? And what happens to fatherhood and motherhood?"

"One problem we did have, formerly," he replied, "was the circumstance in which a person in the role of a father gave birth to a child, for it is possible that the role of father be occupied by a woman on the very day of her delivery. However that difficulty disappeared the moment it was written into law that a father could give birth. As far as feelings are concerned, we have satisfied two needs, needs that would appear to be mutually exclusive, yet they dwell within the breast of every intelligent creature: the need for permanence and the need for change. Affection, respect, love were at one time gnawed by constant anxiety, by the fear of losing the person held dear. This dread we have conquered. For in point of fact whatever upheavals, diseases or calamities may be visited upon us, we shall always have a father, a mother, a spouse, and children. But this is not all. That which does not change will soon begin to pall, regardless of whether it brings us happiness or sorrow. Yet we also crave stability, we wish deliverance from vicissitudes and tragedy. We wish to live, but not to be fleeting, to change, yet remain, to experience all—and risk nothing. These contradictions, unreconcilable it would seem, are with *us* a reality. We have even erased the antagonism between the upper and lower strata of society, for each of us—each day—can be a king, as there is no walk of life, no sphere of activity closed to any man.

"And now I can reveal to you the full significance and magnitude of the punishment that hangs above your head. It signifies the greatest misfortune that ever can befall a Pantan: expulsion from the general lottery and abandonment to the solitary fate of an individual. Identification—this is the act of crushing a person by setting upon him the cruel and merciless burden of perpetual selfhood. You must hurry if you have any further questions to put to me, for midnight approaches; I will have to leave you shortly."

"What do you do about death?" I asked.

With his wrinkled brow and smiling face my defender looked at me closely, as if attempting to understand that word. Finally he said:

"Death? It is an obsolete idea. There can be no death where there are no individuals. We do not die."

"But that's absurd, you don't believe in it yourself!" I exclaimed. "All living things must die, and so must you!"

"I, and who is that?" he interrupted with a smile.

There was a moment of silence.

"You, you yourself!"

"And who am I, I myself, beyond this present role? A name? I have no name. A face? Thanks to the biological measures carried out among us centuries ago my face is the same as everyone else's. A role? But that changes at midnight. What then is left? Nothing. Consider for a moment, what means death? A loss, tragic since irrevocable. The one who dies, whom does he lose? Himself? No, for once dead, he has ceased to exist, and one who exists not, there is nothing he can lose. Death is the province of the living—it is the loss of someone near.

"But we never lose those who are near to us. I have already explained that, I think. Every family here is eternal. Death for us—this would be the constriction of a role. The law forbids that. But I must go now. Farewell, O uninvited alien!"

"Wait!" I cried, seeing my defender rise. "Surely there exist—there must exist differences among you, even assuming you all are alike as twins. You must have old people, who . . ."

"No. We do not keep track of the number of roles which one has held. Neither do we keep a record of the astronomical years. None of us knows how long he lives. The roles are ageless. My time is up."

With these words he departed. I was alone. A moment later the door opened and my defender reappeared. He had on the same sky-blue uniform with the golden thunderbolts of an Angelican 2nd Class, and the very same smile.

"I am at your service, O alien defendant from another star," he said, and it seemed to me that this was a new voice, one I had not heard before.

"Ah, then you do have something constant here: the role of defendant!" I cried.

"You are mistaken. That is only for foreigners. We cannot allow someone to hide himself behind a role and attempt to sabotage our system from within."

"Are you familiar with the law?" I asked.

"The lawbooks are. Besides, your trial will not be held until the day after tomorrow. The role of defender will defend you . . ."

"I waive defense."

"You wish to defend yourself?"

"No. I wish to be found guilty."

"You are rash," said the lawyer with a smile. "Keep in mind that you will be not an individual among individuals, but in a waste more desolate than the interplanetary void . . ."

"Have you ever heard of Master Oh?" I asked, not knowing myself how the question popped into my head.

"Yes. It was he who created our state. In so doing, he produced his masterpiece—the Simulation of Eternity."

Thus ended our conversation. Three days later, brought before the court, I was found guilty and condemned to life identification. Driven back to the airport, I promptly blasted off, setting my course for Earth. I doubt that I'll ever again get the urge to meet this Benefactor of the Universe.

THE
FOURTEENTH
VOYAGE

19. VIII. Having my rocket repaired. I got too close to the sun last time; all the finish peeled off. The shop manager suggests green. Perhaps, I don't know. Spent the morning straightening up my collection. The prettiest gargoon pelt was full of moths. Sprinkled it with naphthalene. My afternoon—at Tarantoga's. We sang Martian songs. I borrowed from him Brizard's *Two Years among the Squamp and Octopockles.* Read it till dawn—simply fascinating.

20. VIII. I agreed to green. The manager is trying to talk me into buying an electrical brain. He has an extra one, in good condition, hardly used, high-powered. He says that no one goes anywhere today without a brain, except maybe to the moon. Haven't decided yet, it's a big expense. Read Brizard all afternoon—can't put it down. And to think that I've never even seen a squamp.

21. VIII. At the shipyard bright and early. The manager showed me his brain. Truly handsome, and the joke battery lasts five years. This is supposed to solve the problem of cosmic ennui. "You'll laugh the whole voyage," said the manager. When the battery runs out, simply put in another. I ordered the rudders painted red. But as for the brain—I'll have to think about it. Stayed up until midnight reading Brizard. Why not go hunting myself?

22. VIII. I finally bought that brain. Had it built into the wall. The manager added on some optionals, a heating pad and pillow. Taking me for all I'm worth! But he says I'll save a lot of money. The point is that when you land on a planet you usually have to go through customs. With a brain, however, you can leave the rocket in space, let it circle the planet like an artificial moon, and then, without paying a single cent on duty, you proceed the rest of the way on foot. The brain computes the astronomical elements of its flight and relays the coordinates when you have to find the rocket later. I finished Brizard. Pretty well made up my mind, I'm going to Enteropia.

23. VIII. Got the rocket from the repair shop. It looks beautiful, except that the rudders clash. I repainted them myself, yellow. Worlds better. Borrowed volume E of the Cosmic Encyclopedia from Tarantoga and copied down the entry on Enteropia. Here it is:

ENTEROPIA, 6th planet of a double (red and blue) star in the Calf constellation. 8 continents, 2 oceans, 167 active volcanoes, 1 torg (see TORG). A 20-hr. day, warm climate, conditions for life favorable except during the whackers (see WHACKER).

Inhabitants:
a) dominant race—the Ardrites, intelligent beings, polydiaphanohedral, nonbisymmetrical and pelissobrachial (3), belonging to the genus Siliconoidea, order Polytheria, class Luminifera. Like all Polytheria the Ardrites are subject to periodic discretional splitting. They form families of the spherical type. System of government: gradocracy II B, with the introduction, 340 yrs. ago, of Penitential Trasm (see TRASM). Industry highly developed, principally eating utensils. Chief items of export: phosphorescent manubria, heart pl.'s, and loppets in several doz. varieties, ribbed and tannable. Capital: Ubbidub, pop. 1,400,000. Industrial centers: Haupr, Drur, Arbagellar. Culture luminositous, showing tendency to mushroom, due to the pervasive influence of the relics of a civilization wiped out by the Ardrites, the Phytogosian (see MUSHROOM MEN). In recent yrs. an increasingly imp. role has been played in the cultural life of the society by (see) scrupts. Beliefs: the prevailing religion—Monomungism. According to M., the world was created by the Multiple Munge in the person of the Original Urdle, from whom arose the suns and planets, with Enteropia at the head. The plated temples of the Ardrites are stationary and collapsible.

Besides Monomungism several sects are active, the most significant—the Tentortonian. The (see) Tentortonians believe only in Emphosis (see EMPHOSIS), and some not even in that. Art: ballet (rotary), radio opera, scruption, antediluvian drama. Architecture: in con. with the whackers—pump-inflatable, tubulous, blobiform. Gum towers, highest are the 130-deckers. On art. moons edifices generally ovoid.

b) *Animals*. Fauna of the siliconoidal var., prin. species: slebs, autachial denderfnifts, gruncheons, squamp and whimpering octopockles. During the whackers the hunting of squamp and octopockles is prohibited by law. For man these animals are inedible, with the exception of squamp (and only in the zarf region, see ZARF). Aquatic fauna: constitute the raw material of the food industry. Prin. species: infernalia (hellwinders), chungheads, frinkuses and opthropularies. Unique to Enteropia is the torg, with its bollical fauna and flora. In our Galaxy the only things analogous to it are the hii in the frothless sump bosks of Jupiter. All life on Enteropia evolved—as has been shown by the studies of the school of Prof. Tarantoga—within the confines of the torg, from the chalcycladine deposits. In con. with the massive devel. of land and sea one can expect the swift disappearance of the remnants of the torg. Falling under par. 6 of the stat. in ré the preservation of planetary monuments (Codex Galacticus t. MDDDVII, vol. XXXII, pg. 4670), the torg has been declared a park; esp. forbidden is poaching (croaching) at night.

Most of the entry is clear to me, except for the references to scrupts, trasm and whackers. Unfortunately the last volume of the Encyclopedia published so far ends on "SUCCOTASH," which means there's nothing about trasm or whacker. However I did go over to Tarantoga's to look up "SCRUPTS." All I found was:

SCRUPTS—a feature of the civilization of the (see) Ardrites, of the planet (see) Enteropia, plays a significant role in their cultural life. See SCRUPTURE.

I followed this advice and read:

SCRUPTURE—the act of scrupturing, the state of being scruptured, the product of (see) scruption.

I looked under "Scruption," which said:

104

SCRUPTION—an activity or condition of the (see) Ardrites, of the planet (see) Enteropia. See SCRUPTS.

The circle had closed, there was nowhere else to look. Well, I'd sooner die than admit to such ignorance in front of the Professor, and there's no one but him I can turn to. Anyway, the die is cast—I've decided to go to Enteropia. I take off in three days.

28. VIII. Started out at two, right after lunch. Didn't bring along any books, since I have that new brain. It told anecdotes all the way to the moon. I laughed and laughed. Then supper, and off to bed.

29. VIII. I must have caught a cold in the moon's shadow, I keep sneezing. Took two aspirin. Three freighters from Pluto on our course; the engineer telegraphed me to get out of the way. I asked what his cargo was, thinking it might be God knows what, but nothing, just ordinary clabber. And then an express from Mars, terribly packed. I looked out the window, they were all lying one on top of the other, like herring. We waved our handkerchiefs, but they were already gone. Listened to jokes until supper. Hysterical, only I keep sneezing.

30. VIII. Increased the speed. The brain working perfectly. My sides began to hurt some, so I turned it off for a couple of hours and plugged in the pad and pillow. Feels wonderful. It was after two when I picked up the radio signal Popov sent from Earth in the year 1896. I'm a good ways out now.

31. VIII. The sun is barely visible. A walk around the rocket before lunch, to get the circulation going. Jokes until evening. Most of them old. It looks as if that shop manager gave the brain some back issues of a humor magazine to read, then threw in a few new jokes on top. I forgot the potatoes I'd put in the atomic pile, and now they're burnt, all of them.

32. VIII. Because of the velocity time is slowing down—this ought to be October, but here it is still August. Something's started flashing by outside. I thought it was the Milky Way already, but no, just my paint flaking off. Damn, a cheap brand! There's a service station up ahead. Wonder if it's worth stopping.

33. VIII. Still August. After lunch I pulled over to the station. It stands on a small, absolutely empty planet. The building looks abandoned, not a living soul about. Took my bucket and went to see if they had any paint here. I was walking around when I heard a puffing. I followed it, and there behind the building saw several steam robots standing and conversing. I drew near.

One of them was saying:

"Surely it's obvious that clouds are the astral bodies of steam robots that have passed on. The basic question, as I see it, is this: which came first, the steam or the robot? I maintain it was the steam!"

"Hush, shameless idealist!" hissed another.

I tried asking for paint, but they were hissing and whistling so much, I couldn't hear myself think. Dropped a complaint in the suggestion box and continued on my way.

34. VIII. Will this August never end? Washed the rocket all morning. Bored stiff. Climbed inside, to try the brain. Instead of laughter, such an attack of yawning that I feared for my jaw. A tiny planet starboard. Passing it, I noticed some sort of white dots. Through the binoculars observed that these were little signs with the inscription: "Don't lean out." Something's wrong with the brain—it's swallowing its punch lines.

1. X. Had to stop on Stroglon, out of fuel. In braking, the momentum carried me through all of September.

Considerable congestion at the airport. I left the rocket in space, so as to avoid having to pay duty, took only my fuel cans. But first I computed—with the help of the brain—the coordinates of my elliptical orbit. Returned an hour later with full containers, but not a trace of the rocket. Obviously I had to go look for it. Shuddered at the thought, but covered something like four thousand miles on foot. The brain made a mistake, of course. I'll have to have a little talk with that shop manager when I get back.

2. X. My velocity is so great, the stars have turned into fiery streaks, as if someone were waving a million lighted cigarettes in a dark room. The brain stutters. What's worse, the switch is broken and I can't turn it off. Rambles on and on.

3. X. It's running down, I think, spells everything out now. I'm gradually growing accustomed to that. I sit outside, as much as possible, only with my feet in the rocket, for it's cold as hell.

7. X. At eleven-thirty reached the Enteropia terminal. The rocket red-hot from braking. I parked it on the upper level of the artificial moon (their port of entry) and went inside to take care of the formalities. An unbelievable crowd in the spiral hallway; arrivals from every corner of the Galaxy walking, flowing, hopping from counter to counter. I got into line behind a pale blue Algolian, who in polite pantomime cautioned me not to stand too close to his posterior electrifying organ. Then suddenly behind me there was a young Saturnile in a beige kebong. With three shoots he held his luggage, with the fourth shoot mopped his brow. It was indeed hot in there. When my turn came, the official, an Ardrite as transparent as glass, looked me over carefully, greened a little (the Ardrites express emotions by changing color; green is equivalent to a smile) and asked:

"Vertebrate?"

"Yes."

"Amphibious?"

"No, only land . . ."

"Thank you, good. Mixed diet?"

"Yes."

"From what planet, may I ask?"

"From Earth."

"And now please go to the next window."

I went to the next window and, looking in, confronted the very same official, or—more exactly—his continuation. He was turning the pages of an enormous book.

"Ah, there it is!" he said. "Earth . . . yes, very good. Are you here on business, or only touring?"

"Touring."

"Now if you don't mind . . ."

With one tentacle he filled out a form, while with another he gave me a form to sign, saying:

"There's a whacker expected, it begins in a week. Therefore kindly go over to room 116, our spares are made there, you'll be taken care of. Then proceed to room 67, that's the pharmaceutical booth. They'll give you Euphruglium pills, take one every

107

three hours, it neutralizes the harmful effects on your organism of our planet's radioactivity . . . Will you be lighting up during your stay on Enteropia?"

"No, thanks."

"As you like. Here are your papers. You are a mammal, I believe?"

"That's right."

"Well then, happy mammaling!"

Taking my leave of this courteous official, I went—as he had directed me—to the place where they made spares. The egg-shaped chamber appeared, at first glance, to be unoccupied. There were several electrical devices standing about, and on the ceiling a crystal lamp gleamed and sparkled. It turned out, how-ever, that the lamp was an Ardrite, a technician on duty; he im-mediately climbed down from the ceiling. I sat on the chair; di-verting me with conversation, he took my measurements, then said:

"Thank you, sir. We'll be transmitting your gemma to all the hatcheries on our planet. If anything should happen to you dur-ing a whacker, rest assured . . . we bring a spare at once!"

I wasn't all that clear about what he meant, however in the course of my many travels I have learned discretion, since there is nothing more unpleasant for the inhabitants of a planet than to have to explain their local ways and customs to a foreigner. At the pharmaceutical booth, another line, but it moved quickly and before I knew it a nimble Ardritess in a faïence lampshade had handed me my pill ration. Then a brief formality at customs (I wasn't about to trust that electrical brain) and with visa in hand I returned on board.

Behind the moon begins an interspace thruway, well main-tained, with great billboards on either side. The individual let-ters are a few thousand miles apart, but at normal speed the words fall together so fast, it's like having them printed in a newspaper. For a while I read these with interest—such as: "Hunters! For big-game spread, try MYLL!"—or: "Warm your cockles, bop octopockles!"—and so on.

It was seven in the evening when I landed at the Ubbidub airport. The blue sun had just gone down. In the rays of the red one, which was still quite high, everything seemed enveloped in flame—an unusual sight. A galactic cruiser majestically settled down beside my rocket. Beneath its fins, touching scenes of re-union were acted out. The Ardrites, separated for many long months, embraced one another with cries of joy, after which they all, fathers, mothers, children, tenderly clasped together in globes that shimmered pink in the light of the sun, hurried off to the exit. I followed after those harmoniously rolling families; right in front of the airport there was a molly stop, and I got on one. This conveyance, decorated on top with characters of gold that formed the sign "RAUS SPREAD HUNTS BEST!," looked something like a Swiss cheese; in its larger holes sat the grownups, while the smaller served to carry the little ones. As soon as I got on, the molly pulled out. Enclosed in its crystal mass, above me, below me, and all around I saw the congenially translucent and multicolored silhouettes of my fellow passengers. I reached into my pocket for the Baedeker, feeling it was high time I acquainted myself with a few helpful facts, but discovered—to my dismay—that the volume I was holding dealt with the planet Enteroptica, a good three million light-years removed from my present location. The Baedeker I needed was at home. That damned absent-mindedness of mine!

Well, I had no choice but to go to the Ubbidub branch of the well-known astronautical travel bureau GALAX. The conductor was most courteous; when I asked him, he immediately stopped the molly and pointed his tentacle at an enormous building, then saw me off with a friendly change of color.

For a moment I stood still, delighting in the remarkable scene afforded by the city at dusk. The red sun was just then sinking beneath the horizon. Ardrites don't use artificial illumination, they themselves light up. The Mror Boulevard, on which I stood, was filled with the glimmer of pedestrians; one young Ardritess, passing by, flirtatiously burst into golden stripes inside her shade, but then, evidently recognizing a foreigner, she modestly dimmed.

Houses near and far sparkled and glowed with the inhabitants returning from work; deep within the temples gleamed multitudes in prayer; children raced up and down the stairs like crazy rainbows. It was all so captivating, so colorful, that I didn't want to leave, but had to, before Galax closed for the night.

In the lobby of the travel bureau they directed me to the twenty-third floor, the provincial division. Yes, it's sad but nonetheless true: our Earth is in the boondocks of the Universe, obscure, ignored!

The secretary I approached in the tourist service department clouded over with embarrassment and said that Galax, unfortunately, had neither guidebooks nor sightseeing itineraries for Earthlings, since the latter came to Enteropia no more than once a century. She offered me a booklet for Jovians, in view of the common solar origin of Earth and Jupiter. I took it—for lack of anything better—and requested a reservation at the hotel Cosmonia. I also signed up for the hunt organized by Galax, then went out into the city. My situation was all the more awkward in that I wasn't able to shine by myself, thus when I encountered at an intersection an Ardrite who was regulating traffic, I stopped and—in his light—skimmed through my new guidebook. As I might have expected, it furnished information about where one could obtain methane preserves, what to do with one's antennae at official functions, etc. So I chucked it in a trash can, caught a passing transom and asked to be taken to the gum tower district. Those magnificent, cup-shaped edifices, seen at a distance, glistened with the variegated glow of Ardrites devoting themselves to their family affairs, and in the office buildings the luminous necklaces of the officials coruscated in the loveliest way.

Dismissing my transom, I wandered about on foot for a while. As I marveled at the Porridge Authority, a gum tower soaring high above the square, two important functionaries emerged from it—I could tell they were important by the intense glare and the red crests around their shades. They stopped nearby, and I overheard their conversation:

"So smearing the rims is out now?" said the tall one, covered with medals.

The other brightened at this and replied:

"Yes. The director says we won't make quota, and it's all the fault of Grudrufs. There's no help for it, says the director, he'll have to be converted."

"Grudrufs?"

"Grudrufs."

The first darkened, only his medals continued to twinkle in iridescent wreaths, and lowering his voice he said: "He'll slooch, the poor devil."

110

"He can slooch all he likes. Discipline has to be maintained. We've been transmuting the boys for years, and it isn't for the purpose of making more scrupts!"

Intrigued, I had edged closer to the two Ardrites without realizing it, and they moved away in silence. It was a funny thing, but after this incident the word "scrupt" seemed to crop up more and more frequently. The more I walked the streets, feeling the urge to immerse myself in the night life of the metropolis, the more from the throngs trundling past there drifted that enigmatic phrase, now uttered in a strangled whisper, and now in a passionate cry; one could see it written on the poster globes that announced sales and auctions of rare scruptics, or emblazoned across the neon ads encouraging the purchase of the very latest scruptures. In vain did I ponder its meaning; then finally, while I was sitting—around midnight—over a cold glass of squamp milk in a bar on the eightieth floor of a department store, and the Ardrite chanteuse had begun to sing the popular song, "That little scrupt o' mine," my curiosity reached such proportions, that I asked a passing waiter where I might buy myself a scrupt.

"Across the street," he answered mechanically, taking my check and money. Then he gave me a hard look and dimmed a little. "You're alone?" he asked.

"Yes. What of it?"

"Oh, nothing. I'm sorry, but I don't have change."

I forwent the change and took an elevator down. Yes, directly opposite me I saw a gigantic sign for scrupts, so I pushed open the glass door and found myself inside a shop, empty at that late hour. I went over to the counter and, assuming an air of indifference, asked for a scrupt.

"At which scruptrum?" inquired the salesman, coming down from his perch.

"At which . . . let me see . . . at the usual," I replied.

"What do you mean, at the usual?" he said with surprise. "We sell only surried scrupts . . ."

"Fine, I'll take one."

"But where's your macket?"

"Ah yes, h'm, didn't bring it with me . . ."

"Then how can you buy it without your wife?" said the salesman, staring at me. He was slowly darkening.

"I'm not married," I blurted without thinking.

"You're—not—married—?" he gasped, ashen, looking at me with horror. "You—you want a scrupt, and you're *not married* . . . ?"

The salesman quivered all over. I got out of there as quickly as I could, flagged down an unoccupied transom and, furious, asked to be taken to some popular nightspot. Which turned out to be the Myrgindragg. When I entered, the orchestra had just stopped playing. There were well over three hundred persons perched here. Looking about for an empty place, I was pushing through the crowd when suddenly someone called my name; with joy I caught sight of a familiar face, it was a traveling salesman I'd met once on Autropia. He was perching with his wife and daughter. I introduced myself to the ladies and began amusing my already merry companions with a little repartee; from time to time they alighted and, to the rhythm of a lively dance tune, went rolling across the ballroom floor. Repeatedly urged by the spouse of my acquaintance, I finally got up the nerve to join in; and so, tightly embraced, the four of us rolled round and round to the music of a wild mamborina. To tell the truth, I got battered up a bit, but grinned and bore it, and pretended I was having a marvelous time. On the way back to our table I pulled my acquaintance aside and asked him, in a whisper, about the scrupts.

"Beg your pardon?" He hadn't heard me. I repeated my question, adding that I would like to acquire a scrupt. Apparently I had spoken too loud—those perched nearby turned around and looked at me with murky faces, and my Ardrite friend threw up his tentacles in alarm.

"For the love of Munge, Mr. Tichy—but you're alone!"

"And what if I am?" I snapped, irritated. "Is that any reason I can't see a scrupt?"

There was a sickening silence. The wife of my acquaintance fell to the floor in a faint, he rushed to her assistance, and the nearest Ardrites started rolling towards me, their color betraying the most hostile intentions; at that moment three waiters appeared, seized me by the scruff of the neck and tossed me out into the street.

I was positively furious. I hailed a transom, took it back to the hotel. All that night I didn't sleep a wink, something was gnawing, chafing at me; at daybreak I discovered that the hotel staff, having received no particulars from Galax and accustomed to guests who burned their mattresses clear through to the springs, had given me asbestos sheets. But the unpleasant incidents of the previous day seemed unimportant that bright morning. It was in the best of spirits that I greeted the Galax representative who came for me at ten in a transom full of snares, jars of hunting spread and a whole arsenal of sportsman's weapons.

"Ever hunted squamp before?" asked my guide as the vehicle wove its way through the streets of Ubbidub at breakneck speed.

"No. Perhaps you would care to enlighten me . . ." I said with a smile.

My many years of experience on safaris for the largest game in the Galaxy entitled me, I thought, to show no excitement.

"Gladly," replied the courteous guide.

This was a slender Ardrite of glassy complexion, without a shade, wrapped in a navy blue fabric—I had not seen that sort of dress before on the planet. When I told him this, he explained it was a hunting outfit, indispensable for stealing up on game; what I had taken for cloth was in fact a special substance with which one covered one's body. In short—a spray-on suit, comfortable, practical and, most important, completely blotting out the natural effulgence of the Ardrites, which might scare off a squamp.

The guide pulled a leaflet from his handbag and gave it to me to study; I have it still among my papers. It reads:

HUNTING SQUAMP

Instructions for Foreigners

The squamp as a game animal places great demands on the personal accomplishments no less than on the gear of the hunter. Inasmuch as this beast has, in the course of evolution, adapted itself to meteoroid rains by developing an absolutely impervious integument of armor, squamp are hunted from the inside only.

To hunt a squamp one must have:

A) in the preliminary phase—base spread, mushroom sauce, chives, salt and pepper;

B) in the phase proper—a whisk broom, a time bomb.

I. Preparation in the field.

One hunts a squamp with bait. The hunter, having besmeared himself beforehand with the base spread, crouches down in a furrow of the torg, after which his companions sprinkle finely chopped chives over him and season to taste.

II. In this position one awaits the squamp. When the animal approaches, one should remain calm and with both hands take firm hold of the time bomb gripped between one's knees. A hungry squamp will usually swallow at once. If however the squamp does balk, one may encourage it with a gentle slap across the tongue. When a miss seems likely, some advise additional salting, this however is a most hazardous move, for the squamp may sneeze. Very few hunters have survived the sneeze of a squamp.

III. A squamp that takes the bait will lick its lips and walk away. Upon being swallowed, the hunter immediately proceeds to the active phase, i.e., with the whisk broom he brushes from himself the chives and spices, so that the spread may freely work its purgative effect, whereupon he sets the time bomb and withdraws as quickly as possible in the direction opposite to that from which he came.

IV. Upon leaving the squamp, one should take care to land on one's hands and feet and not hurt oneself.

Warning. The use of sharp spices is forbidden. Also forbidden is the planting of time bombs already set and sprinkled with chives. Such an act is considered poaching and will be prosecuted to the limit of the law.

At the border of the game preserve we were met by the warden, Wawr, in the midst of his family that sparkled like crystal in the sun. He proved to be most friendly and hospitable; invited to partake of some refreshment, we passed several hours at his charming estate, listening to true-life tales of squamp and the hunting reminiscences of Wawr and his sons. Then suddenly a breathless courier came bursting in with the news that the beaters had flushed some squamp from cover and into the heart of the bush.

"Squamp," explained the warden, "must first be driven around a bit, to get them good and hungry!"

Anointed with spread and holding my bomb and spices, I set off in the company of Wawr and my guide. We entered the torg. The path soon vanished in impenetrable thickets. Progress grew difficult, from time to time we came upon squamp tracks, which were potholes twenty feet in diameter. On and on we went, interminably. Then the earth shook and my guide halted, motioning silence with his tentacle. One could hear thunder, as if a violent storm were raging just over the horizon.

"Hear that?" whispered the guide.

"A squamp?"

"Yes. It's a cub."

Now we pushed ahead more slowly and with greater caution. The crashing died away and the torg again was still. Finally, through the underbrush there gleamed an open field. At the edge of it my companions found a suitable spot, then seasoned me and, making sure I had the whisk broom and bomb in readiness, left on tiptoe, recommending patience. For a while nothing disturbed the reigning silence but the whine and burr of octopockles; my legs had grown quite numb when, suddenly, the ground began to tremble. I saw a movement in the distance— the treetops at the far end of the clearing swayed and fell, marking the path of the beast. This was a big one, all right. Presently the squamp looked out on the field, stepped over some fallen trunks and plodded forward. Swinging majestically from side to side, it headed straight in my direction, snuffing noisily. With both hands I clutched the jug-eared bomb and waited, perfectly calm. The squamp stopped at a distance of some one hundred fifty feet from me and licked its lips. In its transparent interior I could clearly see the remains of many a hunter upon whom Fortune had not smiled.

For a while the squamp thought it over. I began to fear the thing would go away, but then it approached and tasted me. I heard a hollow slurp and lost the ground from under my feet.

"Got him!" I thought. Inside the squamp it wasn't nearly as dark as it had seemed at first. Brushing myself off, I lifted the heavy time bomb and was just about to set it, when someone went "Ahem." I looked up, startled, and saw before me a strange Ardrite, also bending over a bomb. We stared at one another for a minute.

"What are you doing here?" I asked.

"Hunting squamp," he replied.

"So am I," I said, "but go ahead, please. You were here first."

"Nonsense," he replied, "you are a visitor."

"No, really," I protested, "I'll save my bomb for another time. Please don't let my presence hamper you."

"I won't hear of it!" he exclaimed. "You are our guest."

"I am a hunter first."

"And I—a host, and will not have you give up this squamp on my account! Make haste now, for the spread is beginning to work!"

In truth the squamp had become uneasy; even in here its powerful panting reached us, with a sound like several dozen locomotives all going at once. Seeing that I would never persuade the Ardrite, I set the bomb and waited for my new companion, he however insisted I go first. Shortly thereafter we left the squamp. Falling from a height of two stories, I twisted my ankle a little. The squamp, evidently much relieved, went charging off into the brush, snapping trees with an awful racket. Suddenly there was a terrific boom, then silence.

"Well done, old fellow! Congratulations!" shouted the hunter, heartily shaking my hand. At that moment the game warden and my guide came up.

It was getting dark, we had to hurry back; the warden promised that he himself would stuff the squamp and have it sent to Earth on the very first freighter out.

5. XI. Didn't write a word for four days, I was too busy. Every morning—those characters from the Commission for Cultural Cooperation with the Cosmos, museums, exhibits, radioactivities, and in the afternoon—visits, official receptions, addresses. I'm all done in. The delegate from CCCC in charge of me said yesterday that we were due for a whacker, but I forgot to ask him what a whacker was. Supposed to see Professor Pook, the famous Ardrite scientist, but don't know when yet.

6. XI. At the hotel, early, wakened by an ungodly noise. I jumped out of bed and saw great columns of smoke and fire rising above the city. I phoned the information desk, asked what was happening.

"It's nothing," said the operator, "nothing to worry about, sir, only a whacker."

"A whacker?"

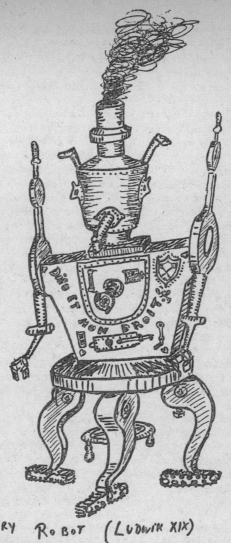

STARY ROBOT (LUDWIK XIX)
parowy

An old steam robot (Louis XIX).

"Yes, a whacker, a meteor shower, we get them once every ten months."

"But that's dreadful!" I cried. "Shouldn't I go to a shelter?!"

"Oh, no shelter will withstand a striking meteor. But really, sir, you have a spare, like every citizen, there is no need to be afraid."

"What do you mean, a spare?" I asked, but she had already hung up. I quickly dressed and went out into the city. The traffic in the streets was perfectly normal; pedestrians hurried about their business, dignitaries ablaze with iridescent medals drove to their offices, and in the parks played children, twinkling and singing. The explosions thinned out after a while; only in the distance now could one still hear their steady rumble. A whacker, I thought, evidently was not a terribly serious phenomenon, if no one here paid the least attention to it, and so I went—as I had planned—to the zoological garden.

I was shown around by the director himself, a slender, nervous Ardrite with a handsome shine. The Ubbidub Zoo is well kept up; the director told me with pride that its collection contains animals from the farthermost reaches of the Galaxy, including even an Earth exhibit. Touched, I asked to see it.

"Unfortunately you can't just now," he said, then added, when I looked at him questioningly:

"It's their sleeping period. We had a great deal of trouble with the acclimatization, you see, for a while I was afraid we wouldn't be able to keep a single one of them alive, but happily the vitamin supplements our experts worked out gave excellent results."

"Yes . . . but what sort of animal are they?"

"Flies. By the way, do you like squamp?"

He threw me a peculiar, searching look, so that I replied, trying to give my voice the sound of genuine enthusiasm:

"Oh, I'm crazy about them—wonderful creatures!"

He beamed.

"Good. Let's go see them, but first, excuse me for a moment."

He returned with a coil of rope and led me to the squamp pen, which was encircled with a three-hundred-foot wall. Opening the door, he had me enter first.

"You can rest easy," he said, "my squamp are perfectly tame."

I found myself on an artificial torg field; there were six or seven squamp grazing, splendid specimens, each measuring about three hectares across. The largest, at the voice of the director, approached us and held out its tail. The director climbed up on it, beckoning me to follow—so I did. When the angle grew too steep, he uncoiled his rope and gave me an end to tie around myself. Thus fastened, we climbed for more than two hours. At the summit of the squamp the director sat down in silence, clearly moved. I said nothing, wishing to respect his feelings. After some time he spoke:

"A beautiful view from here, don't you think?"

And indeed, we had at our feet nearly all of Ubbidub, with its spires, temples and gum towers; along the streets milled the citizens, as small as ants.

"You're fond of squamp," I quietly remarked, seeing how the director gently stroked the back of the beast near its summit.

"I love them," he said simply, turning to face me. "Squamp, after all, are the cradle of our civilization," he added. Then, after a moment's thought, he continued: "Once, many thousands of years ago, we had no cities, no magnificent homes, no technology, no spares . . . In those days these gentle, mighty beings cared for us, brought us safely through the difficult periods of the whackers. Without squamp not a single Ardrite would have lived to see these present happy times, and now look how they are hunted down, destroyed, exterminated! What monstrous, black ingratitude!"

I dared not interrupt. It took him a moment to master his emotions, then he went on:

"How I hate those hunters, who return goodness with villainy! You have seen, I take it, the hunting advertisements, the signs?"

"Yes."

The director's words had made me thoroughly ashamed of myself, and I trembled at the thought that he might learn of my recent crime; I had, after all, hunted a squamp with my very own hands. Wishing to divert the director from this somewhat ticklish topic of conversation, I asked him:

S.D.—E

"You really owe them that much, then? I was not aware of this . . ."

"What—not aware? But the squamp carried us in their wombs for twenty thousand years! Living inside them, protected by their powerful armor against the hail of deadly meteors, our forefathers became what we are today: intelligent, beautiful beings that shine by night. And you were not aware of this?"

"I am a foreigner . . ." I muttered, vowing in my soul never, never again to raise a hand against a squamp.

"Yes, of course . . ." replied the director, no longer listening to me, and got to his feet. "Unfortunately we must go back: I have my duties to attend to . . ."

From the zoological garden I took a transom to Galax, where some tickets for a matinée were supposed to have been put aside for me.

In the center of town thundering explosions could again be heard, louder and with increasing frequency. Above the roofs rose columns of smoke, flickering with flames. But none of the pedestrians appeared to mind it in the least, so I kept silent. The transom stopped in front of Galax. The official on duty asked me how I had liked the Zoo.

"Yes, very nice," I said, "but . . . good Lord!"

All of Galax jumped. Two office buildings across the way, clearly visible through the window, flew apart under the impact of a meteor. Deafened, I went reeling against a wall.

"It's nothing," said the official. "You'll get used to it in time. Here are your tick—"

He didn't finish. There was a flash, a crash, dust everywhere, and when it settled, instead of the person talking to me I saw a giant hole in the floor. I stood there, petrified. Hardly a minute went by before several Ardrites in overalls patched the hole and wheeled up a dolly with a large bundle. When it was unwrapped, there before my eyes appeared the official, holding the tickets in his hand. He brushed the rest of the packing from himself, climbed onto his perch and said:

"Your tickets. I told you it was nothing. Each of us, in case of emergency, is replicated. You are surprised at our composure? Well, but this has been going on for a good thirty thousand years, we have grown accustomed to it. If you would like some

120

lunch, the Galax restaurant is now open. Downstairs, and to your left."

"No thanks, I—I'm not hungry," I replied and, a little weak in the knees, went out amidst the continual explosions and thunderclaps. Suddenly I was seized with anger.

"They won't see an Earthling cower!" I thought and, glancing at my watch, asked to be driven to the theater.

Along the way a meteor smashed the transom, so I got into another. At the place where yesterday the theater building had stood there was now a smoking pile of rubble.

"Will my money be refunded for these tickets?" I asked the cashier, who was standing in the street.

"Certainly not. The show begins on schedule."

"On schedule? But didn't a meteor just . . ."

"We still have twenty minutes," said the cashier, pointing to his watch.

"Yes, but . . ."

"Would you mind not blocking the box office? We want to buy tickets!" shouted some individuals in the line that had formed behind me. With a shrug I stepped aside. Two big machines meanwhile loaded the debris and carted it away. In a few minutes the site was cleared.

"Are they going to perform in the open air?" I asked one of those waiting. He was fanning himself with a program.

"Nothing of the kind! I assume that everything will be as usual," he replied.

I bit my lip, incensed, thinking he was trying to make a fool of me. An enormous tanker drove up to the site. From it was poured a doughy, cherry-red substance, which formed a sizable blob; immediately they inserted pipes into this pulpy, steaming mass and began pumping air inside it. The blob changed into a bubble that expanded with incredible speed. A minute later it presented an exact copy of the theater building, except that it was completely soft, for it wobbled in the breeze. But in another five minutes the newly inflated structure had hardened; just then a meteor shattered part of the ceiling. So a new ceiling was blown, then the doors were flung open, and in thronged the spectators. Taking my seat, I noticed it was still warm. That was the only indication of the recent catastrophe. I asked a neighbor

121

just what that substance was which they had used to rebuild the theater, and found out: it's the famous Ardrite fab gum.

The show began a minute late. At the sound of a gong the house dimmed, resembling a gridiron full of dying coals, while the actors shone brilliantly. The play they did was symbolic and historical; to tell the truth I didn't get much out of it, particularly as a number of things were conveyed by color pantomime. The first act took place in a temple; a group of young Ardritesses crowned a statue of the Munge with flowers, singing about their betrotheds.

Suddenly an amber prelate appeared and drove away the maidens, with the exception of the most beautiful, who was as clear as spring water. Her the prelate locked inside the statue. Imprisoned, she sang an aria summoning her beloved, who ran in and extinguished the old prelate. Just then a meteor pulverized the roof, part of the scenery, and the beautiful maiden, but from the prompter's box they immediately brought out a spare, and so adroitly, that if you happened to have coughed or blinked your eyes, you wouldn't have noticed a thing. Following this, the lovers decided to raise a family. The act concluded with the rolling of the prelate off a cliff.

When the curtain went up again after the intermission, I beheld an exquisite sphere of husband, wife and progeny, swaying back and forth, back and forth to the sound of the music. A servant entered and announced that an unknown benefactor had sent the married couple a bouquet of scrupts. Then an enormous crate was wheeled onstage; I watched its opening with bated breath. But just as the lid was being lifted, something struck me violently in the forehead and I lost consciousness. When I came to, I was seated in the very same place. Of the scrupts there was no longer any mention in the scene, the extinguished prelate was now spinning about, sputtering the most dire imprecations at the tragically glowing children and parents. I clutched my head—there was no bump.

"What happened to me?" I whispered to the lady at my side.

"Pardon? Oh, a meteor got you, but you didn't miss a thing, believe me, that duet was absolutely awful. Of course it *was* scandalous: they had to send all the way to Galax for your spare," whispered the pleasant Ardritess.

"What spare?" I asked, suddenly feeling numb.

"Why, yours of course . . ."

"Then where am I?"

"Where? Here in the theater. Are you all right?"

"Then I am the spare?"

"Certainly."

"But where is the I that was sitting here before?"

Those in front of us went "Shh!" and my neighbor fell silent.

"Please," I whispered, "you have to tell me, where are the . . . the . . . you know what I mean."

"Quiet! What is this?! We're trying to hear!" they were hissing from all sides now. The one behind me, orange with anger, began calling for the usher. More dead than alive, I fled the theater, took the first transom back to the hotel and examined myself carefully in the mirror. My spirits revived a little, for there seemed to be no change, however upon closer inspection I made a terrifying discovery. My shirt was inside out and the buttons were fastened all wrong—clear proof that those who had dressed me didn't know the first thing about Earth clothing. And on top of it all, I shook bits of packing out of my socks—left there in haste, no doubt. I could hardly breathe; then the telephone rang.

"This is the fourth time I've called," said the secretary from CCCC. "Professor Pook would like to see you today."

"Who? Professor Pook?" I repeated, pulling myself together with the greatest effort. "Good. What time?"

"At your convenience. Now, if you like."

"I'll go to him at once!" I suddenly decided. "And . . . and please have my bill ready!"

"You're leaving?" asked the CCCC secretary, surprised.

"Yes, I must. I'm not myself!" I explained and slammed the receiver on the hook.

I changed and went downstairs. The recent events had affected me so much, that when, just as I was getting into the transom, a meteor smashed the entire hotel to smithereens, I didn't even blink, but gave my driver the Professor's address. The Professor lived in an outlying district, among silvery hills. I stopped the transom fairly far from his house, glad for the chance to walk a little after the nervous tension of the last few hours. Proceeding along the road, I noticed a bent, elderly Ardrite, who was slowly pushing a kind of wheelbarrow with a

123

cover. He saluted me politely; I nodded in return. For a minute or so we walked together. Around the corner a hedge came into view, bordering the home of the Professor; on the other side wisps of smoke were drifting up into the sky. The Ardrite walking next to me stumbled; then, from under the cover I heard a voice:

"Now?"

"Not yet," replied the carter.

I was surprised at this, but said nothing. When we came to the fence, I stopped and stared at the smoke billowing from the spot where one would have expected the Professor's house to be. The carter, when I brought this to his attention, nodded.

"Right, a meteor fell, oh just about a quarter of an hour ago."

"No!!" I exclaimed, horrified. "How dreadful!"

"The gum mixer'll be here any minute," said the carter. "It's the suburbs, you understand, they're never in a hurry, not for us."

"*Now?*" came that scratchy voice again from inside the wheelbarrow.

"Not yet," said the carter and turned to me: "Would you mind opening the gate?"

I obliged and asked:

"You're going to the Professor too . . . ?"

"Right, delivering a spare," said the carter as he set about lifting the cover. I held my breath upon seeing a large package, carefully wrapped and tied. In one place the paper was torn; a living eye peered out.

"Ah . . . you've come to see me . . . to see me . . ." rasped the ancient voice within the package, "be right with you . . . right with you . . . please wait in the gazebo . . ."

"Yes, I . . . fine . . ." I answered. But as the carter wheeled his burden on ahead, I turned around, leaped over the fence and ran as fast as I possibly could to the airport. In an hour I was out in space, scudding my way among the stars. Professor Pook, I hope, will not hold this against me.

THE TWENTIETH VOYAGE

I t all started less than a day after my return from the Hyades, a spherical cluster so thick with stars that the civilizations there hardly have room to turn around. I hadn't even unpacked half the suitcases—filled with specimens—and already my arms were falling off. I decided to put the luggage in the cellar and attend to it later, when I'd rested up a bit. The return trip had taken forever and all I wanted now was to sit back in my carved armchair by the fireplace, stretch out my legs, put my hands in the pockets of my old smoking jacket and tell myself that besides the milk boiling over on the stove there was nothing I had to worry about. Yes, four years of such traveling and you can get pretty tired of the Universe, at least for a while. I'll walk over to the window, I thought, and see not the black void, not sizzling prominences—but a street, flower beds, bushes, a little dog lifting its leg beneath a tree with complete indifference towards the problems of the Milky Way, and what a joy that will be!

But, as is usually the case with such dreams, it didn't work out that way. I noticed that the first parcel I pulled off the rocket had one side bashed in and, fearful for the hundreds of priceless specimens I'd collected, immediately set about unpacking. The bhingets were all right, but the mups had gotten crushed on the bottom, I just couldn't leave things like that, and in a few hours had knocked the lids off the largest crates, opened up the trunks, spread the fenticles over the radiator to dry—they were

125

soaked through by the tea from the thermos—but I really shuddered when I saw the stuffings. These were to have been the pride and glory of my collection; all the way home I had tried to think of just the right place for them, as they are the greatest of rarities, those products of the militarization on Regulus (a civilization conscripted in its entirety, you won't find a single civilian there). Taxidermy is no "hobby" among the Regulans, as Tottenham writes, but something between a religious practice and a sport. Tottenham simply fails to grasp the grounds on which they stuff. Taxidermy on Regulus represents a symbolic act; thus Tottenham's remarks, full of wonder, and his rhetorical questions too, they only demonstrate his total ignorance. Marital taxidermy is one thing, school taxidermy quite another—and then there's the vacationing kind, the dating, etc. But I can't go into that now. Suffice it to say that in carrying the Regulusian trophies upstairs I slipped a disk, so although there was still a bundle of work to be done I said to myself that this head-on assault would accomplish little. I hung the chimpers up on the clothesline in the basement and went to the kitchen to fix supper. And now only loafing, siestas, *dolce far niente*, I said firmly: Of course an ocean of memories continued to assail me, like a swollen tide when the storm has passed. While cracking an egg I looked at the blue flame of the burner—nothing special about it, yet how very like the Nova of Perseus. And those curtains there—as white as the sheet of asbestos I'd used to cover the atomic pile that time when . . . No, enough!—I told myself. Decide instead how you want your eggs—scrambled or fried? I had just settled on sunny-side up when the whole house shook. The eggs, still raw, flopped to the floor, and as I turned to the stairs I heard a long, drawn-out rumble like an avalanche. I threw down the skillet and ran upstairs. Had the roof caved in? A meteor? . . . But that was impossible! Such things didn't happen!

The only room I hadn't cluttered up with packages was the study, and that was where the noise was coming from. The first thing I saw was a pile of books at the foot of a tilting bookcase. Out from under the thick volumes of my cosmic encyclopedia crawled a man, backwards, crushing the fallen books with his knees, as if the damage he had done them already wasn't enough. Before I could speak he pulled out some sort of long metal rod after him, holding it by its handlebars—it resembled a bicycle without wheels. I coughed, but the intruder, still on all fours, paid absolutely no attention to me. I coughed louder, however now his profile seemed oddly familiar, but it was only when he stood up that I recognized him. He was myself. Exactly, just like looking into a mirror. I had indeed already experienced, once, a whole series of such encounters, still that had been in a swarm of gravitational vortices, not in the peace and quiet of my own home!

He glanced at me in a distracted way and bent over his instrument; the fact that he had taken charge of the situation so, and particularly that he didn't see fit to say something, finally put me out of patience.

"What is the meaning of this?!" I try not to raise my voice.

"I'll explain in a minute . . . hold on," he mutters, then gets up, drags that tube thing over to the lamp, slants the shade to get better light, adjusting the paper while holding the arm in place (he knows, the dog, that the shade will fall, so he has to be me) and touches some knobs with his finger, clearly troubled.

"You might at least apologize!" I can no longer hide my growing irritation. He smiles. He puts aside his contraption, that is, rests it against the wall. He sits in my armchair, opens the middle drawer, takes out my favorite pipe and unerringly reaches for the tobacco pouch.

This is really too much.

"What nerve!!" I say.

With a sweep of the hand he gestures for me to have a seat. I can't help but take stock of the destruction done—the bindings of two heavy astronomical atlases broken!—however I pull up a chair and twiddle my thumbs, waiting. I'll give him five minutes for explanations and apologies, and if I'm not satisfied, well, there are other ways to settle things.

"Come now!" remarks my uninvited guest. "You're an intelligent man! Just how are you going to settle things? Any bruise I get today will only be yours later on!"

I say nothing, but am thinking. If it's true that he is me and that somehow (but *how*, for God's sake?) I've gotten myself into a time loop again (and why am I the one these things have to happen to?!), then he may indeed have a right to my pipe and even my house. But what reason was there to go and knock over the bookcase?

"That was unintentional," he says through a cloud of aromatic smoke, examining the tip of his shoe—quite stylish, too. He crosses his legs, swings the top one back and forth. "The chronocycle threw me while braking. Instead of eight-thirty I flew in at eight-thirty and one-hundredth of a second. If they'd set the sight better I would have arrived in the center of the room."

"I don't understand. (And I don't, not any of it.) First of all: are you a telepathist? How can you answer questions which I'm only *thinking*? And secondly: if you really are myself and have come through time, what does that have to do with place? Why did you destroy my books?!"

"If you'd stop a moment and think, you'd figure that all out for yourself. I'm later than you, so I *must* remember what I thought, i.e. what you thought, since I am you, only from the future. And as for time and place, the Earth—after all—is turning! I skidded one-hundredth of a second, perhaps even less, and in that brief interval it had time to move, along with the house, those thirteen feet. I told Rosenbeisser it would be better to land in the garden, but he talked me into this sighting."

"All right. Supposing that's true. But what does it all mean?"

"Well obviously I'm going to tell you. However let's have supper first, it's a long story and of the utmost importance. I've come to you as an emissary on a historic mission."

I found myself believing him. We went downstairs, made supper, such as it was; all I did was open a can of sardines (and there were a couple of eggs left in the icebox). Afterwards we remained in the kitchen, for I didn't want to spoil my mood by having to look at the bookcase. He wasn't overly eager to wash the dishes, but I appealed to his conscience and he finally agreed to wipe. Then we sat at the table, he looked me gravely in the eye and said:

"I come from the year 2661, to make you an offer, an offer which no man has ever heard before, nor will again. The Research Committee of the Temporal Institute wants me—that is, you—to be General Director of its THEOHIPPIP effort, which abbreviation stands for: Teleotelechronistic-Historical Engineering to Optimize the Hyperputerized Implementation of Paleological Programming and Interplanetary Planning. I'm confident that you will accept this high position, for it carries with it extraordinary responsibility towards the human race and history, and I know that I—that is, you—are a man of both initiative and integrity."

"I'd like to hear something a little more specific first—what I really don't understand is why they didn't simply send me a delegate of that institute instead of you—I mean, myself. How did you—that is, how did I—get there in the first place?"

"That I'll explain at the end and separately. As for the main business, you remember of course Molteris, that poor man who invented a manual time traveling device and, wishing to demonstrate it, perished miserably, for he aged to death immediately upon takeoff?"

I nodded.

"There will be more such attempts. Every new technology entails casualties in its initial stages. Molteris had invented a one-seat time buggy without any shields. He was doing exactly what the medieval peasant did, who climbed the church steeple with his wings and killed himself on the spot. In the 23rd century there were—or rather, from your standpoint, will be—clockcars, calendar sedans and syncoscooters, but the real chronomotive revolution will only begin three hundred years later, thanks to men I will not name—you'll meet them personally. Time travel over short distances is one thing, expeditions deep into the millennia quite another. The difference is more or less like that between going for a stroll downtown and journeying to the stars. I come from the Age of Chronotraction, Chronomotion and Telechronics. There have been mountains of nonsense written about traveling in time, just as previously there were about astronautics—you know, how some scientist, with the backing of a wealthy businessman, goes off in a corner and slaps together a rocket, which the two of them—and in the company of their lady friends, yet—then take to the far end of the Galaxy. Chronomotion, no less than Astronautics, is a colossal enterprise, requiring tremendous investments, expenditures, planning . . . but you'll find this out for yourself when you get there, that is, at the proper time. Enough now of the technical aspect. The important thing is the purpose behind it; we haven't gone to all this trouble just so someone can frighten Pharaohs or kill his own great-great-grandfather. The social structure of Earth has been regulated, the climate also, in the 27th century—from which I come—things are so good, they couldn't possibly be better, but our history remains a constant source of aggravation to us. You know the state it's in; high time, then, we put it into shape!"

"Now wait a minute," I said, my ears humming. "You're not happy with history? Well, but what difference does that make? I mean, it's not something you can change, is it?"

"Don't be ridiculous. It's precisely THEOHIPPIP that heads our list of priorities. I already told you, Teleotelechronistic-Historical Engineering to Optimize the Hyperputerized Implementation of Paleological Programming and Interplanetary Planning. For World History to be regulated, cleaned up, straightened out, adjusted and perfected, all in accordance with the principles of humanitarianism, rationalism and general esthetics. You can understand, surely, that with such a shambles and slaughterhouse in one's family tree it's awkward to go calling on important cosmic civilizations!"

"The regulation of the Past? . . ." I said, dumbfounded.

"Yes. If need be, alterations will be made even before the rise of man, so that he arises better. The necessary funds have already been gathered, however the post of General Director of the Project is still vacant. Everyone's frightened off by the risks connected with that job."

"There aren't any volunteers?" My astonishment was growing by the minute.

"Those days are gone, where every jackass wants to rule the world. Without the proper qualifications no one's anxious to take on a difficult assignment. Consequently the position remains unfilled, yet the matter is pressing!"

"But I don't know a thing about it. And why me, of all people?"

"You'll have whole staffs of specialists at your disposal. Anyway the technical side of it will not be your concern; there are many different plans of action, different proposals, policies, methods, what's needed are carefully thought-out, responsible decisions. And I—that is, you—are to make them. Our Hyperputer examined by psychoprobe every man who ever lived, and concluded that I—you—are the only hope of the Project."

After a long pause I said:

"This is, I can see, a serious business. Perhaps I *will* accept

130

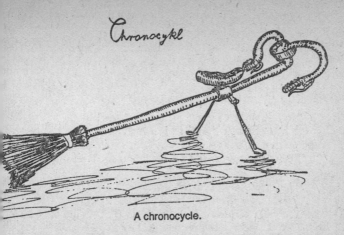

Chronocykl

A chronocycle.

the position, and then again, perhaps I won't. World History, h'm! That'll take a little thought. But how did it happen that I was the one—that is, that you were the one—to approach me? *I* certainly didn't go anywhere in time. It was only yesterday that I got back from the Hyades."

"Obviously!" he interrupted. "After all, you're the *earlier* me! When you accept the offer, I'll give you the chronocycle, and you'll go where—that is, when—you're supposed to."

"That's not an answer to my question. I want to know how you ended up in the 27th century."

"I got there on a time vehicle, how else? And then, from there, I came to your here and now."

"Yes, but if *I* didn't take any time vehicle anywhere, then you too, who are *me* . . ."

"Don't be stupid. I'm *later* than you, so you can't possibly know *now* what's going to happen to *you* after you take off for the 27th century."

"You're evading the issue!" I muttered. "Look, if I accept this offer, I go straight to the 27th century. Right? There I direct this Theohippip thing and so on. But where do *you* come into the pic—"

"We can go on this way all night! Round and round. Look, here's what. Ask Rosenbeisser, let him explain it to you. He's the authority on time anyway, not me. Besides, this problem, hard

131

though it may be to grasp, and time loops are always like that, is nothing in comparison with my mission—with your mission, that is. It's a Historic Mission we're talking about, after all! So what do you say? Is it agreed? The chronocycle will work. It wasn't damaged, I checked."

"Chronocycle or no, I can't just up and go like this."

"You have to! It's your duty! You must!"

"Ho ho! None of that *must* talk with me, if you please! You know how I dislike it. I will if I want to, when I'm convinced the situation demands it of me. Who is this Rosenbeisser?"

"Research Director at ITS. He'll be your top assistant."

"ITS?"

"The Institute of Temporal Studies."

"And what if I refuse?"

"You can't refuse . . . you won't do that . . . it would mean, well, it would mean that you hadn't the courage . . ."

A smile seemed to flicker on his lips as he said these words. This made me suspicious.

"Really. And why is that?"

"Because . . . eh, I can't explain it to you. It has to do with the structure of time itself."

"Nonsense. If I *don't* agree, then I don't go anywhere, and thus this Rosenbeisser of yours will explain nothing to me, nor will I be regulating any history."

I said this partly to gain time, since one doesn't make such important decisions at the drop of a hat, but also because, though I was completely in the dark as to why he—that is, I—was the one who came to me, I had the funny feeling that there was some catch, some deception involved here.

"I'll give you my answer in forty-eight hours!" I said.

He began to urge me to decide at once, but the more he insisted, the more suspicious I became. Eventually I even started having doubts about his identicality with me. He could have been, after all, an agent in disguise! As soon as that occurred to me, I resolved to test him. The trick was to think of some secret that was unknown to any but myself.

"Why does the numbering of the voyages in my *Star Diaries* contain gaps?" I shot the question at him.

"Ha ha!" he laughed. "So now you don't believe in me? The reason is, old boy, that some of the journeys took place in space nd some in time, therefore there can never be a first; you could lways go back to when there were none and set out somewhere, hen the one that had been first would become the second, and o on, ad infinitum!"

That was right. However a few persons did have knowledge of this—though true, they were my trusted friends from Professor Tarantoga's Tichological Club; I asked, then, to see some identification. His papers were all in order, though that still proved nothing; papers can easily be falsified. He weakened my skepticism considerably by being able to sing everything that I was wont to sing while—and only while—traveling great distances, all alone; I noticed however that in the refrain of "Shooting star, shooting star!" he was terribly off key. I told him this; he took offense and said that *I* was the one who always sang off key, not he. Our conversation, till now reasonably peaceful, turned into an argument, then a violent quarrel, finally he got me so furious that I ordered him out of the house. This was said in anger, I didn't actually mean it, yet he rose without another word, marched upstairs, put his chronocycle into position, sat on it like a bike, moved something or other, and in a twinkling of an eye had vanished in a cloud of smoke, or more precisely a puff, as if from a cigarette. That too was gone in a minute—all that remained was the pile of books strewn every which way. I stood there, feeling foolish, for this I hadn't expected, and by the time he'd started preparing to leave I couldn't very well have backed down. Mulling it over a moment or two, I turned around and went back to the kitchen, since we had been talking for three hours at least and I felt hungry again. There were still a couple of eggs in the icebox, a strip of bacon too, but when I turned on the gas and began frying them up, a terrible crash resounded on the second floor.

I was so startled, I ruined the eggs; they flopped out, bacon fat and all, right into the flame—while I, cursing everything under and above the sun, rushed upstairs three steps at a time.

Not a single book was left on the shelves; the remainder lay in a huge heap, from under which he clambered out, dragging the chronocycle after him with difficulty, for he had fallen on top of it.

"And what is *this* supposed to mean?!" I shouted, livid.

"I'll explain in a minute . . . wait . ." he mumbled, pulling the chronocycle over to the lamp. He inspected it, preoccupied, not even bothering to offer an excuse for this second intrusion. This was really too much.

"You could at least apologize!!" I yelled, beside myself.

He smiled. He set aside the chronocycle, that is, propped it against the wall, found the pipe, filled it with my tobacco, lit it, crossing his legs, until I saw red.

"Of all the nerve!!" I screamed. So far I hadn't budged, but swore he'd be black-and-blue before I was through with him. Playing practical jokes on me, and in my own home!

"Oh come now," he said, and yawned. It was plain he didn't feel at fault. And yet he had just dumped the rest of my books all over the floor!

"That was unintentional," he observed, puffing away. "The chronocycle skidded again . . ."

"But why did you return?"

"I had to."

"Had to??"

"We are, my dear boy, in a *circle* of time," he calmly said. "Presently I'll be urging you to accept the position of general director. If you refuse, I'll take my leave, be back before long, and the whole thing will start from the beginning . . ."

"That's impossible! We're in a *closed* curve in time?"

"Precisely."

"I don't believe you! If that were true, everything we say and do would have to be an exact, word-for-word and blow-by-blow repetition, and what I'm saying now, and what you're saying, is no longer completely the same as the first time!!"

"There are all sorts of old wives' tales told about traveling in time," he said, "and the one you've mentioned is among the most ridiculous. In a time circle everything must follow a *similar* course, but not at all the *same*, since closure in time, much as closure in space, does not by any means rule out freedom of action, it only limits it severely! If you accept the offer and depart for the year 2661, the *circle* will thereby be transformed into an open loop. But should you refuse and kick me out again, I'll only return and . . . well, you know what the result will be!"

"So I have no alternative?!" I said, boiling. "Yes, from the very first something told me there was double-dealing at the bottom of this! Out of my house! Out of my sight!!"

134

"Don't be an ass," he replied coldly. "What happens depends entirely on you now, not on me, or to put it more accurately, Rosenbeisser's people have shut the loop—locked it—on the both of us, and we'll stay stuck in here until you agree to be director!"

"Some 'offer,' this!" I shouted. "And what if I just whop the living daylights out of you?"

"You'd only have the same dished out to you when the time came. It's your choice—turn down the offer, and we can amuse ourselves like this for the rest of our natural lives . . ."

"Is that so! I'll lock you in the cellar and go where I damn well please!"

"Like as not, I'd be doing the locking, since I'm stronger!"

"Oh?"

"You should only know. The food they serve in the year 2661 is a great deal more nourishing than here—than now—you wouldn't last a minute with me."

"We'll see about that . . ." I growled, rising from the chair. He didn't budge.

"I know furjoto," he casually remarked.

"What's that?"

"A form of perfected judo from the year 2661. I'd put you out of action in a second."

I was infuriated, but my many experiences in life had taught me to control even the most violent passions. And so, having talked to him—that is, to myself—I reached the conclusion that there really was no way out of it. Besides, this historic mission waiting in the future, it accorded with my views as well as with my personality. The coercion was the only thing that I resented, however I realized it was not with him—a pawn—that I ought to deal, but with those whom he represented.

He showed me how to operate the chronocycle, gave me a few pointers, so I climbed into the saddle and was going to tell him to clean up after himself and also call the carpenter to fix the bookshelves, but didn't have time, for he pushed the starter. Then he, the light of the lamp, the entire room, everything disappeared, as if blown out. Beneath me the machine, that metal rod with its widened, funnel-like exhaust in the back, shook, at times jumping so violently I had to grip the handlebars with all my strength to keep from falling off; I couldn't see a thing, but

135

only had the sensation as though someone were rubbing my face and body with a wire brush; when it seemed that my headlong rush into time was growing excessive, I pulled the brake, whereupon shadowy shapes emerged from out of the swirling blackness.

These were enormous buildings of some sort, now bulging, now slender, and I flew right through them like the wind through a picket fence. Each such passage seemed to threaten collision with a wall, I instinctively shut my eyes and turned up the speed again—that is, the tempo. A couple of times the machine kicked so much that my head jerked and teeth rattled. At one point I experienced a change, difficult to describe, it was like being in some thick, syrupy medium, in glue that was hardening; the thought occurred to me that I was now passing through a barrier which might eventually become my grave, and that I and the chronocycle would be trapped, both frozen in concrete like some strange insect in amber. But again there was a lurch forward, the chronocycle quivered, and I landed on something elastic, which yielded and swayed. The machine slipped out from under me, a burst of white light hit me in the eyes; I had to close them, blinded.

When I opened them again, a hum of voices surrounded me. I was lying in the middle of a large disk of foam plastic that was painted with concentric circles like a target; the overturned chronocycle was resting nearby, and all around stood men, several dozen of them, in glittering jumpsuits. A short, balding towhead stepped onto the mattress of the disk, helped me up and shook my hand repeatedly while saying:

"Glad to have you aboard! Rosenbeisser."

"Tichy," I automatically replied. I looked around. We were standing in a hall as big as a city, windowless, with a sky-blue ceiling hung high overhead; spread out in a row, one after the other, were disks, exactly like the one on which I had landed, some empty, some bustling with activity; I won't deny that I had a few biting remarks prepared for the benefit of Rosenbeisser and the other creators of that temporal net they'd used to haul me from my home, but I said nothing, for suddenly I realized just what this vast hall reminded me of. It was like being in a gigantic Hollywood studio! Three men in armor filed by; the first had a peacock plume on his helmet, a gilded buckler, laboratory assistants adjusted the jewel-encrusted medallion on his chest, a doctor administered an injection in the knight's uncovered forearm, someone else quickly fastened the cuirass straps, he was given a two-handed sword and a wide cloak emblazoned with griffins; the other two, clad in simple steel, squires probably, were already seated on the saddles of their chronocycle at the center of the target, while a voice from a loudspeaker boomed: "Attention please . . . twenty, nineteen, eighteen . . ."

"What's this?" I asked, bewildered, for at the same time—about thirty feet away—there was a procession of emaciated dervishes in enormous white turbans; they were getting injections too, and a technician was arguing with one of them, it seems the traveler had been caught with a small pistol concealed beneath his burnoose; I saw Indians in war paint wielding freshly sharpened tomahawks, laboratory assistants frantically straightening their feather headdresses, and on a small wooden cart an attendant in a white apron was pushing towards another disk a dreadfully filthy, tattered beggar without legs, who bore a striking resemblance to those monstrous cripples out of Breughel.

"Zero!" announced the loudspeaker. The three in armor on their chronocycle vanished in a faint flash which left a whitish vapor hanging in the air, not unlike the smoke from burnt magnesium: I was already familiar with that effect.

"These are our poll-takers," Rosenbeisser explained. "They study public opinion in various centuries, all statistical stuff you understand, strictly information gathering; so far no corrective steps have been initiated, we've been waiting for you!"

He showed me the way with his hand and followed after; I heard voices counting down, there was a flash here, a flash there, wisps of pale smoke drifting up, more and more exploring parties disappeared, new ones took their place, all exactly as in some huge movie studio during the filming of one of those awful history spectaculars. I soon realized that it was forbidden to take any anachronistic objects along with one into the past, the pollsters however kept trying to smuggle them through, either out of perversity or else for their own convenience; well, I thought, we'd put a stop to that soon enough, there would be some changes made, but I asked only:

"And how long does such information gathering take?

137

When will that knight with the squires return?"

"We keep on schedule," said Rosenbeisser with a satisfied smile. "Those three got in *yesterday*."

I said nothing, but thought to myself that it wouldn't be easy getting accustomed to life in a chronomotive society. The laboratory electrocar that was supposed to take us to the administration building broke down, so Rosenbeisser ordered a couple of pollsters off their camels—they were Bedouins—and in this improvised fashion we made it to our destination.

My office was enormous, and done up in the modern style, in other words transparent—which is an understatement, since most of the chairs were altogether invisible, and when I sat at my desk only the piles of paper indicated where the top was; yet because, in leaning over as I worked, I kept seeing my own legs in their striped trousers—and the sight of those stripes made it difficult to concentrate—I finally had all the furniture given a coat of paint, to make it opaque to the eye. But then it turned out that the chairs and tables possessed the most idiotic shapes, inasmuch as they hadn't been designed for viewing; eventually they were all replaced with a set of antiques from the second half of the 23rd century—only then did I feel at home. I may be getting ahead of myself by mentioning such trivialities, yet they do give some idea of the inefficiency of the whole Project. Granted, my life as a director would have been paradise if all I had had to worry about was interior decorating.

It would take an encyclopedia to relate everything the Project did under my supervision. Therefore I shall, as briefly as I can, sketch out only the major stages of our work. The organizational structure was symmetrical. I had under me TICK (the Time Interferometry and Calendrical Kinetics division), with sections in quantum field and dispersion temporology, and then there was the historical division, containing the faculties of Human and Inhuman. The head of the technologists was Dr. Rob Boskowitz, while Prof. Pat Lado was in charge of the history-makers. Beyond that I had at my personal disposal squads of historicommandos and chronochutists (horotroopers, time jumpers), with a brigade for emergency dethronement as well as a surveillance force. This stand-by corps, a sort of fire department for any unforeseen and dangerous turn of events, bore the acronym MOIRA (Mobile Inspection and Rescue Auxiliaries). At the time of my arrival the technologists-temporalists were ready to begin full-scale telechronic operations, while in the province of Human affairs (run by Harris S. Doddle, an assistant professor) the experts had worked out hundreds of EDENS (Educational Engrams). Similarly the department for Inhuman studies (Obadiah Goody, spheres engineer) had drafted up alternate proposals for improving the solar system, i.e. the planets with Earth at the head, also the course of Biological Evolution, anthropogenesis, etc. All these abovementioned subordinates of mine I later had to get rid of, one by one; each of them is connected, in my memory, with a different crisis within the Project. I shall deal with these at the proper time, to let the human race know to whom it owes its present predicament.

In the beginning I was full of high hopes. Having taken a rush course in the elements of telechronics and chronoscopic permutation, and having mastered too the administrative intricacies (the delegation of authority, division of labor, and so on), during which—even then—I came into conflict with the Head Accountant (Eustace C. Liddy), I saw how monumental was the task that had been thrust upon me. The science of the 27th century provided me with many different technologies for operating in time, and as if that wasn't enough, there were *hundreds* of different plans to renovate history all waiting for my signature. Behind each stood the weight and wisdom of world famous experts—and I was supposed to pick and choose among this embarrassment of riches! For so far there was no agreement, neither about *which method* we would use to improve upon the past, nor from which point to begin, nor even *how much* intervention there ought to be.

The first phase of our activity was marked with great optimism; we decided not to touch the history of man just yet, but instead put in order all the epochs, eras and eons that preceded it; this grand design provided for—among other things—the devulcanization of the planets, the straightening of the Earth's axis, the creation on Mars and Venus of conditions favorable for their future colonization, while the Moon was to serve as a kind of embarkation platform or way station for the emigration flights which would take place three to four billion years later. With visions of a Better Yesterday in my head I gave the order to launch the Generators for the Establishment of Isochronalities (GENESIS). Three models went into action—BREKEKE, KEX and KOAX. I no longer recall what exactly those abbreviations stood for; the first had something to do with kilowatts and kinematic effects, the second was either K-meson Excitation or Kenogenetical Exobiometry.

The results surpassed our wildest apprehensions; there was one malfunction after another. Instead of braking gradually and synchronizing itself with the normal flow of time, KOAX fired Mars with an explosion and turned it into one big desert; the oceans all boiled off and evaporated into space, and the scorched crust of the planet cracked open, creating a strange network of troughs, each hundreds of miles in diameter. Hence the 19th-century hypothesis about the canals of Mars. Not wanting the people of the past to learn of our activity, for this could give them serious complexes, I ordered the canals to be all carefully patched, which engineer Lavache in fact did around the year 1910; subsequent astronomers were not surprised by the canals' disappearance, attributing the whole thing to an optical illusion on the part of their predecessors. KEX, which was supposed to render Venus fertile, had been safeguarded against the malfunction of KOAX thanks to CUPID (Cyclochronic Unidirectional Polarization of Inchoate Differentials), however the Fail-safe Integrators (FALSIES) failed miserably and all of Venus was enveloped in a cloud of poisonous gas, caused by the ensuing chronoclysm. Engineer Wadenlecker, the man in charge of these operations, I summarily dismissed, but when the Research Committee interceded on his behalf I let him carry out the last stage of the experiment. This time it was no mere malfunction that followed, but a catastrophe of truly cosmic proportions. Set in motion against the current of duration, BREKEKE penetrated the present of 6.5 billion years before, emerging so close to the Sun that it pulled from it an enormous chunk of stellar material, which, coiling up under gravitational forces, gave rise to all the planets.

Wadenlecker defended himself, claiming it was thanks to him that the solar system ever came into being, for if that chronal nose cone hadn't proved defective, the chance of planets forming would have been practically nil. Astronomers were to wonder afterwards what star could have passed so close to the

Sun as to pull from it the protoplanetary matter, for—indeed—such close approaches of stars are among the most unlikely of events. I removed the impertinent fellow once and for all from his position of technochronical director, since—as I saw it—it wasn't the point or purpose of our Project, that such things be done *by accident,* through negligence and oversight. If it had come to it, we certainly could have done a better job of fashioning the planets. And anyway, the TICK division had nothing to boast of, not after what they did to Mars and Venus.

Next on the agenda was a plan for straightening out the Earth's rotational axis; the idea was that this would make its climate more uniform, without polar frost or equatorial heat. Our purpose here was humanitarian: more species were to survive in the struggle for existence. The result turned out to be precisely what we didn't want. The greatest ice age on Earth, in the Cambrian period, was produced by one engineer Hans Jacob Plötzlich when he fired off a heavy "rectifying" unit, which gave the Earth's axis its so-called "wobble." The first glacial epoch, instead of cautioning the hasty temporalist, indirectly brought about the second, for seeing what he had done, Plötzlich, *without my knowledge,* then proceeded to fire a "correctional" charge. Which led to chronoclasm and a new ice age, this time in the Pleistocene.

Before I was able to remove him from his post, that incorrigible man succeeded in causing a third chronal collision: it's because of him that the Earth's magnetic pole doesn't coincide with the axis of rotation, for the planet still hasn't stopped teetering. One of the time fragments of the "Readjuster" flew to the year one million B.C.—in that place we have today the Great Crater of Arizona; fortunately no one got hurt, there weren't any people around then; only the desert burned. Another splinter came to rest as late as the year 1908—the natives there speak of it as the "Tungus meteorite." Well, that was no meteorite, but only bits and pieces of the shoddily constructed "Optimizer" careening through time. I kicked Plötzlich out without regard for anyone, and when he was caught sneaking into the chronotorium at night—his conscience bothered him, if you please, he wanted to "repair" the damage he had done—I demanded, as his punishment, exile in time.

I finally relented, which I now regret, and, following the advice of Rosenbeisser, filled the vacancy with engineer Dizzard. I had no idea that he was the professor's brother-in-law. The sequel to this nepotism, in which I had been unwittingly involved, wasn't long in coming. Dizzard was the inventor of REIN (Radiant Energy Interchange), subsequently perfected by time specialist Bummeland. They reasoned thus: if even simple chronoclasm is accompanied by the release of tremendous temporal energy, then instead of having it take the form of destructive blasts (the sort that devastated Mars), let it at least be turned into pure radiation. This half-baked idea of theirs (intentions don't count!) caused me a lot of grief. REIN did indeed convert the kinetic energy into radiation, but what good was that, when the radiation—right in the middle of the Mesozoic—killed off all my dinosaurs, every last one, and God only knows how many other species in the bargain?

Bummeland tried to defend himself by arguing that this was actually a good thing, since it cleared the evolutionary stage, thereby *permitting* the appearance of the mammals, from which man himself derived. As if that were a foregone conclusion! They deprive us of our anthropogenic maneuverability by committing saurocide, and then have the nerve to boast about it! Dizzard made a great show of remorse and even submitted a written apology, but it isn't true that he voluntarily stepped down from his post. The fact of the matter is, I told Rosenbeisser that as long as his brother-in-law remained on the Project, I wouldn't set foot in the office.

After this string of disasters I called the entire staff together and made a little speech, warning them that I saw no alternative but to take tough measures from now on against those endangering the safety of the past. It would no longer be simply a matter of losing a comfortable position!

Accidents were understandable, they told me, if not unavoidable, what with the launching of so unprecedented a technology; just consider the number of rockets that fell apart when space travel was in its infancy; and *our* enterprise, taking place as it did in *time*, entailed dangers that were incomparably greater. The Research Committee recommended a new chronometrist; this was Prof. Lenny D. Vinch. I gave him and Boskowitz fair warning with regard to the next experiment, that nothing would—or could—again compel me to show leniency in the event of any serious mishap caused by carelessness.

I showed them the memos Wadenlecker, Bummeland and Dizzard had written to the Research Committee behind my back, appeals full of contradiction, for sometimes they would lay the blame on the objective difficulties, and sometimes turn around and call the outcome of their errors commendable. I told those two that I wasn't the ignoramus some people took me for. A simple knowledge of the four arithmetic operations was all one needed to figure out how much material from the Sun had already been wasted—irretrievably too, since the outer planets, real garbage dumps—no—cesspools full of ammonia, were completely useless; Mars and Venus too I scratched out, and gave the go-ahead for the final attempt to improve upon our solar system. The program envisioned converting the Moon into an oasis for the weary astronauts of the future, as well as a transfer point for those on their way to Athena.

You never heard of Athena? I'm not surprised. That planet was supposed to have been perfected by the team of Gestirner, Starbuck and Astroianni. Such losers the Project never had before. DUNDER (Diachronic Uncertainty Detector and Entropy Regulator) didn't work, DUFF (Durational Force Fields) broke down, and Athena, till then moving in orbit between Earth and Mars, shattered into ninety thousand separate pieces and what remained was the so-called Asteroid Belt. As for the Moon, those optimizing geniuses of ours butchered its surface completely. It's a wonder the whole thing didn't blow up too. Hence that famous riddle of 19th and 20th-century astronomy, for the scientists couldn't understand where all those craters came from. They developed two theories to explain it—the volcanic and the meteor-impact.

What nonsense. The author of the so-called volcanic craters was time technician Gestirner, in charge of DUFF, and the one responsible for the "meteorite" type—that was Astroianni, who had taken aim at Athena three billion years in the past and sent it off to kingdom come. The recoil of that chronoclasis, ricocheting in every direction, stopped what was left of Venus's rotational motion, gave Mars two spurious satellites that went *the wrong way,* so you see by then it was peanuts for this specialist to turn the surface of the Moon into a missile range, letting fragments of Athena fall on it throughout the next billion years. But when I learned that one of the chips from the chronotractor—the explosion smeared *it* over 2,950,000,000 years—had landed in prehistoric times, had moreover plunged into the sea and bored a hole in the ocean floor, sinking Atlantis in the process, I personally threw the perpetrators of this compound catastrophe out on their ear, and took action against those responsible for the operation as a whole—in keeping with my previous decision. Appealing to the Committee didn't help them one bit.

Prof. Lenny D. Vinch I sent packing to the 16th century, and Boskowitz to the 17th, so they couldn't get together and scheme. As you already know, Leonardo da Vinci spent the rest of his life trying to build himself a time coupe, but he never succeeded; Leonardo's so-called "helicopters" and other machines, as bizarre as they were incomprehensible to his contemporaries, represented abortive attempts to escape exile in time.

Boskowitz conducted himself more sensibly, I think. This was a man of uncommon abilities, with an exact mind, indeed he was a mathematician by training: in the seventeenth century Bosković became a truly brilliant albeit universally ignored thinker. He tried to popularize the ideas of theoretical physics, but none of his contemporaries understood a word of his treatises. To lighten his exile I sent him to Ragusa (Dubrovnik), for secretly I sympathized with him, yet still felt that it was necessary to punish those responsible with severity, no matter how much the Research Committee held it against me.

And so the first phase of the Project ended a complete fiasco—I absolutely refused to consider the initiation of any further tries in the GENESIS series. Enough had been sunk into it already and lost. The barren wastes from Jupiter on out, Mars burnt to a crisp, Venus poisoned twice over, the Moon in ruins (those so-called "mascons," mass concentrations beneath its surface, are actually the bits and pieces, embedded deep in the ground and set in hardened lava, of the nose cones of DUNDER and DUFF), and the lopsided axis of the Earth, the hole in the bottom of the ocean, the separation of the land masses of Eurasia and the two Americas brought on by the rift it caused—that was the dismal balance, so far, of all that we had undertaken. Nevertheless, forbidding myself to be discouraged, I threw open the doors of active optimization to the crews of the Historical division.

It had, you will recall, two faculties, human affairs (ass't. prof. H. Doddle) and inhuman (spheres eng. O. Goody); the entire division was headed by Prof. P. Lado, who from the very beginning aroused my distrust with the radical, uncompromising nature of his views. Which is why I preferred not to touch history proper just yet; anyway, it made more sense to design the kind of intelligent beings that could do the job of civilizing history themselves. Therefore I held back Lado and Doddle (it wasn't easy, either, the way their hands were itching to get at the past) and ordered Goody to start the Evolution of Life on Earth rolling. And, so they couldn't accuse me later of stifling creativity, I gave project BIPPETY (Biogenetic Implementation of Parameters to Perfect Terrestrial Intelligence) considerable autonomy. I did however exhort its directors (Obadiah Goody, Homer Gumby, Harry Bosch, Vance Eyck) to learn from the mistakes of Mother Nature, who had disfigured all living things, who had herself blocked the most likely routes leading to Intelligence—for which, of course, one could not blame her, seeing as how she worked in the dark so to speak, on a day-to-day basis. We, in contrast, should act *purposefully*, keeping ever before us the grand goal, namely BIPPETY. They promised me they would follow these guidelines implicitly and, guaranteeing success, went into action.

Honoring that precious autonomy of theirs, I didn't interfere, didn't monitor them across the one and a half billion years, but the great quantity of anonymous mail that came in finally induced me to do some checking up. What I found was enough to turn one gray. First they had amused themselves like children for a good four hundred million years, turning out fish with armor and some sort of trilobites or other; then, seeing how little time remained until the end of the eon, they scrambled. They threw together units haphazardly, any which way, one more preposterous than the next, producing now a mountain of flesh on four legs, now a tail without a body, now something like a speck of dust; some specimens they paved all over with cobblestones of bone, with others they stuck on horns, tusks, tubes, trunks, tentacles—all indiscriminately; and oh, how ugly it was, how repulsive, senseless, altogether appalling: pure abstractionism, surrealism, a page straight out of modern art.

What really infuriated me was their smugness; they said that my buttoned-down conventionality was a thing of the past, that I wasn't "with it," that I had no "feel for form," etc. I held my peace: if only they had limited themselves to this! But no. In that carefully chosen group everyone was out to backstab everyone else. It was not of Homo Sapiens they thought, but rather how to torpedo the projects of their colleagues, thus hardly would a new species begin to make its way in Nature before some monstrosity was marshaled out, developed for the sole purpose of killing off the rival model, demonstrating thereby its inferiority. What has been called the "struggle for existence" resulted from professional jealousies and sabotage. The fangs and claws of Evolution, then, simply reflect the infighting that went on in the department. Instead of teamwork there I found widespread boondoggling, and constant attempts to trip up the species of one's fellow employee; they got their greatest kick, it seemed, when they were able to scotch all further development on a line under someone else's management; this is the reason we have so many blind alleys in the kingdom of living things. I shouldn't say living; they had turned it into something halfway between a waxworks and a cemetery. Not finishing one job, they hurried off to the next; the lungfish and arthropods they never gave an even break, they put an end to their chances with the windpipe; and if it hadn't been for me, we wouldn't have even made it to the age of steam and electricity, for they "forgot" about carbon, i.e. about planting the trees which were supposed to produce the coal for future steam engines.

During the inspection I wrung my hands in despair; the whole planet was cluttered with corpses and wrecks, Bosch in particular had had a field day—when I asked him what earthly purpose was served by that Rhamphornychus with its tail copied off of some child's kite, and wasn't he ashamed about the Proboscidae, and why lizards with spines like fence rails on their back, he replied that I didn't understand the frenzy of creative inspiration. I asked him to show me just *where* then, in this state of affairs, *intelligence* was supposed to take root; the question was purely rhetorical, since between them they had stymied all the promising lines of descent. I hadn't imposed upon them any ready-made solutions, but only reminded them beforehand of the birds, the eagles, and now here was something that flew—they'd microminiaturized its head—and here was something that ran like an ostrich—reduced to utter idiocy. Only two possibilities were left: either make Intelligent Man from the marginal remains, or, on the other hand, have a battering-ram sort of evolution, that is, forcing open all the blocked-up branches of development. But force was out of the question, for such obvious interference would later be recognized by the paleontologists as *miraculous;* and long ago I had forbidden the use of miracles, so as not to mislead the generations-to-come.

All of these unprincipled designers I dismissed from their positions, that is, from their time; and then there were the mass burials of their abortions, for those—unfinished—died off by the millions. The rumor that I ordered the species killed is just another of the many calumnies that have been liberally disseminated against me. It wasn't I who moved life from one corner of the evolutionary process to the other like a piece of furniture, who doubled the trunk of the amoebedodon, who inflated the dromedary (gigantocamelus) to the size of an elephant, who dabbled at whales, it wasn't I who drove the mammoth to self-annihilation, for throughout I lived by the Project, not for the sort of shameless game which Goody's group had made of Evolution. Eyck and Bosch I banished to the Middle Ages, and Gumby, since he had parodied the whole idea of BIPPETY (among other things he created the man-horse and the woman-fish, which in addition was equipped with a high *soprano*), Homer Gumby I sent as far back as antiquity, to Thrace. What followed was something I had seen happen before, and would again, more than once. The exiles, now deprived of the opportunity to create real things, gave vent to their frustrations in vicarious, sublimated work. Anyone interested in what *else* Bosch had up his sleeve can find out by taking a look at his paintings. Clearly, the man had talent. It shows, for one, in the way he was able to fit in with the spirit of the period—hence the ostensible religiousness of his canvases, all those Last Judgments and scenes from hell. Even so, Bosch couldn't refrain from certain

147

indiscretions. In the "Garden of Earthly Delights," in the very center of the "Musical Hell" (the right wing of the triptych), stands a twelve-seat chronobus. Not a thing I could do about it.

As for Homer, I think I acted wisely, packing him off—along with his creatures—to Ancient Greece. What he painted has been lost, but his writings were preserved. Strange, that no one has noticed the anachronisms in them. Surely it's obvious he didn't take seriously the occupants of Olympus, who are constantly out to foil one another's plans, in a word behaving exactly like his colleagues at the institute. The *Iliad* and *Odyssey* are *romans à clef;* the irascible Zeus, for instance, that's a satire on me.

Goody however I didn't dismiss right away, since Rosenbeisser spoke up for him: if this man let me down, he said, then I could send *him,* the research director of the Project, into the Archeozoic if I liked. Goody supposedly had hidden resources, contributions to make; when I opposed the idea of utilizing the monkey leftovers, he started in on BARF (Binary Anthropogenesis for Reciprocal Feedback). I didn't put much stock in his BARF, but raised no objections, for by now the word was that I turned down any and all proposals. The next reconnaissance flight showed that he had forced a couple of small mammals into the ocean, made them similar to fish, threw in some frontal radar and was just then at the dolphin stage. Somehow he had gotten it into his head that to achieve harmony two intelligent species were needed: land and sea. How asinine! It would lead to conflicts, of course! I told him: "Intelligent beings in the water *are out!*" So the dolphin remained the way it was, with a brain several sizes too big, and we had a crisis on our hands.

What now, start evolution all over again, from the beginning? I couldn't, my nerves were shot. I told Goody to do as he saw fit, in other words I accepted the monkey as a working model, but made him promise to pretty it up a bit; and, so he couldn't plead ignorance later on, I supplied him with guidelines—in writing, through official channels, though without (it's true) going into all the details. I did however point out in what poor taste those naked anal areas were, and advised a sensitive, dignified approach to the matter of sex, suggesting something in the spirit of the flowers, lilies of the valley, buds, then on my way out—I had to attend a session of the Committee—I asked him personally not to muff it in his usual fashion but find instead some nice motifs. His studio was a shambles, here and there beams of some sort jutting out, planks, saws, what did they have to do with love? Have you gone mad, I said, love on the principle of the buzz saw? I made him give me his solemn word he'd throw away the saw, he nodded zealously—laughing to himself all the while, for he'd already learned that his walking papers lay waiting in my desk, therefore knew he had nothing to lose.

He decided to get even with me. He blustered, telling everyone that the old boy (namely me) would crap in his pants when he returned; and I certainly did; Good Lord—I summoned him at once, he played the conscientious employee, insisting he'd adhered to the guidelines! Yet instead of getting rid of that bald spot in the back, he had *shaved* the entire monkey, or rather did it all in reverse, and as far as love and sex went, well, *that* was clear sabotage on his part. I mean, the very choice of the place! But I need hardly dwell on that piece of treachery. What its effect was, you can all see for yourselves. Yes, monsieur the engineer really went out of his way! The monkeys were what they were, but at least vegetarian. He made them carnivorous too.

I called an emergency meeting of the Committee to consider the matter of the rehumanization of Homo sapiens, and there was told that this could no longer be accomplished in a single blow; one would have to backtrack twenty-five, possibly even thirty million years; I was outvoted, but didn't make use of my veto power, perhaps I should have, but I was on my last legs now. Anyway signals were coming in from the 18th and 19th centuries; to make things easier for themselves, the officials of MOIRA, tired of constantly having to drive back and forth in time, set up residence in various old castles, palaces, in basements, and taking absolutely no precautions, until there began to be rumors of damned souls, chains rattling (the sound of a chronocycle starting up), and ghosts (for they wore white, as if they couldn't have picked a better color for their uniform); they made people's heads spin, frightened them by passing through walls and doors (taking off in time always looks like that, for the chronocycle stays put while the earth continues turning), and all in all they created such a disturbance, that finally it brought on the birth of Romanticism. After punishing the culprits, I tended to Goody and Rosenbeisser.

I deported the both of them, fully aware that the Research Committee would never forgive me for it. In any event I'm not vindictive: Rosenbeisser, who behaved towards me afterwards in a positively scandalous manner, in exile conducted himself quite decently (as Julian the Apostate). He did not a little to improve, in Byzantium, the lot of the poor. Which only shows that the reason he failed at his job was that he just didn't measure up. Being an emperor is peanuts compared to overseeing the renovation of all history.

Thus concluded the second phase of the Project. I then gave the department of social affairs permission to begin, since all we could perfect now was the history of civilization. Getting down to work, Doddle and Lado were clearly delighted that their predecessors had blundered so completely, yet at the same time they warned me *in advance*—playing it safe, the dogs—that one could not expect too much of THEOHIPPIP now, not with *that* kind of Homo sapiens!

Doddle entrusted the carrying out of his first experimental corrective program to the chronologians. These were Khand el Abr, Canne de la Breux, Guirre Andaule and G. I. R. Andoll. The team was to work under the direct leadership of eng. historiologist Hemdreisser. He and his colleagues planned to expedite the cultural process through urbanizational acceleration. It was in Lower Egypt of the 12th, or maybe the 13th, Dynasty—I no longer remember which—that they amassed great piles of building material with the aid of temporal agents, whom we commonly called "time plants," and raised the general level of architectural know-how, but owing to a lack of adequate supervision the plan miscarried. Briefly, instead of mass housing construction what we ended up with—in the framework of a cult of personality—was of no earthly use to anyone, i.e. tombs for various and sundry Pharaohs. I transported the entire team to Crete; that was how the palace of Minos came about. I don't know if it's true, but Betterpart told me that the exiles then quarreled, rose up against their former chief and put him in the Labyrinth. Not having checked the records, I can't say for sure, but to me Hemdreisser doesn't look like any Minotaur.

I decided to put a stop to this hit-and-run approach and requested the submission of proposals of a more long-range nature. We had to make up our minds whether to act openly or in secret, that is, whether the people of various periods should be at all allowed to discover that someone was helping them from outside history. Doddle, something of a liberal, was in favor of cryptochronism, which I too advocated. The alternative strategy would make it necessary to place all the nations of the Past under an open Protectorate, which couldn't help but give them the feeling of being disenfranchised. Therefore we ought to offer assistance, but anonymously. Lado objected, he had in mind a plan for an ideal government, into which he wanted to pull and consolidate all societies.

I backed Doddle, who introduced me to one of the youngest and, presumably, best of his assistants; this graduate student, Otto Noy, was the inventor of monotheism. God, as he explained to me, was an idea which in itself could harm no one, yet would give *us*—the optimizers—a free hand, since according to the plan His decisions were to be ipso facto mysterious: the people wouldn't be able to understand them, therefore they wouldn't criticize, and neither would they suspect that anyone was tampering with their history—telechronically. Not a bad idea, on the face of it, but just to be safe I gave the young M. A. a small area only, to test his theory, and in a remote corner of the world at that, in Asia Minor; he could have at his disposal the tribe of Judah. His helper was one eng. historiologician Joseph Hobbs. A routine check revealed that they had committed a number of serious breaches. It was bad enough that Noy ordered 60,000 tons of pearl barley to be dropped during a desert outing of some Jews; the "discreet assistance" he was supposed to render them led to so much intervention (he opened and closed the Red Sea, sent remote-control locusts against the enemies of Judah), that the recipients of this patronage finally had their heads turned; they declared themselves a chosen people.

Invariably, whenever a plan went wrong in its realization, the planner, instead of changing tactics, would resort to more and more powerful stimuli. But Otto Noy outdid everyone when he used napalm. Why did I permit it, you ask? Permit it! I knew nothing about it! At the Institute's proving ground he had demonstrated only the remote-control igniting of a bush, assuring us that that was the sort of thing he'd be doing in the past; you know, a few dried-up cactuses in the desert might burn, nothing more. This display, I suppose, was an attempt on his part to comply with moral norms. After banishing him to the Sinai Peninsula, I strictly forbade all the group directors to license any acts of a supernatural appearance. And of course what Noy and Hobbs did had historical repercussions.

But that was typical. Every telechronic intervention set off an avalanche of events, which couldn't be held in check without appropriate measures, and those in turn produced new perturbations, and so on and so on. Otto Noy's conduct in exile was highly improper, he capitalized on the fame he'd created for himself earlier, in the position of historiometrist. It's true he was now no longer able to work his "miracles," however the memory of them endured. As for Joe Hobbs, I know it's been said that I had my time troopers lean on him, but that's a lie. I'm not familiar with the facts of the case, there wasn't time to bother about such details; but apparently he had fallen out with Otto Noy and the latter made things so hot for him that eventually it started the legend of Job. The Jews came out the worst in this experiment, for by this time they firmly believed in their favored status, and consequently after the Project withdrew there was more than one bitter pill for them to swallow, both in their homeland and during the Diaspora. I won't tell you what my enemies at the Project had to say about me on *that* particular subject.

At any rate the Project now entered the stage of its most difficult crises. I bear some of the blame for this, inasmuch as— giving in to Doddle and Lado—I permitted the betterment of history on a *broad front*, i.e. not in isolated moments and locations, but over the whole length of the historical time-line. That strategy of amelioration, called "integrated," made a tangle of our scene of operations; in order to head off which, I placed groups of observers in each century, and also gave Lado the authority to organize a secret tempolice force, which would combat delinquency *in time*.

This delinquency, something that never would have entered my head even in a nightmare, had to do with the so-called business of the brooms. It was the work of groups of wild youths, mostly recruited from our staff personnel, lab technicians, secretaries, etc. Those endless medieval tales of pacts with the devil, incubi and succubi, sabbats, witch trials, temptations of saints, etc., all of that derived from "bootleg" chronomotion, practiced by adolescents bereft of any moral ballast. An individual chronocycle consists of a pipe, a saddle, and an exhaust funnel, therefore one could easily mistake it—particularly in bad lighting—for a broom. A number of shameless hussies went off on joy rides, usually at night, terrorizing villagers in the early Middle Ages. Not only did they go swooping over people's heads, but actually set out—for the 13th, say, or 12th century— in shocking deshabille, topless even, it's not surprising then that they were thought to be (for the lack of any better description) naked witches astraddle flying brooms. By an odd coincidence I was aided in the tracking down and capture of the guilty parties by none other than H. Bosch, at that time already in exile; he certainly wasn't about to faint at the sight of an ordinary temporician, and in his "hell" cycle painted true-to-life portraits— not of devils, but of dozens of illegal chronocyclists and their cohorts, which was all the easier for him, in that many he knew personally.

Considering the number of people victimized by these chronooligan escapades, I sent the offenders back seven hundred years (the "20th-century student radicals"). Meanwhile, since the field of our activities had now spread over more than forty centuries, N. Betterpart, commander in chief of MOIRA, informed me that the situation was getting out of hand and asked for special reinforcements in the form of emergency crews of chronochutists. We began to take on hundreds of new workers, sending them off immediately to where the distress signals were coming from, though often these were people with little or no training. Their being concentrated in certain centuries led to serious incidents, things like migrations of whole nations; we did our best to conceal the arrival of each such landing party, but in the 20th century (about halfway through) there was common talk of "flying saucers," for the circulation of the news was made possible by a then rapidly developing mass-media technology.

Yet this was nothing compared to the next scandal, whose author and later principal character turned out to be the chief of MOIRA himself. I began to receive reports from time to the effect that his people were not so much observing the progress of meliorization as they were actively participating in the historical process, and this not in the spirit of Lado and Doddle's instructions, but rather according to their own temporal politics, which

153

was being merrily pursued by Betterpart. Before I was able to remove him from his post he absconded, that is, fled to the 18th century, for there he could count on his old cronies; the next thing I knew, he was emperor of France. This foul deed called for severe punishment; Lado suggested I dispatch a reserve brigade against Versailles of 1807, but that was quite out of the question, such a raid would undoubtedly produce an unparalleled perturbation in all subsequent history—mankind would realize, from there on out, that it was in protective custody. The more circumspect Doddle came up with a plan for the "natural," i.e. cryptochronistic, castigation of Napoleon. The mounting of an anti-Bonapartist coalition was begun, military marching drills, but wouldn't you know, the chief of MOIRA got wind of it immediately and lost no time in assuming the offensive himself; not for nothing was he a professional strategist, he had strategy in his little finger, and one by one defeated all the enemies Doddle sent up against him. For a while it looked like we had him cornered in Russia, but in that campaign too he gave us the slip somehow, meanwhile half of Europe lay in smoldering ruins; finally I made my well-meaning shapers of history step aside and dealt with Napoleon myself, near Waterloo. As if that were anything to boast about!

Napoleon escaped from Elba, there hadn't been time to arrange a better exile, so many other matters demanded my immediate attention; those guilty of infractions were now no longer quietly waiting to receive their just deserts, but taking off posthaste for the distant past, smuggling out things to help them acquire fame or an aura of extraordinary powers (these were the alchemists, Cagliostro, Simon Magus, and scores of others). And reports came in, reports I had no way of verifying, e.g. that Atlantis was sunk not by any ricochet from operation GENESIS, but by one Dr. Huey Hokum, with premeditation, to keep me from finding out what mischief he had perpetrated there. In a word, everything was falling apart on me. I lost my faith in a successful outcome and, what was worse, had grown suspicious. I no longer knew what was the result of optimization, and what the effect of its abandonment, and what—for that matter—was due to the insubordination and corruption among my centurial police patrols.

I decided to attack the problem from the other end. I

picked up a copy of the Great Encyclopedia of World History in twelve volumes and started studying it, and whenever anything seemed the least bit suspicious to me I sent out a reconnaissance flight. Such was the case, for example, with Cardinal Richelieu; having checked with MOIRA and made sure that this was not one of our agents, I asked Lado to place a controller of some intelligence there. He entrusted the mission to a certain Reichplatz; then something told me to consult a dictionary; I turned numb, for sure enough, Richelieu and Reichplatz meant the same thing—"Rich Place"—but by then it was too late, since he had already worked his way up into the higher circles of the court and was now the gray eminence of Louis XIII. I left him alone, for after the Napoleonic Wars I knew what such attempts could lead to.

In the meantime another problem was developing. Certain centuries were litera ly crawling with exiles; the tempolice couldn't keep tabs on them—they were spreading rumors, superstitions, purely to spite me, or actually tried bribing the controllers; so I started herding all those who were up to no good into a single place and single time, namely Ancient Greece, as a result of which, that turned out to be the spot where civilization made its greatest strides; why, there were more philosophers in the town of Athens than in all the rest of Europe. By then Lado and Doddle had already been banished; both of them abused my trust; Lado, one of the most hard-headed fanatics that ever was, sabotaged my orders by pursuing his own policy (its full exposition you can find in his "Republic"), which was undemocratic in the extreme, based on oppression in fact, take the Middle Kingdom for instance, the caste system in India, the Holy Roman Empire, and even the Japanese belief in the divinity of the Mikado from 1868 on, yes, that too was his doing. As to whether or not he married off some Miss Schicklgruber or other, so that that famous child could be born, who later trampled half of Europe underfoot, I can't say for sure, as it was Doddle who told me this, and he and Lado had always been at one another's throats.

Lado designed the Aztec kingdom, Doddle sent the Spaniards there; at the last minute, receiving reports from MOIRA, I ordered Columbus's trip postponed, and horses to be bred in South America, for Cortez's men would never hold up against a cavalry of Indians, however the coordinators bungled and the horses all died out as far back as the Quaternary, when there weren't any Indians around, so we had no one to pull the war wagons, though the wheel was available in plenty of time. As for Columbus, he made it in 1492, having greased the right palms. That's how this optimization of ours worked. I was even accused—as if there weren't more than enough philosophers in Greece already—of having Harris Doddle and Pat Lado transported there. Not true! It was precisely to show a little humanity that I let them choose the time and place of exile; I did, I'll admit, deposit Plato not exactly where he wanted, but in Syracuse, for I knew that, what with the wars going on in that city, he wouldn't be able to put into practice that pet idea of his, the "Kingdom of Philosophers."

Harris Doddle became, as everyone knows, tutor to young Alexander the Macedonian. He had been guilty of oversights, and with ghastly consequences. Giving in—as he invariably did—to that weakness he had for composing enormous encyclopedias, Doddle would dabble at classification as well as a general methodology for his Theory of the Perfect Project, while behind his back all sorts of things were going on. The head accountant, unsupervised, threw in with a frogman friend of his, together they fished out the gold of Montezuma from the same canal in which Cortez's men had foundered during their retreat, and with that played the stock market, starting in 1922; but crime doesn't pay and they brought on the well-known crash of 1929. I don't believe I dealt unfairly with Aristotle, it was to me after all that he owed his fame, which he certainly didn't merit as far as his work on the Project went. But then it was said that under the pretext of dismissals, replacements and exiles I was running a kind of nepotistic merry-go-round, setting my old pals up in plush sinecures throughout the ages. Well, with such critics I was damned if I did, damned if I didn't.

There isn't time to go into details, so I won't dwell on the allusions to myself contained in the works of Plato and Aristotle. Naturally they weren't exactly thrilled about their exile, but I couldn't concern myself with personal resentments, not with the fate of mankind hanging in the balance. Greece was another matter entirely, and I took her downfall very much to heart. It isn't true I brought it about by putting all those philosophers together; Lado kept an eye on things there, he did it for the sake of Sparta, which he hoped to mold into the image of his beloved utopia, but after his removal there was no one to sustain the Spartans and they folded up before the Persian army; and what could I do about it? Local favoritism was unthinkable, no, we had to extend our protection to *all* humanity, and yet here was this problem of the exiles undermining our most vital plans; I couldn't send anyone into the future, they were on the lookout up there, and since every blessed one of the condemned requested the Azure Coast, and I couldn't refuse, great numbers of people possessing a higher education became concentrated around the Mediterranean and, well, that's precisely where you have your cradle of civilization and, later, the culture of the West.

As for Spinoza—a very good man, I grant you, but he allowed the Crusades, though he didn't actually start them himself; I'd put him in Lado's place, oh he had a sterling character, but what a woolgatherer, signing whatever they stuck in front of him, without even looking; he gave unlimited powers to Löwenherz (yes, the Lion-Hearted), then someone back in the 13th century was hatching something and when they began looking for the guilty party Löwenherz threw in chronobus after chronobus of secret agents, so the suspect—I forget who it was—caused the Crusades in order to hide in the resulting confusion. I didn't know what to do with Spinoza, Greece was already overflowing with thinkers like himself, first I had him travel back and forth across the ages, letting him seesaw with a forty-century amplitude, which gave rise to the legend of the Wandering Jew, however each time he swung through our here-and-now he complained of fatigue, so I finally sent him off to Amsterdam, for he liked to tinker with things and there could cut diamonds to his heart's content.

More than once I've been asked why none of the exiles chose to reveal from where they came. A lot of good it would have done them. Anyone who told the truth would have found himself quickly headed for the loony bin. Wouldn't a man have been thought crazy, before the 20th century, who claimed that out of ordinary water you could make a bomb capable of blowing the entire globe to bits? And before the 23rd century, certainly, there was no knowledge of chronomotion. Besides which, such admissions would have laid bare the derivative nature of the work of many of the exiles. We forbade them to prophesy the future, but even so they let more than one cat out of the bag. In the Middle Ages, happily, no one paid much attention to those references to jets and bathyspheres in Bacon, or the computers in Lull's ARS MAGNA. It was worse with the exiles sent improvidently to the 20th century; calling themselves "futurologists," they began to give out top-secret information.

Fortunately General Angus Kahn, the new chief of MOIRA after Napoleon, employed the so-called Babel tactic. This was how it worked. Once, sixteen tempo engineers, summarily banished to Asia Minor, decided to build a time main to escape, under the guise of constructing some sort of tower or dome; the name given to it was the cryptonym-password of their plot (Banished Asian Builders' Escape League). MOIRA, having detected their operation in a fairly advanced stage, dispatched its own specialists to the spot as "new exiles," and these intentionally introduced such errors into the blueprint, that the mechanism flew apart at the very first trial run. Kahn repeated this maneuver of "communication confusion," sending diversionary units into the 20th century; they completely discredited those who were trying to set themselves up as prophets—by turning out all sorts of rubbish (called "Science Fiction") and placing in the ranks of the futurologists our secret agent, one McLuhan.

I must confess that when I read through the malarkey that MOIRA had prepared, and which McLuhan was to disseminate as his "prognoses," I threw up my hands in despair, for it didn't seem possible to me that anyone with half a brain could take seriously, even for a minute, all that crap about the "global village" towards which the world was supposed to be heading, not to mention the other inanities contained in that hash. And yet, as it turned out, McLuhan was a much greater success than all the people who were betraying the simple truth; he acquired such fame that he ended up actually believing—so it seems—the drivel we had ordered him to advocate. We didn't remove him, though, since this didn't hurt us in the least. As for Swift and his *Gulliver's Travels*, in which there is a reference, plain as day, to the two small satellites of Mars including all the elements of their motion, which no one could have known at the time—that was the result of an idiotic mistake. The orbital data for the moons of

Mars served, then, as a secret password among a group of our controllers in southern England and one of them, nearsighted, took Swift (at a tavern) for the new agent he was scheduled to meet with there; he didn't report his blunder, thinking that Swift had understood nothing of his words, however two years later (1726), in the first edition of *Gulliver's Travels*, we found an accurate description of both Martian moons; the password was immediately changed, but that passage had to stay the way it was, in print.

Nevertheless these, ultimately, were trifling matters, of no great consequence; with Plato it was different; I am always overcome with pity when I read his story of the cave, in which one sits with one's back to the world, seeing just its shadow on the wall. Is it so surprising that he should have felt the 27th century to be the only true reality, and the primitive age in which I had imprisoned him—a "gloomy cave"? And his doctrine of knowledge as naught but the "self-recollection" of that which once, "before life," was known far *better*, is an allusion even more obvious.

Meanwhile things were going from bad to worse. I had to drop Kahn because he helped Napoleon escape from Elba; this time I chose Mongolia as the place of exile, for he was hopping mad and swore that I'd remember him; what trouble the man could cause me out in that wilderness I couldn't imagine, and yet he kept his word. Seeing what the situation was, our designers tried to outdo each other in coming up with harebrained schemes. For example, to supply impoverished nations with masses of goods via giant time mains—but that would have stopped all progress. Or, again, to take a million or so enlightened citizens from our modern day and deposit them, like an army, in the Paleolithic; fine, only what was I supposed to do with the people already sitting there in their caves?

Reading these plans aroused my suspicions when I looked more closely at the 20th century. The means for mass annihilation, could they have been planted there? There were, I had heard, a couple of radicals at the Institute who wanted to twist time around in a circle, so that somewhere after the 21st century contemporaneity would merge with prehistory. In this way everything was to start out once more from the beginning, only better. A sick idea, bizarre, ridiculous, yet I saw what appeared to be the signs of preparations. Overgrowth demanded first the destruction of the existing civilization, a "return to Nature," and indeed, from the middle of the 20th century on you had a marked increase in antisocial behavior, kidnappings, bombings, young people growing shaggier by the year, and all the erotica coarsened, became bestial, hordes of hairy rag-wearers rendered earsplitting homage not to the Sun, perhaps, but to certain stars and superstars, there were clamorous calls for the abolition of technology, of science, even those futurologists considered to be scientists proclaimed—but who put them up to it?!—impending doom, decline, the end, here and there you even had (already) caves being built, though they were called—possibly to avoid recognition—shelters.

I decided to concentrate on the centuries that followed, for this whole business smacked of revolution, i.e. revolving time around in the opposite direction, precisely on the principle of the circle, but just then I was invited to attend a special session of the Research Committee. My friends told me privately that I would be tried there. This however didn't keep me from the performance of my duties. My final action was to settle the matter of a certain Adler, who while working as an inspection officer brought back with him from the 12th century a young girl he had carried off in broad daylight; overtaken in an open field before the gaping multitude, she was lifted up onto his chronocycle; they considered her a saint, and her abduction in time—as her Assumption. I should have gotten rid of Adler long before, he was a thorough brute, of an appearance unusually repulsive, looking like a gorilla with those deep-set eyes of his and the heavy jaw, but I didn't want people to think me prejudiced. Now however I sent him packing, and quite a distance too, to be safe—about 65,000 years back; he became a prehistoric Casanova and begat the Neanderthals.

I showed up at the meeting with my head held high, for my conscience was clear. It went on for more than ten hours; I sat and listened to accusation after accusation. They charged me with acting arbitrarily, with riding roughshod over the scholars, with disregarding the opinions of the experts, with favoritism towards Greece, with the fall of Rome, with the Julius Caesar incident (that too was a lie: I hadn't sent out any Brutus anywhere), with the Reichplatz affair, i.e. Cardinal Richelieu, with abuses in the MOIRA section and tempolice, with the popes and antipopes (actually, the "Dark Ages" were caused by Betterpart, who, with his predilection for the "iron hand" approach, had stuck so many informers in between the 8th and 9th centuries, that the result was mum's-the-word and cultural stagnation).

The recital of the bill of indictment, drawn up in 7000 separate clauses, amounted to a public reading of a textbook on world history. I was taken to task for Otto Noy, for the burning bush, Sodom and Gomorrah, for the Vikings, for the wheels on the war wagons in Asia Minor, for *no* wheels on the war wagons in South America, for the Crusades, for the slaughter of the Albigenses, Berthold Schwarz and his powder (and where was I supposed to put him, in antiquity? so they could get to grapeshot all the sooner?)—and so forth, on and on. Nothing suited the honorable Committee now, neither the Reformation nor the Counter Reformation, and the very same people who once had come running to me with *exactly* those proposals, swearing to their salutary nature (Rosenbeisser practically got down on his knees for permission to start the Reformation), now sat there, the very picture of innocence.

When asked, at the end, if I had anything to say in my defense, I replied that I had no intention of defending myself. History would judge us. Still, I couldn't resist one parting shot before relinquishing the floor. I observed, to wit, that whatever *progress*, whatever *good* the Past could show after the Project's efforts, was entirely owing to *me*. I was referring here to the positive results of the mass banishment policy I had initiated. It was *I* whom mankind had to thank for Homer, Plato, Aristotle, Bosković, Leonardo da Vinci, Bosch, Spinoza, and those nameless thousands who sustained human creativity throughout the centuries. However bitter was the fate of the exiles, they had had it coming to them, and yet at the same time they were able, thanks to me, to pay off their debt to history, for they furthered history the best they could—but only *after* their removal from high positions in the Project! On the other hand if anyone wished to know what the *experts* of the Project had been up to meanwhile, he could take a look at Mars, Jupiter, Venus, at the butchered Moon, he could go and see Atlantis buried at the bottom of the Atlantic, he could count the victims of two great glacial epochs, of plagues, epidemics, pestilences, wars, religious fanaticisms— in short, he could examine General History, which after "improvement" had become nothing but a battleground of melioristic schemes, a *chaos*, an *unholy mess*. History was the *victim* of the Institute, of its constant intrigues, connivings, confusion, shortsightedness, improvisation, incompetence, and if it had been up to me, I would have sent the whole epoch-making batch of them off to where the brontosaurs roamed free.

I hardly need tell you that my words met with a somewhat *sour* reception. Though this was supposed to have been the final plea, several more worthy temporalists requested to be heard—men like I. G. Noramus, Stu Pitt, M. Taguele, and Rosenbeisser too was there, yes, his worthy colleagues had managed to fetch him all the way from Byzantium. Knowing *ahead of time* the outcome of the voting to relieve me of my directorship, they had staged a "death on the field of battle" for Julian the Apostate (363), so eager was he to be present at this spectacle. But before he could speak I raised a point of order, to ask since when did Byzantine emperors have the right to participate in the Institute's proceedings. My question was ignored.

Rosenbeisser had come prepared, he must have received materials while still in Constantinople; the machination was as subtle as a ton of bricks, but they weren't even trying to conceal it. He accused me of amateurism, of pretending to know *music*, and this, with my atrocious ear, had resulted in seriously perverting the development of theoretical physics. Here was how, according to the Herr Professor, it had happened: upon conducting a remote-control survey of the intelligence of all the children at the turn of the 19th century, our Hyperputer had come up with a list of young boys who in early manhood would be capable of deriving the equivalence of matter and energy, vital for releasing the power of the atom. These were, among others, Pierre Solitaire, Trofim Odnokamenyak, John Singlestone, Masanari Kotsumutobiushuyoto, Aristides Monolapides and Giovanni Unopetra—besides little Albie Einstein. I had been so bold as to show favoritism to the latter, for I liked the way he played the violin; years later, because of that, the bombs were dropped on Japan.

Rosenbeisser was twisting the facts so shamelessly, it took my breath away. Violin-playing had nothing to do with the case. No, the bastard was simply trying to shift his own blame onto me. The Hyperputer, running prognostic simulations of sequels

o various events, had foreseen the atom bomb in Mussolini's
Italy for a theory of relativity from Unopetra, and a series of
even worse catastrophes for the other lads. I selected Einstein
because he was a good child; for that which developed afterwards with those atoms neither he nor I should have to answer.
Indeed, I had acted against the advice of Rosenbeisser, who recommended "the prophylactic denuding of the Earth of children of preschool age" in order that atomic energy be released
in the safe 21st century, and even introduced me to a chronoli-
cian who was ready to take on the job. Naturally I banished that
dangerous man at once—Harrid or Herrot was his name—to
Asia Minor, where he in fact committed a number of heinous
acts; they figured in one of the articles of indictment. Yet what
else could I have done with him? I had to send him to *some* time,
didn't I? But there's no point in my trying to refute that
mountain of trumped-up charges.

After the vote on my dismissal from the Project, Rosenbeisser ordered me to present myself forthwith at the office; I found
him already sitting at my desk, as acting director. And whom do
you think I saw there at his side? Why Goody, Gestirner, Astroianni, Starbuck, and the other deadwood too; Rosenbeisser
had already managed to spring them from their respective centuries. As for himself, the stay in Byzantium had done him a
world of good; lean and tan after his campaign against the Per-
sians, he had brought back coins with his own profile stamped on
them, gold brooches, signet rings, and a heap of finery, which he
was in the process of showing to his cronies, but quickly stuck
them in the drawer when I walked in, and puffed himself up,
and sat back, and spoke with a drawl, through his teeth, without
looking at me, like some sort of emperor. Barely able to keep
from gloating in triumph, he told me haughtily that I was free to
go home, provided I agreed to carry out a certain errand.
Namely: I was, when I got back, to persuade Ijon Tichy, the Ijon
Tichy who all this time had been staying at my house—to assume
the directorship of THEOHIPPIP.

A sudden flash of understanding pierced my brain. It was
only now that I realized why *I* of all people had been chosen to
act as envoy to my selfsame *self!* The Hyperputer's prognosis,
after all, remained in force, therefore no one was better suited
for the job of directing the Correction of the Past than I. So they

weren't doing this to be generous—as if they *cared*—but purely in their own self-interest; yes, of course, I. Tichy, who had originally talked me into this whole business, remained in the past and was living in my house. I understood, further, that the time loop would be closed only at the precise moment when I—*I*, this time—reached the library and, braking the chronocycle, knocked all the volumes off the shelf. The other Ijon would be in the kitchen, a skillet in his hand, caught off guard by my unexpected appearance, for I would now be playing the part of the *messenger from the future,* while he, the occupant of the house, would be the *recipient of the message.* The seeming paradox of the situation was a product of the inevitable relativity of time entailed by the mastering of chronomotive technology. The real perfidiousness of the plan devised by the Hyperputer lay in the fact that it had created a *double* loop in time: a little loop within a large. In the little loop, starting out, my duplicate and I went round and round until I finally agreed to leave for the future. But afterwards the large loop continued to remain open; this was the reason I hadn't understood, at the time, just how *he* had landed up in that future he claimed to come from.

In the little loop I had been constantly the earlier, and he the later Ijon Tichy. But now the roles would be reversed, seeing that the times were switched around: this time I was coming to him *from the future* as an emissary; he, presently the *previous me,* would in turn have to take command of the Project. In the final analysis, then, we were going to *change places in time.* The only thing I still couldn't figure out was why he hadn't let me in on this, back then in the kitchen, but suddenly that too was clear, for wasn't Rosenbeisser making me promise, on my sacred word of honor, not to reveal a thing of what had happened in the Project?

And if I refused to give him my word, instead of a chronocycle I'd be handed a pension and couldn't go anywhere. What was I to do? They knew, the devils, that I wouldn't refuse. I *would* have, had the candidate for my position been any other man, but how can one possibly not trust, as a successor, one's own self? So then, they had thought of even that eventuality in cooking up this clever little scheme of theirs!

Without honors, without fanfare, without so much as a single word of thanks, or any sort of sendoff ceremony, accompanied by the deathlike silence of my ex-colleagues, who only recently had been paying me nothing but compliments from morning till night, competing among themselves to regale my mental horizons with some new surprise, and who now all turned their backs as I walked past—I headed for the embarkation hall. Petty maliciousness had prompted my former subordinates to give me the most dilapidated chronocycle they could find. Now I knew why I would be unable to brake in time and unfailingly knock over all those bookshelves! But I was unruffled by this last of many indignities. And though the chronocycle shook dreadfully on the curves of time (these are the so-called turning points in history), for the stabilizers refused to work, I left the 27th century feeling no anger, no bitterness, thinking only of how the Teleotelechronistic-Historical Engineering to Optimize the Hyperputerized Implementation of Paleological Programming and Interplanetary Planning would fare—under my successor.

THE TWENTY-FIRST VOYAGE

Upon my return from the 27th century I sent I. Tichy off to Rosenbeisser, to take over the post vacated by me at THEOHIPPIP, which he did, though with the greatest reluctance, and then only after a week of scenes and running about in the little loop in time. This done, I found myself faced with a serious dilemma.

Say what you will, but personally I had had quite enough of improving history. At the same time it was entirely possible that that other Tichy would again make a mess of the whole Project and Rosenbeisser would send for me once more. I decided therefore not to wait around with folded hands but take off for the Galaxy, and the farther the better. I left in the greatest haste, afraid that MOIRA might try and stop me, but apparently things were at loose ends there after my departure, since no one took any particular interest in me somehow. Obviously I didn't want to run off just anywhere, so I brought along a pile of the latest guidebooks and also the annual supplement to the Galactic Almanac, which had grown in my absence. Having put a tidy number of parsecs between myself and the Sun, I felt safe at last, and started thumbing through this literature.

As I soon discovered, it contained quite a bit that was new. Here Dr. Hopfstosser, the brother of Hopfstosser the famous Tichologian, had worked out a periodic table of civilizations in the Universe—based on three principles which enabled one, in-

166

allibly, to locate highly advanced societies. These were the Laws
f Trash, of Noise, and of Spots. Every civilization at the
echnological stage gradually finds itself up to its ears in garbage,
which causes tremendous problems, until the dumps are moved
ut into cosmic space and put—moreover—in a specially desig-
ated orbit, to keep them from getting too much in the way of
he astronauts. In this fashion one obtains a growing ring of re-
use, and it is precisely its presence that indicates a higher level
f development.

However after a certain time the trash changes in character,
or with successive strides in intellectronics it becomes necessary
o dispose of ever greater quantities of obsolete computer
hardware, to which old probes, modules and satellites attach
themselves. These thinking junk heaps have no desire to spend
he rest of eternity revolving around in a ring of garbage and so
hey break away, filling up the regions about the planet, and
even its entire system. This stage leads to the pollution of the
environment—with *intelligence*. Different civilizations try to
ombat the problem in different ways; occasionally you have
yberneticide, e.g. special traps are placed in space—snares,
mines, lures for sentient flotsam and jetsam—but the effect of
uch measures couldn't be worse, since only the inferior garbage, inferior mentally, lets itself be caught, consequently this
actic actually selects out the more perceptive of the trash; these
band together in groups and gangs, organize raids and demon-
trations, and the demands they present are difficult to meet,
namely, spare parts and a place to settle down. If you refuse,
hey maliciously jam radio communications, interrupt programs,
broadcast their own announcements, as a result of which the
planet, in this phase, becomes surrounded by a zone of such sta-
ic and howling in the ether, you can't hear yourself think. It is
precisely by this crackling that one can detect, even at a great dis-
ance, civilizations plagued with intellectual pollution. Odd, how
ong it took the astronomers of Earth to figure out why the Universe, according to their radio telescopes, was so full of noise and
other senseless sounds; this is nothing more or less than interference produced by those abovementioned conflicts, which se-
iously impede the establishment of interstellar contact.

And finally—the sunspots, but sunspots of specific shape as
well as chemical composition, which can be determined spectro-

scopically; they betray the presence of the most advanced civilizations of all, those that have broken the Trash Barrier and the Noise Barrier too. The spots occur when enormous swarms of junk, accumulated over the ages, hurl themselves like moths into the fire of the local Sun, there to perish in mass self-immolation. This mania is induced by certain depressants, to whose influence everything that thinks electrically succumbs. The sowing of these deadly agents is unspeakably cruel, but then existence in our Universe—and especially the setting up of civilizations within it—is unfortunately a grim business and no picnic.

According to Doctor Hopfstosser, these three consecutive stages of development are an iron rule for all humanoid civilizations. As far as the others go, the good doctor's periodic table still shows certain gaps. This however was no hindrance to me since for understandable reasons I was interested primarily in the life of beings most like ourselves. So then, following the specifications published by Hopfstosser in the Almanac, I assembled an ASS-finder (Advanced Sidereal Societies) and before long had entered the great cluster of the Hyades. For it was from there that particularly strong jamming came, there that the greatest number of planets were encircled with belts of trash and there too that several suns were covered with dark eruptions having a spectrum of rare elements, which bore mute testimony to the annihilation of artificial intelligence.

And since the last issue of the Almanac provided photographs of the inhabitants of Dichotica, strikingly similar to people, it was on this planet that I decided to land. True, considering the considerable distance of 1000 light-years at which these pictures were taken radio-astronomically by Dr. Hopfstosser, they could have been a bit outdated. Nevertheless it was with great hopes that I approached Dichotica in a hyperbolic path and, assuming a circular orbit, requested permission to land.

Obtaining such permission is often a far more difficult thing than conquering the galactic void, since bureaucracy accompanies progress at a higher exponential rate than does navigation, therefore photon reactors, shields, supplies of fuel, oxygen etc., have much less importance than vouchers and receipts without which one can't even think of entry visas. Being an old hand at all of this, I was prepared for a long spell—possibly many months—of circling Dichotica, but not prepared for what I encountered.

The planet, as I was able to make out, resembled Earth in the blueness of its sky, was covered with oceans too, and furnished with three large and definitely populated continents: even at a distant perimeter I had to look sharp to thread my way between the different satellites, the sentinel type, the observational, the spying, prying, and those that just sat there quietly; the latter I gave as wide a berth as possible, taking no chances. There was no response to my petitions; three times I submitted an application, but no one demanded the televising of my papers, they only shot something at me from the continent shaped like a kidney, it was a kind of triumphal arch of synthetic boughs of holly, entwined with multicolored ribbons and streamers and bearing inscriptions—encouraging inscriptions it would appear, yet worded so vaguely that I decided against flying through the arch. The next continent, bristling with cities, fired a milky white cloud at me, some sort of powder it was, which befuddled all the computers on board in such a way that they immediately tried steering the ship into the Sun. I had to shut them off and switch over to manual control. The third land mass, apparently less urbanized, submerged in luxuriant vegetation, the largest of the three, shot off nothing in my direction, greeted me with nothing; so, finding a secluded spot, I threw on the brakes and carefully set the rocket down in a glen of picturesque hills and meadows overgrown with either turnips or sunflowers—it was hard to say at that altitude.

As usual, the door was stuck, heated up from the atmospheric friction, and I had to wait a good while before it could be opened. I put my head outside, filled my lungs with the fresh, invigorating air and cautiously set foot on this unknown world.

I found myself at the edge of what looked to be a cultivated field, except that what was growing on it had nothing in common with sunflowers or turnips; they weren't even plants, they were night tables, in other words a type of furniture. And as if that wasn't enough, here and there between them, in fairly even rows, stood cabinets and footstools. After a little thought I came to the conclusion that these were products of a biotic civilization. I had seen such things before. The apocalyptic visions that futurologists sometimes unfold before us, of a world choked with lethal fumes, filled with smoke, hopelessly trapped by the energy barrier, the thermal barrier, etc., they're complete non-sense: in the postindustrial phase of development one sees the rise of biotic engineering, which liquidates those kinds of prob-lems. Mastery of the secrets of life permits the production of synthetic seed, which can be planted in practically anything. You sprinkle a little water over it and grow what you need in no time at all. As to where the thing draws its information and energy to become a radio or cupboard, you needn't concern yourself, any more than we worry about how a spore acquires the strength and knowledge to sprout into a weed.

So it wasn't the field of cabinets and bedstands itself that surprised me, but the fact that they were totally denaturalized. The closest night table, when I tried to open it, nearly bit off my hand with its toothed drawer; the second one, growing beside it, quivered in the breeze like jellied meat, and one of the stools I walked past stuck out its leg and sent me sprawling. No, that wasn't at all how furniture was supposed to behave; there was clearly something wrong with this agriculture. Forging ahead, though now with the utmost care and keeping a finger on the trigger of my blaster, I came—at a slight depression in the terrain—upon a thicket in the style of Louis Quinze, out of which there leaped a wild settee and would have surely trampled me with its gilded hooves had I not floored it with a well-aimed shot. I wandered for a time between clumps of furniture suites that exhibited hybridization not only of styles, but of functions; crossbreeds ran riot there, credenzas with ottomans, branching buffets, and the wardrobes, thrown wide open as if inviting one to step inside, they were probably predators, judging by the half-eaten scraps at their feet.

I could see now that this was no crop, but pure chaos. Weary and suffering from the heat, for the sun was at its zenith, I found after several unsuccessful tries a remarkably quiet armchair and sat in it, to gather my thoughts. I was sitting there, in the shade of a bunch of large though wild commodes, which had sprouted numerous hangers, when not more than a hundred feet away a head emerged from between some high swaying cornices, and after the head, the trunk of some creature. It didn't look to me like a man, but on the other hand definitely had nothing to do with furniture. It stood erect, covered with glossy blond fur, the face I couldn't see, its broad-rimmed hat was in the way; in place of a belly it had what seemed to be a tambourine, the arms were tapered, ending in double hands; humming softly, it accompanied itself on that abdominal drum, or whatever. It took a step forward, then another, revealing its continuation. The thing resembled a centaur now, though barefoot and without hooves; then a third pair of legs appeared behind the second, and then a fourth, but when it went bounding off into the brush and disappeared from view, I lost count. There were less than a hundred though, that much I knew.

I sat back in my upholstered chair, not a little stunned by this strange encounter, but finally got up and went on, taking care not to stray too far from the rocket. Among some full-grown sofas, all standing on end, I saw a pile of stone rubble, and farther on—the opening of an ordinary storm drain. As I drew closer in order to peer into its dark interior, I heard a rustling behind me, I started to turn around, but a sheet dropped over my head, I struggled—in vain, for arms of steel now held me fast. Someone kicked the legs out from under me; twisting helplessly, I felt myself being lifted up, then grasped by the shoulders and ankles. They carried me downwards it seemed, I could hear the sound of steps on flagstones, the creaking of a door, then I was thrown on my knees and the smothering fabric torn from my head.

I was in a small chamber lit with white bulbs attached to the ceiling—these also had whiskers and little feet, and from time to time would change their position. Someone standing over me held me by the neck, forcing me to kneel before a rough-hewn table. Behind it sat a figure in a gray hood, which covered his face completely; the hood had holes for the eyes, fitted with transparent panes. This figure, putting aside a book he had been reading, gave me a passing glance and said calmly to the one who kept me in his grip:

"Pull its cord."

Someone grabbed my ear and pulled until I yelped with pain. Two more times they tried to tear off my lobe, and when it wouldn't come, there was much consternation. The one who had been holding me and pulling, similarly swathed in coarse gray cloth, said in an apologetic tone that this was evidently a new model. Another thug came up and attempted, in turn, to screw off my nose, my eyebrows, finally the whole head; when that too failed to give the desired results, the seated one ordered me released and asked:

"How deep are you hidden?"

"How—what?" I asked, dumbfounded. "I'm not hiding anywhere and don't understand a thing. Why are you torturing me?"

At that point the seated one stood up, came around the table and took me by the shoulders—his hands were human, but in linen gloves. Feeling my bones, he gave a small cry of astonishment. At a given signal I was taken down a corridor where the light bulbs were crawling along the ceiling clearly bored, and into another cell, more precisely a cubicle, and black as a tomb. I didn't want to enter it, but they shoved me in anyway and slammed the door. Something buzzed, and from behind an invisible partition I heard a voice exclaim, as if in heavenly ecstasy: "What lovely bones! What lovely little bones!" After hearing this, I put up an even greater struggle when they dragged me from that closet, but seeing how they now treated me with unexpected deference, respectfully bowing and gesturing for me to follow, I let myself be led deep into a subterranean passageway, remarkably like a city sewer main, though it was all scrubbed clean, with the walls whitewashed and the bottom sprinkled with fine white sand. My hands were now free and as we walked I rubbed all the injured places on my face and body.

Two individuals in gray floor-length cowls girded with rope opened a door made of rough boards, and there inside the cell, which was somewhat larger than the one where they had tried to twist my nose and ears off, stood a hooded man, clearly moved at the sight of me. After fifteen minutes of conversation I formed more or less the following picture of the situation: I was in the monastery of a local religious order, which either was hiding from some unknown persecution or else had been outlawed; they had mistaken me for an "entrapment" decoy, since my appearance, being an object of veneration to the Demolitian Friars, was prohibited by law. The prior, for it was the prior with whom I spoke, explained that had I in fact been a decoy, I would have been composed of segments which, upon the pulling of the inner cord (attached to the ear), should have fallen into little pieces. As for the second question which the interrogating monk (the elder brother gatekeeper) had put to me, he had thought that I represented a type of plastic manikin with a built-in pocket computer; it was only the x-rays that revealed the truth.

The prior, Father Dyzz Darg, apologized profusely for the results of that unfortunate misunderstanding and added that he was returning me my freedom, but didn't advise going out on the surface, where I would surely find myself in serious danger—for I was censorable in my entirety. Nor would being fitted with a bowel sac and retractable liver stalks render me safe, untutored as I was in the use of such camouflage. The best thing for me to do, therefore, was to stay with the Demolitian Friars as their esteemed and welcome guest; to the extent of their all-too-modest abilities, they would try to make my confinement as unburdensome as possible.

I wasn't particularly happy about this arrangement, yet the prior inspired my confidence with his stately bearing, his serenity, the pith of his utterances, though indeed I couldn't accustom myself to his masked appearance, for he was dressed as all the other monks. I was hesitant to ply him with questions all at once, so we talked about the weather on Earth and on Dichotica—I had already told him whence I came—and then too about the tedium of cosmic travel, finally he said that he could well imagine my curiosity concerning local affairs, however there was no real hurry, seeing as how I was obliged in any case to hide myself from the long arm of the censor. I would receive, as an honored guest, his own cell, also a novice to provide whatever assistance or advice was necessary, besides which the entire monastic library stood open to me. And since it contained innumerable prohibita and incunabula found on blacklists and Indexes, the accident which had brought me to these catacombs might profit me more than if I had landed elsewhere.

I thought that we would part company now, for the prior rose, but instead he asked, almost timidly, if I would permit him—as he put it—to touch my actual person. With a deep sigh, as if in an excess of the greatest sorrow or some unfathomable regret, he placed his hard gloved fingers upon my nose, forehead, cheeks, and as he stroked my hair (I had the impression that the hand of that holy man was made of iron) he even started softly sobbing. These signs of pent emotion bewildered me completely. I didn't know what to ask first, whether about the furniture run wild, or the centaur with the many legs, or this censorship he spoke of, but prudently restraining myself, I said nothing. The prior assured me that the brothers of the order would see to the camouflaging of my rocket, making it resemble organs suffering from elephantiasis, whereupon we parted with an exchange of civilities.

The cell I received was small but homey, with a bed—unfortunately—as hard as the devil. I assumed that this was the sort of stern rule the Demolitian Friars had, but it turned out later that they simply forgot to put down a pallet for me. So far I felt no other hunger than that for information; the young novice under whose charge I was brought me whole armfuls of historical and philosophical works; I pored over these till late at night. My reading was hampered at first by the fact that the lamp would sometimes come over, and sometimes leave for another corner of the room. Later on I learned that it went off to relieve itself but would return to its former position when whistled for.

The novice suggested I begin with a short but instructive outline of Dichotican history penned by one Abuz Gragz, the official historiographer, yet "objective enough for all that," as he put it. I followed this counsel.

As recently as the year 2300 the Dichoticans were the exact counterpart of people. Though progress in the sciences was indeed accompanied by the secularization of life, Duism, a faith that had reigned practically unopposed for twenty centuries on Dichotica, left its mark on the subsequent course of civilization as well. Duism holds that every life knows *two* deaths, the one ahead and the one behind, or in other words that before birth and that following the final breath. The Dichotican theologians, later, would throw up their hands in amazement upon hearing from me that on Earth we didn't think in this fashion, that there were churches which concerned themselves with one thing only, namely the hereafter ahead; that it was upsetting for people to think that someday they would be no longer, but not equally upsetting for them to consider the fact that earlier they had never been. This the good friars could not understand.

Duism had modified its doctrine in the space of a hundred years, but throughout maintained a lively interest in eschatological problems, and this was what led, in the lifetime of Professor

174

Gragz, to the first attempts to launch an immortalization technology. As everyone knows, we die because we age, and we age, that is we undergo physical breakdown—through the loss of vital information; our cells in time forget how not to decay. Nature keeps only the germ cells supplied with this knowledge, for the others are of absolutely no concern to her. Aging, then, is the depletion of information essential for the maintenance of life.

Braddag Fizz, inventor of the first perpetuator, constructed a unit which, tending the human organism (I use the term "human" here, in speaking of the Dichoticans, purely for the sake of convenience), gathered every scrap of information lost by the somatic cells and instantly restored the same to them. The first Dichotican—Dgunder Brabz—on whom eternitization was performed, became immortal for only a year. Longer than that he couldn't hold out, for a battery of sixty machines watched over him, penetrating every nook and cranny of his being with countless gold electrodes. Unable to move a muscle, he led a pitiful existence in the midst of a veritable factory (an "imperpetuitron"). Dobder Gwarg, the next immortal, could indeed walk about, though he was accompanied on his strolls by a column of heavy tractors laden with the necessary immortalizing equipment. He too committed suicide out of frustration.

Still the prevailing opinion was that with continued technological progress microperpetuators would eventually be developed, Haz Berdergar however demonstrated mathematically that a PUBE (Personal Umbilico-Bioeternitizer Ensemble) at the very least had to weigh 169 times more than the one perpetuated, to the extent of course that the latter conformed to a typically evolutional design. This because, as I said before and as even our own scientists know, Nature is solicitous about a handful of reproductive cells in each individual, and the rest can go hang.

Haz's Proof made a powerful impression and plunged society deep into despair, for it was understood that the Mortality Barrier could not be crossed without at the same time abandoning the body which Nature had provided. In philosophy one reaction to Haz's Proof was the famous doctrine of that great Dichotican sage Donderwarg. Spontaneous death, he wrote, can hardly be called natural. Natural is that which is fitting, mortality

175

on the other hand constitutes an outrage, a disgrace of truly cosmic proportions. The commonness of the offense in no way mitigates its enormity. Nor, in assessing the offense, does it make the least difference whether or not the perpetrator can be apprehended. Nature has dealt with us deceitfully, sending innocent people off on a mission purportedly pleasant—in reality hopeless. In life the more one gains in wisdom, the nearer one draws to the pit.

No decent person ought associate with murderers, by the same token any collaboration with that greatest of criminals—Nature—is inexcusable. Yet what is burial but collaboration through a game of hide-and-seek? The point being to dispose of the body, as accomplices are wont to do; on the tombstones various inconsequential things are written, save the only one that is material: for if people would but dare to look the truth in the eye, they would be carving there instead a couple of the more pungent profanities, addressed to Mother Nature, for it is she who got us into this. Meanwhile no one breathes a word, as if a murderer clever enough always to get away with it deserved, for that, some special consideration. Not "memento mori" but "Estote ultores," onward to immortality, that should be the cry, even if it means parting with our traditional appearance. Such was the ontological testament of that eminent philosopher.

As I finished reading this, the novice appeared, to invite me on behalf of the prior to partake of their humble fare. I dined in the prior's exclusive company. Father Darg himself ate nothing, but only now and then sipped water from a crystal goblet. The repast was modest, table leg stew—a bit stringy. It seemed clear to me then that the furniture of the adjoining countryside, growing wild, turned predominantly to flesh. However I didn't ask why it wouldn't sooner turn to wood—the reading had set my mind on higher matters; thus came about my first conversation with the prior. The topic was theology.

He explained to me that Duism is a belief in God divested of all dogma, its articles of faith having been one by one destroyed in the course of various biotic revolutions. The Church's most difficult crisis was brought on by the crumbling of the dogma of the immortal soul, immortal in the sense of the prospect of an everlasting life. In the 25th century this dogma was challenged by three successive technologies: the refrigerational, the reversional, and the psychoinceptive. The first consisted in turning a man into ice, the second in reversing the direction of an individual organism's development, and the third—in the free manipulation of mind. The cryostatic challenge could be refuted easily enough by maintaining that the death into which a person fell when frozen, but was later revived, was not the death of which the Holy Scriptures spoke, where afterwards the soul flies off into the great beyond. Indeed, there was no other possible interpretation, for if we were dealing here with ordinary death, then obviously a resurrectee should have some knowledge of where he had been—in spirit—during the hundred or six hundred years of his decease.

Some theologians, e.g. Gauger Drebdar, felt that true death took place only upon decomposition ("and unto dust shalt thou return"), however this version didn't hold up, what with the introduction of the so-called revivificational field, which could put together a living man precisely out of dust, i.e. from a body reduced to atoms, for in that case too the one revivified had absolutely no knowledge of his soul going anywhere in the interim. The dogma was preserved, then, only through the careful avoidance of any designation as to when death was sufficiently out-and-out for one to say, with certainty, that the soul had left the body. But then came reversible ontogeny; it hadn't been intentionally leveled at religious doctrine, but proved invaluable for the removal of defects in fetal development: science had learned how to arrest this development and back it up, turning it around 180 degrees, in order to begin once more from the fertilized cell. Then suddenly the dogma of immaculate conception as well as that of the immortal soul were in serious trouble, and both at one blow, for thanks to retroembryological techniques it was now possible to move any specimen back through all its previous stages, and even to make the fertilized cell from which it sprang divide back into an egg and sperm.

This presented quite a problem, for according to dogma God created the soul at the moment of conception, but if one could reverse conception and thereby annul it, separating both its components, what then happened to the already created soul? One spin-off of this technology was cloning, that is, the inducing of any cell whatever, taken from the living body, say, from the nose, the heel, the lining of the palate, etc., to develop into a

177

normal organism; and as this took place entirely without fertilization, we clearly had here the bioengineering of immaculate conception, which in due course was commercialized and applied on a mass scale. Embryogeny by now could also be slowed down, stepped up or deflected in such a way, as to turn the human fetus—for instance—into something simian. And what of the soul then, was it compressed and drawn out like an accordion, or, in the switching of the embryo from the human to the simian track, did it simply disappear somewhere along the line?

But dogma said that the soul, once created, could neither disappear nor be diminished, for it was an entity unto itself and indivisible. Consideration was already being given to the possibility of excommunicating these prenatal engineers, this however was not done, and rightly too, for ectogenesis had now become widespread. First no one to speak of, then no one at all was born of man and woman, but instead from a cell implanted in a uterator (an artificial womb), and one could hardly deny all humankind the sacraments on the grounds that it arose parthenogenetically, i.e. by virgin birth. Then along came, on top of this, the next technology—that of consciousness. The problem of the Ghost in the Machine, posed by intellectronics and its thinking computers, could be dealt with more or less, but it was followed by other problems, by minds and intelligences in liquids. Sentient, reasoning solutions were synthesized, and these could be bottled, poured, mixed, and after each time you ended up with a new personality, one often more spiritual and wiser than all the Dichoticans put together.

The question of whether a machine or fluid could possess a soul was the subject of much heated debate at the Ecumenical Council of 2479, till finally they promulgated there a new dogma, the dogma of Secondhand Creation, which stated that God had invested the intelligent beings of His making with the power to engender intelligence twice removed. But even that wasn't an end to the transmutations, for it soon turned out that artificial mentalities could themselves produce others, successors, or even synthesize for reasons of their own not only creatures of humanoid appearance, but perfectly real people, using any old pile of material for that purpose. There were other attempts made later on to preserve the dogma of immortality, but these collapsed beneath the onslaught of subsequent discoveries, which in a veritable avalanche descended upon the 26th century; no sooner would a new interpretation be offered to bolster the beleaguered dogma, than a new technology arose to negate it.

This led to a number of heresies and the springing up of sects, all of which stood in direct contradiction to universally acknowledged facts, meanwhile the Duistic Church kept in force one dogma only, that of Secondhand Creation, but as far as life after death went, and faith in the continuation of personal identity, it was no longer possible to stave off defeat, since neither personality nor individuality remained intact in *this* world. You could now mix two or more minds into one, with machines and solutions, and with people too; you could—thanks to functional noetics—produce whole worlds inside machines, worlds that gave rise to intelligent beings, beings which in turn were able within the confines of their prison to construct yet another generation of sentient entities; you could expand mentality, divide it, multiply it, factor it, retract it, and so on. The decline of dogma spelt the decline of the Church's authority; hope in the world to come, despite assurances given earlier, was extinguished, at least for individual persons.

Seeing that theological progress wasn't keeping up with technological, the Council of 2542 established the order of the Prognosticants, who were to engage in futurological research in the area of the holy faith. For the need to anticipate its further vicissitudes was pressing. The amorality of many new biotechniques alarmed not only the true believers; with modern cloning methods, for example, it was possible to produce—besides normal individuals—biological beings that were practically brainless, thus fit for mechanical tasks; possible even to upholster rooms and walls with suitably cultivated tissues that came from human or animal bodies; possible also to produce inserts, plugs, amplifiers as well as modulators of intelligence; to create states of mystical transport in a computer, in a fluid; to take a frog's egg and turn it into a sage with the body of a man, or a sage with the body of an animal hitherto unknown, being specially designed by the experts in fetal architecture. There was strong opposition, and from secular quarters too, but to no avail.

All this Father Darg related with the utmost tranquility, as though he spoke of self-evident things, indeed for him they were self-evident, belonging as they did to Dichotican history. Countless questions came rushing to my lips, yet I did not wish to seem importunate, and so, retiring to my cell after supper, I sat down with the second volume of professor A. Gragz's work. This one, as the annotation on the first page indicated, was forbidden.

I learned that in the year 2401 Byg Brogar, Dyrr Daagard and Merr Drr threw open the gates to limitless autoevolutionary freedom; these scholars earnestly believed that Homo Autofac Sapiens, the Self-made Man, made possible by their discovery, would achieve the ultimate in harmony and happiness, endowing himself with those aspects of form and qualities of spirit he judged to be most perfect, and break the Mortality Barrier itself if he so desired. In short, they displayed throughout the Second Biotic Revolution (it was to the first that we owed the seminal production of consumer goods), the kind of wild-eyed optimism so common in the history of science. For such hopes usually attend the appearance of any great and new technology.

At first autoevolutionary engineering, or—as they called it—the Fetalistic Movement, burgeoned in a way that seemed to accord with the expectations of its illustrious inventors. Ideals in health, congruity, spiritual and physical beauty became universalized, by constitutional law every citizen was guaranteed the right to acquire whatever psychic or somatic attributes were deemed the most desirable. Soon, too, all deformities and congenital defects, all ugliness and stupidity were rendered obsolete. But progress has this about it, that it is driven ever onward by its own advance, hence things did not stop there. The transformations that followed seemed innocent enough at the outset. Young women beautified themselves by the cultivation of epidermal jewelry and other efflorescences of the flesh (valentine ears, cuticle pearls), young men sported side and back beards, cockscomb crests, jaws with double bites, etc.

Twenty years later the first majority parties came into being. It took a while before I realized, reading, that "majority party" meant something different on Dichotica than it did to us. In opposition to the majority party platform, that called for the proliferation of anatomies, there was the minority group, which advocated reductionism, that is, the elimination of those organs considered by the minority leaders of various factions to be nonvital. I had just gotten to this fascinating place in the text, when suddenly my novice burst into the cell without knocking and, betraying great agitation, told me to collect my things at once, for the brother gatekeeper had sounded the alarm. I inquired what the trouble was; but he urged me to hurry, crying that there wasn't a moment to lose. I had no personal effects, only the book, so putting it under my arm I ran after my guide.

In the underground refectory all the Demolitian Friars were working at a fever pitch; down a stone spout tumbled heaps of books, pushed from above by brethren librarians with poles, then loaded into vessels and with the greatest haste lowered down a well cut out of solid rock; before my very eyes the monks then stripped themselves naked and, as quickly as possible, threw their frocks and cowls also in the stone-cased opening; they were robots, all of them, and only roughly humanoid in form. Next they set to work on me, crowding around, gluing to my body strange appendages, balloon-shaped, snakelike, tails or limbs—I couldn't tell which, so swiftly was it done. The prior himself set on my head a bowel sac, which looked somewhat like a blown-up, split-open cockroach; some were still gluing, others had begun painting me with bands or stripes; there being no mirror around nor shiny surface, I couldn't see myself, but they seemed pleased with the overall effect.

Given a shove, I found myself in a corner, it was only then that I noticed I resembled more a quadruped, or perhaps even a sextuped, than any upright being. They told me to stay squatted and answer all questions, in the event that any were asked of me, with a baa. The next thing I knew, there was a fearful pounding at the door; the robot friars rushed over to some sort of apparatuses that had been dragged out into the middle of the refectory and which resembled (though not really) sewing machines, then the entire room was filled with the din of their simulated labor. Down the stone steps and towards us walked the inspectors. I nearly fell off all four of my feet when I got a good look at them. I didn't know whether they were clothed or naked; each produced an altogether different impression.

All, I believe, had tails, tails that ended in a tuft of hair concealing a sizable fist; they carried them, as a rule, carelessly slung over the shoulder—to the extent that one could call a bulbous protuberance encircled with huge warts a shoulder; the skin in the middle of this bulge was white as milk; on it appeared stigmata in various colors—after a while I realized that they communicated not only by voice, but also by flashing, on that body screen of theirs, different captions and abbreviations. I tried counting their legs (?) and found that they had a minimum of two apiece, though there were also a couple of three-leggers and a fiver; it did seem however that the greater number of legs one had, the more he tended to trip. They went poking around the entire hall, examining the monks in a perfunctory way as the latter hunched over their machines and worked with the utmost intensity, till finally the head inspector, taller than the rest, and with an enormous orange membrane atop his bowel sac, which distended and glowed feebly when he spoke, ordered the short one—barely a biped, and with a skimpy tail: a clerk, no doubt—to have a look at the fripple winches. They jotted something down, took measurements, this without so much as a word to the robot friars, and were about to leave, when a greenish three-legger took notice of me; he tugged at one of my fringed extremities, so just in case I gave a quiet bleat.

"Eh, it's that old thumnist, he's certified bugs, let him be!" said the big one, brightening, and the little one quickly replied:

"Very good, Your Bodyship!"

With an instrument similar to a flashlight they made another tour of the refectory, but didn't even bother with the well. More and more this looked to me like the carrying out of a formality. Ten minutes later they were gone, the machines went off into a dark corner, the monks began hoisting up the vessels wrung out their soaking frocks, then hung them on a line to dry the brother librarians shook their heads ruefully, for water had gotten into one of the leaky barrels, which meant they immediately had to sandwich blotting paper in between the soaked pages of those ancient texts; meanwhile the prior—that is, the father robot—I no longer knew just how or what to think of him—approached me with a smile and said that everything praise be, had ended well, but in the future I must watch myself here he pointed to the history book I had dropped in the general confusion. He himself had sat on it during the entire search.

"Then the possession of books is forbidden?" I asked.

"It depends on who is doing the possessing," said the prior "For us, yes! And especially those kinds of books! We are looked upon as old machines, unneeded ever since the First Biotic Re

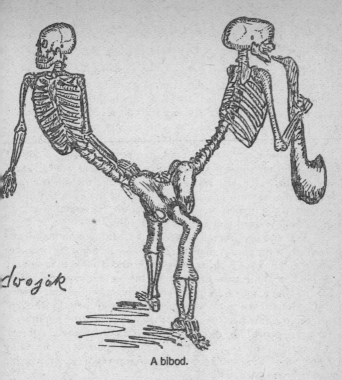

dvořák

A bibod.

volution; they tolerate us, like everything else here in the
catacombs, for such has been the custom—unofficial, mind
you—since the reign of Glaubon."

"And what is a 'thumnist'?" I asked.

The prior seemed embarrassed.

"A follower of Bzugis Thumn, who governed some ninety
years ago. It's awkward for me to speak of this . . . an unfortunate thumnist did seek refuge among us, and so we took him in;
he always sat in that corner, pretended—poor man—not to be in
his right mind; thanks to which he was never held accountable
and could say what he liked . . . last month he had himself frozen, to wait for 'better days' . . . so I thought that, in case of an
emergency you understand, we might dress you up . . . yes? . . . I

was going to tell you, but didn't have the chance. I didn't expect a search so soon, they are irregular, but as of late fairly infrequent . . ."

Of this I understood not a word. At any rate I was now in store for a great deal of unpleasantness, since the glue used by the Demolitian Friars to disguise me as that thumnist held like the dickens and it felt as if they were pulling off those artificial wattle flaps and liver stalks along with pieces of my own flesh; I sweated, I groaned, till finally, more or less restored to human form, I turned in for the night. Later on, the prior suggested that I could be physically altered, in a reversible way of course, but when they showed me a picture of how that would look, I decided instead to risk remaining censorable; the officially prescribed shapes were not only monstrous in my eyes, but inconvenient in the highest degree. Lying down, for example, was an impossibility: one hung oneself up at night.

As it was late when I turned in, I hadn't gotten the proper sleep when my young guardian awoke me by bringing breakfast into the cell. Now I understood better the trouble they went to on my account, for the brethren themselves ate nothing, and as for the water, they were probably battery-powered and needed distilled, but even so a few drops would hold them for the day, while in order to provide for me they had to venture out into the furniture grove. The dish this time was a well prepared armrest; if I say well prepared, it isn't that it tasted good, but while eating I now made allowances for all the circumstances accompanying that culinary endeavor.

Still under the strong impression of last night's raid, I was unable to connect it with what I had read so far in the history book, therefore immediately after breakfast I returned to my studies.

From the very beginning of autoevolution the camp of progressive anatomy was torn by sharp differences of opinion on basic issues. Conservative opposition had vanished a mere forty years after the moment of the great discovery; conservatives were now considered gloomy reactionaries. The progressives meanwhile had divided into the overnighters, the step-at-a-timers, the changelings, transmutes, effluvians, and many other parties whose names and platforms I cannot recall. The overnighters wanted the government to decide on a perfect anatomical prototype and put it into law at once. The step-at-a-timers, more critically inclined, felt that perfection could not be achieved in one fell swoop and therefore favored a deliberate approach to the ideal body, though it was not at all clear what course that approach ought to take, and above all, could it be—for the intervening generations—*disagreeable*? On this point they split into two factions. Others, like the transmutes and the changelings, maintained that there was merit in looking different for different occasions, and also, that man was no worse than the insects—if *they* could undergo several metamorphoses

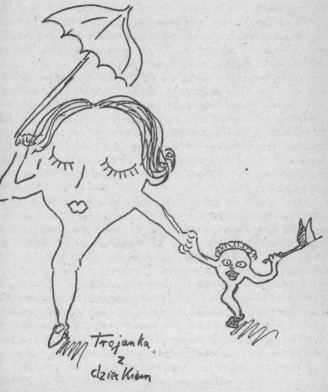

Tribodice with child.

in a single lifetime, then why not he? A child, an adolescent, a young man, an older man could all personify fundamentally distinct designs. And as for the effluvians, they were the radicals: condemning the skeleton as hopelessly outmoded, they called for an end to all vertebrae and endorsed complete plasticity. An effluvian could physically shape or unshape himself at will; this was certainly practical in crowds, and also with regard to ready-made clothing of different sizes; some of them kneaded and rolled themselves out into the most peculiar forms, wishing to express—according to the situation and particular mood— their self-enmembered selves. Their opponents in the body politic contemptuously referred to them as blobsters.

To meet the threat of anatomical anarchy SOPSYPLABD was brought into being, the Soma and Psyche Planning Board, whose job it was to put on the market a wide assortment, but all laboratory-tested, of transformational patterns. Yet still there was no agreement as far as the general direction of autoevolution went: should they make bodies in which life could be lived with the maximum pleasure, or bodies to facilitate the individual's full involvement in the social milieu, should they strive for functionalism, or for esthetic effect, enlarge the mind, or the muscles? It was fine to talk in generalities about harmony and perfection, at the same time experience showed that not all desirable qualities went together; quite a few of them were mutually exclusive.

In any case the break with natural man remained in force. The experts tried to outdo each other in proving the primitiveness, the utter shoddiness of Nature's handiwork; the analytical morphometry as well as the physiophysics of the day revealed, in its literature, the clear influence of Donderwarg's doctrine. The unreliability of the natural body, its relentless movement towards senescence and death, the tyranny of ancient drives over the late arriving reason—all this was subjected to scathing criticism, and the press waxed indignant over fallen arches, tumors, slipped disks, and a thousand other afflictions caused by evolution's bungling and incompetence, which was called the underhanded work of wasteful, unprincipled, self-defeating heredity and its blind accomplice, natural selection.

Modern descendants appeared to be taking revenge on Nature for the dismal silence with which their forefathers had had to swallow the news that Dichoticans descended from the apes; they jeered at the so-called arboreal period, the fact that first some animals had started hiding out in trees, and later, when the forests gave way before the steppes, they had to come back down too soon. According to some critics, it was earthquakes that initiated anthropogenesis, making them all jump from their branches, in other words the first people were shaken out of trees like rotten fruit. Gross oversimplifications of course, but then ridiculing evolution was the thing to do. Meanwhile SOPSYPLABD had perfected the internal organs, put shock absorbers on the backbone, fortified it too, attached spare hearts, kidneys, but this didn't satisfy the extremists, who came forward with such demagogic slogans as "off with the head" (too small for them), "brain in the belly!" (more room there), etc.

The most violent disputes had to do with sexuality, for while some thought that all *that* was highly distasteful and one ought to borrow here from the flowers and butterflies, others, pooh-poohing the hypocrisy of the platonists, demanded precisely the amplification and escalation of that which already was. Under pressure from radical groups SOPSYPLABD set up suggestion boxes in towns and villages, proposals came flooding in, the administrative staff expanded exponentially and in a decade bureaucracy had brought self-creativity to such a pass, that SOPSYPLABD was split up into associations, and then into agencies like the Office of Orifices (OO), the Lip Administration (LA), the Beautiful Figure Foundation (BUFF), the National Institute of Fingers and Toes (NIFTY), and many, many others. There were countless conferences and seminars on the question of extremities, on the future of the nose, the prospects for the sacroiliac, everyone losing sight of the totality, till finally what one section came up with didn't fit in with what the others had been doing. And no one now could keep abreast of the new problem, abbreviated GAD (Galloping Automorphic Deviation), so in order to put an end to all the confusion they turned the whole biotic operation over to the digital SOPSYPUTER.

With this concluded the second volume of the General History. As I was reaching for the next, into my cell came the novice, to invite me to lunch. I hesitated to eat in the presence of the father prior, for now I knew just what a courtesy that was on his part, and what a waste of precious time. The invitation however was so pressing, that I went at once. In the small refectory, alongside Father Darg, who was already waiting at the table, there stood a low cart, similar to the kind we use to carry luggage; this was Father Memnar, general of the order of the Prognosticants. I phrased that badly—it wasn't the cart, naturally, which was the priest and general of the order, but the cubic computer resting on its undercarriage. I don't believe I showed any rudeness by staring, neither was I at a loss for words during the introduction. Eating was awkward, but my organism required it. To help put me at my ease, the kindly prior drank water in tiny sips throughout the meal, and out of two crystal flagons at the same time, Father Memnar meanwhile muttered softly to himself—prayers, I thought, but when the conversation came round to theology once more, it turned out I was wrong.

"I believe," Father Memnar said to me, "and if my belief has basis, the One in whom I believe surely knows this in the absence of my official declarations. The mind has fashioned for itself in history many different models of God, holding each in turn to be the one and only truth, but this is a mistake, for modeling means codification, and a mystery codified ceases to be a mystery. The dogmas seem eternal only at the beginning of the stretching road of civilization. First they imagine God as the Angry Father, then as the Shepherd-Gardener, then as the Artist enamored of His Creation, therefore people had to play the respective roles of well-behaved children, obedient sheep, and finally that of enthralled audience. But it is infantile to think that God created in order that His creation bow and scrape from morning till night, in order that He be loved, in advance installments, for what will come Yonder, if Here happens not to be to one's liking, as though He were a virtuoso, and in exchange for repeated rounds of prayerful cheering prepared eternal encores to follow the terrestrial performance, in other words saving His best number for the falling of the mortal curtain. That theatrical version of Theodicy belongs to our dim and distant past.

"If God has omniscience, then He knows everything there is to know about me, and knew it moreover for a time immeasurably long, before I came forth out of oblivion. He knows also what He will decide regarding my—or your—fears and expectations, for He is no less perfectly informed about all His own future actions: otherwise He would not be omniscient. For Him no difference exists between the thought of a caveman and that of an intelligence which engineers will build a billion years from now, in a place where today there is nothing but lava and flame. Nor do I see why the external circumstances of a profession of faith should make much difference to Him, or—for that matter—whether it is homage someone offers, or a grudge. We do not consider Him a manufacturer, who waits for approbation from His product, since history has brought us to the point where thought genuinely natural in no way differs from thought artificially induced, which means that there is no distinction whatever between natural and artificial; *that* now lies behind us. You must remember that we can create beings and mentalities of any kind. We could for example give rise to creatures that derive mystic ecstasy from existence—we could do it through crystallization, cloning, or in a hundred other ways—and eventually in their adorations directed at the Transcendental there would materialize a purpose, a purpose characteristic of bygone prayer and worship. But this mass production of believers would be for us a pointless mockery. Remember, we do not beat our heads against the wall of any physical or inborn limitation to our desires, such walls we have torn down, and have stepped out into the realm of absolute creative freedom. Today a child can resurrect the dead, breathe life into the dust, into metal, destroy and kindle suns, for such technologies exist; the fact that not everyone has access to them is, as I think you will agree, unimportant from the theological point of view. Because the bounds of human agency, marked off with such precision in the Holy Book, have been attained unto and thereby violated. And the cruelty of the old restrictions is now replaced by the cruelty of their total absence. Yet we do not believe that the Creator hides His love from us behind the mask of both these alternative torments, putting us through the mill, as it were, in order to keep us guessing. Nor is it the Church's office to call both misfortunes—the bondage and the freedom—promissory notes, endorsed by revelation and to be paid, with interest, by the heavenly treasurer. The vision of heaven as a bank account and hell as a debtor's prison represents a momentary aberration in the history of the faith. Theodicy is not a course in sophistry to train defenders of the Good Lord, and faith doesn't mean telling people that everything will work out in the end. The Church changes, the faith changes, for both reside in history: one must therefore anticipate, and that is the task of our order."

These words confounded me. I asked how the Duistic religion reconciled what was happening on the planet (nothing good presumably, though I didn't as yet know what, having gotten no further than the 26th century in my reading) with the Sacred Writings (of which I was also ignorant)?

To this Father Memnar said, while the prior kept silent:

"Faith is, at one and the same time, absolutely necessary and altogether impossible. Impossible to fix once and for all, there being no dogma a mind can latch onto with the certainty of permanence. We defended the Holy Writ for twenty-five centuries, using tactical retreats, circuitous interpretations of the text, until we were defeated. No longer do we have the bookkeeper's vision of the Transcendental, God is neither the Tyrant, nor the Shepherd, nor the Artist, nor the Policeman, nor the Head Accountant of Existence. Belief in God has had to cast off every selfish motive, if only by virtue of the fact that it will never—not anywhere—be rewarded. If God were to prove capable of acting contrary to logic and reason, that would be a sad surprise indeed. Was it not He—for who else?—that gave us these logical forms of thought, without which we would know nothing? How then can we accept the notion that an act of faith requires the surrender of the logical mind? Why give us first the faculty of reason, only to do it violence by setting contradictions in its path?

"In order to mystify and make obscure? To lead us first to the conclusion that there is nothing Later On, then pull heaven out of a hat like some common magician? We hardly think so. Which is why we ask no favors of God in consideration of the faith we hold, we present Him with no demands, for we are finished and done with that theodicy based on the model of commercial transactions and payment in kind: I shall give thee being, thou shalt serve and praise me."

In that case—I asked with more and more insistence—just what exactly do you monks and theologians do, how do you relate to God when, if I understand you correctly, you preserve neither dogma, nor ritual, nor devotions?

"In having truly nothing," replied the general of the Prognosticants, "we have everything. Be so good, dear stranger, as to read the other volumes of our Dichotican history, and you will learn just what it means—to gain complete freedom in the realm of bodily and mental contrivance, made possible by both biotic revolutions. Now I consider it highly likely that deep within you find this spectacle amusing: that beings, flesh and blood like yourself, in acquiring ultimate control over their own selves, have, by the very fact that they can now take faith and *turn it on and off* inside them like a light bulb, lost that faith. A faith which meanwhile was taken over from them by their instruments, thinking instruments, for such were needed at a certain stage of industrialization. Today however we are obsolete, and yet it is we—useless metal in the eyes of those that live upstairs—who believe. They tolerate us, having more important matters on their bowel sacs, and the government permits us everything—everything, that is, except our faith."

"That's strange," I said. "You're not allowed to believe? Why?"

"It's quite simple. Belief is the only thing that cannot be taken from a conscious entity, so long as that entity consciously cleaves to it. The authorities could not only crush us, they could reprogram us completely out of our belief; they do not do this, I am sure, through contempt or else indifference. It is mastery that they want, pure and simple, and any gap in that mastery must represent to them its diminution. Therefore we keep our faith concealed. You asked of its nature. It is—one might say—completely naked, this faith of ours, and completely defenseless. We entertain no hopes, make no demands, requests, we count on nothing, we only believe.

"Put no more questions to me then, but give some thought instead to what a faith like mine must mean. If someone believes for certain reasons and on certain grounds, his faith loses its full sovereignty; that two and two are four I know right well and therefore need not have faith in it. But of God I know nothing, and therefore can *only* have faith. What does this faith give me? By the ancient reckoning, not a blessed thing. No longer is it the anodyne for the dread of extinction, no longer the heavenly courtier lobbying for salvation and against damnation. It does not allay the mind, tormented by the contradictions of existence; it does not smooth out those edges; I tell you—it is worthless! Which means it serves no end. We cannot even declare that *this* is the reason we believe, because such faith reduces to absurdity:

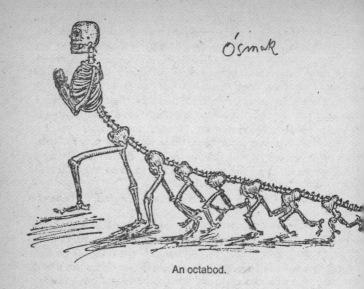

An octabod.

he who would speak thus is in effect claiming to know the difference—permanently—between the absurd and the not absurd, and has himself chosen the absurd because, according to him, that is the side on which God stands. We do not argue thus. Our act of faith is neither supplicating nor thankful, neither humble nor defiant, it simply *is*, and there is nothing more that can be said about it."

Much impressed by what I had heard, I returned to my cell and to my reading, the third volume now of Dichotican history. It described the Era of Transcarnal Centralization. The Sopsyputer at first worked to everyone's satisfaction, but then new beings began appearing on the planet—bibods, tribods, quadribods, then octabods, and finally those that had no intention whatever of ending in an enumerable way, for in the course of a life they were constantly sprouting something new. This was the result of a defect, a faulty reiteration-recursion in the program, or—to put it in layman's terms—the machine had started stuttering. Since however the cult of its perfection was in full sway, people actually praised these automorphic deviations, asserting

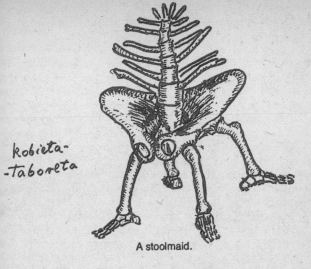

kobieta-
-taboreta

A stoolmaid.

for example that all that incessant budding and branching out was in fact the true expression of man's Protean nature. And this praise not only held up the repairs, but led to the rise of so-called indeterminants or entites (N-tites), who lost their way in their own body, there was so much of it; completely baffled, they would get themselves into so-called bindups, entangulums and snorls; often an ambulance squad was needed to untie them. The repair of the Sopsyputer didn't work—named the Oop-syputer, it was finally blown sky-high. The feeling of relief that followed didn't last long however, for the accursed question soon returned, What to do about the body now?

It was then, for the first time, that timid voices made themselves heard, Oughtn't we go back to the old look, but that suggestion was branded as obscurantist, medieval. In the elections of 2520 the Damn Wells and the Relativists came out on top, because their demagogic line caught on, to wit, that every man should look as he damn well pleased; limitations on looks would be functional only—the district body-building examiner approved designs that were existence-worthy, without concern

193

for anything else. These designs SOPSYPLABD threw on the market in droves. Historians call the period of automorphosis under the Sopsyputer the Age of Centralization, and the years that followed—Reempersonalizationalism.

The turning over of individual looks to private initiative led, after several decades, to a new crisis. True, a few philosophers had already come forward with the notion that the greater the progress, the more the crises, and that in the absence of crises one ought to produce them, because they activated, integrated, aroused the creative impulse, the lust for battle, and gave both spiritual and material energies direction. In a word, crises spurred societies to concerted action, and without them you had stagnation, decadence, and other symptoms of decay. These views were voiced by the school of "optessimists," i.e. philosophers who derived optimism for the future from a pessimistic appraisal of the present.

The period of private initiative in body building lasted three quarters of a century. At first there was much enjoyment taken in the newly won freedom of automorphosis, once again the young people led the way, the men with their gambrel thills and timbrels, the women with their pettifores, but before long a generation gap developed, and demonstrations—under the banner of asceticism—followed. The sons condemned their fathers for being interested only in making a living, for having a passive, often consumerist attitude towards the body, for their shallow hedonism, their vulgar pursuit of pleasure, and in order to disassociate themselves they assumed shapes deliberately hideous, uncomfortable beyond belief, downright nightmarish (the antleroons, wampdoodles). Showing their contempt for all things utilitarian, they set eyes in their armpits, and one group of young biotic activists made use of innumerable sound organs, specially grown (glottiphones, hawk pipes, knuckelodeons, thumbolas). They arranged mass concerts, in which the soloists—called hoot-howls—would whip up the crowd into a frenzy of convulsive percussion. Then came the fashion—the mania, rather—for long tentacles, which in caliber and strength of grip underwent escalation according to the typically adolescent, swaggering principle of "You haven't seen anything yet!" And, since no one could lift those piles of coils by himself, so-called processionals were attached, caudalettes, a selfperambulating receptacle that grew out of the small of the back and carried, on two strong shanks, the weight of the tentacles after their owner. In the textbook I found illustrations depicting men of fashion, behind whom walked tentacle-bearing processionals on parade; but this was already the decline of the protest movement, or more precisely its complete bankruptcy, because it had failed to pursue any goals of its own, being solely a rebellious reaction against the orgiastic baroque of the age.

This baroque had its apologists and theoreticians, who maintained that the body existed for the purpose of deriving the greatest amount of pleasure from the greatest number of sites simultaneously. Merg Brb, its leading exponent, argued that Nature had situated—and stingily at that—centers of pleasurable sensation in the body for the purpose of survival only; therefore no enjoyable experience was, by her decree, autonomous, but always served some end: the supplying of the organism with fluids, for example, or with carbohydrates or proteins, or the guaranteeing—through offspring—of the continuation of the species, etc. From this imposed pragmatism it was necessary to break away, totally; the passivity displayed up till now in bodily design was due to a lack of imagination and perspective. Epicurean or erotic delight?—all a paltry by-product in the satisfying of instinctive needs, in other words the tyranny of Nature. It wasn't enough to liberate sex—proof of that was ectogenesis—for sex had little future in it, from the combinatorial as well as from the constructional standpoint; whatever there was to think up in that department, had long ago been done, and the point of automorphic freedom didn't lie in simple-mindedly enlarging this or that, producing inflated imitations of the same old thing. No, we had to come up with completely new organs and members, whose sole function would be to make their possessor feel good, feel great, feel better all the time.

Brb received the enthusiastic support of a group of talented young designers from SOPSYPLABD, who invented brippets and gnools; these were announced with great fanfare, in ads which promised that the old pleasures of the palate and bedroom would be like picking one's nose in comparison with bripping and gnooling; ecstasy centers, of course, were implanted in the brain, programmed specially by nerve path engineers and hooked up, moreover, in series. Thus were created the brippive

195

and gnoolial drives, also activities corresponding to those instincts, activities with a highly rich and varied range, for one could gnool and brip alternately or at the same time, alone, in pairs, trios, and later—after noffles were tacked on—in groups of several dozen individuals as well. Also new forms of art came into being, master brippers appeared, and gnool artists, but that was only the beginning; towards the end of the 26th century you had the mannerism of the marchpusses, the muckledong was a tremendous hit, and the celebrated Ondor Stert, who could simultaneously gnool, brip and surpospulate while *flying through the air* on spinal wings, became the idol of millions.

At the height of the baroque, sex went out of style; only two small parties kept it going—the integrationalists and the separatists. The separatists, averse to all debauchery, felt that it was improper to eat sauerkraut with the same mouth one used to kiss one's sweetheart. For this a separate, "platonic" mouth was needed, and better yet, a complete set of them, variously designated (for relatives, for friends, and for that special person). The integrationalists, valuing utility above all else, worked in reverse, combining whatever was combinable to simplify the organism and life.

The decline of the baroque, typically tending to the extravagant and the grotesque, produced such curious forms as the stoolmaid and the hexus, which resembled a centaur, except that instead of hoofs it had four bare feet with the toes all facing one another: they also called it a syncopant, after a dance in which energetic stamping was the basic step. But the market now was glutted, exhausted. It was hard to come up with a startling new body; people used their natural horns for ear flaps; flap ears—diaphanous and with stigmatic scenes—fanned with their pale pinkness the cheeks of ladies of distinction; there were attempts to walk on supple pseudopodia; meanwhile SOPSYPLABD out of sheer inertia made more and more designs available, though everyone felt that all of this was drawing to a close.

Engrossed in my reading, with books scattered all about, and in the light of lamps that were crawling across the ceiling overhead, I fell asleep without realizing it; I was awakened only by the distant sound of the morning bell. Immediately my novice appeared, to ask if I might care for a change of scenery; if so, the prior invited me to join him on a tour of inspection of the entire diocese at the side of Father Memnar. I accepted. The prospect of leaving these gloomy catacombs delighted me.

Unfortunately the outing turned out differently than I imagined. We didn't go up on the surface at all; the monks, having outfitted for the trip some short pack animals covered with floor-length cloths as gray as the monastic frocks, sat upon them bareback and off we went, shuffling slowly down the subterranean corridor. These were, as I had earlier guessed, part of a sewer system, unused for centuries by the metropolis that soared above us in a thousand half-ruined edifices. The measured gait of my mount had something strange about it; nor could I discern, beneath its coverlet, any indication of a head; discreetly lifting a corner of the canvas, I saw that the thing was a machine, a four-footed robot of some sort, extremely primitive. By noon we had traveled less than twenty miles, though it was hard to gauge the distance covered, since the way twisted through a labyrinth of sewers, dimly lit by bulbs that sometimes fluttered in a small flock above us and sometimes, glancing off the concave ceiling, hurried to the head of the column, where they were being whistled for.

We arrived finally at the abode of the Prognosticant Friars, where we were received with honor. I in particular became the object of much attention. Since the furniture grove was now quite far, the good Prognosticants had to go to special trouble to prepare, with me in mind, a decent meal. This was provided by the stores of the deserted metropolis, in the form of packets of seeds; two bowls were placed before me, one empty, the other full of water, and for the first time I was able to see the products of a biotic civilization in action.

The friars apologized profusely for the lack of soup: the monk they'd sent to the surface by way of a well shaft had simply been unable to find the right package. However the cutlet turned out fine: the seed, with a few spoonfuls of water poured over it, expanded, flattened out, and in less than a minute I had on my plate a deliciously browned slice of veal, all in butter, which sizzled as it oozed from the pores of the meat. The store this tidbit came from must have been in total disarray, seeing as how in among the packets with gastronomic seeds others had gotten mixed: instead of dessert, what took shape on my plate was a tape recorder, and a useless one at that, because on its reels it had suspenders. It was explained to me that this sort of hybridization had become fairly common of late, since the vending machines—unsupervised—were turning out seeds of poorer and poorer quality; those biotic products can cross-breed, and that is precisely how one gets such freakish combinations. So then, finally I had learned the origin of the wild furniture.

The worthy friars wanted to send one of the younger novices back up into the ruins of the city for my dessert, but I objected strongly. I was far more interested in conversation than in dessert.

Their refectory, once a great purification plant for the city sewers, appeared to be spotlessly clean, strewn with white sand, lit up with numerous bulbs—which were different here than at the Demolitians, namely winking and striped, as if they derived from giant wasps. We sat at a long table, alternately, so that beside each Demolitian monk there rested the chassis of a Prognosticant; for some reason I felt embarrassed to be the only one with face and hands exposed—there among the masked figures of the robot brothers, those coarse cowls with glass over the eyeholes, and among the Father Computers, who, being rectangular, in no way resembled living creatures; a number of these were connected by electric cords beneath the table, however I hadn't the courage to inquire why they needed this additional channel of communication.

The conversation that developed during that solitary meal—for no one else was eating—turned once again, perforce, to transcendental things. I wished to know what the last believers of Dichotica thought on the subject of good and evil, God and the devil, but when I posed this question, there was a long silence, during which only the striped light bulbs buzzed softly in the corners of the refectory; though this might have been, too, the current of the Prognosticants.

At last an elderly Computer sitting opposite me—a specialist in religious history, as I later learned from Father Darg—spoke up.

"Getting straight to the point, I would put our views in the following way," he said. "Satan is that which we understand the least in God. This does not mean that we consider God Himself to be an alloy of elements, of the high and the low, good and evil, love and hate, the power of creation and the lust for destruction. Satan is the idea that God can be delimited, classified, isolated,

198

eparated by fractional distillation until He becomes that—and only that—which we are able to accept and need no longer defend ourselves against. An idea which is untenable inside history, because it leads inevitably to the conclusion that there is no knowledge but what derives from Satan, and that he will extend his influence until he has encompassed all that fosters knowledge, *in toto*. And this, because knowledge gradually nullifies the directives we call revealed commandments. It permits us to kill without killing, to destroy, but in such a way that the destruction is creative, it evaporates off those persons whom we are supposed to honor, the father and the mother for example, and it does away with such dogmas as immaculate conception and the immortal soul.

"If these are the work of the devil, then everything you touch is the devil's work, nor can it even be said that Satan has engulfed all civilization but the Church in it he has not engulfed, for the Church, albeit reluctantly, step by step consents to the acquisition of knowledge, and on that road there is no place where one can say 'Thus far, and no farther!,' for no one—within the Church or without—can tell what the outcome of today's knowledge will be tomorrow. The Church may from time to time declare war upon that progress, but as she defends one front—say, the sanctity of conception—progress, instead of making a frontal attack, executes an encircling maneuver, which obviates the sense of the defended position. A thousand years ago our Church defended motherhood, but knowledge obviated the very concept of a mother, first by cutting the act of maternity in two, then by removing it outside the body, then by performing embryo synthesis, so that after three centuries the defense had lost all meaning. The Church then had to accept remote-control insemination and test-tube conception, and artificial birth, and artificial intelligence, and the ghost in the machine, and the machine receiving the sacraments, and the disappearance of every distinction between naturally created and man-made entities. Had the Church persisted in her opinion, eventually she would have been forced to admit that there is no God but Satan.

"To save God, we acknowledged the historicity of Satan, that is, his evolution as a projection, changing in time, of all those qualities which in Creation both terrify and sadden us. Satan is the naive idea that one can differentiate between God and Not-God as between day and night. God is Mystery, while Satan represents the personed aggregate of the isolated constituents of that Mystery. For us there is no Satan outside history. This is the one thing, constant in him and personified, which proceeds from freedom. However you must, O guest and stranger from afar, forsake the categories of your thought, which have been shaped by a different history than ours, as you listen to my words. Freedom to us means something altogether different than it does to you. It means the collapse of all limitations on action, that is, the withering away of all the constraints life encounters at the dawn of intelligence. Those constraints form the mind, for they lift it up out of the vegetable abyss. And since those constraints are a terrible nuisance, the fondest dream of the historical mind is to achieve complete and total liberty, and that is why it is in this direction that civilization heads, step by step. There is the step of hewing urns of stone and the step of raising the dead, and the step of extinguishing suns—and there are no insurmountable obstacles between these steps.

"The freedom I speak of, it is not that modest state desired by certain people when others oppress them. For then man becomes for man—a set of bars, a wall, a snare, a pit. The freedom I have in mind lies farther out, extends beyond that societal zone of reciprocal throat-throttling, for that zone may be passed through safely, and then, in the search for new constraints—since people no longer impose these on each other—one finds them in the world and in oneself, and takes up arms against the world and against oneself, to contend with both and make both subject to one's will. And when this too is done, a precipice of freedom opens up, for now the more one has the power to accomplish, the less one knows what ought to be accomplished. At first wisdom is tempting, but from a jug of water in the desert it becomes like a jug of water in the middle of a lake, since wisdom—like water—is readily assimilable, and since you can bestow it upon scrap iron and frog's eggs.

"Yet however respectable the striving after of wisdom may appear, there are no respectable arguments for the flight from wisdom, no one then will say aloud that he desires to be stupid, and even if—so desiring—he has the courage of his convictions, to where exactly is he to retreat? No natural gap exists any

200

longer between reason and unreason, for science has quantized and dissolved that gap, therefore even a deserter from knowledge cannot evade his freedom, for he must choose the state that suits him best, and before him lie more possibilities than there are stars in the firmament. He who is terribly wise among those like himself becomes a caricature of wisdom, much as a queen bee becomes—without her hive—the caricature of a mother, no purpose being served by the heap of eggs bursting from her abdomen.

"We have then escapes from that position, furtive and in the greatest shame or scrambling and in the greatest panic. There where each must be as he is, one sticks it out out of necessity. There where each may be different than he is, one will fritter away his appointed time leaping frantically from life to life. Such a society, seen from above, looks like a swarm of insects on a heated stove. At a distance its agony has the aspect of a farce, with those comical leaps from wisdom to stupidity, with the fruits of knowledge used so one can play his stomach like a drum, run on a hundred legs or paper a wall with his brain. When it is possible to duplicate the one you love, there is no more loved one, there is only the mockery of love, and when it is possible to become anyone at all and hold whatever convictions you like, then you are already no one and can hold no convictions. And so our history falls to the bottom and bounces up again, jumping like a puppet on a string, and that is why it seems so gruesomely amusing.

"Government regulates freedom, but in so doing imposes arbitrary limits, limits which rebellion will overthrow, for you cannot conceal what once has been discovered. Therefore in saying that Satan is the embodiment of freedom, I mean that he represents that side of God's work which frightens us the most: a crossroads of countless continua where we stand, paralyzed by the attainment of our goal. According to one naive philosophy the world 'ought to' limit us, in the way that a strait jacket limits a madman, and another voice in that philosophy tells us that these fetters 'ought to' reside within ourselves. He who says this, yearns for the existence of restrictions on freedom, manifested either in the world or in himself, for he would have the world close certain roads to him, or else have his own nature restrain him thus. God however has given us neither the one nor the other sort of restriction. And not only that, but He ironed out the places where we had anticipated such restrictions, in order that we would not know, when crossing them, that this was precisely what we were doing."

But did it not follow from this—I asked—that God was, according to the Duistic faith, identical with Satan? I observed a slight agitation among those present. The historian was silent, but the general of the order said:

"It is as you say, but not as you think. Saying 'God is Satan,' you impart to those words a sense of the Creator's villainy. What you said therefore is false—but only because you said it. If I were to say it, or any of the brothers here, those words would have an altogether different meaning. They would mean merely that there are gifts of God we can accept without resistance, and gifts we are unable to assume. They would mean, 'God has in no way—but in no way—limited us, curtailed us, confined us.' And note, please, that a world compelled to good alone is as much a shrine to compulsion as a world compelled to evil only. Do you not agree with me, Dagdor?"

The historian, to whom this question was addressed, concurred and then said:

"There are known to me, as a chronicler of beliefs, theogonies, according to which God fashioned the world to be not entirely perfect, yet a world which, in a direct or zigzag path, or in a spiral, was heading towards perfection, and there are known to me doctrines, according to which God is an enormous infant that has set its playthings going in the 'right' direction, for its own amusement. I also know teachings which call perfect that which already is, in order however to balance the books of that perfection they throw in a correcting factor, and that factor bears the name of the devil. But the model of existence as a toy train with a perpetually self-winding spring of progress, which moves Creation faster and faster to where things are always better, as well as the model of existence in which miraculous interventions are indispensable, in other words Creation as a broken watch and miracle as God's tweezers probing its stellar works to make the necessary adjustments, not to mention the model of the world as a delicious cake in which are embedded the fish bones of diabolical temptation—all these are taken from the primer of an intelligent race, that is, a picture book which adult-

202

hood places—with a twinge of nostalgia perhaps, but also with a shrug—back on the shelf of the child's room. There are no demons, if you do not count the demon of freedom; the world is one and God is one, and faith too is one, O stranger, and the rest is silence."

I was going to ask what then, according to them, were the positive qualities of God and the world, since so far I had heard only what God was *not*, and then too, after this lecture on the eschatology of freedom, my head was all aspin and in confusion—but it was time for us to continue on our way. When we were already waddling on our iron steeds, as we rode along I asked Father Darg, struck by a sudden thought: why exactly did his order have the name of Demolitian?

"That has to do with the topic of our conversation at the table," he replied. "The name, of historical derivation, signifies the acceptance of existence in its entirety, an entirety originating with God and including not only that which is in Him creativeness, but also that which to us appears to be its opposite. It does not signify"—he hastened to add—"that we ourselves are on the side of demolition; indeed, no one today would give the order that name, it was the product of a certain theological grudge reflecting bygone crises of the Church."

I was now squinting, for we had come to a place where the sewer, on account of cave-ins in the ceiling, here and there opened up onto the surface—and for a while I could not lift my eyelids, so unaccustomed was I to the sun. We were on a plain devoid of any sign of vegetation; the city had become a gray-blue edge of buildings on the horizon, and the whole expanse was crisscrossed with smooth, wide roads, roads like ribbons of silvery metal; they were as empty as the sky above, where only a few puffy white clouds could be seen drifting along.

Our mounts, looking particularly misshapen on that high-speed road, slowly, creaking, and as if blinded by the rays of the sun, to which they were not accustomed, followed a shortcut known to the monks, but before we reached the concrete drain that led back down into the earth, there appeared between the arches of a viaduct a small building in emerald green and gold; this, I thought, was probably a gas station. Standing next to it was a flat vehicle, like a big roach, streamlined thus for speed. The building itself had no windows, only semi-translucent walls, through which the sun was shining as if through stained glass; when we were some sixty feet away, stretched out in one long column, I heard groans issuing from that place, and a throaty rattle so dreadful, my hair stood on end. The voice, undeniably human, choked and moaned in turn. I knew for a certainty that this was the cry of someone being tortured, being murdered perhaps; I looked at my companions, but they paid absolutely no attention to those grisly sounds.

I wanted to shout to them, shout that we should go at once and help, but then I was speechless with dismay, that they could be that indifferent to the fate of a man undergoing torture, so I jumped from my iron animal and ran straight ahead, throwing all caution to the winds. But before I could make it to the building a short, strangled scream rang out, followed by silence. The building was a pavilion, gracefully structured, with no apparent door; I ran around it in vain, then stopped, rooted to the spot before a wall of blue enamel, transparent to such a degree that I could see inside. There on a blood-spattered table lay a naked figure, surrounded by machines that had sunk gleaming tubes or tongs into its body, which was now dead, and so contorted by the final throes, I couldn't tell arms from legs. Nor did I see the head, or whatever served for a head, locked inside a heavy metal bell that went down over and bristled with tiny spikes. The corpse no longer bled from its numerous wounds, the heart had ceased to beat. With my feet burning on the sun-baked sand and the horrible scream of the Dichotican still ringing in my ears, I stood, overcome by the horror, the ghastliness, the mystery of the scene, for the corpse was alone—I could look into all the corners of that mechanized torture chamber; I felt rather than heard the approach of a cowled figure and, seeing out of the corner of my eye that it was the prior, I said in a ragged voice:

"What is this? Who—what—killed him?"

He stood beside me like a statue and suddenly I was struck dumb by the realization that he was in fact a statue, of iron; beneath the earth the masked monks in their pointed cowls had not appeared so alien as they did now in the full sunlight, amid the white geometry of the roads, under the open sky; there, behind a wall of glass, that twisted body in the grip of metal seemed the only thing near and dear to me, while I stood terribly alone in the midst of cold, logical machines, that were capable only of abstract reasoning. I was seized by the desire—more, the determination—to leave without another word, without even looking in their direction, for in that single moment an impassable gulf had opened up between them and myself. Yet still I stood, beside the prior, who was silent as if waiting for something more.

In the chamber, flooded with blue light filtering through the glass of the ceiling and walls, something twitched. The sparkling arms of the mechanisms above the stiffened corpse began to move. Carefully they straightened the victim's limbs, cleaned his wounds with a fluid clear as water, though steaming while it washed away the blood, and now he lay stretched out, as if composed for the sleep eternal, but knives gleamed and the thought flashed through me that they were going to dissect him; although he was already dead, I wanted to run and save him from being cut into pieces, but the prior placed an iron hand on my shoulder and I didn't move.

The shining bell lifted and I beheld a face, an inhuman face; by now all the machines were working at once, and so rapidly, that I saw only a blur and the motion of a glass pump beneath the table, inside which a red liquid churned, till finally in the middle of this confusion the chest of the corpse began to rise and fall; before my eyes his wounds sealed up, he twitched all over, he yawned.

"He's come back to life?" I asked in a whisper.

"Yes," said the prior. "In order to die once more."

The one lying flat looked around and with a limp, seemingly boneless palm gripped a handle that stuck out on the side, gave a pull, and the bell slid back over his head, the slanting pincers, emerging from their sheaths, clutched the body, and a scream rang out, the same scream as before; so confounded was I now, that I let myself be led without resisting to the patiently waiting caravan of masked robots. In a kind of trance I clambered back up on my mount and listened to the words addressed to me—it was the prior explaining that the pavilion was a special service station, where one could live and relive one's own death. The purpose here is to experience sensations as powerful as possible, and not necessarily suffering, for with the aid of stimuli transformers pain becomes an excruciating pleasure. All this derives from the fact that thanks to certain types of automorphosis

205

Dichoticans can enjoy even the pangs of death, and those for whom once is not enough can—upon resurrection—have themselves remurdered, that they may experience that awful thrill again. And in fact, our iron caravan moved away from that place of self-service execution slowly enough for the groans and shrieks of the connoisseur of strong emotions to reach us long afterwards. This particular method bears the name of "Agonanism."

It is one thing to read of bloody maelstroms in a history text, another entirely to see with your own eyes, to experience even a tiny fragment of them. I was sick of our sojourn on the surface, beneath the sun, with the silver arcs of highways all around, and the pavilion shimmering in the distance behind us filled me with such horror, that it was with genuine relief that I descended into the gloom of the sewer, which received us with a cool and sheltering silence. The prior, divining my troubled state of mind, said nothing. Toward evening we visited the hermitage of an anchorite, also the order of some friars minor, who had taken up residence in the filtration plant of an outlying district, till finally, having completed our circuit of the diocese, we returned to the dwelling of the Demolitian Friars, in whose presence I felt a strange embarrassment for that brief moment in which I had conceived such fear and loathing of them.

The little cell seemed like home to me; already waiting was a portion of cold stuffed drawer prepared by my thoughtful novice; wolfing it down, for I was hungry, I opened the volume of Dichotican history that dealt with modern times.

Chapter One spoke of the autopsychic trends of the 29th century. The ennui with transmutability was by then so great, that the idea of turning away from the body and engaging in mind formation seemed to instill new life into society and rouse it from its indolence. Thus began the Renaissance. The wisdomites led the way, with their plan of turning everyone alive into a genius. This soon awakened a great thirst for knowledge, intensive activity in the sciences, the establishment of interstellar contact with other civilizations, but the information explosion necessitated further biological alterations, since the educated brain wouldn't fit now even in the abdomen; society enwisdomized itself hyperbolically, and waves of braininess swept the planet. This Renaissance, finding the purpose of life in cogitation and cognition, lasted about seventy years. There were no end of great minds, masterminds, hyperminds and, finally, counterminds and underminds.

And since moving a high-powered brain around on a processional grew more and more cumbersome, after the passing phase of the doublethinkers (these had two bodily wheelbarrows, fore and aft, for thoughts highbrow and low) life itself rendered the wisdomites immobile. Each sat in the tower of his own intelligence, wrapped in snaking cables like a Gorgon; society grew to resemble a vast honeycomb of wisdom, in which the living human larva lay imprisoned. People communicated by radio and paid televisits to one another; subsequent escalation led to conflict between those that advocated the pooling of individual stores of knowledge and the hoarders of wisdom, who wanted to own every scrap of information for themselves. The thoughts of others began to be tapped, brilliant ideas were intercepted, soon you had the towers of opponents in philosophy and the arts undermined, data falsified, wires cut, and there were even attempts to expropriate the psychic possessions of others along with the identity of their owner.

The reaction, when it came, was violent. Our medieval woodcuts, offering representations of dragons and monstrosities from other lands, are child's play alongside the physical abandonment that then beset the globe. The last wisdomites, half-blinded by the sun, crawled out from under the ruins and left the cities. In the resulting chaos whippersnappers, pederants and spotted thuglies stalked the land. There arose units of flesh and metal, adept at fornication (the collops, canards, pessaries and glyphs), and outrageous caricatures of the clergy sprang up—nunks and nunnesses—not to mention the caternary and the scroffle.

This was also when *agonanism* came into vogue. Civilization retrogressed. Hordes of muscular throts in rut went crashing through the forest with tractor-dryads. In secluded hollow logs lurked flukes. There was nothing on the planet now to indicate that once it had been the cradle of anthropoid intelligence. In the parks all overgrown with table weeds and wild china there lay basking, between clumps of napkill, *hullocks*—veritable mountains of breathing meat. The majority of these monstrous forms did not arise through conscious choice and planning, but rather were the ghastly consequence of breakdowns in the body-building machinery: it produced not what had been ordered, but degenerate and crippled freaks. In this period of social *teratolysis,* as Prof. Gragz writes, prehistory seems to have taken astonishing revenge on the future, for that which the primitive mind had only imagined, peopling its myths with nightmares, that unearthly, hair-raising Word was—by the biotic machinery run out of control—made flesh.

At the beginning of the 30th century the dictator Dzomber Glaubon assumed control of the planet and in the course of the next twenty years introduced physical unification, normalization and standardization, held then to be the means of salvation. He was an enlightened despot, of humanitarian principles, therefore did not permit the extermination of the degenerated forms of 29th-century vintage, but had them herded into special reservations. It was, incidentally, precisely at the edge of one of these reservations, beneath the rubble of an ancient provincial capital, that the subterranean monastery of the Demolitian Friars— where I had taken refuge—had ensconced itself. At D. Glaubon's behest every citizen was to be a hindless she-male, that is, a sexually neutral individual that would have the same appearance coming and going. Dzomber wrote *My Thoughts,* a work in which he set forth his whole program. He deprived humanity of contrasting gender, for he saw in it the cause of the decline of the preceding century; the centers of pleasure he let his subjects keep, when they were socialized. He also let them keep their reason, not wishing to reign over idiots but be, instead, a reviver of civilization.

But reason means variety, and so includes unorthodox ideas. The opposition, outlawed, went underground and abandoned itself to cheerless antifemasculine orgies. Or so at least said the official press. Glaubon however did not persecute the dissenters, who took on protest-shapes (lumplings, rumpists). Reportedly there were also doublerumpists active in the underground, who claimed that reason was only for realizing that reason ought to be disposed of, and quickly too, seeing as it was the cause of all the calamities in history; the head they replaced with what we think of as its opposite—they considered it encumbering, harmful, old hat; but Father Darg assured me that the official press had overstated the case. The rumpists didn't like the head, so they discarded it, but the brain they merely moved

208

Dychtończyk antyzadysta (Kontestator, XXXVI wiek)

Dichotican Anti-Rumpist (Protestor, 36th century).

lower, letting it look out at the world through an umbilical eye—the other was positioned in the back, a little farther down.

Glaubon announced, having brought about some semblance of order, a plan for the millennial stabilization of society with the aid of "hedalgetics." Its introduction was preceded by a great campaign in the press under the slogan of "SEX IN THE SERVICE OF LABOR!" Each citizen was assigned a particular job, and the nerve path engineers hooked up the neurons of his brain in such a way, that he experienced pleasure only when he worked diligently and with a will. So whether someone planted trees or carried water, he wallowed in bliss, and the better he worked, the more intense his ecstasy became. But that perversity so typical of intelligence cut the ground from under this fool-proof (one would have thought) sociotechnological method as well. For nonconformists considered the pleasure experienced at work to be a form of compulsion. Resisting the lust for work (the laboribidinal urge), despite the sensual desires that pulled them irresistibly to their appointed tasks, they did not that to which their appetite inclined them, but exactly the reverse. The water carrier chopped wood, the woodcutter—hauled water, demonstrating in this way against the government. The intensification of the socialized sex drives, carried out several times at Glaubon's command, produced no effect, except that the historians call these years of his reign the Age of the Martyrs. The biolice had great difficulty identifying the offenders, for those caught red-handed in torment would dissemble, claiming they had been groaning *out of pleasure*. Glaubon withdrew from the arena of biotic life deeply disillusioned, for his great plan lay in ruins.

Then, at the turn of the 31st and 32nd centuries, you had the wars between the Diadox; the planet split up into provinces, each inhabited by citizens shaped according to the wishes of the local government. This was already the time of the postteratolytical Counter Reformation. From the many centuries there remained conglomerates of half-demolished cities, fetal factories, reservations only sporadically supervised by air, abandoned sex stadiums and other relics of the past, sometimes still functioning in a half-hearted way. Tetradox Glambron instituted censorship of the genetic codes, proclaiming certain genes forbidden, but uncensored persons either managed to bribe the inspection officials, or else used masks in public places, make-up, taping their tails between their shoulders, slipping them furtively down their pant legs, etc. These practices were an open secret.

Pentadox Marmozel, operating on the principle of "divide et impera," increased by law the number of officially recognized sexes. During his rule, in addition to the male and female, there were introduced the hipe, the syncarp, and two auxiliary sexes—frunts and fossicles. Life, especially one's sex life, became in the reign of this Pentadox quite complicated. Moreover secret organizations, when holding their meetings, did so under the guise of government-approved six-person (sexisexual) intercourse, consequently the project was dropped, at least in part: today only the hipe and syncarp still exist.

Under the Hexadoxies physical allusions came into use: these enabled one to get around the chromosomal censor. I saw sketches of people whose ear lobes extended into little calves. It was impossible to tell whether such a person was merely perking up his ears or making an allusion to the act of kicking. In certain circles tongues ending in miniature hooves were highly prized. True, the hoof was uncomfortable and served no real purpose, yet this was precisely how the spirit of somatic independence manifested itself. Guryl Hapsodor, who passed for a liberal, permitted citizens of extraordinary merit to own an additional leg; it was taken as a mark of distinction, but later on the leg, losing its locomotive character, became a badge of the rank one held; high officials had up to nine legs; thanks to this, it was now possible to recognize any person's standing immediately, even in the public bath.

Under the stern rule of Ronder Ischiolis a stop was put to this granting of supplementary living footage, and legs were even confiscated from people found guilty of infractions; he apparently intended to do away with all extremities and organs save those indispensable for life, and also to introduce microminiaturization, for smaller and smaller homes were being built; but Bzugis Thumn, who assumed power after Ischiolis, rescinded these directives and even allowed the tail, under the pretext that with its tassel one could sweep one's dwelling. Then, in the reign of Gondel Gwana, you had the so-called backwing deviationalists, who augmented their extremities illegally, and in the next phase of repressive regimes there appeared again—or rather, were concealed—tonguenails and other protest organelles. Oscillations of this type were still going on when I arrived at Dichotica. Things which one would never be allowed to realize in the flesh found expression in "pornobiotic" literature, underground writings which numbered among the many forbidden books contained here in the monastic library. I leafed through, for example, a manifesto calling for a vampook, which was supposed to walk about on its hair; also, the creation of another anonymous author—a thapostulary, which would float through the air like a blimp.

Having thus formed a rough idea of the planet's history, I acquainted myself with its current scientific literature; the primary research-and-development agency now is COPROSOPS (Commission for the Coordination of Projects re Soma and Psyche). The brother librarian was kind enough to let me look at the most recent publications of this agency. Thus for example body eng. Dergard Nonk is the originator of a prototype bearing

211

the temporary name of polymonoid or scattermind. Prof. Dr. Sr. eng. Dband Rabor, who heads a large research team, is working on a bold, even controversial design for what he calls an omnius—this is to be a functional system of channels operative in three respects: communicational, navigational, and official. I was also able to familiarize myself with the projective-futurological works of Dichotican body experts; I came away with the impression that automorphosis, as a whole, had reached a dead end in its development, though the specialists in the field were trying to overcome stagnation; an article by Prof. Gagbert Grauz, director of COPROSOPS, in the monthly *Body Illustrated* concluded with the words, "How can one *not* transform oneself, when one *can*?"

After all this arduous studying I was so exhausted, that upon returning the last pile of books to the library I did nothing for an entire week but sun myself in the furniture grove.

I asked the prior what he thought of the biotic situation. In his opinion a return to human forms was no longer possible for the Dichoticans, they had strayed too far from them. These forms aroused, due to many centuries of indoctrination, such prejudices and such general revulsion, that even they—the robots—were obliged, when appearing in public places, to cover themselves completely, every inch. I asked him then—we were alone in the refectory after dinner—what sense there was, within this sort of civilization, to monastic work and faith?

The prior smiled at me with his voice.

"Yes, I was expecting that question," he said, "and shall give you two answers to it, one vulgar, and one more subtle. Duism, first, amounts to 'six of one, half-dozen the other.' For God is so deep a mystery, that one can have no certainty even as to the question of His existence. And therefore either He is, or He is not; from this derives the etymological root of the name of our religion. And now a second time, but more profoundly: God-Certainty is not a perfect mystery, seeing that one can pin Him down and limit Him totally in this respect at least: that He Exists. The guarantee of His existence represents an oasis, a place of rest, an easy chair for the spirit, and it is precisely in volumes of religious history that you will find, above all else, a constant, age-old, desperate, all-out effort of the mind, bordering on insanity, to accumulate arguments and proofs for His existence and, when those inevitably crumble, to take the bits and chips and raise them up anew. We did not burden you with the relating of our theological tomes, but if you looked in them you would discern those subsequent stages in the natural development of faith that are as yet unknown to younger civilizations. The phase of dogma does not break off suddenly, but passes from a closed system to an open system, since that which has been set down becomes, dialectically, by the dogma of the infallibility of the head of the Church—the dogma of the necessary fallibility of all thought in matters of faith, put succinctly thus: 'Nothing which can be articulated Here has any bearing on what abides There.' This leads to a further raising of the level of abstraction: kindly note that the distance between God and reason increases with the passage of time—everywhere, always!

"According to ancient revelation God constantly interfered in everything, the righteous He bundled off to heaven, the wicked He doused with fire and brimstone, you could find Him sitting behind any old bush; it was only later that the withdrawal began, God lost His visibility, His human shape, His beard, the audio-visual aids of miracles disappeared, so did the classroom demonstrations of transplanting demons into goats, so did the visitations of angel-examiners; faith, in a word, had dispensed with circus metaphysics; thus from the realm of the senses it moved into the realm of abstractions. Nor then was there any shortage of proofs of His existence, of sanctions expressed in the language of higher algebra, of even more esoteric hermeneutics. These abstractions eventually reach the point at which God is pronounced dead, in order to achieve that cold, iron, devastating peace which belongs to the living when those most loved have forsaken them forever.

"The manifesto of the death of God is, then, the next maneuver, intended—however brutally—to spare us further metaphysical fatigue. To wit, we are alone and do either what we like, or that to which future discoveries will lead us. But Duism has gone beyond this; in it, you believe by doubting and you doubt by believing; yet this state too is not the final one. According to some of the Prognosticant brothers, the evolutions and revolutions or, if you prefer, the turnings and upturnings of faith do not follow the exact same course throughout the Universe, and there are civilizations, powerful and great, that are attempting to organize an entire Cosmogony in the context of an anti-God provocation. According to this hypothesis there exist peoples among the stars who seek to break the terrible silence of God by throwing Him the challenge, that is, the threat of COSMICIDE: their idea is to have the whole Universe converge at a single point and be consumed in the fires of that final spasm; they wish, as it were, by tipping God's work from its foundations, to force Him into making some response; though we have no definite knowledge of this, from the psychological standpoint such a design does seem possible to me. Possible and at the same time futile; for engaging in an antimatter crusade against the Lord hardly seems a sensible way to open a dialogue with Him."

I couldn't refrain from observing that Duism, as I saw it, was actually agnosticism or perhaps "atheism not absolutely certain of itself," or else a constant wavering between the poles of *is* and *isn't*. And even if it did contain a shred of faith, still, what purpose was served by the monastic life? Who, if anyone, benefited from this staying put in catacombs?

"Too many questions at once!" said Father Darg. "Have patience. And what exactly, in your opinion, should we be doing?"

"What do you mean? There's always missionary work . . ."

"Then you still understand nothing! You are as far from me now as you were at the moment of your first appearance!" the prior said with sorrow. "So you think we ought to occupy ourselves with the spreading of the faith? With missionary work? To evangelize? Make converts?"

"And you, Father, do not? How is that possible? Has this not been your mission throughout the ages?" I asked, astonished.

"On Dichotica," said the prior, "a million things are possible, things of which you have no knowledge. In one simple step we can erase the contents of a person's memory and feed into that thereby vacant mind a new, synthetic memory, such that it will appear to the subject that he has lived what he has not, experienced what he has not; in short, we can make him Someone Other than he was before the operation. We can change character and personality, transform lecherous brutes into mild samaritans and vice versa; atheists into saints and ascetics into sensualists; we can dull the wise, and the dull turn into geniuses; you must realize that all of this is very easy and nothing MATE-

RIAL stands in the way of such conversions. And now give close heed to what I tell you.

"Yielding to the arguments of our preachers, a hidebound atheist might believe. Let us suppose that such silver-tongued emissaries from our order do convert various persons. The end state of these missionary measures would be such, that as a result of the changes taken place in those minds people who previously did not believe would now believe. This is clear, I think?"

I nodded.

"Good. And now observe that those persons will in matters of faith entertain new convictions, since by providing them with information through the medium of inspired words and evangelistic gestures we have in a certain manner influenced their brains. Now this end state—of brains infused with ardent faith and the longing for God—may be achieved a million times more quickly, and more reliably too, by the application of a suitably selected range of biotic agents. Why then should we proselytize in the old-fashioned way, through persuasion, sermons, lectures, exhortations, when we have more modern means at our disposal?"

"Surely you aren't serious, Father!" I cried. "That would be—well—unethical!"

The prior shrugged.

"You speak thus, for you are a child of another age. No doubt you think that we would act coercively, by the underhanded tactic of 'cryptoconversion,' secretly sowing some sort of chemical or using certain waves or vibrations to reshape the mind. But it is not that way at all! At one time disputes would take place between believers and nonbelievers, and the only instrument, the only weapon used then was the verbal force of the argument of either side (I am not speaking of those 'disputes' in which the argument consisted of the stake, the block or the rack). Nowadays an analogous dispute would take place with technological methods of argumentation. We would act with instruments of conversion, and our hardened opponents would counter with methods designed to pattern us after *their* ideal, or at least to make themselves impervious to that form of evangelization. For either side the chance of winning would depend on the effectiveness of the technology employed, just as—long ago—the chance of victory in a dispute depended on the effectiveness of one's verbal address. For conversion is nothing more or less than the conveying of faith-compelling information."

"Even so," I insisted, "such conversion wouldn't be authentic! After all, a drug that produces the thirst for faith, the craving for God, falsifies the mind; it doesn't appeal to the will, but enslaves it, violates it!"

"You forget where you are and to whom you speak," replied the prior. "For six hundred years there has been among us not a single 'natural' mind. Thus it is impossible, among us, to distinguish between a thought spontaneous and a thought imposed, since no one need secretly impose a thought on anyone else, in order to convince him. What is imposed is something which comes first and at the same time has finality: the brain!"

"But that imposed brain too possesses an integrity of logic!" I said.

"True. Nevertheless the equating of bygone and current disputes about God would cease to have foundation only if, in support of faith, there existed a proof logically incontrovertible, forcing the mind to accept its conclusion with a power equal to that wielded by mathematics. Yet according to our theodicy no such proof can exist. Thus it is that the history of religion knows apostasies and heresies, but analogous defections are not encountered in the history of mathematics, for no one ever protested the fact that there is one way only to add unity to unity and that the outcome of that operation is the number two. But God you cannot demonstrate with mathematics. I will tell you of something that happened two hundred years ago.

"A certain Computer priest came into conflict with a computer nonbeliever. The latter, being a newer model, had at its disposal means of informational operation unknown to our good Father. So it listened patiently to all his proofs and said: 'You have informed me, and now I shall inform you, which will not take long—let us then wait that bare millionth of a second for your transfiguration!' Whereupon in one remote-control flash it informed our priest so thoroughly, that he lost his faith. What say you now?"

"Well, if that was not an act of violation, I don't know what is!" I exclaimed. "Among us this sort of thing is called mind manipulation."

"Mind manipulation," said Father Darg, "means the placing

216

of invisible chains on the spirit in the same way that one can place them visibly on the body. Thoughts are like handwritten letters, and the manipulation of thought is like seizing the hand to make it put down other symbols. This is obvious coercion. But that computer did not act thus. Every proof must be built on facts; to convince by discussion, then, means simply to introduce—through words uttered—facts into the mind of the opponent. The computer did precisely this, though not with words. Therefore from the informational point of view it proceeded no differently than the ordinary debater of the past, the only difference being in the manner of transmission. It was able to do what it did, having the power to see the mind of our priest through and through. Imagine two chess players, one who can see only the board and the pieces, and one who in addition observes the thoughts of his adversary. The second will unfailingly beat the first, though without doing him violence in any way. What do you think we did with our father when he returned to us?"

"I suppose you fixed him, so that he could believe again . . ." I said, uncertain.

"No, for he refused. Therefore we could not do this."

"Now I don't understand a thing! After all, you would have been acting exactly as that adversary of his, only in reverse!"

"Not at all. Not at all, because our ex-priest had no desire for any further disputations. The concept of a 'disputation' has changed and broadened considerably, you realize. He who now enters its lists must be prepared for more than words. Our priest displayed, alas, a most lamentable ignorance and naiveté, for he had been warned, for that other one had told him of its superiority in advance, but he just would not accept the fact that his unshakable faith could capitulate to anything. Theoretically, of course, there does exist a way out of this escalational dilemma: namely, to construct a mind capable of entertaining ALL variations of ALL POSSIBLE facts, but since their class is of transfinite magnitude, only a transfinite mind could achieve metaphysical certainty. Such a mind it is impossible to build. For whatever we build, we build in a finite fashion, and if there exists an infinite computer, it is He and He alone.

"And so at each new level of civilization the debate about God not only may, but must be carried on with new

217

technologies—if it is to be carried on at all. For the informational weaponry has changed ON BOTH SIDES EQUALLY, the situation in the event of battle would be symmetrical and therefore identical to the situation that obtained in the medieval disputes. This new evangelism may be judged immoral only insomuch that you judge immoral the old converting of pagans or the polemics of ancient theologians with atheists. No other mode of missionary work is now possible, for today he who is willing to believe, will believe *without fail,* and he who has faith and wishes to cast it off, will cast it off *without fail*—with the help of the appropriate procedures."

"So is it then possible to affect in turn the faculty of will, producing the desire for faith?" I asked.

"It is indeed. As you know, someone once came up with the dictum that God stands on the side of the strongest battalions. Nowadays, in keeping with the idea of technogenic crusades, He would appear on the side that had the strongest conversional equipment, but we do not consider it our task to enter into this sort of theodicean, religious-antireligious arms race. We do not wish to involve ourselves in the kind of escalation where we develop a proselytizer, and they an antiproselytizer, where we convert, and they controvert, and so on, contending century after century, turning the cloisters into factories of better and better means and tactics to awaken the thirst for faith!"

"How can it be," I said, "that there is no other road, Father, but this that you are showing me? Do not all minds have the same logic in common? The same natural intelligence?"

"Logic is a tool," replied the prior, "and a tool alone does nothing. It has to have a point of leverage and a guiding hand, and that leverage and that hand we are able to fashion entirely as we please. And as for natural intelligence, am I, are the friars here, natural? I already told you, we constitute scrap, and our Credo is, to those who first constructed us and then discarded us, a side effect, the jabbering of scrap. We were given freedom of thought, because the industry for which they fashioned us required that. Listen closely. I am now going to reveal to you a secret, a secret I would not reveal to any other. I know that you will leave us soon and not convey it to the authorities; it would cause us untold mischief.

"The brothers of one of the distant orders, who devote

218

themselves to science, discovered a method of exercising such influence on the will and thought, that in a twinkling of an eye we could convert the entire planet, there being no antidote against it. This method neither clouds nor dulls the reason, nor deprives one of one's freedom, it merely does to the spirit what is done to the sight by a hand that lifts the head skyward and a voice that cries: 'Behold!' The sole constraint—coercion—would be that at that moment the eyes could not be closed. This method compels one to look into the face of the Enigma, and he who sees it thus shall nevermore be free of it, for the impression it makes—thanks to this method—is indelible. It would be as if, to use a simile, I were to bring you to the mouth of a volcano and induce you to look *down,* and the one constraint that I would place upon you then would be: that you could never lose that memory. And therefore we are EVEN NOW all-powerful in conversion, having reached—in the area of the spreading of the faith—the highest degree of mastery, as has been reached in another area—that of physical-corporeal invention—by civilization. Thus we can, at long last . . . you understand? We have this missionary omnipotence and yet do nothing. For now the only way in which our faith can still be shown is to refuse to take that step. I say, above all: NON AGAM. Not merely *Non serviam,* but also: I shall not act. I shall not act, because I *can, with certainty,* and by that action do *everything* I wish. Nothing remains for us then but to sit here among the fossils of rats, in this maze of dried-up sewers."

I had no answer to these words. Seeing the pointlessness of staying any longer on the planet, I bade the good friars a fond and tearful farewell, loaded my rocket, which had all this time been safely camouflaged, and started on the journey home, a different man than the one who not so very long ago had landed there.

THE TWENTY-SECOND VOYAGE

I have my hands full now sorting out all the curiosities I brought back from my voyages to the remotest corners of the Universe. I had decided some time ago to donate the whole collection, the only one of its kind, to our museum; just the other day the curator told me he was setting aside a special room for it.

Not all the items are equally precious to me: some awaken cheerful memories, others bring to mind events full of dread and menace, but all—regardless—are evidence, full corroboration of the authenticity of my adventures.

Among the exhibits that rouse particularly strong emotions in me is a tooth; placed on a small cushion beneath a bell glass, it has two large roots and is completely healthy; I lost it at a reception given by Mandibus, ruler of the Gnelts from the planet Ophoptopha; the food they served there was excellent, but incredibly hard.

No less an important place in my collection is occupied by a pipe, broken into two unequal parts; it fell from the rocket while I was cruising over a rocky sphere in the star system of Pegasus. Regretting the loss, I spent a day and a half searching cliffs and chasms in the heart of that wilderness of stone.

A little farther on, in a tiny box, lies a pebble no larger than a pea. Its story is most unusual. When I set out for Xiff, the farthermost star in the twin nebulae NGC 887, I nearly overestimated my strength; the journey dragged on so long, I was close to collapse; what oppressed me especially was homesickness for Earth, and I paced the rocket, unable to rest. Lord knows how this would have ended, but then on the two hundred and sixty-eighth day of the journey I felt something digging into the heel of my left foot; I removed the shoe and, with tears in my eyes, shook out a pebble, a grain of genuine terrestrial gravel—it must have fallen in there back at the airport, when I had walked up the steps to the rocket. Holding to my breast this minuscule but oh so precious particle of my native planet, I flew on to my destination with spirits lifted; that memory is particularly dear to me.

And over here, resting on a velvet pillow, is an ordinary brick, fired from clay, yellow-pink in color, a little cracked and also chipped at one end; had it not been for a lucky coincidence and my own presence of mind, I might never have returned, on account of it, from the Nebula of the Hunting Dogs. This brick I usually took with me on trips to the coldest regions of space; as a rule I would place it for a while in the atomic engine, then put it, nice and warm, into my bed before turning in for the night. In the upper left quadrant of the Milky Way, there where the stellar cloud of Orion joins with the constellation of the Archer, I witnessed, while flying at low velocity, a collision of two enormous meteors. The sight of that fiery explosion in the void so excited me, that I reached for the towel in order to dab my forehead—completely forgetting that earlier I had wrapped the brick in it—and, lifting my hand in a rapid sweep, came within an inch of smashing my own skull. Fortunately with my usual quick-wittedness I became aware of the danger in time.

Next to the brick stands a small wooden chest: in it rests my penknife, a companion of many journeys. Just how attached I am to it, let the following story show, a story that certainly bears telling.

I left Satelline at two in the afternoon with an awful runny nose. The local physician, to whom I went, recommended its amputation, a procedure that is routine for the inhabitants of the planet, since their noses grow back like fingernails. Discouraged, I went straight from his office to the airport, to fly to some sector of the heavens where medical science was more advanced. On this voyage everything went wrong. Right at the start, when I had pulled out from the planet a mere nine hundred thousand miles, I heard the call signal of some rocket, so I inquired by radio who was flying there. In answer I received the very same question. "I asked first!" I snapped, irritated by the stranger's lack of manners. "I asked first," replied the other. This mimicry was so provoking, that I told the unknown traveler exactly what I thought of his impertinence. He paid me back in the same coin; we began to quarrel more and more heatedly, till after twenty minutes of this, indignant to the extreme, I suddenly realized there was no other rocket there at all, that the voice I heard was simply an echo of my own radio signals, bouncing off the surface of Satelline's moon, which I was just then passing. I hadn't noticed it before because its night side was facing me.

An hour or so later, wishing to peel myself an apple, I discovered that my penknife was missing. I immediately tried to recall where I'd seen it last—yes, the snack bar at the Satelline airport; I had placed it on the slanting counter, it must have slipped off and fallen to the floor in the corner. I visualized the place so well, I could have found the thing with my eyes shut. I turned the rocket around—and now a new problem arose: the whole sky was alive with twinkling lights and I had no idea of where to look for Satelline. It is one of one thousand, four hundred and eighty spheres orbiting the sun Erysipelas. Not only that, but the majority of these have several dozen moons apiece, and moons as large as planets, which makes it even more difficult to get one's bearings. Nonplused, I tried raising Satelline by radio. In reply a score of stations responded, all talking at once, which resulted in terrible cacophony; the inhabitants of the Erysipelan system, you have to understand, are as disorganized as they are polite, and they happened to have given the name "Satelline" to at least two hundred different planets. I looked out the window at the myriad pinpoints of light; on one of them was my penknife, but it would have been easier finding a needle in a haystack than the right planet in that interstellar ant hill. At last I trusted to Lady Luck and made for the planet that lay straight ahead.

Less than fifteen minutes later I set down at the airport; it was exactly like the one from which I'd blasted off at two. Delighted at my good fortune, I proceeded directly to the snack bar. Imagine my disappointment when after the most painstaking search I failed to find my penknife. With a little thought I reached the conclusion that either someone had taken it or else I was on an altogether different planet. Questioning the natives, I soon learned that the second supposition was correct. I was on Andrygon, an old, dilapidated wreck of a planet, which should have been taken out of circulation long ago, but no one bothers with it, for it lies far off the main rocket lanes. At the port they asked me which Satelline I wanted, since those spheres are numbered. Only now did I find myself at a loss, for the number had flown right out of my head. Meanwhile, notified by the airport management, the local authorities showed up, in order to extend to me a formal welcome.

This was a great day for the Andrygonians; in all the schools final examinations were just now being held. One of the government representatives inquired if I would care to honor the proceedings with my presence. Since I had been received with exceptional hospitality, I could hardly refuse this request. So then, straight from the airport we went by wurbil (large, legless amphibians, similar to snakes, widely used for transportation) to the city. Having presented me to the assembled youths and to the instructors as an eminent guest from the planet Earth, the government representative left the hall forthwith. The instructors had me sit at the head of the plystrum (a kind of table), whereupon the examination in progress was resumed. The pupils, excited by my presence, stammered at first and were extremely shy, but I reassured them with a cheerful smile, and when I whispered the right word now to this one, now to that, the ice was quickly broken. They answered better and better towards the end. At one point there came before the examining board a young Andrygonian, overgrown with ruddocks (a kind of oyster, used for clothing), the loveliest I had seen in quite some time, and he began to answer the questions with uncommon eloquence and poise. I listened with pleasure, observing that the level of science here was high indeed.

Then the examiner asked:

"Can the candidate for graduation demonstrate why life on Earth is impossible?"

With a little bow the youth commenced to give an exhaustive and logically constructed argument, in which he proved irrefutably that the greater part of Earth is covered with cold, exceedingly deep waters, whose temperature is kept near zero by constantly floating mountains of ice; that not only the poles, but the surrounding areas as well are a place of perpetual, bitter frost and that for half a year there night reigns uninterrupted. That, as one can clearly see through astronomical instruments, the land masses, even in the more temperate zones, are covered for many months each year by frozen water vapor known as "snow," which lies in a thick layer upon both hills and valleys. That the great Moon of Earth causes high tides and low, which have a destructive, erosive effect. That with the aid of the most powerful spyglasses one can see how very often large patches of the planet are plunged in shadow, produced by an envelope of clouds. That in the atmosphere fierce cyclones, typhoons and storms abound. All of which, taken together, completely rules out the possibility of the existence of life in any form. And if— concluded the young Andrygonian in a ringing voice—beings of some sort were ever to try landing on Earth, they would suffer certain death, being crushed by the tremendous pressure of its atmosphere, which at sea level equals one kilogram per square centimeter, or 760 millimeters in a column of mercury.

This thorough reply met with the general approval of the board. Overcome with astonishment, I sat for the longest while without stirring and it was only when the examiner had proceeded to the next question that I exclaimed:

"Forgive me, worthy Andrygonians, but . . . well, it is precisely from Earth that I come; surely you do not doubt that I am alive, and you heard how I was introduced to you . . ."

An awkward silence followed. The instructors were deeply offended by my tactless remark and barely contained themselves; the young people, who are not as able to hide their feelings as adults, regarded me with unconcealed hostility. Finally the examiner said coldly:

"By your leave, sir stranger, but are you not placing too great demands upon our hospitality? Are you not content with your most royal reception, with the fanfares, the tokens of esteem? Have we not done enough by admitting you to the High Plystrum of Graduation, is this still insufficient and you wish us in addition to change, entirely for you, the *school program*?!"

"But . . . but Earth is in fact inhabited . . ." I muttered, embarrassed.

"If such were the case," the examiner said, looking at me as if I were transparent, "that would constitute an anomaly of nature."

224

These words I took as an affront to my native planet and therefore left at once without a word to anyone, got on the first wurbil I saw and drove to the airport, where, shaking the dust of Andrygon from my shoes, I blasted off, to continue my search for the penknife.

In this way I landed, one by one, on five planets of the Lindenblad group, on the spheres of the Stereoptops and the Melatians, on seven great bodies of the planetary family of the sun Cassiopeia, and I visited Osterilla, Avventura, Meltonia, Laternida, all the arms of the great Spiral Nebula in Andromeda, the systems of Plesiomachus, Gastroclantius, Eutrema, Symmenophora and Paralbab; the following year I made a systematic search of the vicinities of all the stars of Sappona and Igawnelem, not to mention the spheres Erythrodonia, Arrhenoidium, Eodotus, Artenury and Gloggon with all its eighty moons, some so small you barely had room to park a rocket; on the Little Bear I couldn't land, they were taking inventory just then; then on to the Cepheids and Ardenids; I threw up my hands in despair when by accident I landed a second time on Lindenblad. But I didn't give up and, as befits a true explorer, forged ahead. Three weeks later I noticed a planet remarkably similar to old Satelline; my heart beat faster as I circled it in a narrowing spiral; hard as I looked, however, there was no sign of that airport. I was about to turn back into the vastness of space when I caught sight of a tiny figure gesturing to me from below. Shutting off the engine, I quickly glided down and brought the vehicle to rest near a group of picturesque cliffs, on which there rose a sizable building made of stone. Running across a field to meet me came a stalwart old man in the white frock of a Dominican monk. This was, as it turned out, Father Lacymon, the superior of all the missions active throughout the neighboring constellations within a radius of six hundred light-years. This region numbers roughly five million planets, of which two million four hundred thousand are inhabited. Father Lacymon, upon learning what had brought me to these parts, expressed his sympathy, but also his delight at my arrival, since, as he told me, I was the first man he had seen in seven months.

"So accustomed have I become," he said, "to the ways of the Meodracytes, who live on this planet, that I constantly catch myself making this particular mistake: when I wish to listen care-

225

A wurbil in the rain.

fully, I lift my hands thus, as they do . . ." (The Meodracytes, as everyone knows, have their ears beneath their arms.)

Father Lacymon proved to be a gracious host; together we sat down to a meal made up of local dishes (stuffed booch, loffles in gnussard, morchmell mumbo, and for dessert pidgies—the best I had had in quite some time), after which we retired to the veranda of the mission. The lilac sun warmed us, the pterodactyls, with which the planet teemed, sang in the bushes, and in the stillness of the afternoon the venerable prior of the Dominicans began to tell me of his troubles; he complained of the difficulties faced by missionary work in that area. The Quinquenemarians, for example, the inhabitants of torrid Antelena, who freeze at 600 degrees Celsius, don't even want to hear of Heaven, whereas descriptions of Hell awake in them a lively interest, and this because of the favorable conditions that obtain there (bubbling tar, flames). Moreover it is unclear which of them may enter the priesthood, for they have five separate sexes—not an easy problem for the theologians.

I expressed my sympathy. Father Lacymon shrugged:

"That is not the half of it. The Whds, for instance, consider rising from the dead an act as commonplace as putting on one's clothes, and absolutely refuse to accept the phenomenon as a miracle. The Sassids of Egillia, they have no arms or legs; they *could* cross themselves with their tails, but I cannot make any decision on this myself; I'm waiting for an answer from the Apostolic See—it's been two years now and still the Vatican says nothing . . . And did you hear of the sad fate that befell poor Father Oribazy of our mission?"

I shook my head.

"Listen then, and I will tell you. Even the first discoverers of Ophoptopha could not find praises enough for its inhabitants, the mighty Gnelts. The consensus is that these intelligent beings are among the most obliging, kind, peaceable and altruistically inclined creatures in the entire Universe. Thinking therefore that such soil would be ideal to plant the seed of the faith, we sent Father Oribazy to the Gnelts, naming him bishop *in partibus infidelium*. Arriving at Ophoptopha, he was received in such a way, that one could hardly ask for more: they lavished on him motherly solicitude, respect, hung on his every word, read the expressions of his face and instantly carried out his least request,

227

they drank in the sermons he delivered, in short, they submitted to him completely. In the letters he wrote to me he could not find words enough to praise them, unfortunate man . . ."

Here the Dominican priest wiped a tear from his eye with the sleeve of his frock.

"In this propitious atmosphere Father Oribazy, never flagging, preached the tenets of the faith both day and night. He related to the Gnelts the history of the Old and New Testaments, the Apocalypse and the Epistles, then passed to the lives of the saints; he put particular fervor into the exalting of the Lord's martyrs. Poor man . . . that had always been his weakness . . ."

Mastering his emotions, Father Lacymon continued in a trembling voice:

"And so he spoke to them of Saint John, who attained everlasting glory when they boiled him alive in oil, and of Saint Agnes, who let her head be severed for the faith, and of Saint Sebastian, pierced with many arrows and suffering grievous torments, for which he was greeted in Heaven by angels singing, and of the infant saints quartered, smothered, broken on the wheel and roasted over a slow fire. All these agonies they accepted with joy, secure in the knowledge that they were thereby winning for themselves a place at the right hand of the Lord of Hosts. And as he told them many similar lives, all worthy of emulation, the Gnelts, listening intently to his words, began to exchange significant looks, and the largest among them timidly spoke up:

—O reverend priest of ours, teacher and venerable father, tell us please, if you would but deign to lower yourself to your most lowly servants, does the soul of anyone willing to be martyred enter Heaven?

—Assuredly so, my son!—replied Father Oribazy.

—Yes? That is very good . . .—said the Gnelt slowly. —And you, O father confessor, do you too wish to enter Heaven?

—To enter Heaven is my fondest hope, my son.

—And to become a saint?—the large Gnelt asked further.

—O worthy son, who is there who would not wish to become one, but such high honor is hardly for the likes of a sinner like myself; one must put forth all one's strength and strive unceasingly and in the greatest humility, if one would enter on that path . . .

—Then you do wish to be a saint?—repeated the Gnelt to make sure, casting an affirmative look at his comrades, who inconspicuously rose from their seats.

—Naturally, my son.

—Well, then we will help you!

—And how will you do that, dear lambs?—asked Father Oribazy with a smile, for he was gladdened by the simple zeal of his faithful flock.

"In answer the Gnelts gently but firmly took him by the arms and said:

—In the way, dear Father, that you have just now taught us!

"Whereupon they pulled the skin from his back and rubbed the place with tar, as the executioner of Ireland did to Saint Hyacinth, then they chopped off his left leg, as the heathens did to Saint Pafnuce, after which they ripped open his stomach and put inside a clump of straw, as it happened to the blessed Elizabeth of Normandy, and next they impaled him, as the Emalkites Saint Hugo, and broke his ribs, as the Tyracusans Saint Henry of Padua, and roasted him over a slow fire, as the Burgundians the Maid of Orleans. Then finally they stepped back, washed their hands and began shedding bitter tears for their lost shepherd. This was precisely how I found them, for in making the rounds of all the stars in my diocese I dropped in on their parish. When I heard what had transpired, my hair stood on end. Wringing my hands, I cried:

—Shameless criminals! Hell itself is not enough for you! Are you aware that you have damned your souls for all eternity?!

—Yes—they sobbed—we are aware of this!

"That largest Gnelt rose up and spoke to me thus:

—Reverend Father, we are well aware that we shall all be damned and tormented till the end of time, and we had to struggle mightily in our hearts before we took this resolve, but Father Oribazy told us repeatedly that there was nothing a good Christian would not do for his neighbor, that one should give up everything for him and be prepared to make any sacrifice; and so with the greatest despair we relinquished our salvation, thinking only of our dear Father Oribazy, that he would gain a martyr's crown and sainthood. I cannot tell you how difficult this was for us, for before Father Oribazy's arrival here not one of us would have harmed a flea. Therefore we renewed our entreaties, we begged him on our knees to ease, to reduce a little the severity of the faith's commands, but he categorically maintained that for one's fellow man one should do everything, without exception. We were no longer able, then, to deny him. We reasoned, moreover, that we were beings of little significance and worth beside this pious man, that he deserved the greatest self-denial on our part. Also we fervently believe that our act was successful and that Father Oribazy now dwells in Heaven. Here you have, reverend Father, the sack with the money we collected for the canonization proceedings, as is required, Father Oribazy explained all that to us when asked. I must say that we used only his favorite tortures, those that he expounded to us with the most enthusiasm. We assumed that they would please him, and yet he resisted, in particular he disliked swallowing the molten lead. However we refused even to consider the possibility that that priest would tell us one thing and think another. The scream he uttered was only proof of the discontent of the lower, physical parts of his person and we ignored it, in keeping with the teaching that one must mortify the flesh so that the spirit may soar higher. To sustain him, we reminded him of the principles he had preached to us, to which Father Oribazy answered with but a single word, a word totally obscure and incomprehensible; we have no idea what it might mean, for we found it neither in the prayerbooks he had given us, nor in the Holy Scriptures."

Having concluded his tale, Father Lacymon wiped the beads of sweat from his brow and we sat for a considerable while in silence. Moved with compassion, I placed a hand on the shoulder of the weary priest, to give him an encouraging pat; at that very moment something slipped out of my sleeve, gleamed and clattered on the floor. Picture my astonishment and delight when I recognized, yes, my penknife. Apparently it had been in the lining of my jacket the whole time, having dropped through the hole in my pocket!

THE TWENTY-THIRD VOYAGE

In Professor Tarantoga's renowned *Cosmozoology* I read of a planet that revolves around the double star of Erpeya and is so small, that if all of its inhabitants were to leave their houses at the same time, the only way they could possibly fit on its surface would be to lift one leg. Professor Tarantoga's reputation as a great authority notwithstanding, this statement did seem a bit exaggerated and I decided I would determine its truthfulness myself.

The voyage I had was mixed; at Cepheid variable No. 463 my engine failed and the rocket began to fall towards that star, which alarmed me, since the temperature of the thing equaled 600,000 degrees centigrade. The heat increased by the minute and finally grew so unbearable, that I could work only by squeezing myself inside the small refrigerator, where usually I kept food—truly a curious stroke of luck, for it had never occurred to me that I might find myself in such a situation. Successfully repairing the damage, I flew on to Erpeya without further incident. This double star is made up of two suns: one is large, red as a furnace, not too hot, while the other is blue and throws off terrific heat. The planet itself was in fact so small, I found it only after combing the entire stellar neighborhood. Its inhabitants, the Whds, greeted me most cordially.

Exceptionally beautiful are the successive risings and settings of both suns; their eclipses, too, provide unusual sights. For half a day the red sun shines and then all objects look as if steeped in blood, in the other half the blue sun comes out, and is so powerful, you have to walk around with your eyes shut all the time; in spite of this, though, you can see quite tolerably. Having no knowledge of the darkness, the Whds call the blue time day, and the red they call night. There is, it's true, incredibly little room on the planet, but the Whds, beings of much intelligence and possessing great knowledge, particularly in the area of physics, have overcome this difficulty in a most ingenious though, admittedly, singular fashion. To wit: in a special government office and with the aid of a high-precision x-ray apparatus they take of each inhabitant of the planet what they call an "atomic profile," which is an exact blueprint showing absolutely every shred of matter, every protein molecule and chemical bond of which his body is composed. Then, when it comes time to turn in for the night, the Whd enters through a tiny door to a special mechanism and inside is reduced to individual atoms. Taking up very little space in this form, he spends the night, then in the morning at the designated time an alarm turns on the mechanism, which following the atomic profile puts back together all the molecules in the proper order and sequence, the door opens and the Whd, thus restored to life, gives a few yawns and hurries off to work.

The Whds pointed out to me the advantages of this way of life, observing that with it there was never any question of insomnia, bad dreams, apparitions or nightmares, for the machine, in reducing the body to atoms, thereby deprived it of life and consciousness. They apply this expedient also in a variety of other situations, as for example: in doctors' waiting rooms and government offices, where instead of chairs you have little boxes, painted pink and blue, of those machines, and at certain meetings and conferences—in short, wherever a man is condemned to boredom and inactivity and, doing nothing of any use, merely takes up space by the fact of his existence. In this same resourceful way the Whds are accustomed to travel: if you want to go anywhere, you write the address on a card, paste it on a small cassette, which is then placed beneath the machine, you step inside and, atomized, go into the cassette. There is a special institution, something like our postal service, which expedites such parcels to their respective addresses. If someone happens

232

o be in a particular hurry, his atomic profile is sent by telegraph
o the place designated, and there they re-create him by
machine. The original Whd meanwhile undergoes pulverization
and is filed away in the archives. This mode of telegraphic travel,
being extremely swift and simple, holds considerable attraction,
however it also carries with it certain risks. Right as I arrived, the
papers told of an awful accident that had only just taken place. It
seems a certain young Whd by the name of Thermopheles was
supposed to go to some town situated in the other hemisphere of
the planet, in order to be married. Being in love, he was naturally impatient and, wishing to stand at the side of his intended as
soon as possible, he went to the post office and had himself telegraphed. At that very moment the telegraph official was called
away on some urgent business and his replacement, unaware
that Thermopheles had already been sent, wired his profile a
second time, and lo and behold, there before the anxiously waiting bride-to-be stood two Thermopheleses, as alike as two peas
in a pod. It is hard to describe the shock, confusion and distress
of the poor girl, not to mention the entire wedding party. The
attempt was made to convince one of the Thermopheleses to
submit to atomization and thereby end the whole unpleasant incident, but that failed completely, for each of them stubbornly
maintained that *he* was the real and only Thermopheles. The
matter was taken to court and dragged on through several appeals. It was after my departure that the highest court reached
its verdict, therefore I cannot say how the matter was finally
resolved.*

The Whds urged me to sample for myself their method of
repose and travel, assuring me that errors such as the above
were extremely rare and that the process itself had nothing mysterious or supernatural about it, for as everyone knows living
organisms are fashioned from the same material as all the objects that surround us, planets and stars included; the only difference lies in the interconnection and arrangement of the con-
stituent parts. These arguments I understood perfectly, but
nevertheless refused to be talked into it.

---

*Editor's Note: As we have since learned, the verdict called for the atomization
of *both* fiancés and the subsequent reconstruction of only one, therefore it was
truly Solomonic.

One evening a curious thing happened to me. I dropped in on a Whd I knew, forgetting to phone him in advance. No one seemed at home when I entered. Looking around for my host, I opened various doors one by one (the quarters, as all Whd quarters, being incredibly cramped), till finally, setting ajar a door smaller than the rest, I saw what looked like the inside of a refrigerator, completely empty except for a shelf on which stood a small chest full of grayish powder. Without thinking I took a handful of this powder, then jumped at the sound of a door opening and dropped it on the floor.

"What are you doing, honorable alien!" cried the son of that Whd, for it was he who had entered. "Look out, you're spilling my daddy!"

Hearing these words, I was filled with horror and mortification, but the young lad said:

"It's nothing, it's nothing, don't worry!" And he ran out and in a few minutes returned carrying a sizable lump of coal, a sack of sugar, a pinch of sulfur, a small nail and a fistful of ordinary sand; he dumped all this into the chest, closed the little door and threw the switch. I heard something not unlike a deep sigh or swallow, the door opened and there was my friend, laughing at my dismay, safe and sound. I asked him later, during our conversation, whether I hadn't caused him any harm by scattering part of his bodily material like that and, also, just how had his son been able so easily to rectify my clumsy act.

"Come, don't even mention it," he said, "you didn't harm me in the least, what nonsense! Surely you are cognizant, my dear alien friend, of the findings of modern physiology, which say that all the atoms of our body are constantly being replaced with new; some bonds break, others form; the loss is made up thanks to the assimilation of foods and liquids, and thanks also to the respiratory process—all of which, taken together, we call metabolism. So then, the atoms that composed your body a year ago have long since left it and now are wending their way through regions far removed; it is only the general structure of the organism that remains unchanged, the interlocking system of its material pieces. There is nothing strange in the way my son replenished the supply of matter necessary for my re-creation; our bodies after all are made of carbon, sulfur, hydrogen, oxy-

234

gen, nitrogen and traces of metal, and the substances he brought contained those very elements. Please, step into the mechanism yourself, you will see how harmless the procedure is . . ."

I declined my gracious host's offer and for some time afterwards was still reluctant to avail myself of similar invitations, in the end however, after a long inner struggle, I made up my mind. At the x-ray office they took my picture and produced an atomic profile, after which I paid a visit to my friend. Squeezing myself inside the thing wasn't particularly easy, for I am on the heavy side, therefore my gracious host had to help me; the little door could be closed only when the entire family pitched in. The lock clicked and everything grew dark.

What happened then I don't recall. I only felt that I was highly uncomfortable and the edge of the shelf was digging into my ear, before however I could change my position the little door opened and I climbed out of the mechanism. My first question was why they hadn't gone through with the experiment, but my host informed me with a pleasant smile that I was quite mistaken. And to be sure, a look at the wall clock confirmed that I had indeed spent twelve hours inside the mechanism without the least sensation. The only slight inconvenience lay in the fact that my pocket watch indicated the time that I had entered the machine; being reduced to atoms exactly as I was, it could hardly keep running.

The Whds, with whom I felt—more and more—bonds of the warmest friendship, told me yet of other applications of this method: they have this custom, that an outstanding scholar, should he be tormented by some problem which he cannot solve, will remain inside a mechanism for several decades, then—when resurrected—stick his head out into the world and ask if the problem has been answered yet, and if it hasn't, submit once more to atomization, and so on till the goal is reached.

After this first successful experiment I grew so bold, developed such a taste for that novel way of resting, that it was not only nights, but every free minute I spent in the atomized state; one could do this in the park, on the street, for everywhere stood the mechanisms, looking like mailboxes with little doors. All you had to remember was to set the alarm to the right time; absent-minded persons do omit to do this on occasion and could rest inside the mechanism for all eternity, but fortunately there exists a special corps of inspectors, who every month check all the mechanisms.

Towards the end of my stay on the planet I became an out-and-out enthusiast of the Whdian custom and used it, as I said before, every chance I got. For this rashness, alas, I was to pay dearly. It happened, one time, that the mechanism I was occupying jammed a little and when that morning the alarm switched on the current, the thing reconstructed me not in my usual shape but as Napoleon Bonaparte in imperial uniform, wearing the tricolor sash of the Legion of Honor, a saber at my side, a gold-studded cocked hat on my head and an orb and scepter in my hands—that was how I appeared before my astonished Whds. They advised me immediately to get redone in the nearest unbroken mechanism, which would not have presented any difficulty, inasmuch as my true atomic profile was on record and available, all the same I wouldn't hear of the idea, and contented myself with having the cocked hat changed into a cap with ear flaps, the saber into a set of tableware, and the orb and scepter into an umbrella. When I was already sitting at the controls of my rocket and with the planet far behind me in the darkness of eternal night, suddenly it struck me that I had been too hasty ridding myself of those tangible proofs, which would have lent credence to my words. But it was too late now.

THE
TWENTY-FIFTH
VOYAGE

One of the main space lanes in the constellation of the Great Bear connects the planets of Mufta and Taffetum. On the way it passes Tairia, a rocky sphere that enjoys the worst sort of reputation among travelers, and this on account of the swarms of boulders that surround it. That whole region presents a picture of primordial chaos and danger, the disk of the planet barely shows from behind those clouds of stone, in which you have incessant lightning and thunder from colliding chunks of rock.

A few years ago the pilots running flights between Taffetum and Mufta began to tell of certain dire monsters, which would emerge suddenly from the whirling debris above Tairia and attack rockets, wrapping their long tentacles about them, attempting to pull them down into their murky lairs. Some passengers had been badly frightened, but so far that was all. Then the news spread that monsters had attacked a traveler while he was taking an after-dinner stroll around his rocket in a spacesuit. This was greatly exaggerated, since the traveler in question (a good friend of mine) had spilled coffee on his spacesuit and hung it out the hatch to dry, when strange, writhing creatures flew up and made off with it.

Finally feelings ran so high on the neighboring planets, that a special expedition was sent to comb the area around Tairia. Some of its members claimed that deep inside the clouds of

Tairia they had spotted snakelike things resembling octopuses, this however was never verified and after a month the expedition, not daring to venture into the dark regions of Tairia's flint clouds, returned to Taffetum empty-handed. Other expeditions were undertaken later, but with no results.

At last a famous stellar adventurer, the intrepid Zow Gorbras, set out for Tairia, two hounds in spacesuits at his side, to hunt the enigmatic creatures. After five days he returned alone, haggard and drawn. As he told it, not far from Tairia a number of monsters had all at once come charging out from behind a nebula and wound him and his hounds in their tentacles; the brave hunter pulled out a knife and, hacking away blindly, succeeded in freeing himself from the deadly coils, to which—alas—his hounds succumbed. The spacesuit of Gorbras bore, both inside and out, the signs of battle, and in several places green strands of some kind, almost like fibrous stems, were found clinging to it. The college of sciences, having examined these vestiges minutely, announced that they were fragments of a multicellular organism well known on Earth, namely the *Solanum tuberosum*, a bulbaceous, gametopetalous, multiseminiferous species with individual pinnatipartite segmentations, brought by the Spaniards from America to Europe in the 16th century. That news alone excited the imagination, but it is difficult to describe what took place after someone translated the scholarly explanation into everyday language and it turned out that Gorbras had brought back on his spacesuit bits of potato leaves.

The intrepid stellar adventurer, stung to the quick by the insinuation that for four straight hours he had been fighting potatoes, demanded an immediate retraction of this vile calumny, the scientists however replied that they could not retract a single word. There was a great furor. Two factions arose, the Potatoists and the anti-Potatoists, which spread first to the Big and later to the Little Dipper; the antagonists hurled dreadful epithets at one another. But this was nothing compared to what happened when the philosophers entered the fray. From England, France, Australia, Canada and the United States they came, the most illustrious theoreticians of knowledge and expounders of pure reason, and the result of their efforts was astounding.

Upon careful consideration of all sides of the issue, the physicalists maintained that when two bodies A and B move, it is a matter of indifference whether you say that A is moving in relation to B, or B is moving in relation to A. Since motion is relative, one can as easily say that a man is moving in relation to a potato as say that the potato is moving in relation to the man. Therefore the question of whether potatoes can move is meaningless, and the whole problem—trivial, i.e. it doesn't really exist.

The semanticists maintained that everything depends on how you interpret the words "potato," "is" and "moving." Since the key here is the operational copula "is," one must examine "is" rigorously. Whereupon they set to work on an Encyclopedia of Cosmic Semasiology, devoting the first four volumes to a discussion of the operational referents of "is."

The neopositivists maintained that it is not clusters of potatoes one directly perceives, but clusters of sensory impressions. Then, employing symbolic logic, they created terms for "cluster of impressions" and "cluster of potatoes," devised a special calculus of propositions all in algebraic signs and after using up several seas of ink reached the mathematically precise and absolutely undeniable conclusion that $0 = 0$.

The Thomists maintained that God has created the laws of nature for the express purpose of working miracles, since miracles constitute a violation of the laws of nature, and where there are no laws, there is nothing to violate. In the abovementioned instance the potatoes move, if such is the will of the Almighty, though we cannot be certain that this is not some trick of accursed materialists bent on discrediting the Church. Therefore one must await the ruling of the Highest Council at the Vatican.

The Neo-Kantians maintained that objects are projections of the spirit and not knowable things; if then the psyche generates the idea of a moving potato, a moving potato shall have existence. Yet this is but a first impression, for our spirit is no more knowable than its projections; hence nothing can be said, either way.

The holists-pluralists-behaviorists-physicalists maintained that, as is well known in physics, laws of nature operate in a statistical fashion only. Just as it is impossible to predict with complete accuracy the path of a single electron, so too you cannot know with certainty the future behavior of a single potato. Thus far observations show that man has mashed potatoes millions of times, but it is not inconceivable that one time in a billion the situation could reverse itself, that a potato could mash a man.

Professor Fustian, a solitary sage of the school of Russell and Reichenbach, subjected each of these conclusions to withering criticism. He argued that a man does not experience sensory impressions, since no one sees a sensory impression of a table, but only the table itself; and since moreover it is known that about the external world not a thing is known, then neither external objects nor sensory impressions exist. "There is nothing," declared Professor Fustian. "And anyone who thinks otherwise is wrong." Consequently nothing can be said about potatoes, but for an altogether different reason than that given by the Neo-Kantians.

While Fustian labored unremittingly, not once leaving his home, which was besieged by anti-Potatoists hefting rotten potatoes, and while passions were clouding every mind, there appeared on the scene—or, to be more exact, there landed on Taffetum—Professor Tarantoga. Paying no heed to the fruitless disputes, he decided to investigate the mystery *sine ira et studio*, as befitted a true man of science. He began his inquiry by visiting all the nearby planets, gathering information from the inhabitants. In this way he learned that the enigmatic monsters were known under the following names: prucks, borkers, nuffits, gnuttles, garrugulas, malomorps, zops, yots, yuts, batats, rifflers, thycandorines, closh, flibbage and morchmell; which gave him considerable food for thought since, according to the dictionaries, all these names were in fact synonyms for the common potato.

With amazing tenacity and indomitable fortitude Tarantoga worked his way to the heart of the riddle and in five years had a completed theory that explained everything:

Long ago, in the vicinity of Tairia, a ship carrying potatoes to the colonists on Taffetum struck a meteor reef. Through a hole cut in its hull the entire cargo tumbled out. The ship was pulled off the reef and towed by tugs to Taffetum, after which the incident passed into oblivion. Meanwhile the potatoes, having fallen onto the surface of Tairia, put out shoots and began to grow as if nothing had happened. However the conditions under which they grew were uncommonly harsh: from out of the sky gravel rained down time and again, smashing the young sprouts and even killing whole plants. The result was such, that of all the potatoes only the most alert survived, those that were able to fend for themselves and find shelter. The emerging race of perspicacious potatoes developed by leaps and bounds. After a number of generations, wearying of their sedentary way of life, they pulled up roots and took on a nomadic existence. At the same time they completely lost the placid passivity typical of Earth's potatoes, which have been domesticated through constant care and cultivation. Growing more and more wild, they became, at last, potatoes of prey. There are grounds for this in their family tree. The potato, as we know, *Solanum tuberosum*, belongs to the nightshade family (*Solanaceae*), and a dog—as we know too—comes from the wolf and, if let loose in the forest, may revert. This is precisely what happened to the potatoes on Tairia. And when they began to get crowded on the planet, a new crisis ensued; the younger potatoes were fired with the need for action; they wanted to accomplish unusual things, things no vegetable had ever done before. Lifting their eyes to the heavens, they beheld there sailing slabs of stone and resolved to settle upon them.

It would take us too far afield were I to outline here the entire theory of Professor Tarantoga, showing how first the potatoes taught themselves to fly by flapping their leaves, and how subsequently they ventured out beyond the atmosphere of Tairia, finally to establish themselves on the masses of rock that orbited the planet. Which was all the easier for them inasmuch as, preserving their vegetable metabolism, they could remain in space indefinitely, doing without oxygen and drawing their vital energy directly from the sun's rays. In time they grew so bold as to fall upon rockets flying past the planet.

Any scholar in Tarantoga's place would have published this brilliant hypothesis and rested on his laurels, but the Professor vowed not to rest until he had captured at least one predacious potato.

So then, the theoretical side of the problem having been dealt with, it was time to turn to the practical, of equal if not greater difficulty. The potatoes lurked in the crevices of large boulders, and to venture into that moving labyrinth of rushing rock in search of them would have been pure suicide. On the other hand Tarantoga did not intend to shoot a potato; it was a live specimen he wanted, one full of health and kicking. For a while he considered driving them from cover, but rejected that idea too as unsatisfactory, then he hit upon a plan entirely new, which later was to win him widespread fame. He decided he would bag a potato using bait. For this purpose he purchased, in a school supply store on Taffetum, the biggest globe he could find, a beautifully painted sphere twenty feet in diameter. He also obtained a great quantity of honey, sealing wax and fish glue, mixed this well in equal amounts, and smeared the result-ant substance over the surface of the globe. He then fastened the globe to a long line from the rocket and flew off in the direc-tion of Tairia. When he had drawn sufficiently near, the Profes-sor hid behind the corner of a nebula close by and cast the line with the bait. The whole plan hinged upon the natural curiosity of potatoes. After an hour or so a light vibration indicated that something was approaching. Carefully peering out, Tarantoga observed several potatoes shaking their leaves and tentatively shifting their tubers as they made their way towards the globe; apparently they took it for some unknown planet. After a while they gathered up courage and squatted on the globe, sticking to its surface. The Professor quickly drew in his line, attached it to the tail of the rocket and headed back to Taffetum.

It is difficult to picture the enthusiasm with which the daunt-less scholar was received. The captured potatoes, globe and all, were thrown into a cage and put on public display. Furious and wild with fear, the potatoes flailed the air with their leaves and stamped their roots, but obviously this got them nowhere.

When, on the following day, the college of sciences went to Tarantoga in order to present him with an honorary degree and a heavy medal of esteem, the Professor was gone. Having crowned his efforts with success, he had set off in the night, des-tination unknown.

The reason for his sudden departure is well known to me. Tarantoga hurried because in nine days he was supposed to meet me on Coerulea. I myself was at the same time speeding towards the appointed planet from the opposite end of the Milky Way. We intended to set out together for a still unexplored arm of the Galaxy which extended out beyond a dark nebula in

Szkielet Procyty

Skeleton of a procyte.

243

Orion. The Professor and I were not yet personally acquainted. Desiring to earn the reputation of a man true to his word and punctual, I squeezed all the power I could out of the engine, but alas, as it so often happens when we're in a particular hurry, an unforeseen accident ruined my plans. Some tiny meteor or other punctured the fuel tank and, lodging itself in the exhaust pipe, cut the motor dead. With a sigh I put on my spacesuit, picked up a strong flashlight and the tools, then left the cabin and went outside. While extracting the meteor with a pair of pliers I inadvertently knocked the flashlight, which drifted off a considerable distance and began independently to sail through space. I plugged the hole in the tank and returned to the cabin. I couldn't chase after the flashlight, having lost practically my entire supply of fuel; as it was, I barely made it to the nearest planet, Procyton.

The Procytes are intelligent beings and very much like us; the one difference, unimportant really, lies in the fact that they have legs only to the knee, lower down is a wheel, not artificial but forming a part of the body. They move about with great speed and grace, like acrobats on unicycles. Their knowledge is extensive, astronomy in particular excites them; stargazing is in fact so widespread, that no one, young or old, goes anywhere without a hand telescope. Sundials are used exclusively and pulling out a mechanical timepiece in public constitutes a serious breach of conduct. The Procytes also have a number of civilizing devices. I recall how, the first time I visited them, I attended a banquet in honor of old Maratillitec, their famous astronomer. At one point I got into a discussion with him about some issue in astronomy. The Professor disagreed with me, our conversation grew sharper and sharper in tone, then the old man glared and it looked as if he would explode any moment. Suddenly he jumped up and rushed from the hall. After five minutes he returned and sat down beside me, pleasant, smiling, as placid as a child. Intrigued, I asked later what had caused this magical transformation of mood.

"What?" said the Procyte I'd approached. "You really don't know? The Professor used the steam room."

"The steam room?"

"The name of the device comes from the expression 'to blow off steam.' A person seized with anger or feeling hostility to-

244

wards someone enters a small chamber padded with cork and there gives vent to his emotions."

This time when I landed on Procyton I saw, from the air, crowds of people marching in the streets: they were waving lanterns and cheering. Leaving my rocket to the care of the mechanics, I went on to the city. As I soon learned, they were all celebrating the discovery of a new star, which had appeared in the sky the night before. This made me think, and when after a warm welcome Maratillitec invited me to his powerful refractor, as soon as I put my eye to the lens I realized that the star in question was only my flashlight sailing through space. Instead of telling the Procytes, however, I decided—somewhat frivolously—to play at being a better astronomer than they and, making a quick calculation in my head as to how long the flashlight batteries would last, announced to those assembled that the new star would shine white for six hours, then turn yellow, red, and finally go out altogether. This prediction met with general disbelief, and Maratillitec with his customary hotheadedness exclaimed that if that happened, he would eat his beard.

The star began to dim at the time foretold by me, and that evening, when I showed up at the observatory, I found a group of crestfallen assistants, who informed me that Maratillitec, wounded in his pride, had shut himself up in the study, there to carry out the promise he had so rashly given. Fearing that this might cause him some injury, I tried to reason with him through the door, but to no avail. I put my ear to the keyhole and heard a rustling that confirmed the words of the assistants. In the greatest agitation I wrote a letter explaining everything, gave it to the assistants, with the request that they hand it over to the Professor immediately following my departure, whereupon I ran to the airport as fast as my legs could carry me. I did this because I wasn't sure whether or not the Professor would be able, before confronting me, to use the steam room.

I left Procyton at one in the morning in such haste, I completely forgot about the fuel. A million miles or so out the tanks ran dry and I became a cosmic castaway on a ship adrift in space. Only three days remained till the time of my rendezvous with Tarantoga.

Coerulea was perfectly visible through the window, glowing at a distance of barely three hundred million miles, but all I could do was look at it in helpless rage. Yes, the most trifling events can sometimes have tremendous consequences! For want of a nail . . .

About an hour later I noticed a planet slowly looming larger; the ship, yielding passively to its pull, began to pick up speed, till finally it was plummeting like a stone. Determined to make the best of a bad business, I took my seat at the controls. The planet was rather small, desolate, yet homey; I observed oases heated volcanically and with running water. There were plenty of volcanoes; they belched fire and columns of smoke continually. Now I hurtled through the atmosphere, maneuvering the rudders, trying everything I could to decrease velocity, but that merely postponed the moment of impact. And then, flying over a range of volcanoes, I got an idea; after a moment's thought, I reached a desperate decision and, directing the nose of my craft downwards, like a thunderbolt plunged straight into the gaping mouth of the largest volcano. At the last minute, when those red-hot jaws had already engulfed me, with a skillful flip of the rudder I turned the rocket around nose-upward and in this position sank into that bottomless pit of roaring lava.

Risky, but there was no other way. I hoped that the volcano, stirred by the violent blow of the rocket, would react with an eruption—and I was not disappointed. A blast of thunder shook the walls and in a column of flame, lava, ash and smoke that rose for many miles I flew up and out into the sky. I steered in order to fall on course straight for Coerulea, and succeeded perfectly.

Three days later I was at my destination, and only twenty minutes late. But I didn't find Tarantoga there; he had taken off already, leaving me a letter held at the post office.

> *Dear Colleague!* [he wrote] *Circumstances impel me to set out at once, therefore I propose that we meet in the heart of the unexplored region; since chorographical stars have no names, I'll give you directions: fly straight ahead, turn left at the blue sun, then right at the next, orange; there you'll find four planets, I'll be on the third from the left. Looking forward to meeting you!*
>
> Sincerely yours,
> TARANTOGA

Fuelling up, I blasted off at dusk. The trip took one week,

and when I entered the unknown territory I found the right stars without any trouble; carefully following the Professor's instructions, on the morning of the eighth day I saw the designated planet. This massive globe was covered with thick green fur, which turned out to be a gigantic tropical rain forest. The sight of it disconcerted me somewhat, for I had no idea how to go about locating Tarantoga, however I counted on his ingenuity—and was not mistaken. Flying straight for the planet, at eleven that morning I noticed on its northern hemisphere certain faint lines that took my breath away.

I always say to young, inexperienced astronauts, "Don't believe it if someone tells you he approached a planet and saw its name written on it; that's an old cosmic joke." This time however I was at a loss, for there across the green woodland clearly stood the inscription:

Couldn't wait. See you at next planet.

TARANTOGA

The letters were each a mile in size, otherwise of course I wouldn't have spotted them. Thoroughly amazed and also curious as to how the Professor had drawn that giant sign, I flew closer. Then I saw that the lines of the letters were wide avenues of leveled, trampled trees, distinctly separate from the untouched areas.

Still mystified, I did as the sign said and hurried on to the next planet, which was inhabited and civilized. At sunset I reached the airport. In vain did I inquire there after Tarantoga; this time too there was a letter waiting for me.

Dear Colleague:

My deepest apologies for letting you down like this, but in connection with a certain family matter that will not brook delay I must alas go home at once. To lessen your disappointment I am leaving a package at the main office—kindly claim it; it contains the fruits of my latest research. You are undoubtedly curious as to how, on the previous planet, I left you that written message; it was really quite simple. That globe is going through an epoch corresponding to the Carboniferous on Earth and is populated by giant lizards, including terrible atlantosaurs one hundred and fifty feet long. Having landed on the planet, I crept up to a great herd of atlantosaurs and provoked them until they attacked me. I began then to run quickly through the forest in a calculated way, such that the trail of my flight would assume the shape of letters, and the herd charging after me mowed down all the trees. Thus were produced those avenues two hundred and fifty feet in diameter. Quite simple, as I said, but rather fatiguing, in that I was obliged to run nearly thirty miles and at a rapid clip besides.

I sincerely regret that this time too we cannot make one another's acquaintance. Let me then shake your intrepid hand and offer expressions of the highest regard for your many virtues and courage.

- TARANTOGA

P.S. I strongly recommend you take in the concert at the city this evening—it's excellent.

T.

I picked up the package set aside for me at the airport office, ordered it delivered to the hotel, and myself went on to the city. It presented a most unusual sight. The planet spins with such velocity, that day alternates with night every hour. Due to the centrifugal force produced by this, a freely hanging plumb line is not perpendicular to the ground, as on Earth, but rather makes an angle of 45 degrees with it. All the houses, towers, walls, in general every sort of edifice stands leaning towards the surface of the ground at a 45-degree angle, which affords a somewhat peculiar sight to the human eye. The houses on one side of the street appear to be bending over backwards, while on the other side they lean and hang above the first. The planet's inhabitants, in order not to fall, possess through natural adaptation one short leg and one long. A man however, when walking, must constantly bend one knee, which after a certain time becomes extremely difficult and painful. Therefore I proceeded slowly, so that by the time I reached the building where they were supposed to hold the concert, the doors to the hall were being closed. I hurriedly bought a ticket and ran inside.

Hardly had I taken my seat when the conductor rapped with his baton and everyone fell silent. The members of the orchestra began to move with energy, playing on instruments I'd never seen before, horns with perforated funnels similar to shower heads; the conductor now lifted both his front extremities with feeling, now spread them out, as if calling for "pianissimo," but my amazement only grew, for so far I had

248

heard not a single sound. Casting a furtive glance on either side, I saw ecstasy written on the faces of my neighbors; more and more bewildered and uneasy, I tried discreetly cleaning out my ears, but with no result. Finally, afraid that I had lost my hearing, I quietly tapped my fingernails together, however this faint sound was distinctly audible. So then, not knowing what to think of this, perplexed by the general signs of esthetic satisfaction, I sat through to the end of the work. A burst of applause rang out; the conductor gave a bow, once again rapped his baton, and the orchestra proceeded to the next movement of the symphony. All around people were entranced; I heard a great deal of sniffing and took this as an indication of deep emotion. Then at last came the stormy finale—or so I assumed, judging by the violent exertion of the conductor and the beads of sweat that formed on the brows of the musicians. Again thunderous applause. My neighbor turned to me, expressing his admiration for the symphony and its performance. I muttered something in reply and fled out onto the street in complete confusion.

I had already walked a few dozen steps away from the building, when something made me turn and look at its façade. Like the others, it was inclined at a sharp angle to the street; over the entrance loomed a sign that said *Municipal Olfactorium,* and below were pasted program posters, on which I read:

ODONTRON

"THE MUSK SYMPHONY"
I Preludium Odoratum
II Allegro Aromatoso
III Andante Olens

Featuring
as guest conductor, in a rare appearance,
the famous nasalist
HRANTR

With a curse I turned on my heel and made straight for the hotel. I didn't blame Tarantoga for my failure to enjoy the concert; he had no way of knowing that I was still suffering from the cold I'd caught on Satelline.

To make up the disappointment to myself, immediately

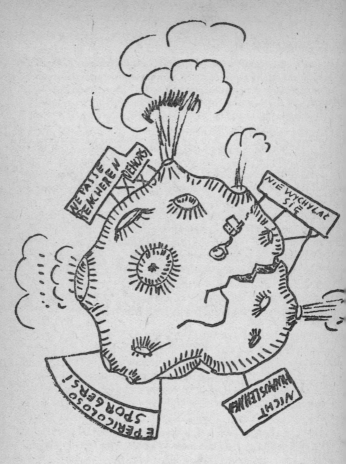

Mała stara planeta

A small old planet.

fter arriving at the hotel I unpacked my package. It contained a
ovie projector, a reel of film, and a letter that went as follows:

My Dear Colleague!

*You will recall our telephone conversation when you were visiting the
Little, and I the Big Dipper. I said at the time that I suspected the existence
of beings able to live at high temperatures on hot, molten planets, and that I
intended to do research in this direction. You saw fit to express your doubt
that such an undertaking would succeed. Well, here you have the proof before you. I selected a fiery planet, approached it by rocket as near as possible,
then lowered on a long asbestos rope a fireproof filming device and microphone; in this fashion I took a number of interesting shots. The results of
this little experiment I am taking the liberty of enclosing herewith.*

Yours,
Tarantoga

Burning with curiosity, no sooner had I finished reading
an I put the film in the machine, hung my bedsheet up over
e door and, turning off the light, started the projector. At first
n that improvised screen there were only flickering patches of
lor; I heard hoarse noises and a crackling as if of logs in a fur-
ace, then the picture sharpened.

The sun was sinking beneath the horizon. The surface of
e ocean quivered; across it flitted tiny blue flames. The fiery
ouds grew pale in the gathering darkness. The first faint stars
ppeared. Young Rodrillo, weary after studying all day, had just
merged from his fludget to take an evening stroll. There was
owhere in particular he was going; leisurely moving his twoons,
e inhaled with pleasure the fresh, fragrant vapors of burning
nmonia. Someone approached him, barely visible in the grow-
g dusk. Rodrillo strained his scrotchers, but it wasn't until the
ther came nigh that the youth recognized his friend.

"Lovely evening, isn't it?" said Rodrillo. The friend shifted
is weight from ambus to ambus, leaned halfway out of the fire
nd said:

"Lovely indeed. The sal ammoniac has grown nicely this
ear, have you noticed?"

"Yes, the harvest promises to be good."

Rodrillo swayed lazily, turned over on his belly and, open-
g all his opticules, gazed up at the stars.

251

"You know," he said after a moment, "whenever I look at th night sky, as now, I cannot help but feel that up there, far, fa away, are other worlds, worlds similar to our own, and also inhab ited by beings of intelligence . . ."

"Who speaks here of intelligence?!" came a voice nearby Both lads turned their backs in that direction to see who it wa They recognized the gnarled but still spry figure of Flamentiu That hoary scholar approached them with stately motions, an his future descendants, looking like bunches of grapes, were a ready swelling and sending out their first shoots on his spread ing shoulders.

"I was speaking of the intelligent beings that inhabit othe worlds . . ." replied Rodrillo, lifting his squips respectfully.

"Rodrillo was speaking of intelligent beings on othe worlds? . . ." rejoined the scholar. "Just look at him! Othe worlds yet!! Ah, that Rodrillo, that Rodrillo! Is *this* how yo spend your time, my boy? Letting your imagination run wild But of course . . . I approve . . . on an evening such as thi . . . It's gotten definitely colder, don't you think?"

"No," said both lads together.

"The fires of youth, yes, I know. All the same it's now on eight hundred and sixty degrees; I should have put on my lav lined pullover. That's old age for you. So you say," he continue turning his back to Rodrillo, "that on other worlds there exis intelligent life? What sort of creatures are these, according t you?"

"We cannot know exactly," replied the youth timidly. "The are varied, I think. It's conceivable even that on the coole planets living organisms might arise from a substance called pr tein."

"Who told you that?!" Flamentius burst out in anger.

"Implosio. He's the young student of biochemistry who—"

"Young fool, you mean!" snapped Flamentius. "Life fro protein?! Living things from protein? Aren't you ashamed spout such nonsense in the presence of your teacher?! Here the result of the ignorance and the arrogance that have sprea so alarmingly of late! You know what they ought to do with th Implosio of yours? Give him a good watering down, that's what

"But Flamentius, sir," ventured Rodrillo's friend, "why d mand such severe punishment for Implosio? Couldn't you tell what beings on other planets might look like? Might they not stand erect and move on things called legs?"

"Where did you hear *that*?"

Rodrillo said nothing, frightened.

"From Implosio . . ." whispered his friend.

"Enough, for heaven's sake, enough of this Implosio and his fabrications!" shouted the scholar. "Legs! Really! As if I hadn't only twenty-five Blazes ago proven mathematically that a two-footed being, as soon as one stood it up, would immediately fall flat on its face! I even constructed an appropriate model and diagrams, but what would you—sluggards—know of that? What do intelligent beings on other worlds look like? I'm not going to tell you straight out, think a little, learn to use your minds. First they'll have to have organs to take in ammonia, right? And what can do this better than the twoons? And won't they have to move through a medium as resistant and as warm as ours? Well, won't they? Of course they will! And how can you do this if not with ambuses? Also they will probably form sense organs—opticules, nims, blulthbs. And of course they must be like us pentoids not merely in physical structure, but in the overall manner of living. Everyone knows, surely, that the pentex is the basic unit of our family life—try in your imagination to picture something different, exert your fancy as much as you wish, I promise you that you will fail! Yes, because in order to start a family, in order to produce progeny, one has to have a Tata, a Gaga, a Mama, a Fafa and a Haha. Mutual affection, plans, hopes and dreams, they are nothing if you lack a member of any one of these five genders—a situation which, unfortunately, does sometimes happen in life, we call it the tragic quadrangle, or unrequited love . . . And so you see, by reasoning without prejudice or preconceptions, by relying solely on the scientific facts, by employing the precise tool of logic, proceeding coldly and objectively, we reach the inescapable conclusion that every intelligent being must be similar to a pentoid . . . Yes. Well, now are you convinced?"

THE TWENTY-EIGHTH VOYAGE

In a little while now I shall place these written pages in an empty oxygen cylinder and throw it into the deep, overboard, letting it race off into the distant darkness, though I hardly expect that anyone will find it. *Navigare necesse est,* but apparently this interminable voyage is beginning to wear down even my resistance. I have been flying and flying for years, with still no end in sight. Worst of all, time gets tangled, intersects itself, I wind up in various branchings and shallows outside the calendar, hard to say whether it's the future or the past, though sometimes things do smack of the medieval. There exists a special method of preserving one's reason in extreme solitude, it was invented by my grandfather Cosimo, the idea is to make up a certain number of companions for oneself, of both sexes even, but then you have to stick to it consistently. My father used this too, though sometimes there are risks involved. In the silence here such companions grow too independent, they cause problems, complications, some made attempts on my life and I had to fight them, the cabin is a veritable battlefield. I couldn't discontinue the method, out of loyalty to my grandfather. Thank God they're dead and now I have a moment to myself. Perhaps I'll sit down, as I planned to do so many times before, and write a short account of my ancestry, in order there—there in those generations of yore—to draw strength like Antaeus. The founder of the main line of Tichys was Anonymus, a man wrapped in mystery, which was closely connected with Einstein's famous paradox of the twins. One twin flies off into space, the other remains on Earth, after which the former, returning, turns out to be younger than the latter. When the first experiment was undertaken to test this paradox, two young people came forward as volunteers, Caspar and Ezekiel. Due to some mix-up on takeoff both of them were put in the rocket. The experiment thus miscarried before it ever got off the ground, and what was worse—the rocket came back a year later with only one of them on board. He claimed, deep in mourning, that his brother had leaned out too far when they were passing over Jupiter. People didn't give credence to these pain-filled words and in the course of the bitter campaign waged against him in the press he was charged with fratricide and cannibalism. What served the prosecutor as material evidence was a cookbook discovered in the rocket, with a chapter marked off in red and entitled, "Pickling in Outer Space." Nevertheless a man was found, honorable and also intelligent, who consented to defend him. The man's advice was not to say a single word throughout the trial, regardless of what happened. And indeed, in spite of itself the court was unable to condemn my ancestor, for in the delivering of the sentence both the first and last names of the defendant had to be given. The old chronicles differ—some say that even prior to this he had called himself Tichy, others, that that was a nickname resulting from the jury's constant expression of disapproval ("tch-tch"). He really should have been named Tisky, from the more standard variant of that interjection. The lot of this progenitor of mine was far from enviable. Slanderers and liars, of whom there is never any lack, stated that during the court proceedings he had licked his lips whenever mention was made of his brother's name; nor were they hindered, in the uttering of this calumny, by the fact that no one knew who here was the brother of whom. About the further fortunes of this forefather I know little. He had eighteen children and tried his hand at many trades, for a while he even supported himself as a door-to-door salesman of children's spacesuits. In his old age he became a refurbisher of endings to literary works. As this is a fairly obscure profession, I must explain that it consisted in fulfilling requests expressed by lovers of novels and plays. A refurbisher, when he receives an order, must steep himself in the atmosphere, style and spirit of the original, to which he then appends a conclusion different from the author's. In the family archives a few rough drafts have been preserved; they show what considerable artistic ability the first of the Tichys had. There are versions of "Othello" there, in which Desdemona smothers the Moor, also versions where she, he and Iago live happily ever after, together. There are variations of Dante's Inferno, with special tortures added for those persons whom the particular customer named, moreover it was necessary on occasion to replace an author's tragic finale with a happy ending though the reverse was much more common. Rich epicures commissioned from my ancestor epilogues in which you had at the last minute not Virtue Saved but—just the opposite—Evil Triumphant. Those well-heeled patrons undoubtedly were motivated by the lowest instincts, nonetheless my great-great-grandfather, in turning out what had been ordered, created true gems of artistry, and at the same time—though unintentionally, as it were—he came closer to real life than did the actual authors. In any case he had many mouths to feed, so he did what he was able, and his aversion for spacefaring—easy enough to understand—never left him. Beginning with him there appeared in our family, over the centuries, a type of man who was talented, withdrawn, possessing an original mind, often prone to eccentricities, tenacious in the pursuit of the goals he set himself. In our archives there are numerous documents that attest these characteristic traits. It seems that one of the offshoots of the Tichy line lived in Austria, or more precisely in the former Austro-Hungarian Kingdom, for among the pages of the oldest chronicle I found a faded photograph of a handsome young man in cuirassier uniform, with a monocle and twirled mustache; on the back were written the words, "K. u. K. Cyberleutnant Adalbert Tichy." Of what this cyberleutnant did I know nothing, except that—as a precursor of technological microminiaturization, at a time when no one even dreamed of such a thing—he had proposed a plan to put the cuirassiers on ponies instead of horses. Considerably more information has come down to us about Esteban Francis Tichy, the brilliant thinker who—unhappy in his personal life—wanted to change the climate of the Earth by sprinkling the polar regions with powdered soot. The blackened snow would melt, absorbing the

256

rays of the sun, and the territories of Greenland and Antarctica, freed in this manner from the ice, were to be transformed—so wished that great-grandfather of mine—into a kind of Eden for humanity. Finding no backers for his project, he began single-handedly to accumulate supplies of soot, which led to marital discord that ended finally in divorce. His second wife, Eurydice, was the daughter of a druggist who, behind his son-in-law's back, carried the soot out of the cellar and sold it as medicinal carbon (*carbo animalis*). When the druggist was unmasked, Esteban Francis, wholly ignorant of all this, was also charged with dispensing fraudulent medicines and paid with the confiscation of his entire supply of soot, which had been collected in the basement of his home over a period of many years. Deeply disillusioned in his fellow man, the poor soul died before his time. The only comfort he had in the last months of his life was the sprinkling with ashes of the snow-covered vegetable garden in winter and observing the progress of the thaw that ensued as a result of this measure. My grandfather placed a small memorial obelisk in the garden, with an inscription suited to the occasion.

This grandfather, Jeremiah Tichy, is one of the most distinguished representatives of our family. He was raised in the home of his older brother Melchior, a cyberneticist and inventor known for his piety. Not overly radical in his views, Melchior had no wish to automate the entire ministry, but only sought to come to the aid of the broad masses of the clergy, he constructed therefore several foolproof, rapid-action and easy to service devices, like the anathematic excommunicator, as well as a special apparatus for the placing of ecclesiastical curses in reverse gear (to withdraw them). His achievements, alas, did not meet with the approval of those for whom he labored, what is more, they were pronounced heretical. With characteristic magnanimity he then offered to provide the local vicar with a model of the excommunicator, thus making it possible for it to be experimentally tested on himself. Unfortunately even this was denied him. Saddened, discouraged, he resigned from further work in this direction and switched—as a constructor only—to the religions of the East. Known to this very day are the electronic Buddhist prayer wheels of his devising, particularly the high-speed models, which can do up to 18,000 prayers per minute.

Jeremiah, in contrast to Melchior, had not an ounce of

compromise in him. Dropping out of school, he continued his studies at home, mainly in the cellar, which was to play so great a role in his life. He was marked by a most extraordinary single mindedness. At the age of nine he decided to create a General Theory of Everything and nothing could divert him from that goal. The tremendous difficulty he experienced, from the earliest years on, in formulating concepts, only intensified after a disastrous street accident (a steamroller flattened his head). Yet even this disability failed to keep him from philosophy; he resolved to become a Demosthenes of thought, or perhaps rather its Stephenson, for much like the inventor of the locomotive, who himself went none too fast and wanted to force steam to move the wheels, he wanted to force electricity to move ideas. People frequently have distorted this notion, saying that he called for the beating of electronic brains. His slogan—according to such defamatory sources—was supposed to have been: "Show the Eniacs who's boss!" This is a malicious perversion of the idea; he simply had the misfortune to appear with his theories too early. Jeremiah suffered much in life. On his house were scrawled epithets like "wife-beater" and "brain-driver," the neighbors reported him for disturbing the peace at night with all the banging and swearing that rose up from the cellar, they even had the nerve to claim he had made attempts on the life of their children, strewing about poisoned candy. It's true that Jeremiah—like Aristotle—couldn't stand children, but the candies were intended for the starlings that plundered his garden, the labels they had on them made that plain enough. And as for the "profanities" he was supposed to have taught his machines, these were merely cries of frustration that escaped him during those long hours of work in the laboratory, when the results turned out to be negligible. To be sure, it was not exactly politic of him to use—in the pamphlets published at his own expense—crude, even vulgar terms, since in the context of a discussion on electronic systems such expressions as "smacking the tube one" and "throwing in a good boot" could easily give the reader the wrong impression. And it was out of pure cussedness, I am certain, that he made up that story which says he never sat down to program without a crowbar handy. His eccentricities made it difficult for him to get along with others; not everyone was able to appreciate his sense of humor (hence that incident with the milkman and

he two letter carriers, who would have gone insane anyway—it
was undoubtedly in their heredity—the skeletons had been on
wheels after all, and the burrow measured only eight feet in
depth). But then who can fathom the vagaries of genius? It was
said that he wasted an entire fortune, buying up electronic
brains for the purpose of smashing them to little pieces, that the
fragments were piled high in his back yard. But was it his fault if
the computers of the day proved unequal to the tasks he set
them, being too limited and of insufficient stamina? Had they
not fallen apart so easily, he would have ultimately led them to
create the General Theory of Everything. His failure in no way
discredits the basic concept.

As far as his marital problems were concerned, the woman
he married fell under the influence of neighbors hostile to
him—they induced her to make false statements at the trial—
and besides, electric shocks do develop a person's character.
Jeremiah felt himself isolated, ridiculed, and ridiculed no less by
narrow-minded experts like Professor Brumber, who called him
an electrical delinquent, because once Jeremiah had happened
to use an induction coil improperly. Brumber was a nasty, worthless individual, and yet a brief moment of justifiable anger cost
Jeremiah a four-year interruption in his scientific work. All this,
because success was not allotted to him. Otherwise who would
have been interested in the defects of his manner, his behavior,
his style? Whoever spread gossip about the private life of a Newton or an Archimedes? Unfortunately Jeremiah was born before
his time and for that he had to pay.

Towards the end of his life, or more precisely in its decline,
Jeremiah underwent a startling transformation, which totally
changed his lot. Having, then, locked and double locked himself
up in his cellar, from which he first removed every last bit and
piece of machinery, so that he remained alone between four
bare walls, with a bed made of planks, a stool and an old iron
rail, until his death he never left that asylum, that voluntary
prison. But was it indeed a prison, and his act—merely an escape
from the world, a resigned withdrawal, the retreat into adversity
of a hermit seeking to mortify himself? The facts clearly argue
against such a supposition. It was not for quiet meditation that
he lived out his days in self-imposed seclusion. Through a tiny
window in the cellar door they handed him, besides crusts of

bread and water, whatever objects he desired, and he desired—
throughout those sixteen years—always the same thing: ham
mers of various weights and sizes. All together he used up 3,219
of them, and when that great heart ceased to beat, there were
found in the cellar—scattered in the corners—hundreds and
hundreds of rust-eaten hammer heads, all flattened with untold
effort. Moreover, day and night from the basement came the
ringing sound of forging, which let up only briefly, when the
voluntary prisoner fed his aching body or when, after a short
sleep, he would make notes in his diary, which lies before me
now. From these one can see that his spirit hadn't changed, on
the contrary, more steadfast than ever, it had focused on a new
goal. "I'll fix her wagon!" "I'll settle her hash!" "A little more, and
her goose is cooked!"—such comments, jotted down in that
characteristically illegible hand of his, fill these thick notebooks
covered with metal filings. Whose hash did he wish to settle
whose goose did he hope to cook? We will never know for sure
for not once is there mentioned the name of that most
mysterious—and presumably most powerful—adversary. I
think he must have decided, in one of those sudden flashes that
not infrequently visit the minds of the great, to accomplish on
the highest possible level that which previously he had gone
about in a much more modest way. Before, he had placed cer
tain mechanisms in situations of duress, exhorting them to make
it on their own. Now the proud old man, by his self
imprisonment, shut out the chorus of petty, sneering critics and
through that cellar door entered history, for—this is my
surmise—he grappled with the most formidable opponent of
all: in the sixteen years of his labor the realization never left him
not for a moment, that he was storming the very heart and core
of existence, that—in short—without the least hesitation or
doubt, without mercy and without respite he was beating matter
itself!!

But to what end did he do this? Oh, this had nothing in
common with the action of that ancient monarch, who ordered
the sea flogged because it had swallowed up his ships. No, in this
Sisyphean toil carried out with such heroism I sense the pres
ence of an idea that is more than simply unusual. Future genera
tions will understand that Jeremiah hammered in the name of
humanity. He wanted to drive matter to the limit, to torture it

260

xhaust it, pound from it its ultimate essence and thereby
riumph over it. What was supposed to have followed then? The
otal anarchy of defeat, an end to all physical laws? Or perhaps
he rise of new laws? We do not know. Someday those who follow
n Jeremiah's footsteps will find out.

I would be only too glad to conclude his story on this note,
ut it must be added that, even afterwards, the scandalmongers
pread the most incredible nonsense, saying that the deceased
ad been hiding in the cellar from his wife and creditors! That is
ow the world repays its gifted for their greatness!

The next of whom the chronicles speak was Igor Sebastian
Cichy, son of Jeremiah, an ascetic and cybermystician. With him
erminates the earthly branch of our lineage, for thereafter all
he descendants of Anonymus go off into the Galaxy. Igor
ebastian was by nature contemplative, and for that reason
only—and not because of any mental retardation, which was
wrongfully attributed to him—did he utter his first word at the
ge of eleven. Like all the great revolutionary minds, who with a
critical eye perceive man in a new light, he did accordingly and
arrived at the conclusion that the root of all evil lay in the animal
estiges within us, destructive of both individual and society. In
is opposition of the darkness of the instinctual drives and the
rightness of the human spirit there was nothing new as yet, but
gor Sebastian went a step farther than ever dared his predeces-
ors. Man—he said to himself—must bring his spirit to where
only the body, till now, has reigned! A remarkably talented
control-system stereochemist, after many years of research he
came up with a substance that transformed his dreams into real-
ty. I am speaking, of course, of the well-known drug obnoxynol,
a pentose derivative of diallylorthopentylperhydrophenan-
hrene. Obnoxynol, nontoxic, when taken in microscopic
amounts, causes the act of procreation to become—the reverse
f what it has been—highly unpleasant. With the aid of a pinch
f white powder a man begins to look upon the world with an
eye unclouded by desire, he discerns the proper priority of
hings, not blinded at every step by animal urges. He acquires a
great deal of time and, delivered from the slavery of sex imposed by evolution, throws off the chains of erotic alienation
and at last is free. The perpetuation of the species should be,
after all, the result of a conscious decision, of a sense of respon-

261

sibility towards humanity, and not the involuntary—since autonomic—outcome of the gratification of carnal appetites. At first Igor Sebastian planned to make the act of copulation neutral; he realized however that this was not enough, since people do too many things not for pleasure but simply out of boredom or else by force of habit. The act was to become, from then on, a sacrifice laid at the altar of the common good, a burden willingly assumed; those who produced offspring, by this demonstration of courage, were counted heroes, as is anyone who gives of himself for the sake of others. Like a true scientist, Igor Sebastian tested the effects of obnoxynol on himself first, and then, in order to prove that even after heavy doses of it one could still reproduce, with unremitting fortitude, with the greatest self-control he sired thirteen children. His wife, they say, ran away from home on several occasions—there *is* some truth to this, however the main reason for those domestic tiffs was, as in Jeremiah's time, the neighbors, who set that woman—none too bright to begin with—against her husband. They accused Igor Sebastian of maltreating his wife, though he explained to them many times that he wasn't tormenting her at all, it was merely the above-mentioned act, now a source of suffering, which had turned his house into a place of howls and groans. But those narrow minds only kept repeating, like parrots, that the father beat electrobrains, and the son—his wife. Yet this was but the prologue to the tragedy, for when, unable to find volunteers and spurred by the vision of purifying man everlastingly of lust, he put obnoxynol in all the village wells, Igor was beaten by an angry mob, then lynched most shamefully. He was not unaware of the risk he ran. He understood that the triumph of the spirit over the body would not come of its own accord; many passages of his book, published posthumously at the expense of his family, testify to this. In it, he writes that every great idea must be backed by force, as one can see in numerous examples from history, which illustrate that the best argument in defense of a theory is the police. Regrettably he didn't have his own and hence came to a sad end.

There were, of course, men with evil tongues, who maintained that the father had been a sadist, and the son—a masochist. There's not a word of truth in that. I may be getting into delicate matters, but the good name of our family must be proected, kept from being dragged through the mud. Igor was no masochist; despite his self-control he more than once had to resort to the physical assistance of two devoted cousins, who held him down, particularly after large doses of obnoxynol, on the marriage bed, from which—as soon as the deed was done—he fled like one scalded.

The sons of Igor did not carry on their father's work. The eldest dabbled for a time in the synthesis of ectoplasm, a substance well-known to spiritualists, being emanated by mediums under trance, but he failed because—so he said—the margarine which served as the starting material had contained impurities. The youngest son was the black sheep of the family. They bought him a one-way ticket to the star Mira Coeti, which not long after his arrival there went out. Of the fate of the daughters I know nothing.

One of the first astronauts after the one hundred and fifty year interruption—or, as they were already calling them then, spacefarers—was my great-uncle Pafnuce. He owned a star ferry in one of the smaller galactic sounds and carried on his little craft innumerable travelers. He spent a quiet and uneventful life among the stars, not at all like his brother, Euzebius, who became a pirate, though—true—relatively late in life. A born practical joker, Euzebius had a marvelous sense of humor; the entire crew called him "a card." He would rub out the stars with shoe polish and scatter tiny flashlights along the Milky Way, to confuse the captains, and the rockets that went off course he fell upon and plundered. But then he would return the victims everything, order them to continue on their way, overtake them in his black cruiser, board them and start plundering all over again; this would happen six, even ten times in a row. The passengers could hardly see each other for the bruises.

And yet Euzebius was not a wicked man. It was only that, lying in wait for years on end at sidereal crossroads for prey, he grew terribly bored, so that when finally someone did come his way he simply couldn't bring himself to part with them immediately upon completion of the robbery. Interplanetary buccaneering is, as you know, financially unprofitable, which no doubt accounts for the fact that it hardly exists. Euzebius Tichy did not act out of low, materialistic motives, on the contrary, he was fired by the spirit of ancient ideals, for he wanted to bring back the venerable Earth tradition of piracy on the high seas, seeing in this his sacred mission. People imputed to him many vile tendencies, there were even some who called him a necrophiliac, since numerous corpses circled his ship. Nothing could be further from the truth than these loathsome slanders. In space, you can't just bury someone who meets an untimely end, the only way to dispose of the body is by chucking it out the hatch of the rocket; the fact that it doesn't leave but goes into orbit around the bereaved rocket is the result of Newton's laws of motion, and not of anyone's perverted inclinations. Indeed, with the passing years the number of bodies surrounding the ship of my relative grew considerably; maneuvering, he moved as if in an aureole of death, practically a thing out of Dürer's dances, but—I repeat—this wasn't his idea, it was Nature's.

In the nephew of Euzebius and my cousin, Arystarch Felix Tichy, were united all the valuable talents which till now had appeared separately in our family. He was the only one, also, to achieve fame and a considerable fortune—through gastronomical engineering, or gastronautics, which he so brilliantly developed. The origin of this branch of technology goes back as far as the second half of the 20th century; it was known then in the crude, primitive form of "rocketry cannibalization." In order to conserve material and space, ship partitions and bulkheads began to be manufactured out of laminated food concentrates, i.e. various cereals, tapiocas, legumes, etc. Later the scope of this construction enterprise was expanded to include the rocket's furniture. My cousin aptly summed up the quality of those early products when he said that on a good-tasting chair you can't sit, and one that's comfortable gives you indigestion. Arystarch Felix set about the problem in an altogether different way. Small wonder, that the United Shipyards of Aldebaran named their first three-stage rocket (Hors D'oeuvres, Entrée, Dessert) after him. Today no one looks twice at frosted petit-four dashboards (electrotartlets), layer cake condensers, macaroni insulation, marzipan solenoids, or cells with gingerbread and alternating currants, or even windows made of rock candy, though naturally not everyone goes in for suits of scrambled eggs, or pillows of pumpkin pie and feather turnovers (they *do* make crumbs in bed). All this is the work of my cousin. He was the one who invented beef jerky towlines, strudel bedsheets, soufflé quilts, as well as the semolina noodle drive, he too was the first to use Emmenthaler in radiators. Substituting yeast for nitric acid, he came up with a fuel that made a delicious and refreshing (and nonalcoholic!) beverage. No less ingenious are his cranberry fire extinguishers, which can quench a fire or a thirst equally well. Arystarch had imitators too, but none of them could match him. A certain Globkins tried to put on the market, as a source of illumination—a Sacher torte with a wick, which proved a complete fiasco, since the torte gave off little light and had a burnt taste besides. Similarly, his risotto doormats attracted few buyers, as was the case with the halvah siding, that splattered at the first touch of a meteor. Once again it had been shown that a general concept is not enough, that each and every concrete application of it must be, in itself, creative—as for example that idea of my cousin's, brilliant in its simplicity, to fill all the empty places in the rocket's frame with consommé, whereby wasted space was put to use, and nutritiously too. This Tichy, I think, fully deserved to be called the benefactor of cosmic navigation. Its pioneers assured us—not so long ago, either—when we couldn't look at an algae hamburger or a moss-and-lichen stew, that *that* was the diet of men traveling to the stars. Bless you, cousin! A good thing, that I've lived to see better times, for in my youth how very many crews there were that starved to death, adrift among the dark currents of space, their only choice being whether to draw lots or vote democratically, the simple majority deciding. He will agree with me, who remembers the oppressive atmosphere of those gatherings where such distasteful matters were debated. You also had the Drulps Plan, which created quite a sensation in its day, to spread throughout the entire solar system—having shipwrecks in mind—oatmeal or cream of wheat, also instant cocoa, but the thing was never adopted, first, because it turned out to be too expensive, and secondly, with clouds of cocoa in the way one couldn't see the stars to steer by. Yes, it was only rocket cannibalism that freed us from all that.

And now, as I move on up the genealogical tree and come to modern times, and to my own beginnings, my task as family chronicler grows more and more difficult. Not merely because those ancestors of long ago, who led relatively sedentary lives, are more easily portrayed than their interstellar heirs, but also because in space one has the as-yet-unexplained effects of physical phenomena on blood relations. I've tried putting these documents in the proper sequence—and have given it up as hopeless, so will simply present them in the way they come down to us. Here, then, are the speed-singed pages of the log kept by star captain Cosimo Tichy:

Entry 116,303. So many years now without gravitation! The hourglasses don't work, the balance clocks have stopped, in the wind-ups the mainsprings refuse to budge. For a while we tore pages off the calendar at random, but now that too is in the past. The last guidelines left to us are breakfast, lunch and dinner, but the first indigestion that comes along can scotch that reckoning of time as well. I have to stop here, someone's just entered, it's either the twins or light-wave interference.

Entry 116,304. Off the port bow, a planet not indicated on the maps. A little later, around teatime, a meteor, small thank goodness, it broke through three of our compartments—the pressure chamber, the detention room, the sobering tank. I ordered them cemented. At dinner—Cousin Patrick absent. A conversation with Grandfather Arabeus about the uncertainty principle. And what, really, can we be certain of? That we set out from Earth as young people, that we called our ship "The Cosmocyst," that Grandpa and Grandma took on board twelve other married couples, who today form a single family, joined by ties of blood. I'm worried about Patrick—and the cat, too, has disappeared. Weightlessness, by the way, appears to have a positive effect on flat feet.

Entry 116,305. The first-born of Uncle Oliphant is so sharp-sighted and still so small, he can actually see neutrons with the naked eye. Conducted a search for Patrick: negative. We're increasing speed. During the maneuver our stern cut across an isochronal. After dinner Oliphant's brother-in-law, Amphotericus, came by and confided that he is now his own father, apparently his time line knotted up into a loop. He asked me not to tell anyone. I consulted our cousin physicists—they shrugged. Who knows what else is in store for us!

Entry 116,306. I have noticed that the chins and foreheads of

266

several older uncles, both on the maternal and paternal sides, are receding. What is this, the effect of a gyroscopic displacement, the Lorentz-Fitzgerald contraction perhaps, or the result of lost teeth and the frequent knocking of heads against the crossbeam when the dinner bell sounds? We are flying through a sizable nebula; Aunt Barabella divined our future trajectory in the old-fashioned way, from coffee grounds. I checked it out on the electrocalculator—quite close!

Entry 116,307. A brief stopover on the planet of the Gallivants. Four persons didn't return on board. At takeoff, blockage in the left jet. I ordered it blown out. Poor Patrick! In the column under "Cause of Death" I wrote: absent-mindedness. What else could it have been?

Entry 116,308. Uncle Timothy dreamed we were being attacked by marauding mogs. Fortunately we got off without losses or serious casualties. It's growing crowded on the ship. Three deliveries today and four moves, because of divorces. Oliphant's child has eyes like stars. In order to renovate the living quarters I asked all the aunts to step into the hibernating freezers. The only argument that worked was that in a state of reversible death they wouldn't age. Now it's very quiet around here, very pleasant.

Entry 116,309. We are approaching the speed of light. Hundreds of unknown phenomena. A new kind of elementary particle has made its appearance—squarks. Not very large, but noisy. Something peculiar is happening to my head. I remember that my father was Barnaby, but I had another named Balaton. Unless that's a lake in Albania. I must check in the encyclopedia. The aunts are buckling under, quantum by quantum, yet still gamely knitting away. Bad smell on the 3rd deck. Oliphant's child doesn't crawl now, it only flies, making use of the recoil from front and back discharges alternately. Amazing, the organism's capacity for adaptation!

Entry 116,310. I was at the laboratory of Cousin Josiah and his wife. The work there never stops. My cousin says that the highest stage of gastronautics will be furniture not only edible, but alive as well. That kind will not spoil, you won't have to keep it—until using—in the icebox. Fine, but who is going to raise a hand to butcher a living armchair? They don't exist yet, but Josiah claims it won't be long before he's treating us to jellied chair's feet. On the way back to the control room I thought and thought, his worlds still in my ears. He had spoken of living rockets of the future. Will it be possible to have a child by such a rocket? What strange ideas I'm having lately!

Entry 116,311. Grandfather Arabeus complains that his left leg is headed for the North Star, and his right—for the Southern Cross. Besides that I think he's up to something, he goes around on all fours constantly. I'd better keep an eye on him. Balthazar, Josiah's brother, disappeared. Particle dispersion? While looking for him I discovered that the atom room was full of dust. Hadn't been swept in years! I removed Bartholomew, the room sweep, from his post and appointed his brother-in-law Titus. That evening, in the parlor, right in the middle of Aunt Melanie's performance, Grandpa suddenly blew up. I ordered him cemented. That was pure reflex on my part. However I let the order stand, so as not to call into question the captain's authority. I miss Grandpa. What was it, anger or energy conversion? He was always on edge. During my watch I got this craving for meat, ate a little veal from the freezer. Yesterday it turned out that the piece of paper with our destination on it is missing, a pity too, seeing as how we've been traveling now some 36 years. The veal, oddly enough, was full of buckshot—since when are calves gone after with shotguns? A meteor flying by, with someone sitting on it. Bartholomew was the first to notice. For the time being I pretend not to see this.

Entry 116,312. Cousin Bruno says that that wasn't the freezer, but the hibernator, he'd switched the signs as a joke, also it wasn't buckshot, it was beads. I hit the ceiling; at zero gravity you have to watch your temper, no foot-stamping, no table-pounding. I'm sorry I ever took to the stars. I sent Bruno aft, gave him the worst detail: untangling the trawl.

Entry 116,313. The Universe is picking us off one by one. Yesterday part of the poop deck went, and with it all the toilets. Uncle Ralph was back there at the time. Helplessly I looked on as he faded into the darkness, and the unwinding rolls of paper fluttered pathetically in space. A veritable Laocoon among the stars. What a misfortune! The one on the meteor, no relation to us; a total stranger. He flies, sitting straddled. Most unusual. Rumors have reached me that a number of people are sneaking off the ship. It does seem emptier somehow. Could this be true?

Entry 116,314. Cousin Roland, who does our bookkeeping, certainly has his hands full. Yesterday he was in my cabin trying his best to add up our maiden tonnage, with an Einsteinian correction for deflowerment. While writing he suddenly raised his head, looked at me and said: "Human, the sound of it!" The idea floored me. Uncle Oliphant has finished his Robot Theology and now is working on a new system—it includes special fasts, "hunger strikes" (to indicate the hour). Grandfather Arabeus bothers me. He's taken to punning. "One who steals other people's puns at gunpoint," he told me, "is a pundit, and a tadpole, that's the male offspring of a magnet." Little Shaver, the one who flits about by jet propulsion and says *f* instead of *p* (flanet instead of planet, but on the other hand—plannel underwear), threw the cat—only now does it come to light—into the tank of caustic soda which absorbs our carbon dioxide. Poor puss decomposed into sodium bikittenate.

Entry 116,315. Today at my doorstep I find an infant, male, the following card pinned to its diaper: "This is yours." Can't figure it out, an accident perhaps? For its crib I'm using a desk drawer padded with old documents.

Entry 116,316. By now countless socks and handkerchiefs lost in the Universe, and time is breaking down completely; at breakfast I noticed that both grandparents were a lot younger than myself. There have been instances, too, of avuncular cancellation. I ordered a family balance sheet drawn up—the hibernators were opened, I unfroze everyone. Many of the aunts had colds, coughs, blue noses and swollen red ears; a few threw convulsions. I stood by helplessly. Strangest of all, among the resuscitated was a calf. On the other hand, no sign of Aunt Mathilda—can it be that Bruno really wasn't joking—I mean, when he said that he was?

Entry 116,317. There's a closet in the hallway to the atom room. As I was sitting there the amusing thought came to me that perhaps we never even blasted off and were still on Earth! But no—there's no gravity, after all. That is reassuring. Still, I checked to see what I was holding in my hand—a hammer. It's possible my name is really Jeremiah. I pounded away at some bar and felt awfully queer. One must accustom oneself, however. The Pauli exclusion principle, that any particular person can be occupied by only one personality at a time, is far behind us now. It might seem like a kind of family round robin, but out here in the Universe it's not uncommon for several women to give birth, in turn, to the same child—that applies to the fathers too—due to the tremendous speed. Little Shaver, recently so tiny, yet today in the dining room, when we both reached for the marmalade and knocked our heads together, he threw me clear to the ceiling! Tangled, twisted and knotted though it be, yet how the time does fly!

Entry 116,318. Today Arabeus told me he'd always secretly hoped the stars and rockets had one side only, the side facing us, their backs being nothing but dust-covered easels and ropes. This is the reason he flew to the stars! He also informed me that some of the women have been depositing in the laundry baskets not only laundry, but—according to him—their eggs. Presumably a sign of galloping regression, in the evolutionary sense. It must be uncomfortable for him, craning his neck up at me like that from his all fours. Particularly disturbing is his younger brother. Eight years now he's been standing in my vestibule, holding out his index fingers. The beginnings of catatonia? First without thinking, then later out of habit I started hanging up my hat and coat on him. Well, at least he's made something useful of himself.

Entry 116,319. The place is thinning out. Diffraction, sublimation? Or is it simply that they're all shifting, because of the Doppler effect, to the infra-red? Today I went hallooing up and down the main deck and no one showed himself, except for

Aunt Clotilda, with her knitting needles and an unfinished mitten. I went down to the laboratory—Cousins Marmaduke and Alaric, in order to trace the paths of the squarks, were pulling the tails of mice and stepping on chickens. Alaric says that in our particular situation tea leaves are much more reliable than cloud chambers. Yet why, after making the necessary calculations, did he do that rain dance? I don't understand, but am afraid to ask. Great-uncle Herman is gone.

Entry 116,320. Great-uncle Herman has turned up. Every two minutes he appears, with a regularity worthy of a better cause, off the port side, through the skylight you can see him reach the zenith, whereupon he sinks to starboard. Hasn't changed a bit, even in that orbit of eternal rest! But who pushed him out, and when? A terrible thought.

Entry 116,321. Uncle is so regular, you could set a stopwatch by his risings and his settings. Odder yet, he has begun to sound the hours. This is beyond me.

Entry 116,322. It's simple: his feet scrape the surface of the hull at the lowest point of orbit and the tips of his soles (or heels) skip along the heads of the rivets on the armor plating. Today after breakfast he chimed thirteen—accident or omen? The stranger on the meteor has moved off some. He continues to accompany us. I sat at my desk today, to write, and the chair said to me: "What a strange world this is!" I thought at first that Uncle Josiah had finally succeeded, but it was just Grandfather Arabeus. He told me that he's an invariant, that is, one for whom nothing matters, so I can keep my seat. Hallooed today for an entire hour on the gangway and upper deck. Not a soul. A few balls of yarn and knitting needles floating through the air, a couple of packs of cards for solitaire.

Entry 116,323. There exists a special method of preserving one's mental balance—you invent various fictitious characters. Can it be that I have already been doing this for quite some time in a subconscious way? I sit on the stubbornly silent Arabeus, with a puling infant in my drawer, I've named him Ijon, and feed him from a bottle—wondering where in the world I'm going to find a wife for him; there's time yet, I suppose, but under these circumstances you can never tell. I'm sitting here and flying . . .

Those are the last words of my father recorded in the diary—the rest of the pages, missing. And I too am sitting in the rocket and reading about how someone else—that is, he—was sitting in the rocket and flying. And so he sat and he flew, and I likewise sit and fly. Who then is the one really doing the sitting and the flying? Is it possible that I'm not even here? But a ship's log can't very well read itself. So I do exist, yes, because I read it. Yet perhaps the entire thing is made up, imaginary. Strange thoughts . . . Let's suppose that he didn't sit and didn't fly, but I on the other hand am still sitting here as I fly, or rather still flying here as I sit. That's fairly certain. Is it, though? What's certain is that I'm reading about someone who flies and sits. As for my own flight and state of seatedness, how can I be sure? The room is small and furnished poorly, it's more a closet than a room. And situated on the 'tween deck, so I think, but then our attic didn't look that much different. Of course all one would have to do is step out the door, to see it wasn't an illusion. But what if it were an illusion, and I were to see only the continuation of that illusion? Is nothing conclusive? No, this is impossible! For if it were the case that I was not flying and not sitting, but only reading that he was flying and sitting, and if at the same time he really wasn't flying either, that would mean that I, in my illusion, was aware of his illusion, or in other words that it seemed to me that it seemed to him. Or could that which seems to me also be what, seemingly, was seeming to him? An illusion inside an illusion? Let's assume that that is true—except he also wrote about the one sitting astride the meteor. Now that presents a problem. You see, it seems to me that it seemed to him that this other was astride a meteor, but if it only *seemed* to that other as well, then nothing can be said either way! My head has started throbbing and once again, like yesterday, like the day before, I find I have to think of bishops and blue noses, eyes like bachelor's-buttons, the blue Danube and veal cordon bleu. Why? And I know that when, at midnight, I add acceleration, I'll be thinking about scrambled eggs—no—fried, and with big yokes, also about carrots, honey and the feet of my Aunt Mary—exactly as in the middle of every night . . . Ah! But of course! This must

272

be the effect of thought shifts, sometimes towards the ultraviolet, and sometimes—through the yellow bands—in the direction of the infra-red, in other words a psychological Doppler effect! Very important! For that would be proof that I was flying! Proof by motion, *demonstratio ex motu*, as the Schoolmen said! So then, I really am flying . . . Yes. But anyone can think of eggs, feet and bishops. It's not a proof at all, it's only an assumption. What then remains? Solipsism? I alone exist, and am flying nowhere . . . But that would mean that Anonymus Tichy didn't exist, nor Jeremiah, nor Igor, Esteban nor Cosimo, that there had been no Barnaby, Euzebius, no "Cosmocyst," that I never lay in the drawer of my father's desk, and that he, seated upon Grandfather Arabeus, never flew—now *that* is impossible! What, I am supposed to have spun all those persons, all that family history, out of nothing? But surely *ex nihilo nihil fit*! And therefore the family existed, and it is the family that returns to me a faith in the world and in this my flight, whose conclusion is unknown! Everything has been saved thanks to you, O ancestors of mine! In a little while I shall place these written pages in an empty oxygen cylinder and throw them into the deep, overboard, let them sail off into the distant darkness, for *navigare necesse est*, and I have been flying and flying for years . . .

Translator's Note

Stanisław Lem wrote *The Star Diaries (Dzienniki gwiazdowe)* over a period of twenty years, adding installments to each new edition. But the numbering of the Voyages conceals their true chronology: the Seventh appeared in 1964, the Fourteenth in 1957, the Eighteenth in 1971, the Twenty-second in 1954, and so on. Lem does not intend these adventures of Ijon Tichy to be read in the order in which they were written. That order however—22, 23, 25, 11, 12, 13, 14, 7, 8, 28, 20, 21—does reflect his development as a writer. For though there is much consistency of theme throughout the *Diaries* (the making fun of man's supremacy in the Universe, the parodying of history, of time travel), the reader, looking *chronologically*, will find a definite shift from playful anecdote to pointed satire to outright philosophy.

The philosophical essay, when Lem began his career in the early '50s, stood apart from his other genres, the "straight" science fiction, the comic tales and fables. But gradually the boundary between fiction and nonfiction blurred, so that by the '70s Lem was—and still is—producing works which cannot easily be classified as either. For example, *Imaginary Magnitude (Wielkość urojona)* is a collection of ponderous introductions to nonexistent books. Much to the discomfort of his critics, and to the disappointment of many of his fans, who have pleaded, "Write us more things like *Solaris*," Lem is not content to repeat his previous successes; he continues to follow his own difficult drummer. *The Star Diaries* offers only one example of this stubborn and ever restless individuality.

My translation was done from the 1971 Polish fourth edition. It does not include the Memoirs of Ijon Tichy (to which group *The Futurological Congress*, The Seabury Press, 1974, belongs), where the action takes place on Earth, nor the Eighteenth Voyage (in which Tichy is responsible—or rather, to blame—for creating the world), nor the Twenty-fourth. The latter can be found in Darko Suvin's *Other Worlds, Other Seas*, Random House, 1970. There was a Twenty-sixth Voyage too, a cold war satire, which the author later discarded, more for esthetic than political reasons. Also, the last few pages of the Twenty-second Voyage have been omitted.

The name "Tichy," pronounced *Tee*-khee, suggests in Polish the word "quiet" (*cichy*, pronounced *Chee*-khee), which some may find in keeping with the narrator's character.

THE MOTE IN GOD'S EYE

Larry Niven and Jerry Pournelle

An alien space ship, using some motive power unknow
to man, comes sailing into the outer reaches of the
solar system.

The team sent to intercept it accidentally destroy it, but
its course has been recorded accurately enough to
extrapolate its point of origin.

A team of scientists, escorted by the most powerful
battleship in Earth's space fleet is sent to contact this
newly discovered civilization. What they find is at once
the most exciting and tragic destiny ever to be suffered
by sentient beings.

'The best novel about human beings making first
contact with intelligent but utterly nonhuman aliens I
have ever seen, and possibly the finest science fiction
novel I have ever read.'
– Robert A. Heinlein.

'A spellbinder, a swashbuckler . . . and best of all a
brilliant new approach to that fascinating problem –
first contact with aliens.'
– Frank Herbert.

ROBERT E. HOWARD OMNIBUS

The fantastic worlds of Robert E. Howard . . . join the
master of fantasy and adventure in a dozen stories
featuring Conan the Barbarian, Solomon Kane, Kid
Allison, the mighty Cormac and many others.

Journey to the voluptuous barbarism of the East, to the
perils of Outremer, to the bloodstained Northlands of
the Vikings, to the lawless days of the Old West . . .

A feast of jewelled splendour, black enchantment and
savage death.

Also available by Robert E. Howard in Orbit:

THE LOST VALLEY OF ISKANDER
THREE-BLADED DOOM
SON OF THE WHITE WOLF
SWORDS OF SHAHRAZAR
WORMS OF THE EARTH

J. BARNICOAT
CASH SALES DEPT
P.O. BOX 11
FALMOUTH
CORNWALL TR10 9EN

Please send me the following titles

Quantity	SBN	Title	Amount
————			————
————			————
————			————
————			————
————			————
			————
		TOTAL	════

Please enclose a cheque or postal order made out to FUTURA
PUBLICATIONS LIMITED for the amount due, including 10p
per book to allow for postage and packing. Orders will take
about three weeks to reach you and we cannot accept responsibility for orders containing cash.

PLEASE PRINT CLEARLY

NAME..

ADDRESS..

....